Additional Acclaim f[...]

"A modern master . . . Dybek is in[...]

"May propel Dybek into the top rank of living American writers."
—*Chicago* magazine

"These pieces are infused with Dybek's moral intelligence and wisdom, and achieve a kind of elegiac quality."
—*Esquire* magazine

"Beautifully realized . . . a tour de force of American magical realism . . . this book is undoubtedly his best."
—*Chicago Sun-Times*

"Stuart Dybek's new novel in stories...includes a remarkable lyricism and structural spontaneity. . . . Readers . . . will undoubtedly hear parts of their own stories in Perry Katzek's."
—*The Boston Globe*

"*I Sailed with Magellan* is a lovely collection of lyrical pieces."
—Alan Cheuse, NPR's *All Things Considered*

"Not only does Dybek masterfully evoke the intricate, singing web of urban life . . . he also aligns the longings and aspirations of his empathically rendered characters with Chicago's often forbidding, sometimes radiantly beautiful cityscape. . . . [*I Sailed with Magellan*] places him in a constellation of writers that includes Joyce in *The Dubliners,* Italo Calvino, Gabriel García Márquez, and Chicago's own Leon Forrest."
—Donna Seaman, *Chicago Tribune*

"Dybek's book . . . is a kind of marvelous parade . . . full of scruffy energy and dangerous surprises, funny and heartbreaking, both."
—*The Buffalo News*

"Every story in Stuart Dybek's latest book is original, operatic, and unexpected."
—*Bookforum*

"These are wonderful stories, shot through with humor, violence, and love. The writing is strong and sure, the characters precisely drawn, the worlds of childhood and adolescence described vividly, and the war-wounded delineated with realistic truth. *I Sailed with Magellan* is an intense, compelling book."
—*The Providence Journal*

I Sailed with Magellan

Stuart Dybek

Picador
Farrar, Straus and Giroux
New York

The author would like to express gratitude to the Lannan Foundation for an award that bought time to write, and to the Rockefeller Foundation for a residency at the Bellagio Study and Conference Center, where some of this work was written. Thanks also to Paul D'Amato for the generous use of his photo *Isela, Girl in Spray (from open pump)* on the cover, and to Perry Higman, whose translation of "El Conde Arnaldos" is quoted on the epigraph page. A special thanks to Tracy Kidder.

www.picadorusa.com

For information on Picador Reading Group Guides, as well as ordering, please contact the Trade Marketing department at St. Martin's Press.
Phone: 1-800-221-7945 extension 763
Fax: 212-677-7456
E-mail: trademarketing@stmartins.com

Grateful acknowledgment is made to the editors of the periodicals in which these stories have appeared: "Song," *Harper's;* "Live from Dreamsville," *Chicago Magazine* (as "Old Grandma's Rocking Chair") and The Pedestal (as "I Sailed with Magellan"); "Undertow," *The Atlantic Monthly;* "Breasts," *Tin House;* "Blue Boy," *TriQuarterly;* "Orchids," *DoubleTake;* "Lunch at the Loyola Arms," *The New Yorker;* "We Didn't," *Antaeus;* "Qué Quieres," *TriQuarterly;* "A Minor Mood," *The Iowa Review;* "Je Reviens," *Harper's.* Thanks are also due to the anthologies in which "We Didn't" was reprinted: *The Norton Anthology of Short Fiction; Getting It On,* Soho Press; *The Best American Short Stories 1994,* Tobias Wolff, editor; *Prize Stories 1994: The O. Henry Awards.*

Designed by Jonathan D. Lippincott

Library of Congress Cataloging-in-Publication Data

Dybek, Stuart, 1942–
    I Sailed with Magellan / Stuart Dybek.
        p. cm.
    ISBN 0-312-42411-6
    EAN 978-0312-42411-4
    I. Title.

PS3554.Y313 2003
813'.54—dc21   2002049052

First published in the United States by Farrar, Straus and Giroux

First Picador Edition: October 2004

10 9 8 7 6 5 4 3 2 1

For Adeline Dybek

1913–2003

In memory everything seems to happen to music.
    —Tennessee Williams, *The Glass Menagerie*

Yo no digo esta canción
sino a quien conmigo va.

I shall never teach you this song
unless you sail away with me.
    —Anonymous, "El Conde Arnaldos"

Contents

I Sailed with Magellan

Song

~~~~~~

Once I was a great singer. Caruso Junior they called me, and Little *der Bingle*. Crooners like Bing Crosby and Sinatra were still big in those days. My repertoire included "Clang, Clang, Clang Went the Trolley," the song behind my ambition to become a streetcar conductor. I knew the nameless tune my mother sang when we waited for the El: "Down by the station early in the morning, see the little puffer-billies all in a row"; and my uncle Lefty had taught me a version of "Popeye the Sailor Man" that went, "I'm Popeye the Sailor Man, I live in a garbage can, I eat all the junk and smell like a skunk, I'm Popeye the Sailor Man, I am."

But none of those was the song for which I was famous, the song requested over and over. They'd hoist me onto the bar, where I'd carefully plant my feet among the beer bottles, steins, and shot glasses, and, taking a breath of whiskey air, belt out "Old Man River." I'd learned the song by listening to my father's mournful baritone while he shaved for work. It wasn't a popular song of the time, not one you'd find on the mob-owned jukeboxes in those taverns where "That's Amore" or the "Too Fat Polka" were as likely to be thumping from the speakers as "Hound Dog." But the men drinking there had all toted that barge and lifted that bale and got a little drunk and landed in jail, too, and had the scars to prove it. The noisy bar would quiet, small talk deferring to lyrics.

"He's sure got a deep voice for his age," someone would invariably comment.

When I finished the song, holding the last note as if I dove down to the dark river bottom for it, they cheered and showered me with loose change and sometimes a few dollar bills.

"What's the little man drinking?" they asked Uncle Lefty.

"What'll it be, champ?" Lefty would relay to me.

"Root beer," I'd shout, and root beer it was.

I'd sit with my feet dangling over the bar, slugging from a heavy stein. Singing gave one a thirst. Then Uncle Lefty, who'd also had a few on the house, would comb his nicotine-stained fingers through my hair, straighten my buttons as if tuning me up, and lift me from the bar, gently, like a musical instrument he was packing away, an instrument that he carried with him—one that sometimes rode his shoulders—as he made the rounds from tavern to tavern.

We'd go from Deuces Wild on Twenty-second to the Pulaski Club across from St. Kasmir, and from there we'd hit the Zip Inn, where Zip, who'd lost his right arm in the Big War, tended bar. Zip always kept the empty sleeve of his white shirt neatly folded and clamped with a plastic clothespin—red, blue, yellow, green—he changed the colors the way some guys changed their ties. The walls of his bar were hung with framed photographs of the softball teams he'd sponsored, and there was also a photo of a young Uncle Lefty with his boxing gloves cocked, taken when he fought in the Golden Gloves tournament.

"Ah, my fellow Left-wingers," Zip would greet us.

"Quit trying to pass yourself off as a genuine southpaw," Lefty would tell him. "You ain't fooling nobody."

"I admit it. I'm a convert, but hey, converts are the true believers. Fact is, my right arm is killing me today. Means rain."

"Zip, it's pouring already," Lefty said, peeling a hard-boiled egg he'd helped himself to from the bowl on the bar. "Think we'd stop in a dive like this if we weren't getting soaked?"

Both Zip and I glanced out the door propped open with the doorstop of a brass spittoon. Sunbeams fuming with blue to-bacco smoke streamed into the dim tavern. Zip looked at me and shrugged.

Uncle Lefty snatched the checked bar rag from Zip's left shoulder and toweled off my hair as if I was dripping wet. "Phan-tom pain brings phantom rain," he said by way of explanation.

"Perry," Zip said, "your uncle is a very strange man."

"Zip," Lefty asked, "did I ever mention this kid can sing?"

And later, my pockets jangling with tips, we'd open invisible um-brellas and step from Zip's into the phantom rain, on our way to Red's on Damen, or to the frigid, mint blue bar at Cermak Bowl, where, I believed, air-conditioning was invented, or to Juanita's, a bar that also served tacos, or to the VFW, which had slot ma-chines. There were more taverns in the neighborhood than we could visit in a single afternoon. At every stop it was the same: "Old Man River," applause, bar change, and root beer, until Un-cle Lefty, who was downing two boilermakers to every drink of mine, would caution, "You're gonna have a head of foam when you pee. Don't tell your mother how many you've had or we'll both be in Dutch with her."

My mother was Lefty's older sister. It was from her that I'd heard how Lefty had wanted to be a musician ever since he was a kid. As a child, Lefty had chronic bronchitis, and my mother re-membered him spending his sick days home from school devising instruments from vacuum-cleaner attachments. He'd give the family a concert at night, humming through his homemade horns while moving his fingers as if tootling up and down the scale. My mother said that Lefty could perfectly imitate the sound of any wind instrument so long as he had a vacuum-cleaner nozzle or a cardboard tube that he could pretend to blow.

When he was thirteen, Lefty saved enough money from his paper route to buy a trumpet, but a week after buying it, he had a front tooth broken in a school-yard fight, which ruined his embouchure. So he traded in the trumpet for a tenor saxophone, and took the precaution of signing up for boxing lessons at St. Vitus, where Father Herm, a priest who was an ex-heavyweight, trained boys to fight in Catholic Youth Organization bouts. For months, Lefty monopolized the full-length mirror on my mother's bedroom door, shadowboxing himself into a sweat. The opponent in the mirror was Bobby Vachata, the kid who'd broken Lefty's tooth, though no one suspected Lefty's boxing obsession was fueled by revenge until he gave Vachata a beating and brought a furious Father Herm to the house. Lefty was expelled from the St. Vitus CYO, and for the next year the proceeds from his paper route went to pay Vachata's dental bills.

When he wasn't shadowboxing, Lefty was in the basement "practicing his sax." That's what he called it, my mother said, though he wasn't actually playing the horn any more than he'd played the vacuum-cleaner attachments. The family could hear the sound rising through the heating ducts as he slurred and honked and wailed—a mimicry so convincing that, if you didn't know, you'd think there was a virtuoso down there, who could play any song at will. But my mother knew his fingers were still moving along imaginary scales, and his pretend playing no longer seemed cute to her as it had back when Lefty would give them concerts after dinner. Something about all that music at once unexpressed and yet erupting from her younger brother, all that sound swirling nonstop in his head, made her afraid for him. Then, one evening, she heard Lefty suddenly stop improvising on "How High the Moon." There was silence followed by a metallic squawk and then another squawk and another, notes croaked haltingly, the way lyrics might be sounded out by a deaf person learning to sing: "some . . . where there's mu . . . sic how high the moon?" She realized that Lefty had finally fit a reed into the mouthpiece and was teaching himself to play.

By high school Lefty had grown into a welterweight and was training for the Golden Gloves at Gonzo's Gym on Kedzie, where the mostly lighter-division Mexican fighters boxed. He'd taught himself to play the sax almost as proficiently as he'd once faked playing it. With a few buddies from Farragut High, he started the Bluebirds, which Lefty described as a bebop polka band. They played taverns for parties and weddings with Lefty on sax and vocals. It was difficult to imagine him singing because of the raspy whisper he spoke in, but my mother said when he was young, Lefty could croon like Mel Tormé, a singer known as the Velvet Fog. Lefty had returned from a Korean POW camp and a subsequent yearlong detour at a VFW mental hospital in California with a chronically hoarse, worn-away voice. It was a voice a rock singer might have envied, but rock and roll wasn't the music Lefty grew up playing. When he shipped out for Korea, the music from World War II had still hung in the air. His war didn't have its own music, and years later, when he stepped back into America, the country's allegiance had shifted to another beat. The raspy voice was the only voice of his I heard live, but I once listened to a scratchy 45 rpm record he'd sent to my mother from San Diego while on leave before his troopship sailed for Japan. Lefty crooned an a cappella "I'll Be Seeing You," and even on that disk of flimsy acetate, when he hit the words "I'll be looking at the moon, but I'll be seeing you," I could hear the velvet foggy vibrato of his voice and turned to say so to my mother, but she'd left the room. It was the last I ever saw of that record.

My mother had made me promise never to ask Uncle Lefty
about the war—a promise I kept—not that I wasn't curious, but I
didn't want to do anything that would jeopardize our outings together. Now that he'd finally returned home from Korea, everyone expected he'd resume playing in a band, but the only thing
Lefty seemed interested in playing anymore were the ponies. My
parents would never have allowed him to take me to the track, so
sometimes on Saturday afternoons Uncle Lefty would tell them
we were going across town to a Cubs game. Instead, we'd head
for Cicero, where the sulkies were running at Sportsman's Park.
And after Sportsman's we'd celebrate our winnings, whether
there were any or not, by taking our singing routine to the taverns of Cicero.

Later, we'd empty our pockets on the drumskin-tight army
blanket of the neatly made bed in Lefty's bare, rented room with
its marbled blue linoleum floor. We'd count our take, and Lefty
would say, "We're in the peanuts and caramel now, champ," the
same phrase he used when he'd hit a long shot.

Even my mother had never been to his one-room, third-floor
flat on Blue Island Avenue—a street that failed to live up to its
name. I'd imagined the lake visible at the end of the block, gulls
mewing, and water lapping the wooden back porches as if they
were docks. It was a vision Lefty had prompted when he told me
the street was named for a ghostly island that sometimes still rose
on the horizon of the lake, an island once inhabited by the Blue
Island Indians that sank from sight when the last warrior died.
Maybe my lifelong longing for islands came from the promise of
that street name.

Pigeons, not gulls, paced the window ledges. One of Lefty's
Mexican neighbors kept a pigeon coop on the roof, and the
birds' constant cooing seemed like a cool windless breeze wafting
through Lefty's room. A few times, Lefty took me up through the
trapdoor to see the pigeons. "Welcome to Dreamsville," he'd say

and pull me up onto the hot, pebbled tar roof that looked over Blue Island and beyond to a city of holy spires. I recalled over-hearing my mother talking in a worried way to my father about Lefty drunkenly staggering up to the roof at night to play his sax. The cops had been called to get him down.

"You can't feel guilty about not taking care of your nutcase brother," my father said. "He's living his own life and won't listen to nobody anyway."

I didn't understand what was so crazy; it made perfect sense to me that he'd go up to Dreamsville to play a duet with the pigeons.

Except for an audience of pigeons and neighbors whom he woke from a sound sleep at three in the morning, Lefty no longer played in public. His old combo, the Bluebirds, had broken up when he'd left for Korea. Lefty's best buddy from the Bluebirds, a guy we called the Bruiser, still drummed in a local band that played for weddings. You could hear the Bruiser from a block away, his bass beat a sonic boom, his rimshots carrying like gunfire. We'd follow the beat to the open side door of a tavern hall and stand watching the dancers whoop around the dance floor while the Bruiser thundered behind a wheezy, sad-sack polka band.

"See that drummer," Lefty told me, "his god was Gene Krupa."

There was an amazing recording of the Benny Goodman band's "Sing, Sing, Sing" on the jukebox at the Zip Inn, with Krupa exploding on tom-toms. Lefty played it whenever the Bruiser joined us there for a drink. They always set a shot of Jim Beam on the bar for Deke, the Bluebirds' guitar player who'd been killed in Korea. I wondered who drank it after we left.

It was one of those Saturdays in summer when we'd gone to Sportsman's—I'd hit a winner with a horse named You Bet Your Dupa—and we were in Lefty's room on Blue Island, listening to the Cubs lose to the Giants so I could report on the game, when he told me he was thinking of moving back to California. I'm glad we weren't at a tavern, because before I could stop myself, I began to cry.

"Hey, come on, champ, don't feel that way. I'll be back. Look, I got something special I been meaning to show you. Check it out." He slid a beat-up case from under the bed and let me pop the latches. It opened with a whiff of brass and another scent, one that later in life I'd recognize as a mingling of cork grease, bamboo, and dried saliva. There was a note of perfume from a black slip stuffed in the bell of the horn. The bell was engraved with cursive I couldn't read, the keys were capped in mother-of-pearl. The saxophone gleamed from the plush emerald lining like pirate treasure in an encrusted chest. Like a piano on an empty stage, it seemed to emit silence. I pressed the keys, and the felt pads resonated against the holes. Just thumping the keys made a kind of music.

"Try it on." Lefty fit the neck strap over my head and attached the sax to the little hook. The weight of the horn pulled me forward.

"Too big for you," he said. "Here's one more your size." He reached beneath the bed and came up with a compact little case and snapped it open to reveal a disassembled clarinet cushioned in ruby velvet. "Learn to play this and the sax will come easy. You like that Benny Goodman's 'Sing, Sing, Sing,' don't you?"

I shook my head yes, afraid I'd blubber if I tried to talk.

"Know why this has your name on it?"

"Why?" I wasn't sure if he was really giving me the clarinet.

"Because you can hear it, right?" He held up a finger like a conductor raising a baton.

I listened. All I heard were pigeons. "What?" I asked.

"The phantom music, you know, like Zip's right arm. It's there even if no one else hears it."

I had no idea what he was talking about, but I nodded yes. I wanted that clarinet.

"I can hear you feel it when you sing. Who taught you to whistle so good?"

"I taught myself," I told him, which was true. I'd learned to whistle by practicing under an echoey railroad viaduct at the end of our street.

"That's what I'm talking about. It's there all the time. It kept me company when I was *in*." He didn't say in the army or in the war or in Korea or in the POW camp or in the VA hospital. Just *in*, and that was the only time he even mentioned so much as that.

When I brought the clarinet home, it caught my mother by surprise. She'd suspected Lefty had pawned his horns in order to pay his bar tabs and gambling debts. I didn't tell her he was leaving for California. I asked if I could keep it, and she said maybe. Maybe Uncle Lefty would give me a lesson sometime, she said, but it was better not to ask him because he didn't need that kind of pressure right now. Maybe I should think of it as simply taking care of his clarinet for him until someday maybe he'd want to play it again himself.

I promised her that if he ever did, I'd give it back. I meant it, too, because I couldn't understand why somebody who was once in the Bluebirds and could play for people on an instrument like that golden saxophone would ever stop playing. I thought that if I could play a horn like that, I'd never give it up no matter what happened. I knew I'd never stop singing.

Yet all it took to end my career was Sister Relenete, who during my first choir practice stopped the choir in the middle of "Silent Night," looked directly at me, and asked, "Who is singing like a tortured frog?"

It was a shock: the shock of humiliation. After my command performances of "Old Man River" just a few years earlier, I'd joined the Christmas Choir in third grade expecting to be a star. Those rounds with Uncle Lefty had left me feeling special. I was a standout all right, but for the wrong reason. It was an awakening of a kind I hadn't had before, but I grasped it immediately, not doubting for a moment that the nun's appraisal was right. I wasn't prone to blushing, but I felt the hot, dizzying rush of blood to my face. Sister Relenete directed us to begin again, and this time I moved my lips, only pretending to sing. After a few bars Sister Relenete signaled a pause and said, "Much better!"

I never returned to choir practice. I didn't fall silent though. Stifled song can assume so many shapes. Instead of being a singer, I became a laugher. Not that it occurred to me then that clowns are, perhaps, failed singers. All it would take to set me off was some odd little thing: Denny "the Fish" Mihala's answer in fourth grade to Sister Philomena's question "If birds come in flocks, and fish in schools, what other kinds of groupings can you name?"

Mihala's hand shot up and he said, "A dozen donuts!"

It wasn't the first time one of Mihala's answers broke up the class. Once, during a spelling exercise, he was asked to use the word *thirsty* in a sentence. It was a fateful question, one that would earn him his nickname, a question he seemed utterly stumped by. He looked frantically around the classroom for help, then pointed at the goldfish bowl and said in his thick Chicago accent, "Da fish are tirsty."

When Fish answered "A dozen donuts," even Sister Phil smiled momentarily, then she shushed the class and said, "Thank you, Denny, very original thinking, but the question was more about groups of animals. What about cows or wolves?"

Fish stared mutely at her.

Camille Estrada raised her hand and said, "A pack of wolves, a herd of wild horses, a pride of lions, a swarm of locusts, a pod of dolphins . . ."

The lesson moved on, but I couldn't let go of such moments. They kept replaying the way an insult or a slight lodges in the mind of someone with a temper—probably the way that Uncle Lefty replayed the fight in which Bobby Vachata broke his tooth, depriving Lefty, in a single blow, of his natural inclination to play trumpet. Instead of rage, it was hilarity rising in me. The more I tried to gain control over myself, the more I thought of what had triggered the laughter. Fish's answer, "A dozen donuts," wasn't that funny in and of itself, but there seemed to me something infinitely comic about the way he'd thrust his hand up in order to share his inspiration with the class, and in Sister's response, "Thank you, Denny, very original thinking." I'd disappear under my desk as if tying a shoe or looking for a dropped pencil, but the laughter would find me. I'd rest my head on my arms pretending to nap at my desk while my sides heaved with barely smothered laughter—laughter that, despite my better interests, was proving more irrepressible than song.

The nun had seen this act before. "Perry, are you a loon or what? Go think about your behavior in the cloakroom until you grow up enough to join us."

Banished to the cloakroom, where I'd been spending increasing amounts of time, I'd stand in the meditative company of my classmates' hanging coats, free to surrender to spasms of laughter.

The worst, most achingly ecstatic laughing fits came on during obligatory weekday morning mass. Usually the mass was either the feast day of a martyr or a requiem, the priests' vestments red or black. I'd follow the liturgy for a while in my St. Joseph missal, then slip into the stupor of another medieval morning that reeked of incense. But sometimes there'd be a diversion, like the time in fifth grade when my buddy the Falcon—Angel Falcone—who was sitting beside me, managed to toe up the padded kneeler during the Gospel without anyone noticing. At the Offertory, when the kids in our pew went to kneel, the whole row of knees hit the marble floor. The Falcon had the gift of remaining deadpan. I laughed for both of us even as I knelt, trying to choke the laughter back, pretending to be coughing or blowing my nose while my eyes teared. Then, from rows behind us, I heard the wooden beads of the nun's floor-length cinch of rosary rapping rapid-fire against the pew as she furiously rose and rushed from her seat and down the aisle to where I knelt, pushing kids aside to get to me, yanking me up and dragging me down the center aisle into the vestibule.

"Laughing like a fool in God's presence. He's hanging on the cross for your sins and you're laughing at His suffering like the Romans and Jews! You don't deserve to be a Christian. Stop it! Stop it this instant or I'll slap that smile off your face."

"Make like you're smiling," Sid Sovereign told me. "Not like that! Did I say make like a shit-eating grin? What are you, retarded? Pay attention. *This* is a smile."

I watched him demonstrate the proper smile. Eyes fierce, he smiled without showing his teeth. That was a relief, because he had small, rotten-looking teeth—tobacco-stained like his bristly gray mustache, which was yellowed where the smoke blew from his nostrils. He balanced his Lucky Strike on a cigarette-tarred music stand and into his tight-lipped smile fit the mouthpiece of his clarinet and exhaled an open-fingered G. I almost expected to see cigarette smoke puff from the bell of the horn.

"You see *my* cheeks bulging? I'm not blowing up a goddamn balloon, I'm playing the clarinet. You try. Sit up straight, how do you expect to breathe with posture like that? Now, smile. No, dammit! This is a smile." He jabbed his fingers into the corners of my mouth, remolding my face. I could feel my face not cooperating with either of us, and I tried to concentrate and disregard my hurt feelings. My first clarinet lesson was not going the way I'd anticipated.

My father had decided that since Uncle Lefty had given me the clarinet, the time had come for me to take lessons.

"Someone who can play can always make a buck on the side," he reasoned, and for my father a buck on the side was reason enough. He hated to see things wasted, and that included a clarinet sitting idly in a case. But maybe there was more to it than he was willing to admit. In his way, my father loved music. On Saturday nights he'd record *The Lawrence Welk Show* on his new reel-to-reel tape deck, an expense he justified because he'd never have to buy another record, not that he ever bought records. He sang most every morning as he got ready for work with a gravity that woke the house. "The voice of the Volga Boat Man is heard in the land," my mother would say. He sang with facial expressions that caused him to cut himself shaving. He shaved with a straight razor rather than wasting money on blades, and he bled as he sang, the foam on the razor stained pink and his face stuck up with bloody clots of toilet paper. I was afraid that, reaching for a note, he'd cut his throat. The songs he sang were from a lamentable past I could barely imagine—"Old Man River," "Brother Can You Spare a Dime?" "That Lucky Old Sun":

> Up in the mornin', out on the job,
> work like the devil for my pay,
> but that lucky ole sun, got nothin' to do
> but roll around heaven all day . . .

When I was little I used to think I was the son he was singing about.

Uncle Lefty had said he'd teach me to play, but, as my father pointed out, that had been several years ago, and Uncle Lefty had yet to return from California—in fact, we weren't sure where he was. Besides, the word was out from Johnny Sovereign that his older brother, Sid, had been released from jail and needed the money. Whether it was a cheap haircut or cut-rate music lessons, my father couldn't pass up a deal.

Sid Sovereign had done time in Florida for passing bad checks. Now he was back in Chicago, trying to go straight. Sid's brother Johnny lived with his wife and their kids, Judy and Johnny Jr., in a two-flat around the corner from us. Their alley fence was camouflaged in morning glories, and behind it was a screened-in sandbox protected from cats where Johnny Jr. and my younger brother, Mick, played together. Johnny Sovereign ran the numbers in our neighborhood, Little Village. That makes him sound like a big shot, but everyone knew he was just a small-time hood, which in Little Village didn't attract much more notice than if he was a mailman. Johnny was well connected enough, however, to get Sid the patronage job of band director for the Marshall Square Boys' Club. There, in a room smelling of liniment, where basketballs and boxing gear were stored in a pad-locked cage along with drums and tubas, Sid gave private lessons.

Sid hated giving lessons. He hated kids. He kept cotton balls in the cellophane sleeve around his pack of Luckies. He opened his Luckies with meticulous care and utilized the cellophane sleeve to hold matches, loose change, business cards, phone numbers on shreds of paper, and cotton balls. During a lesson, after the first few shrieks on the horn, he'd yell, "Fuckaduck, kid! Are you trying to ruin my hearing?" and reach for the cotton balls. A few more shrieks and he'd bounce up as if to smack you, then instead open a locker stuffed with boxing gloves and take a swig from a half-pint bottle. When I first saw him do it, I thought he was drinking liniment. He sat back down smelling of booze. Though I'd yet to master smiling, we were on to breathing.

"In little sips," he said, "and don't let the goddamn horn waggle in your mouth. The mouthpiece just rests on your bottom lip and the upper teeth bite down." He tested my embouchure by grabbing the horn and giving it a shake that made me feel as if my bottom teeth cut through my lip. "It should be firm so I can't jiggle it around like this. Little sips and then exhale just touching the reed with your tongue, like saying *thoo*." He demonstrated without his horn, and boozy spit sprayed in my face. "Little sips! You're trying to eat the horn. You're not playing a hot dog. Did you think you were at a hot-dog lesson?" He rammed the mouthpiece down my throat so that the reed scraped the roof of my mouth. "Can you play like that? Well? It's a question. Are you deaf? Maybe that's the problem here."

I tried to answer with the horn in my mouth. It was like trying to talk at the dentist's. I shook my head no. I was sweating. My face threatened to betray me, but no way was I going to further humiliate myself before this man. And no way was I giving up on music a second time.

"All right, try again: *thoo*."

I *p-thooed* a squawk that pretty much expressed my feelings, and Sid Sovereign flinched, then shouted, "Little sips, little sips!" and grabbed my nose, pinching it shut, forcing me to breathe little sips through my mouth, but the effect was that of throwing a switch, one that opened the valves of my shameful tears.

Despite this inauspicious start, I was marching—my maroon cape flaring behind me—down Cermak Road to the joyful cacophony of "When the Saints Go Marching In."

True, at third clarinet I was bringing up the rear; true, Sid Sovereign had told me, "You'd be tenth clarinet if we had a part for it"; and true, I was mostly lost and faking the notes. I had a hard enough time keeping up with the band when we practiced sitting down. Every so often I'd blow a middle C that would fit

in. Sometimes, having lost my place on the sheet music, middle
C was all I played, as if adding a drone. Sid Sovereign, directing
the band, didn't seem to mind. In fact, he suggested I might want
to fake it till my tone improved. He gave the same advice to
Miguel Porter, another third clarinet marching beside me.

By now we were supposed to have memorized the music
for the upcoming band competition at Riverview, a legendary
amusement park on the North Side, but since this was a dress rehearsal, we were allowed to have our parts on miniature music
stands clipped to our instruments. The maroon capes and matching maroon and gold-brimmed caps, and the white spats that I
buttoned over my PF flyers had been provided by Sid Sovereign.
It was summer, and the capes and caps were wool, and despite
their mothball smell, moth-eaten. They looked to be from another era, the Great Depression, maybe. We suspected Sovereign
had ransacked some long-forgotten storeroom in the Boys' Club
system. I admired the ornate satiny uniforms that the softball
teams sponsored by neighborhood taverns wore, but I had mixed
feelings about parading around in this kind of getup. I wanted to
be in the band on our way to Riverview—the most magical place
in the city—but not dressed as a dork.

It seemed out of character for Sovereign to be putting so
much energy into the Riverview competition. He'd made the
brass players polish their horns, and he'd added today's late afternoon rehearsal to our regular Saturday band practice. Maybe the
change in him had something to do with Julio Candido's mother,
Gloria, who'd begun attending our rehearsals, an audience of one
who filled the band room with a tropical perfume that couldn't all
be coming from the white flower in her black hair. Julio's father,
wanted for murder, had fled back to Mexico years ago. Mrs. Candido drove Julio to band practice, to school, and everywhere in
her white Buick convertible, not a car that a woman employed as
a singing cocktail waitress at Fabio's, a mob hangout in the Ital-

ian neighborhood just across Western Avenue, could normally afford.

The band room was actually the half-court basketball gym. Usually it smelled of fermented sweat. Mrs. Candido sat beneath the basket on a folding chair, dressed in a sleeveless white summer sheath, her bronze legs crossed, the toe of a white high heel tapping the air to whatever beat Sid Sovereign conducted. He'd begun conducting instead of hiding sunk in depression behind his office door, smoking and drinking while we blared directionless in the gym, as had been his routine before Mrs. Candido started showing up. The cotton was gone from his ears. He'd even written music for us to play while we marched before the judges at the Riverview competition—a piece to get their attention, something contemporary to go with the classic "When the Saints Go Marching In."

"A little something original," he bragged to Mrs. Candido before he struck up the band, "something you can bet nobody else will be playing."

Sovereign had transcribed and arranged Bill Haley and the Comets' hit, "Rock Around the Clock," for marching band.

His arrangement began with the glockenspiels tapping out "One o'clock, two o'clock, three o'clock," and then the whole band shouting out *"Rock!"* The tubas picked it up: "Four o'clock, five o'clock, six o'clock," and we shouted *"Rock!"* Then the other instruments—flutes, cornets, trombones—counted out the remaining hours on the clock, winding up to our final *"Rock!"*—a shout punctuated by the drums, which launched the entire band into a swinging march beat we emphasized by swinging our horns as we played.

Mrs. Candido drove slowly along Cermak, part of the parade. It was hot and sunny, but the top was up on the Buick as it always was, no matter how bright the day. It made me wonder why she wanted a convertible.

Sid Sovereign, wearing a kid-size maroon cape that looked on him like an askew napkin, led us with the kind of baton that twirlers throw. A cigarette bobbed from the corner of his lip, and his gait wouldn't have passed the walk-a-straight-line test at a DUI stop. He was definitely marching under the influence and probably couldn't have managed to be out here sober. He signaled for us to turn down California Avenue. Mrs. Candido got caught at a red light, and Sovereign held us up, marching in place until the Buick turned down California, too. He had told us that we were only going to march once around the block, but we'd already gone farther than that and were on our fourth chorus of "When the Saints." As soon as her white convertible caught up with us again, we marched the few blocks to the elevated station for the Douglas Park "B." In the blaze of sunlight, the shadows of the El tracks and girders latticed the pavement. It felt cooler stepping into them, and our playing was graced with the resonance that shadow imparts to sound. I could see the people waiting on the platform for the "B" grinning down at us. A two-car El train clattered over, the screech of its braking steel wheels about as in tune as we were. Sid Sovereign signaled with the baton for us to stop playing but to continue marching in place.

I figured the El was the point he'd been heading for and now we'd turn back to the Boys' Club. The El station was the kind of boundary that doesn't show up on street maps. East of the tracks was Little Village, with its Ambros and Two-Twos and Disciples graffiti; west was a narrow stretch of No-Man's-Land and then the African American neighborhood of Douglas Park, embossed with the graffiti of the Insane Unknowns.

The "B" train overhead clapped its doors shut and rattled off downtown to its own rhythm.

"Oh, yeah!" Sovereign hollered, waving the baton as if directing the train's departure. The baton had become his scepter, and he saluted Mrs. Candido, who had all the windows open and

waved back. She was wearing sunglasses and a picture hat that
looked too big for the interior of the Buick—one more reason to
drop the top. Sovereign regally sceptered at the commuters descending from the station. They looked surprised to see a band
awaiting their arrival.

"Oh, yeah!" Sovereign yelled to no one in particular. "I feel
we could march all the way to Riverview!"

I pictured the Blue Streak, Shoot the Chutes, Aladdin's
Palace, and the Rotor, a ride whose centrifugal force pinned you
to a wall, defying gravity when the floor dropped out.

"I think he's on speedballs," Miguel Porter said.

"Okay, my little hepcats, my little mariachis," Sovereign
yelled. "Okay, now let me hear it! A one, two, and glockenspiels,
yeah!"

The glocks started pinging "One o'clock, two o'clock, three
o'clock." We all shouted *"Rock!"* and Sovereign gave a little hop
and landed yelling *"ka-POW!"* This was the one part of the song
I could keep up with, and I was into it, too. The bystanders from
the El train cheered. Sid Sovereign yelled, "Oh yeah, baby, tubas!
Tubas give it to me, baby, oh yeah, let me have it!" We gave it to
him: an oompahed "four o'clock, five o'clock, six." Sovereign
pointed the baton straight ahead, and to the roar of *"Rock!"* and
of a "B" train screeching in, we marched under the tracks and out
the other side into No-Man's-Land.

The pavement thumped beneath our synchronized, rock-
steady, maroon columns, and for the first time I managed to keep
my place in the music and dared to play louder, suddenly recalling a dream in which Uncle Lefty's clarinet could play itself. Playing felt automatic, as if the band glided on a conveyor belt of the
music we blew before us. People, more and more of them black,
stepped from doorways and threw their upper-story windows
open to gape. Pumping the baton like a drum major, Sid Sovereign led us through stop signs without stopping as if we had the

immunity of a funeral. When the green of Douglas Park appeared, Mrs. Candido began honking her horn, and Sid Sovereign, pretending to toot the baton as if it were a clarinet, and
yelling, "Oh yeah, baby, *pow, pow, pow*! bass drum!" bowed in her
direction. He must have thought she was musically tooting her
automobile horn, adding a touch of Spike Jones, though what
she actually signaled was, Where the hell are you taking my little
Julio?

Sovereign hadn't noticed that our parade had grown longer.
We'd attracted a group of black kids who'd been hitting a softball
in the park. Other kids from Douglas Park had joined them. They
were marching in the gutter beside our column, and still more
were running in our direction. Maybe Sovereign thought that
music afforded us some dispensation and that everyone simply
wanted to join in the fun as if we were Alexander's Ragtime
Band.

It almost looked that way at first. The new paraders from
Douglas Park seemed to be enjoying themselves—laughing at
our uniforms, marching backward, colliding into our ranks, and
yelling, "*Pow! Pow! Pow!* motherfucker." A lanky guy in a shower
cap codirected us with a softball bat, mimicking Sovereign's baton technique. We marched with our eyes fixed straight ahead, as
if oblivious to the growing chaos at our flanks and the shouts of
"You disturbing the peace!" But it was impossible to ignore the
guy in the shower cap suddenly whacking the bass drum with the
bat, radically changing the beat. We were heading along a sidewalk across the street from the park when out of an upper-story
window someone emptied a pot of water into the tubas. A bottle
crashed down. Voices yelled, "Hey! Shut that honky shit up
down there!" The bass drum player was in a tug-of-war with a kid
who wanted the trophy of a fuzzy mallet, while the shower-
capped guy with the bat kept banging the drum.

We were double-timing, triple-timing, nearly jogging and still playing—I was back to droning middle C—and a confetti of garbage fell from windows and roofs. Sovereign was hit in the head—for an instant it appeared his skull had exploded, but it was just a tomato. He staggered and, looking stunned, directed us to turn down a side street. Mrs. Candido, blaring her horn nonstop, screamed, "Julio! Julio!" Julio broke ranks and ran for the car as a half-eaten pizza Frisbeed down, splatting the convertible top and windshield. It looked comical to see Mrs. Candido's wipers working as she gunned away. I wished I was in the Buick with Julio—they wouldn't hear a peep from me about the top being up—and when the car disappeared I felt abandoned.

A band member's trombone was now in the possession of a guy whose biceps were not tattooed but branded with gang insignia, and who was busy working the slide to produce brassy lip-farts. A kid about my age, smiling cheerfully beneath the brim of a White Sox hat nesting on an Afro, grabbed for my clarinet. I wrenched it away, filled with sudden panic over having to tell Uncle Lefty, if he ever returned from California, that I'd lost his horn. The band broke into a disorganized jog, and then we were running, abandoning horns and glockenspiels, the drummers trapped in their harnesses, every man for himself in full retreat. I cut from the pack, down another side street and another.

The itchy cape flared behind me, tugging at my throat, perfect for someone to grab and pull me down. Voices shouted, but I didn't turn to see who was chasing. My ill-fitting hat flew off, then my sheet music, and next the clip-on music stand, but I kept a grip on the clarinet. I was fast, the fastest kid in my school. I might be tenth clarinet, but I was first in every footrace, and the spats buttoned above my PF flyers seemed to make me faster still, as if I'd added winged heels. I thought I was fleeing in the direction of No-Man's-Land but wasn't sure. The streets were a blur and I had a stitch in my side, but I kept running. On an impulse I turned down a side street I hoped would lead back onto California. My gym shoes splashed through water, not puddles but a current that swirled the rubbish out of the gutters. The street was flooded: every hydrant opened, boards jammed in their geysering mouths, fanning pressurized water into the prismatic mist of phantom rainbows. I was in a strange neighborhood that expressed its anarchy in water, a village on the shore of pouring hydrants. Its inhabitants wore wet clothes plastered to their bodies and cavorted through the torrents. A young Spanish girl in shorts stood beside the fountain of a red fire pump, her arms spread as if she were balancing on ripples. She was humming aloud to herself—a tune without a language, maybe her secret fire-pump song.

"Hey, Clarinet Boy," she singsonged, and I stopped and stood, catching my breath. "Play something," she said and gestured for me to come through a curtain of spray. And, as if I belonged there, I stepped to the shelter of where she waited beneath a cascading canopy of water.

"What you want to hear?" I asked, as if I could play anything.

Live from Dreamsville

~~~~~~

Their voices floated across the musty mud smell of the gangway into our room. Mick and I sat at the edges of our beds and listened, laughing until we were afraid we might be heard, then burying our faces in our pillows to muffle the laughter. Next door, Jano was drunk and cursing. His gravelly voice slurred from some cavity deep within the dilapidated frame house.

"Hurry up the goddamn food," he kept repeating, and every time he said it, Kashka would fire back, "Don't get a hard-on."

"Hurry up the goddamn food."

"Don't get a hard-on!"

We got a whiff of food frying in the smoky crackle of lard.

"Phewee!" Mick whispered. "It smells like they're cooking a rat."

We both dove for our pillows, choking with laughter. I buried my face until it got sweaty and I could smell the feather ticking. Mick was still laughing; it sounded as if he was being strangled.

"Cool it," I said, "or Sir'll hear us."

"Don't get a hard-on," Mick said.

We pushed our faces against the screen, trying to peer into Kashka's house. Her window was a little below ours and off to the right so that we couldn't see much beyond the torn bedspread half-draped across it. Even where we could see, the windowpane was the color of soot. A bare lightbulb gleamed through black-

ened glass. There were crickets in the gangway among the ragweed, trilling louder than the distant sirens rushing to some
calamity.

Mick climbed onto the inside windowsill, squatting to get a
better look. We were sleeping in our underwear because it was
hot, though despite the heat we both resolutely wore homemade
nightcaps cut from one of Mom's old nylons. They fit tightly over
our heads to hold our Brylcreemed d.a.'s in place. I reached up
and pinched his ass.

"*Ow!*" he yelled, and banged his head on the sash.

"Shut up, you want Sir to hear? Get down, ya lubber."

"Where's the goddamn food?" Jano demanded, his voice getting louder, moving toward us.

"Don't get a hard-on."

"How can I without you?"

We tried very hard to stifle our laughter because we wanted to
hear what would happen next.

"Don't tear my goddamn dress . . . for crissakes take it easy,
Janush." Kashka's rough voice sounded different than I'd ever
heard it when she called him Janush. We heard a heavy thunk and
then a clank like a pot falling from a table.

"You're hurtin my titties." She moaned. "Suck 'em, don't bite
'em, Janush."

Then, except for an occasional groan, they got quiet, and we
lay straining to hear, the word *titties* still hanging in the gangway
like an echo that refused to fade. I'd always figured women, even
Kashka, referred to them as their *bosom* or *breasts*, words more
dignified than *titties*. Titties were for girls, something blossoming, maybe the size of tangerines. Kashka was built like a squat
sumo wrestler. She had the heaviest upper arms I'd ever seen,
rolls of flab wider than most people's thighs, folding like sleeves
over her elbows. She didn't have titties, she had watermelons,
and Jano, missing half his teeth, was sucking them. I listened for

the slurping but heard nothing. I wondered what Mick was making of it all. I wasn't sure how much he really understood about sex yet. The creaking of their house became audible, as if a galleon was anchored beside our window, and the moans resumed, louder and more frequent, though no sexier than those that came from behind the frosted glass of Dr. Garcia's office, sounds we always regretted overhearing as we waited our turns in the dental chair. Then, mercifully, they fell silent.

"What do you think they're doing?" Mick asked.

I thought of different possibilities but said nothing.

"Hey," he asked, "you going to sleep?"

I lay listening to him tossing in his bed, flapping his sheets.

"I know you're up, ya swab. You're just fakin," he said.

My eyes were closed, though he couldn't see me in the dark.

"If you're sleeping, then you won't hear me calling you Toes. I won't lose any points. Ha-ha, Toes! Hey, Toes? Toesush?"

I totaled up his lost points, grinning in the dark. Minus five for each time he called me Toes. Those were the rules according to the Point System. Mick wasn't old enough yet to go alone to the movie theater on Marshall Boulevard, and if he wanted to tag along with me on Saturdays, he had to lose less than a hundred points during the week. He could gain points for doing things for me, too, like folding my papers before I delivered them. Or sometimes he'd get something on me and blackmail me for points not to tell Sir. He'd just lost fifteen and was already a hundred and twenty in the hole.

"Hey, Toes, you eat boogers."

Invasion of the Body Snatchers was coming this weekend, and Mick really wanted to see that.

I heard him getting out of bed, and I tensed, keeping my eyes closed and trying not to break up. I could feel him standing over me.

"Hey, Toesush," he whispered.

I heard him rubbing his fingers together near my face, beneath my nose. He was chuckling maniacally. "I guess you really are sleeping," he said, then got back in bed.

We lay there completely quiet for a while.

"I'm sure glad you're sleeping, because you know what I did? I cleaned my kregs and sprinkled the toe-jam on your face."

My not saying anything was really driving him nuts. He shut up for a long time after that. When I figured he was about to drop off to sleep, I started to snore.

"Shut up! I know you're fakin'."

I mumbled in my sleep and snored louder, and he bounced up again and gave my bed a shake. I rolled over with a groan as if in the middle of a dream. He gave me a jab in the back, then threw himself into bed.

He was turned toward the wall, convinced against his best judgment that I really was asleep, and trying now to sleep himself. Except for the *ding* of a freight train blocks away and a single cricket still trilling in the gangway, it was very quiet.

"You just lost a hundred points, matey," I said.

He kind of flinched, then pretended *he* was sleeping.

"You might as well forget about that movie. I bet it's really gonna be great, too. The coming attractions were fantastic. Oh well, I guess you didn't want to see it anyway. That's why you're not saying anything. At least you ain't gonna beg. Which is smart because there's no way I'm changing my mind. Not after having toe-jam sprinkled in my face. And getting socked in the back. That was a test. Now I know what kind of stuff goes on when I really am sleeping. Well, okay, good night, I'm going to Dreamsville."

I tucked the sheet over my head and curled up in the middle of the mattress. Both of us knew he no longer believed in Dreamsville, but neither of us was about to admit it. A year ago he'd still been convinced I had a secret trapdoor in my bed that led to a clubhouse full of sodas, malts, popcorn, candy, a place where the stray dogs and cats in the neighborhood gathered at night. In Dreamsville, animals could talk. Sometimes celebrities like Bugs Bunny would drop in.

Mick would hear fragments of our merrymaking, muffled as if the trapdoor had been left ajar: my voice saying, "Hi, Whiskers. Hi, Topsy. Oh, hi there, Mousie Brown, you here tonight?"

Whiskers was our cat, supposedly out for the night. Topsy was Kashka's ginger-colored watchdog. He was supposed to guard the chickens she kept illegally, but he'd let me sneak over her fence, and while he wagged his tail, I'd untie the clothesline noosed around his neck and boost his back end over the fence into the alley. Whenever we managed an escape, he'd spend the rest of the day following Mick and me around the streets until Kashka or one of her demented wino friends caught him again. Though Kashka had never caught me in the act, she knew I was the one springing Topsy, and hated me for it, not that I cared. Mick and I loved Topsy and had planned to steal him for good when we got old enough not to need Sir's permission to keep him, but a couple of weeks ago I'd sprung him and the dogcatchers caught him. Kashka had just replaced him with a black puppy.

Mousie Brown was the name of Mick's favorite stuffed animal, one he slept with until a night when, sick with flu, he puked all over it. When Moms tried to clean it, the fur washed off, leaving behind a raggedy, bald lump that reeked of vomit, so she threw it out on the sly.

They'd all bark and meow hello, and Mousie Brown might squeak, "Have a Dad's old-fashioned root beer, Perry."

It was during the winter, back before there was a Point System, that Mick still believed in Dreamsville. I'd made it up as a joke, one I didn't expect he'd take seriously, but he must have wanted to believe, and once he did, he wanted to go to Dreamsville, too. In winter, I slept beneath a *piersyna*—a big old feather tick our grandmother had brought from Poland—and once I disappeared beneath it into Dreamsville, Mick would get out of bed and try to lift the *piersyna* up to get at the trapdoor. I'd lie tucked into a ball, holding the *piersyna* to me, with him on top tugging at it, punching me through the goose feathers, getting worked up so loud sometimes that Sir would hear the noise and charge in swinging a belt or a shoe or whatever was handy, an attack he called a "roop in the dupe." Seeing the covers ripped and me getting my *dupa* beat tended to weaken Mick's belief in Dreamsville. Though for a while I was able to convince him that, in order to preserve the secret, I'd come up through the trapdoor just before Sir whisked off the covers. Since Mick was getting rooped, too, he couldn't really be sure. Then one night, instead of first yelling down the hall that we better get to sleep, Sir snuck up on us and suddenly stepped into the room, flicking on the light and stripping the *piersyna* off me where I lay bunched up in the middle of the mattress.

"What the hell do you guys yak about so much in here anyway?" he asked.

As usual we both pretended to be groggy, as if he'd just awakened us from a sound sleep.

"You're the older guy, Perry," he said to me. "You should be setting him a good example instead of this fooling around every night. You know he's like a monkey—copies whatever you do. Then in the morning your mother's gotta fight with you guys to get up for school and she's nervous the rest of the day."

I lay there hoping he'd control his temper, feeling naked in the light, and diminished, like the room made suddenly tiny without its darkness. Finally, he switched the light back off and left. I guess when he was angry enough to come in swinging, he didn't like the light on any more than I did.

A few nights after that I decided that I'd finish off Dreamsville before Mick did. He'd already stopped begging me to take him there. I was under the *piersyna* talking in my pirate accent to the animal crew: "Whiskers, pass the peanuts, matey, and squirt a ducat of catsup on these fries. Yum, tasty! Purr, purr. Squeak, squeak. Hey, Mousie Brown, hoist that case of cold pop off the poop deck, yo-ho-ho, pass that cotton candy, please. Pass the popcorn, pass the pop, pass the poop, me hardies."

We both exploded into laughter. When the laughter would let up, one of us would say, "Pass the poop, me hardies." Mick laughed so hard he had to go to the bathroom, but I convinced him it would be a mistake to let them know he was still awake and talked him into pissing out the window.

It was cold and raining. We quietly slid up the window, then the storm window. The radiator was in front of the window, and Mick had to slide over it in order to sit on the sill. I held on to him so he wouldn't fall.

"I'm getting soaked," he complained, and I started laughing hysterically again. "What's so funny?"

"You must be totally crazy hanging out a window and pissing."

"Okay, get me in," he demanded.

"Oh-oh, you know what?"

"What?"

"I bet Kashka's looking out her window and saw what you just did."

"Get me in, get me in!" He was getting frantic, struggling for leverage.

"She's probably coming around the back way to grab your legs and pull you outside."

"Come on, quit fooling around, get me in." He sounded ready to cry, so I let him in.

"My pajamas are all wet. Now I can't sleep." He was wearing his flannel pirate pajamas.

"Let that be a lesson to never piss out a window."

Even though Mick no longer believed in Dreamsville, it still got to him when I'd disappear under the sheet, like now, describing scenes from *Invasion of the Body Snatchers* as if I had my own private screening room down there.

"The pods are coming! Aaayyiiii! Everyone's a pod! This is the scariest movie I ever saw."

"If you were up, why didn't you say so? I was just seeing if you were fakin'."

"Almost too horrible to look at!"

"I didn't really mean it."

"Hold it. Stop the movie a second. I think I hear something. What? Did you wake up?"

"I didn't mean it."

"Didn't mean what?"

"Whatever I lost points for."

"Like what?"

"Calling you Toes."

"Okay, even though I ought to take extra off for *ush*ing me, you can have the fifteen points back. Anything else?"

"Like sprinkling toe-jam in your face."

"Jesus Christ! You might as well forget apologizing for that."

"I swear I didn't really do it."

"Don't lie. I felt it. I smelled it."

"Honest to God! I didn't do it! I was just rubbing my fingers together making the noise."

"His fingers sure smell a lot like his kregs, ladies and gentlemen." *Kregs* was a name Mick had coined for the spaces between toes.

"I did it just like you did the peanut butter."

"Just because I'm laughing don't mean I believe you," I said, breaking up just thinking about it. A few days earlier, while Mick was reading a *Mad* comic, I'd snuck up on him with a glob of peanut butter on a sheet of toilet paper, smeared it on his arm, and told him it was shit. At first he didn't believe me, so I told him to smell it. He did and started screaming, "You really did it! You're crazy! I'm telling Moms!" I tackled him before he could get away and began trying to smear the glob off his arm into his mouth. He was fighting back hard, yelling I'd gone completely crazy, wrenching his face away, spitting it out every time I got it near his lips. I thought once he tasted it he'd see the joke, but I had a hard time getting him to believe that it was only peanut butter.

"You only gave me seventy-five points for not telling about that, so it's not fair I lose a hundred for this."

"All right, you want to get a hundred points back?"

"How?"

"Stick your head out the window and tell Kashka you love her."

"Go to hell! I wouldn't do that for a million stinking points."

"I'll give you fifty if you just admit it to the ladies and gentlemen."

"Admit what?"

"The truth, just say it out loud: Ladies and gentlemen, I admit it, I love Kashka."

"No, it's not fair."

"Okay, ladies and gentlemen, he had his chance. He didn't want to see the movie anyway."

I disappeared under the sheet again and began to snore. Suddenly, I felt him land on top of me. He'd jumped from his bed

onto mine and was trying to strangle me through the sheets while
kneeing me in the back.

"Hey, take it easy," I said, "or Captain Roopus will hear." But
he wouldn't stop. "This is gonna cost your scurvy ass another
hundred points."

That made him punch all the harder. He tried to gouge my
eyes through the sheet. "I don't care what you do," he said.

"Sir's gonna hear."

"I don't care."

I squirmed loose, grabbed my pillow, and smashed it in his
face, sending his head thudding off the wall.

"They'll hear that for sure. Better get in your own bed."

Mick was half-crying. "I don't care. I'll tell them everything.
I'll tell about the Point System. I'll tell I saw you playing with
matches."

He tried to break away toward the bedroom door. I grabbed
him by his undershirt and tried to wrestle him down, but it tore
away.

"I'm gonna tell you ripped my T-shirt."

"No tell, no tell, Mickush," I pleaded.

"Don't *ush* me."

He managed to open the door and slip out with me still
pulling on his arm. "No tell, no tell," I kept whispering. It was
too late to force him back. We were halfway down the dark hallway. The fluorescent light in the kitchen was still on and lit up the
end of the hall. Their voices carried to us. Mick stopped.

They were arguing. We could hear them very clearly. Moms
was already at that point when her hands shook; we could hear
the tremors in her voice. When what she called her "nerves" got
bad enough, her lower jaw would tremble, too, as if she was on
the verge of a fit. She would continue trying to talk even though
she could no longer control her voice, and it sounded as if she
was gagging on words stuck in the back of her throat. Her attacks

of nerves had begun a couple years earlier. Usually, they'd come
on at night. I'd wake to her walking the apartment in the dark,
talking to herself, praying, crying. Sometimes, thinking us asleep,
she'd enter our room and sit shaking at the foot of my bed. Once,
Mick woke, heard her crying, and began crying, too, so now
when the attacks came she'd lock herself in the bathroom and
turn on the water taps.

"You gotta get ahold of yourself before you're in the same
boat as your brother, Lefty," Sir was saying. "I'm gonna call that
phony-baloney doctor and tell him I'm taking those da-damn
pills he's giving you to the police."

There was a crash like a dish breaking. "I-yi-yi c-c-can't stand
it," Moms gagged out.

"He's turning you into an addict," Sir said. "You take the pills
and act like a zombie, and without them you fall apart."

"Y-y-you ever t-t-try li-li-living without any sympathy? I-yi-yi
can't stand it." Something else broke.

"Go on, act like a da-damn nut and break it all so I can work
harder to support us."

"I'll give you all the points back. I'll take you to the movie," I
whispered. "Come on back to bed."

Mick followed me, both of us creeping back to the room. I
closed the door, and it was dark again. We climbed into our beds
and lay there not saying anything.

I was nearly asleep when the whining started from across the
gangway. At first it was just there, a night sound like the crickets,
sirens, and freights, but it grew louder and sharper and I realized
I was feverish with sweat and sat up.

"It must be their new dog," Mick said.

"Jesus, what's the matter with him? I never heard a dog sound
like that."

We tried to look through the screen again, but all we saw was the bulb behind the bedspread. Then we heard Kashka's voice.

"Janush, stop beating on him."

The whining went on.

"That sonofabitch, that dirty bastard. He's torturing that puppy in there." I threw myself back in bed and started punching the pillow until the whining stopped. In the quiet I could feel my lungs heaving and realized I'd been holding my breath. Then the whining started again.

"Why's he doing it?" Mick asked.

"I'll get him for this, the sonofabitch. I'll steal that dog and burn their goddamn house down. I'm not kidding. I'll wait till the bastard's passed out drunk and get him with a brick. I'm going to call the Humane Society tomorrow."

"For shitsake, Jano, stop beating the goddamn dog," Kashka yelled. She sounded more irritated by the noise than anything else.

"You said you wanted him mean, not like the other one, didn't you?" Jano answered. "This is when you gotta get them if you want 'em mean."

He kept at it as if proving his point. There was an even worse sound, like a choking squeal, and I could imagine Jano holding the dog up by the clothesline they kept tied around his neck while his hind legs danced off the floor.

"Shut up!" Jano shouted, and it was abruptly silent.

"Maybe he killed him," Mick whispered.

I pulled the nylon stocking from my head and peeled my undershirt off and put it on the radiator. It was soaked through with sweat. I lay back down and waited, my insides braced for the whining to start again. It was quiet, but I couldn't relax.

"Want to have a Radio Show?"

"Okay, you start," Mick said.

"Hello again out there, ladies and gentlemen, this is your

friendly announcer, Dudley Toes, coming to you live from Dreamsville in the heart of Little Village over station KRAP, brought to you by Kashka Marishka's dee-licious melt-in-your-fat-mouth Frozen Rat DeLuxe Dinners!"

"And Jano's Hard-on Pickles. The only pickles especially made for shoving up your nose."

"Thank you, Mick the Schmuck, and now, ladies and gentlemen, let's get the show on the road with the thing you've all been waiting for. Hey, ladies and gentlemen! Wake the hell up! I said the thing you've all been waiting for!"

Applause, cheers, boos from Mick's bed.

"And here it is! The Great Singing Competition between the world's two greatest singers—Tex Robe and Boston Blackhead!"

"I'm Tex Robe," Mick said. "I made it up."

"But you made it up for me. And I made Boston Blackhead up for you. There's no reneging on Blackhead, old buckaroo. Now shut up till it's your turn, or you're disqualified. Right, ladies and gentlemen?"

"Right, right, right," the ladies and gentlemen answered from the sides of their mouths.

"And here he is, ladies and gentlemen, Tex Robe singing the great new hit 'Saxophone Boogie'!"

> Saxophone Boogie, yeah yeah,
> Saxophone Boogie, yeah yeah,
> Saxophone Boogie, yeah yeah,
> Oh man, that music's cool!
> You hear the saxophone
> When you're sittin there at home,
> Hear that saxophone
> And know you're not alone,
> Hear the saxophone
> When you're sittin there in school,

Oh man, that music's cool.
Saxophone Boogie, yeah yeah . . .

"Let's hear it for Tex Robe, ladies and gentlemen!"
Thunderous applause.
Then it was Boston Blackhead's turn. The ladies and gentlemen cheered again. Some booed and hissed. Boston Blackhead
began to sing in a quavery, haunting voice, the voice of a ghost,
of an ancient mariner.

"Oh no, ladies and gentlemen, not that, any song but that,"
the master of ceremonies implored, but it was too late. There was
no stopping the song, the same song that Mick had been singing
on and off over the past months, ever since I'd brought a book on
explorers home from the library, and, adrift on our beds in the expanse of darkness, we circumnavigated the world. Instead of returning the book on time, I'd hid it along with a flashlight
behind the radiator, and after the house was quiet I'd read in a
whisper about the five ships and two hundred and seventy-seven
men who'd set sail, about the Patagonian Giants with their
strange words—*ghialeme* for fire, *settere* for stars, *chene* for hand,
gechare for scratch—words we began to use, as in "I hear you
gecharing your balls, matey." They passed the Cape of Desire, the
Cape of Eleven Thousand Virgins, the Land of fire—*ghialeme*
—under the Southern Cross, past the Unfortunate Isles, the
Robber Islands. There were doldrums, shipwrecks, mutinies,
demasting storms. "My men die fast, but we approach the East
Indies at fair speed. . . . I know a ship can sail around the world.
But God help us in our suffering." Their ankles swelled enor-
mously, their teeth dropped out, the flesh of penguins stunk in
the hold, they soaked the leather wrappings from the masts in
seawater for days, ate sawdust and wood chips. Three years, forty
thousand miles, only eighteen men returned.

I sailed with Magellan, ooo-ooo-ooo
Oh, oh, oh,
I sailed with Magellan . . .

Each time Mick sang it, the song got weirder, rambling without any one melody, its scale sounding foreign like a Muslim prayer, Mick never pausing, even if I laughed, he'd just keep singsonging on into a kind of trance . . . I sailed with Magellan, oh, oh, oh . . . boiled our shoes . . . ate our sails . . . without teeth . . . chewed our ship down to the nails . . . I sailed with Magellan, ooo-ooo-ooo

Oh, oh, oh . . .

It kept getting softer and softer until finally he faded out. I could hear his breathing heavy and rhythmic and knew he was sleeping. The light across the gangway went out, leaving the room a shade darker. After a while, when the dog felt it was safe to softly whimper, I knew Kashka and Jano were sleeping, too.

~~~~~~

Swimsuits on beneath our clothes, a towel each, and the bar of brown laundry soap Sir always brought, we rumbled out of the neighborhood in his latest bargain, a Kaiser the green of an army tank—one that had seen combat. At Twenty-third, Mick and I shouted for him to swing onto the flooded side street where a plank propped before an open hydrant made for an illegal fountain, but he ignored us, and we headed down Cermak, stop and go, never fast enough to make a breeze, past the lumberyards on Ashland, and the huge electric plant where Moms used to work, and the turnoff to Maxwell Street, then through Chinatown, with its crowded streets and pagodaed restaurants where it was rumored illegal fireworks were sold.

"Full of tourists," Sir said. "Only place in Chicago where you see tourists."

"Why don't we ever stop and look around Chinatown?" Mick asked.

Sir just gave him a raised brow.

After Chinatown the street turned shabby, trash in the gutters, factories and gutted apartment buildings side by side. Black people sat on the doorsteps, escaping the heat.

"Roll up the windows," Sir said. "Hot nights like this anything can happen around here."

We rolled them partway, but it was too stuffy. It had been in the nineties all week. The State Street El station looked as if it were silhouetted against the radiation from an atomic blast. The platform's shadow stretched in perfect detail, like an enormous negative superimposed on the street. Beneath its shady girders was a bar, its open door like an amplifier reverbing blues guitar. Black men sweating through their shirts and women in silky, sleeveless dresses congregated in front, foaming beer bottles in hand. They laughed and swayed, and the women fanned themselves to the music. They looked as if they were having a good time. We stopped for the light under the slatted shadows of the El tracks.

"Lookit! Lookit!" Sir yelled. "The guy with the chicken!"

"Where at?" Mick whirled in the backseat. He'd only heard about the Chickenman till now.

A bony, brown man, legs like stilts, shirt out over his trousers, strutted down State, nodding left and right as if the street were lined with people watching a parade. A white chicken perched at attention on his head. He passed the bar and stopped at the curb. The chicken stepped from his head to his shoulder, ruffled its feathers, and white droppings hit the sidewalk. Then it gently twisted its neck and rubbed its faded pink comb along the man's cheek.

The light changed. Sir stepped on the gas. The Chickenman blew us a kiss. I could see black kids running to catch up with him and wished I could follow him, too.

"He goes all over the city with that chicken," Sir said. "Perry and I see him sometimes at Maxwell Street, right sonnyboy?"

"About every Sunday," I said. For the last year, since I turned thirteen, Sir had been taking me along to Maxwell, an open-air bazaar that some people called Jewtown. He said he wanted to teach me how to shop. I didn't want to go at first, until I realized

the big shopping day on Maxwell was Sunday morning, and that
going with Sir got me out of going to church.

"Maxwell Street *is* your father's church," Moms would kid.

Mick, still too young for Jewtown, was stuck going to Sunday
mass.

"That Chickenman had that chicken pecking corn right off his
tongue," Sir told Mick. "Poor crazy goof."

I remembered a Sunday in spring when we'd seen the Chickenman close his mouth over the head of the chicken as if preparing
to swallow it whole. The chicken didn't seem to mind. That was
on Maxwell Street amidst crowds of people browsing and heat-
edly bargaining in different languages. Sir led me from one rick-
ety stall to another, stopping to pick through boxes of used
faucets, lengths of pipe, elbow joints, fittings heaped in musty,
tangled piles on canvas tarpaulins lining the curbs. As usual, he
was looking for some specific part—a three-quarter fitting—and,
as usual, I was supposed to be helping him find it, though I had
no idea what a three-quarter fitting was.

His ability to gauge instantly the dimensions of things both
mystified and intimidated me. It was a gift I seemed to lack completely, one expressed in a language I was ignorant of, with a vocabulary one needed to gain admittance into the practical world
of men. We might be rumbling in the Kaiser down a busy street
like Western Avenue, and Sir would suddenly hit the brakes and
stop in the middle of traffic before a piece of scrap that other cars
swerved to avoid. While Mick and I slouched in humiliation below the dash, Sir would get out of the car, pick up the scrap, and
singing aloud, wholly oblivious to the motorists honking and
cursing as they pulled around him, he'd carefully fasten it to the
homemade carriers he'd suction-cupped to the roof. He carried
rope in case of such lucky finds, though in the absence of rope,
twists of wire coat hangers served just as well. A coat hanger fas-

tened the tailpipe to the Kaiser, and we'd gone through a phase when coat hangers held the screen door to its hinges, secured the lids of trash cans, and appeared in a variety of other ingenious applications. Mick had remarked that he expected Sir to start using coat hangers as belts for our trousers and laces for our shoes. When—still singing—Sir got back in the car, we'd ask: "Yo, Dad, don't you think the Kaiser is junky enough without stopping to pile more junk on top?"

He always had the perfect comeback. "Do either of you guys know what a good two-by-four is going for by the foot?"

Not only did I not know the price per foot but I didn't know how by looking at a piece of busted lumber he could recognize its dimensions.

That Sunday on Maxwell Street, back in spring, it was a three-quarter fitting we were after, and I especially hated sorting through used plumbing. I couldn't help imagining the flood of excrement that had flushed through those moldy gray parts. I was lagging behind, thumbing through a carton stuffed with old comic books, when a gypsy girl came out of one of the store-fronts on Maxwell and slipped an arm around my father's waist. Her earrings dangled nearly to her bare shoulders. Her peasant blouse scooped across the crease between her smallish, pointy breasts. A red scarf bandannaed her black hair, and her eyes were violet with mascara. Beneath the makeup, she didn't look that much older than me.

"You got black hair like gypsy," she said to Sir. "Want gypsy good time? I give you."

Sir took off walking, shaking her arm off, trying to ignore her. Suddenly, he slapped his wallet, pinning her hand to his back pocket. "Let go," he said.

Instead, she reached a hand around and grabbed his crotch and, still smiling, stared up at him, whispering something I couldn't hear. It stopped him in his tracks.

"Da-dammit," he said, screwing up his face as if he'd swallowed something sour, then shot a harried look back at me, a look I interpreted as *Don't tell Mother.*

They stood stalemated, nobody on the street paying the least attention, the gypsy massaging the front of his trousers while Sir tried to work her hand out of his back pocket without the wallet coming with it. I just stood there, too, instantly entranced by her, until I saw two gypsy men stepping out of the same doorway toward my father.

A cop, gnawing a Polish sausage dripping sauce, ambled across the street and headed them off.

"Giving you trouble?" he asked Sir.

"Forget it," Sir said, face still registering a sour taste. "I don't want no trouble."

As we walked away, I turned and saw the cop slip his arm around the girl's shoulder, taking a bite from the sausage he held in one hand while his other hand nonchalantly slid into her blouse so that a bare breast almost lifted over the elastic neckline, flashing the tan areola of a nipple I didn't quite see. I watched the girl disappear back into the doorway of the storefront. Sir caught the look on my face.

"They get you inside there and *shlish*," he said, drawing a finger across his throat. "Girls like that carry a disease that'll make you walk like Charlie Chaplin."

It was the first advice he ever gave me about sex and, thankfully, the last.

We saw the Chickenman that day, stilt-legged, balanced on a hydrant above the passing crowds, with the chicken rising from his head like a weather vane. The bird hopped to his shoulder, and the man's mouth widened to a gaping hole in which the chicken bobbed his head. The mouth closed, and when the chicken slowly spread its wings, it looked as if the man's head might fly from his body.

I'd described the whole scene more than once to Mick on nights when I'd lie in the dark and think about the girl before I went to sleep, wondering where the gypsies had gone. Mick especially liked the part about her grabbing Sir by the balls.

We knew we were close when we passed Donnelly's, a block-long factory where telephone books were printed. I could feel the pneumatic exhalation of its giant, racketing presses, smell the scorched ink of all those compressed names and numbers and the sweat of the night shift, who stared out like convicts behind mesh screens. Then traffic accelerated, and as we pulled onto the Outer Drive the sudden coolness made my head light. Soldier Field rose on the left, and the lake stretched past the breakwater and farthest sailboats, shimmering pink under a sun that glazed the park trees.

"Workin on the railroad, workin on the farm, all I got to show for it's the muscle in my arm," Sir sang in a voice he lowered to a baritone he considered operatic. He often sang when he drove. "I had a Caruso-quality voice as a kid," he'd tell us, "but ruined it imitating trains."

Mick was rolling around in the backseat with his hands over his ears, groaning as if having convulsions.

"At least he's not singing 'Brother Can You Spare a Dime?' " I said.

"And it looks like I'm never gonna cease my wanderin."

"He's *never* gonna cease his wanderin," I said to Mick.

Mick and a black kid in the backseat of a car in the lane beside us were giving each other the finger. The kid tried to spit into our Kaiser, but his spit blew back on him. We all busted up, including the kid.

Sir was pumping the brakes as cars weaved in front of him.

"Da-damn nuts," he yelled, jockeying for the turning lane. "It's really dog eat dog on this thing."

Brakes grinding, we shimmied off the exit for Twelfth Street Beach and crawled along the aisles of the parking lot looking for a space. Finally, Sir had to drive over the sidewalk and park on the grass. There were a lot of other cars parked on the grass.

"Can't give us all tickets," he said.

We slipped our jeans off. Sir hid his watch and wallet under the seat.

"Leave the windows open a crack, so when we come back it's not like a da-damn oven in here."

"Where's the door opener?" Mick asked.

"Just climb out this way," Sir said.

"No," Mick insisted, "I demand the door opener."

I handed it to him over the seat, and he began to mash at the buffalo. Only the door on the Kaiser's driver side opened, so we carried around a sawed-off broom handle we called the door opener. The Kaiser had no inside door handles. Before the Kaiser-Frazer company went out of business, it had advertised its designs as the automobiles of the future. To their engineers, the future meant push buttons, so they'd replaced door handles with push buttons embossed with the Kaiser trademark, a buffalo. By mashing the buffalo with just the right amount of force, we sometimes got the passenger door to open. We'd turned it into a competition. This time Mick got it on five tries—average.

Sir checked to make sure everything was locked while Mick and I hopped barefoot across scorching asphalt to the beach.

"Don't step on any da-damn broken glass or we'll have a real mess," Sir hollered behind us. "I don't know why the punks have to break the bottles instead of throwing them in the trash." He paused to kick a bottle neck through a sewer grate. He was still wearing his socks and unlaced factory shoes, though he'd stripped down to his old maroon bathing trunks with the gold buckle and the leaping aqua blue swordfish over the coin pocket. People didn't wear swimsuits like that anymore. Sometimes seeing it made me weak inside with a feeling that I couldn't name but that had to do with all the times I'd seen him wear it before, times when I was little—younger than Mick was now—when Moms would always come with us to the beach, times before she got nervous, before we'd hear her pacing the house in the dark in the middle of the night crying to herself. Seeing the maroon bathing suit made me think of the old maroon Chevy, the first car I remembered. I thought my father had driven home from the Army in it. It had a running board he'd let me ride on while he parked.

It was a car we'd pack once a year with shopping bags full of old clothes and jars of jam and the dill pickles Moms canned. Leaving Moms behind, my father and I would drive a long time into what seemed to me to be countryside because the streets were shadowy with trees. We'd arrive at a high iron gate and follow a road that curved through park-like grounds where people in wheelchairs were pushed by attendants in white. We'd park and enter a cavernous building of gray stone, tote our shopping bags down corridors acrid with disinfectant, and wait before a bank of windows that looked out on lawn. An old man with stunned eyes and a jawline grizzled in gray would be wheeled in to where we waited. The three of us would sit silently together. There was never any talk, not even in Polish, a language my father relied on for secrecy. My father took the old man's veined, stony hand and traced its battered knuckles. Before we left he'd kiss that hand. We never stayed long, and I'd forget about our trip until a year later, when we'd again load shopping bags into the maroon Chevy and drive into what felt like a déjà vu.

After a few such visits I asked, "Dad, who is that old guy?"

"Grandpa," he answered, the only time I ever heard him use the word. After that we never went back. If my father continued to visit, he did so secretly. Only later did I learn that the place to which we drove was Dunning, the state mental hospital that people then commonly called the insane asylum.

The beach house was shaped like an ocean liner with a huge orange smokestack. Lights glowed from its portholes; the air smelled like red hots and popcorn. People padded barefoot through sandy puddles slopped along the concrete decks, shouting in different languages. Men showered in open stalls in front of changing rooms, spraying sand off kids little enough to go naked.

As always, Mick and I stopped at a huge concrete drinking fountain where water gurgled from a dozen metal pipes, water rusty tasting and cold as if pumped straight from the lake. When he leaned for a drink, I plugged two of the pipes with my fingers and water shot up Mick's nose. He chased me down to the lake, his cheeks bulging with a mouthful of water to spit.

"Doesn't it feel kinda stupid running into the lake with your mouth full of water?"

He opened his mouth for a comeback, and the water dribbled out, breaking me up. I waded out laughing, and he came after me, both of us splashing sheets of water at each other. I dove under, and when I came up, Mick was chest deep, jogging up and down in time to the waves while milling his arms through the air as if he were doing the Australian crawl. His cheeks bulged; he'd gulped a mouthful of lake water to spit.

"You really think you're swimming?" I yelled, recalling how I'd once done the same thing. But the Army helicopter whirring in overhead drowned out my voice. Everyone stopped and stood looking up as the helicopter hovered in to land behind the barbed wire of Meigs field, an airstrip that bordered the beach.

We'd always come here to Twelfth Street Beach. It was where

Sir taught me to swim. But tonight he was going to take us off the Rocks, where the water was deep.

"The Rocks is where we used to swim when I was a kid," he said, "me and my friends. We used to get out there around eight in the morning and not take the streetcar home till after dark. That was the life. Johnny Weissmuller used to swim off the Rocks with us."

"Who's Johnny Weissmuller?" Mick asked.

"Who's Johnny Weissmuller? You never seen *Tarzan of the Apes*?" Sir beat his chest and gave an ape call. People on the blankets glanced at him and laughed in a friendly way. He was different whenever he got around water—younger, grinning, kidding around.

"So who were you guys? The Apes?" Mick asked, always quick to get one in on Sir. Mick had made up the nickname Sir one night when we were all watching *Leave It to Beaver* and Dad said how nice it was that Wally and Beaver called their father "Sir."

"Apes is right—you shoulda seen us. Talk about tan! Italians would call me *paisano*. You shoulda seen this lake. People don't realize how da-damn dirty it's getting. When I was a kid you could see the bottom off the Rocks."

"What's down there?" I asked.

"A bunch of rocks. But who knows how old? They coulda been there when this was Indian country. Hell! Maybe rocks from back when it was all glacier with saber-tooths and mammoths. We used to dive down to see who could bring up the biggest rock. Weissmuller could swim faster and farther than any of us—one time I tried to swim to the pumping station with him, but hell, more than halfway I gave up. I coulda made it out there, but I was afraid about getting back. He didn't tell me a boat was gonna pick him up. But I could dive deeper and stay down longer than anyone, even old Tarzan. Things were so clean then we used to swim in the Chicago River."

"You mean the Drainage Canal!"

"With the floating turds?" Mick asked.

"It was still a river in some places, not a sewer. It was beautiful."

The breeze off the Rocks felt almost chilly. It blew straight in over a horizon that was a blinding gleam, and beyond the horizon I could picture the forests of Michigan. I tried to recapture the daydreams I'd had all week about coming out to the lake; I tried to remember how stuffy it would be tonight when we got back home.

There weren't any women. Men and teenagers plunged and swam in the deep green swells. Water bucked over the lip of the concrete walkway. I stared into the lake and couldn't imagine touching bottom.

"Want me to lower you in by the arms and cool you off?" Sir asked Mick. Mick was watching the swells hump in, standing well back from the edge.

"No, I'm gonna climb the rocks."

Just behind the concrete walk, enormous limestone blocks were piled in jagged, steplike tumbles as if some ancient city lay in ruins after a tidal wave.

"Okay, you do that"—Sir laughed—"and keep an eye on the towels." He slipped his shoes and socks off, put his car keys in one heel and shook them into the toe.

Spray showered over the concrete. I felt like going with Mick. The walkway vibrated when the waves whumped in as if it were hollow underneath. The sun was slipping lower in the hazy lilac sky. Mexican teenagers with gang tattoos whapped at each other with wet towels, their gold crosses swinging from their necks as they pushed each other in.

Sir gave an ape call.

Everyone turned for a moment and looked at him.

He backed up against the limestones and sprinted toward the water, hurtling off the concrete edge. His body arced like that of a man shot from a cannon—legs together, arms against his sides, so that when he hit the water it was headfirst, arms still pressed to his body. A spume thumped up, then showered back around his point of entry.

The guys standing next to me cheered.

We waited. Mick gathered up the towels and his shoes. Sir hadn't come up. People began to stare at us. I studied his socks stuffed in his shoes, then looked at Mick. He glanced away. Go find a lifeguard, I was getting ready to say, when Sir's head shot up, hair flattened slick as a seal.

"The old torpedo dive!" he shouted. "Come on in, Perry! Don't ever try the old torpedo unless you know there's nothing sticking up underwater."

Two Mexican guys who'd cheered raced for the water and torpedoed in on either side of Sir. They came up snorting and coughing and rubbing their eyes.

Sir sidestroked around them, laughing.

"Come on, sonnyboy!"

I'd never dived into deep water before. I was shivering and wasn't sure I remembered how to swim.

A Mexican kid, not much older than Mick, stood beside me. He was drying himself off with his shirt and shivering too, except he was dripping wet.

"Cold?" I asked, gesturing at the water.

"*Muy, muy.*"

"Strong undertow today," a guy with a mustache said. He looked like he could be the shivering kid's older brother. "Somebody drowned this morning and they still ain't found his body, man."

I'd heard of the undertow off the Rocks, of people being

pulled out into the lake, sucked under. I watched the bobbing swimmers for anyone being drawn away.

Sir was backstroking along the concrete edge, waves boosting him almost level with the walkway.

"Gimmie the soap!"

I got the bar of laundry soap and flipped it out to him. He floated on his back, lifting his toes and ankles high out of the water as if he were rocking on a hammock, and soaped his feet and legs, then rubbed the soap into lather in his black chest hair. I'd never seen anyone else bring soap to the lake, and for the first time a possible reason occurred to me: maybe when he was a boy they didn't have a bathtub. Whatever the reason, he didn't seem concerned that it looked weird to see a man washing while he was swimming.

"Perry, you're not coming in?"

"How come it's so wavy?"

"Must be the wake of that big ship passing by." He laughed and pointed. "Way out there."

There *was* a massive shadowy form against the dusky horizon, vaguely outlined by the light dying around its edges, and I recalled my uncle Lefty telling me about Blue Island, a ghost island Indian burial ground.

"*Murciélago! Murciélago!*" the Mexican guys started yelling.

Everyone was diving for the water.

"What is it?"

"Bat." The kid next to me grinned, then jumped in.

It boomeranged out of the bug-clouded floodlights, leathery, soaring at forehead level, and I dove.

For a moment, the foam of my dive felt like crushed ice. When I shot up, a wave broke over my head and I snorted some water, but I was swimming. Sir's head splashed up from underwater right beside me.

"Want the soap?"

I shook my head no. "It's great! Terrific!"

"Sure, just takes making the plunge and a little getting used to."

I felt used to it already, clean and hard, letting the cold wash away a week of sweat. The water seemed more and more comfortable so that, when a breeze skimmed over, I sank deeper, breaststroking, riding the waves. Like Sir had told me, it was easier to swim in deep water. I could feel it buoying me and practiced the crawl, lifting my arms high and rolling my face in the water, hoping Mick was watching. Sir streaked under me, the white soles of his feet gleaming like fish scales.

"How do you swim underwater so long?"

"Easy—the secret in water is to relax, don't listen to little nervous voices. Never fight it and you'll be all right. Take three deep breaths." He demonstrated, huffing in and out slowly three times. "And when you dive if your ears start to hurt, swallow like on an elevator. Keep your eyes open."

He flipped and speared down.

I inhaled three times quick and ducked under, trying to follow him. When I surfaced, he was still under. I knew I'd wimped out, and could have stayed down longer if I hadn't listened to the frightened voice urging me to come up for air.

"Hey, Mick!" I hollered.

I slowly inhaled six breaths and dove. The water was silvery green, and my hands finned before me like two perch. I was drawing my body through layers, each colder than the last, my eyes blurrily peering through increasing dimness, and my ears starting to ache with pressure. I swallowed, which helped some, kicked deeper, and as I heard the inner voice begin prompting me to shoot back up, I saw bottom, the same bottom Sir had seen when he swam with Johnny Weissmuller. There were no Mastodon tusks. It was gray, littered with mossy rocks, rolling beer cans, swaying silty seaweed.

I kicked hard and wrenched a slimy rock out of the mud, and the bottom clouded up so that I couldn't see. My ears were roaring, and instead of ascending, I was being carried along the bottom, my head near to exploding from holding my breath, and even though I couldn't see I was suddenly sure that the ocean liner on the horizon was passing overhead, its enormous hull turning the water dark, diesel churning the shaft of the great propeller that swept me along the bottom until I dropped the rock. Within the dreamlike moment that breath-holding expands, I could feel the current along the bottom rushing into the cavern under the walkway and realized the undertow didn't pull you out, it sucked you in, under the city, into the pipes, that was why they couldn't find the bodies. I knew the boy who'd drowned was curled in a fetal position, ghastly white, hair swaying as he pitched under the Rocks. It was me. I was going to die choosing numbness rather than panic. My Adam's apple swelled in my throat, forcing my mouth open. A hand was pushing on the seat of my suit, I opened my eyes, my father stared at me underwater, bubbles came from his mouth as he moved his lips like he was trying to tell me something important.

Stars were out over the lake. The bronzed dome of the Planetarium glowed otherworldly over the ridges of limestone. Mick stood at the edge of the Rocks waving and yelling, "Come on in . . . I wanna go home . . . mosquitoes!"

Behind him floodlights were enveloped in bugs. They landed drowning in kicking circles on the oily troughs of swells. The surface glistened, rocking with moonlit suds. Sir was surrounded by Mexican kids, all shampooing with the laundry soap, laughing, dunking, flinging handfuls of lather.

"Me Tarzan!" they shouted, howling ape calls across the water.

I was still coughing and spitting up, ears plugged and ringing.

"Don't swallow too much water," Sir said, looking at me. "People do their business in it."

"I'm going in for a while." I dog-paddled away, then hung in the water, letting a warm jet of pee run through my suit. Then I timed a wave and let it boost me up the rusty metal rungs sticking from the concrete. The sides went straight down, scarred with watermarks. It wasn't hollow under the walkway after all.

I sat on the edge of the Rocks watching the beacons from Meigs field crisscross as winking planes cranked in for the night.

"How's it goin?" The same young Mexican kid squatted down beside me. His lips were still chattering. He was dragging at a wet cigarette.

"I thought that big ship out there came in."

"Those red lights way out there, man?"

"Yeah."

"That's the pumping station," he said, and before I could say *I know* he whirled and called something in rapid Spanish to his brother.

His brother came over, grinning.

"See that guy in the water?" I said quickly. "He swam all the way out there once."

The kid passed me the cigarette, wet paper sticking to his fingertips. I glanced over at Sir. He was propelling on his back, holding the soap over his head while the others thrashed after him trying to catch it.

"Tarzan! Me Tarzan!" they were yelling.

I took a drag and passed it to the older brother.

"Man," he said, "even the *real* Tarzan ain't gonna swim out there." He inhaled deeply, squinting out past the glowing ash.

The red lights blinked on and off in the descending darkness. They seemed to be slowly moving.

Breasts

~~~~~~

Sundays have always been depressing enough without having to do a job. Besides, he's hungover, so fuck Sunday. Taking somebody out on Sunday is probably bad luck.

And Monday: no wheels. He's got an appointment with the Indian at the Marvel station on Western. That man's a pro—can listen to an engine idle and tell you the wear on the belts, can hear stuff already going bad that won't break for months. The Indian is the only one he lets touch the Bluebird, his powder blue, 312 Y-block, Twin Holley, four-barrel T-bird.

Tuesday, it's between Sovereign and hauling more than a month's laundry to the Chink's. Not to mention another hangover. He strips the sheets, balls them into the pillowcases, stuffs in the towels. He's tired of their stink, his stink, of dirty clothes all over the floor, all over the apartment. He's been wearing the same underwear how long? He strips naked and stares at himself in the bedroom mirror. His reflection looks smudged, and he wipes the mirror with a sock, then drops to the carpet to do a hundred push-ups—that always sharpens the focus.

He manages only seventy, and then, chest pounding hard enough to remind him that his father's heart gave out at age forty-five, lights a cigarette. He slaps on some Old Spice, slips back into his trousers and shirt without bothering to check the mirror, stuffs another pillowcase with dirty clothes, and since he's cleaning, starts on the heaps of dishes unwashed for weeks. Then, wham, it hits him like a revelation: who needs all this shit? Into trash bags go not only pizza cardboards and Chinese food cartons but bottles, cans, cereal boxes, plates, bowls, glasses, dirty pots. The silverware can stay. Next, it's the refrigerator's turn: sour milk, moldy cheese, rancid butter, all the scummy, half-empty bottles of mustard, mayo, pickles, jam, until the fridge is completely empty except for its cruddy shelves.

He removes the shelves.

Now he's got room for the giant mortadella that Sal brought from Italy. Sal came back from his trip bearing gifts and saying, *"Allora!"* whatever that means. The mortadella is scarred with wounds from another souvenir Sallie brought him, a stiletto. He's wanted an authentic stiletto for his knife collection, and this one is a piece of work, a slender pearl handle contoured to slide the thumb directly to the switch, and the most powerful spring he's ever seen on a knife. When the six-inch blade darted out, the knife actually recoiled in his hand. It felt as if the blade could shoot through Sheetrock, let alone flesh. He tested it on the mortadella, a thick sausage more muscular than Charles F-ing Atlas. He wondered if the knife could penetrate the rind, and was amazed when the thrust of the spring buried the blade to the hilt. It was a test he found himself repeating, and the mortadella, now propped in the empty refrigerator, looks as if it's seen gladiatorial combat, like Julius F-ing Caesar after Brutus got done with him.

Whitey calls. "Joey, you take care of business?"

"Still in the planning stage."

"Well, the decision's been made, you know? Let's not be indecisive on this."

"No problem, Whitey."

Taking care of business. Last Saturday night at Fabio's what Whitey said was "Blow the little skimming fuck's balls off and leave him for the birds."

"Not like there's vultures circling the neighborhood," he told Whitey, and Whitey said, "Joey, it was a manner of fucken speaking."

Okay, *allora!* motherfucker, no more procrastination. He can haul out the garbage, drop his laundry at the Chink's, *and* take care of Johnny Sovereign. Let's get this fucking thing over with even though he hasn't made a plan yet and that's not like him. Things are chancy enough without leaving them to chance. The man who's prepared, who knows exactly what he's going to do, always has the advantage. What seems inevitable as fate to such a man, to others seems like a surprise. Problems invariably arise, and he wants to be able to anticipate them, like the Indian who can listen to an engine and hear what will go bad. He wants to see the scars that appear before the wounds that caused them.

With a cotton swab he oils the .22, then sets the Hoppe oil on a glass ashtray on his dresser beside the Old Spice so it doesn't leave a ring, and tests the firing mechanism. He fills the clip with hollow-point shells and slides it into the Astra Cub, a Spanish-made Saturday night special that fits into the pocket of his sport coat. The sport coat is a two-button, powder-blue splash—same shade as the Bluebird. He'd conceal the stiletto in his sock, but he's stuffed all his socks into the dirty laundry, which forces him to dig inside the pillowcases until he comes up with a black-and-pink argyle with a good elastic grip to it. He can't find the match, so he puts the argyle on his right foot and a green Gold Toe on the left—nobody's going to be checking his fucking socks—then slides the stiletto along his ankle.

From his bedroom closet he drags out the locked accordion case that belonged to his grandfather. There's a lacquered red accordion inside that came from Lucca, where Puccini lived. In a cache Joe made by carefully detaching the bellows from the keyboard is an emergency roll of bills—seven G's—and uppers, downers, Demerol, codeine, a pharmacopoeia he calls his painkillers. In a way, they're for emergencies, too. Inside the accordion case there's also a sawed-off shotgun, a Walther PPK like the one James Bond uses, except this one is stolen and has the serial number filed off, and a Luger stamped with a swastika, supposedly taken off a dead German officer, which his father kept unloaded and locked away. After his father's death, Joe found ammo for it at a gun show. There's a rubber-banded cigarillo box with photos of girlfriends baring their breasts, breasts of all sizes, shapes, and shades of skin, a collection that currently features Whitey's girlfriend, Gloria Candido, and her silver-dollar nipples. She told Joe the size of her nipples prevented her from wearing a bikini. It's a photo that could get Joe clipped, but he's gambling that Gloria Candido is clever enough to play Whitey. Whitey's getting old, otherwise a punk-ass like Johnny Sovereign wouldn't be robbing him blind.

Capri St. Clair is in the cigarillo box, too, not that she belongs with the others. Her letters he keeps in his bureau drawer. She was shy about her breasts because the left was wine-stained. No matter that they were beautiful. To her, it was the single flaw that gives a person something to hide. Joe understood that, though he didn't understand her. There's always some vulnerability that a personality is reorganized to protect, a secret that can make a person unpredictable, devious, mysterious. Capri was all those, and still he misses her, misses her in a way that threatens to become his own secret weakness. Her very unpredictability is what he misses. Often enough it seemed like spontaneity. He doesn't have a photo of her breasts, but one surprising afternoon he shot a roll of her blond muff. He'd been kidding her about being a bottle blonde, and with uncharacteristic swagger she hiked her skirt, thumbed down her panties, and said, "Next time you want to know is it real or is it Clairol, ask them to show you this." She'd been sitting on his windowsill, drinking a Heineken, and when she stood the sun streamed across her body, light adhering not just to her bush but to the golden down on her stomach and thighs, each hair a prism, and a crazy inspiration possessed him with the force of desire, so strong he almost told her. He wanted to wake to that sight, to start his day to it, to restart his life to it, and maybe end his life to it, too. The breasts could stay stashed in the cigarillo box, but he wanted a blowup on his bedroom wall of her hands, the right lifting her bunched skirt and the left thumbing down her turquoise panties. He took the roll of film to Walgreens to be developed, and when he picked it up, photos were missing. He could tell from the weight of the envelope, but went down the Tooth Care aisle to open it and be sure. He returned to the photo counter and asked the pimply kid with "Stevorino" on his name tag who'd waited on him, "You opened these, didn't you? You got something that belongs to me."

"No way," the kid said, his acne blazing up.

"Zit-head, I should smash your face in now, but I don't want pus on my shirt. It's a nice shirt, right? So, see this?" Joe opened his hand, and a black switchblade the width of a garter snake flicked out a silver fang. "I'm going to count to five, and if I don't have the pictures by then, I'm going to cut off Stevo's dickorino right here to break him of the habit of yanking it over another man's intimate moments."

"Okay," the kid said, "I'm sorry." He reached into the pocket of his Walgreens smock and slid the pictures over, facedown.

"How many of my boob shots have you been snitching, Stevorino? What is it? You think of me as the Abominable Titman, the fucken Hugh Hefner of St. Michael's parish? See me coming with a roll of Kodak and you get an instant woodie?"

"No, sir," the kid said.

Joe went outside and sat in his idling car, studying the photos, thinking of Capri, of the intensity of being alone with her, of her endless inventions and surprises, but then he thought of her deceptions, their arguments, and of her talk of leaving for L.A. It was there, in the car with her photos on the dashboard, that he let her go, accepted, as he hadn't until that moment, that she had to want to stay or it wasn't worth it. He didn't let thinking of her distract him from his plan of action, which required watching the Walgreens exit. A plan was the distinction between a man with a purpose and some joker sitting in a car, working himself into a helpless rage. Two hours passed before the kid came out. He was unlocking his bicycle when he saw Joe Ditto.

"Mister, I said I was sorry," the kid pleaded.

"Stevo, when they ask how it happened say you fell off your bike," Joe said, and with an economically short blur of a kick, a move practiced in steel-toed factory shoes on a heavy bag, and on buckets and wooden planks, hundreds, maybe thousands of times until it was automatic, took out the kid's knee.

Joe never did get around to making that blowup of Capri. He hasn't heard from her in months, which is unlike her, but he knows she'll get in touch, there's too much left unfinished between them for her not to, and, until she's back, he doesn't need her muff on the wall.

Tuesday afternoon at the Zip Inn is a blue clothespin day. That's the color that Roman Ziprinski, owner and one-armed bartender, selects from the plastic clothespins clamped to the wire of Christmas lights that hangs year-round above the cash register. With the blue clothespin, Zip fastens the empty right sleeve of his white shirt that he's folded as neatly as one folds a flag.

It's an afternoon when the place is empty. Just Zip and, on the TV above the bar, Jack Brickhouse, the play-by-play announcer for the Cubs. The Cubbies are losing again, this time to the Pirates. It's between innings, and Brickhouse says, It's a good time for a Hamm's, the official beer of the Chicago Cubs.

"Official," Zip says to Brickhouse, "that's pretty impressive, Jack."

To the tom-tom of a tribal drum, the Hamm's theme song plays: "From the land of sky blue waters," and Zip hums along, "from the land of pines, lofty balsam comes the beer refreshing, Hamm's the beer refreshing . . ."

Hamm's is brewed in Wisconsin. Zip has a place there, way up on Lac Courte Oreilles in the Chain of Lakes region famous for muskies. It's a little fisherman's cottage no one knows he has, where he goes to get away from the city. A land of sky blue waters is what Zip dreamed about during the war. Daydreamed, that is. If Zip could have controlled his night dreams, those would have been of sky blue water, too, instead of the nightmares and insomnia that began after he was wounded and continued for years. Sometimes, like last night, Zip still wakes in a sweat as sticky as blood, with the stench of burning flesh lingering in his nostrils, to the tremors of a fist hammering a chest—a medic's desperate attempt to jump-start a dead body. No matter how often that dream recurs, Zip continues to feel shocked when in the dark he realizes the chest is his, and the fist pounding it is attached to his missing right arm.

When he joined the Marines out of high school, his grandmother gave him a rosary blessed in Rome to wear like a charm around his neck and made him promise to pray. But Zip's true prayer was one that led him into the refuge of a deep northern forest, a place he'd actually been only once, as a child, on a fishing trip with his father. He summoned that place from his heart before landings and on each new day of battle and on patrol as, sick with dysentery, he slogged through what felt like poisonous heat with seventy pounds of flamethrower on his back. He'd escape the stench of shit and the hundreds of rotting corpses that the rocky coral terrain of Peleliu made impossible to bury, into a vision of cool freshwater and blue-green shade scented with pine. When I make it through this, that's where I'm going, he vowed to himself.

Sky blue water was the dream he fought for, his private American Dream. And so is the Zip Inn, his tavern in the old neighborhood. He's his own boss here. Zip uncaps a Hamm's. It's on the house. The icy bottle sweats in his left hand. He raises it to his lips, and it suds down his throat: he came back missing an arm, but hell, his buddy Domino, like a lot of guys, didn't come back at all.

He can't control his night dreams, but during the day, Zip makes it a practice not to think about the war. Today, he wishes for a customer to come in and give him something else to think about. Where's Teo, that odd Mexican guy who stops by in the afternoon and sits with a beer, humming to himself and writing on napkins? The pounding in his temples has Zip worrying about his blood pressure. He has the urge to take a dump but knows his bowels are faking it. The symptoms of stress bring back Peleliu— the way his bowels cramped as the amtrac slammed toward the beach. They lost a third of the platoon on a beachhead called Rocky Point to a butchering mortar barrage that splintered the coral rock into razors of shrapnel. Zip stands wondering, how does a man in a place so far from home summon up whatever one wants to call it—courage, duty, controlled insanity—in the face of that kind of carnage, and then say nothing when two goombahs from across Western Avenue come into *his* place, the Zip Inn, and tell him it would be good business to rent a new jukebox from them? Instead of throwing those parasites out, he said nothing. Nothing.

Only a two-hundred-dollar initial installation fee, they told him.

The two of them smelling of aftershave: a fat guy, Sal, the talker, and Joe—he'd heard of Joe—a psycho for sure with a Tony

Curtis haircut and three-day growth of beard, wearing a shark-skin suit and factory steel-toes. The two hoods together like a pilot fish and a shark.

"Then every month only fifty for service," fat Sal said, "and that includes keeping up with all the new hits. And we service the locked coin box so you won't have to bother. Oh yeah, and to make sure nobody tries to mess with the machine, we guarantee its protection—only twenty-five a month for that—and believe me when we say protection we mean protection. Nobody will fuck with your jukebox. Or your bar."

"So you're saying I pay you seventy-five a month for something I pay fifteen for now. I mean the jukebox don't net me more than a few bucks," Zip told them. "It's for the enjoyment of my customers. You're asking me to lose money on this."

"You ain't getting protection for no fifteen bucks," Sal tells him.

"Protection from what?" Zip asked.

The hoods looked at each other and smiled. "*Allora*." Sal shrugged to Joe, then told Zip, "A nice little setup like you got should be protected."

"I got Allstate," Zip said.

"See, that kind of insurance pays *after* something happens, a break-in, vandalism, theft, a fire. The kind we're talking here guarantees nothing like that is going to happen in the first place. All the other taverns in the neighborhood are getting it too. You don't want to be the odd man out."

"A two-hundred-dollar installation fee?" Zip asked.

"That covers it."

"Some weeks I don't clear more than that."

"Come on, man, you should make that in a night. Start charging for the eggs," Sal said, helping himself to one. "And what's with only six bits for a shot and a beer? What kinda businessman are you? Maybe you'd like us to set up a card game in the back room for you on Fridays. And put in a pinball machine. We're getting those in the bars around here, too."

"Installation was fifty for the box I got. Service is fifteen a month."

Joe, the guy in the sharkskin suit, rose from his barstool and walked over to the jukebox. He read some of the selections aloud: "Harbor Lights," "Blue Moon," the "Too Fat Polka," "Cucurrucucu Paloma," "Sing, Sing, Sing."

"These songs are moldy, man," Joe said. "Where's Sinatra, where's Elvis the Pelvis? Your current jukebox dealer's a loser. They're gonna be out of business in a year. Their machines ain't dependable. Sallie, got a coin?"

"Here, on me," Zip said, reaching into the till.

"No, no, Sallie's got it."

"Yeah, I got it," Sal said, flipping a coin to Joe.

"Requests, Mr. Zip?" Joe asked.

"I hear it anytime I want."

"So, what's your favorite song?"

"Play, 'Sing, Sing, Sing,' " Sal said, yolk spitting from his mouth. "Did you know Benny Goodman's a yid from Lawndale? Lived on Francisco before the *tutsones* moved in."

Joe dropped in the coin and punched some buttons. Zip could hear from the dull *clunk* that the coin was a slug.

"Goddamn thing ate my quarter!" Joe exclaimed. "I fucken hate when machines snitch from me. Newspaper boxes are the worst. Selling papers used to be a job for blind guys and crips. No offense, Mr. Zip, I'm just saying a paper stand was decent work for these people, and then they put in newspaper boxes. I'm trying to buy a *Trib* the other day and the box eats my quarter. Know what I did to that newspaper box?"

"Here," Zip said. "Here's a refund."

"But, see, Mr. Zip, it's bad business to be covering for these lousy fucking jukes. You know if you whack them just right it's

like hitting the jackpot." Joe kicked the jukebox knee high and its
lights blinked out. From the crunch, Zip knew he'd kicked in
the speaker. "No jackpot? Well, guess it ain't my lucky day." Joe
laughed. "So, listen, Mr. Zip, we got a deal to shake hands on?"
Joe extended his hand. Then, eyeing Zip's clothespinned sleeve,
Joe withdrew his right hand and extended his left.

"Let me think it over," Zip said. He didn't offer his hand. He
wasn't trying to make a statement. It was the only hand he had.

"No problem," Joe said. "No pressure. Give it some careful
thought. I'll come by next week, maybe Friday, and you can give
me your answer." He pulled out a roll of bills, snapped off a
twenty, and set it on the mess of eggshells Sal had left on the bar.
"For the egg."

Big shots leaving a tip stolen from the pocket of some work-
ingman. After they walked out of his bar, Zip snapped open his
lighter and watched the burning twenty turn the eggshells sooty.
In the war, he'd operated an M2 flamethrower. They must have
figured a kid his size could heft it, lug the napalm-filled jugs, and
brace against the backward thrust of the jetting flame. Its range
was only thirty yards, so Zip had to get in close to the mouths of
caves and pillboxes that honeycombed the ridges where the Japs
were dug in ready to fight to the death. He had to get close
enough to smell the bodies burning. A flamethrower operator
was an easy target and always worked with a buddy, whose job it
was to cover him. Zip's buddy on Pelelui was Dominic Morales,
from L.A. They called him Domino. During a tropical downpour
on a ridge named Half Moon Hill, Domino was killed by the
same mortar blast that took off Zip's right arm. They were both
nineteen years old, and all these years later that astonishes Zip
more than it ever did at the time. Nineteen, the same age as kids
in the neighborhood shooting each other over who's wearing
what gang colors in some crazy, private war. He thought he'd
paid his price and was beyond all that, but now Zip stands be-

hind the bar waiting for the days to tick down to Friday, when
Joe Ditto comes back. Zip could call the cops, but he can't prove
anything, and besides, hoods wouldn't be canvasing taverns if the
cops weren't on the take. Calling the cops would be stupid. What
if he simply closed down the bar, packed his Ford, drove north
into the mist of sky-blue waters?

Zip recalls putt-putting out just after dawn in his aluminum
boat into a mist that hadn't burned off the water yet. The lake
looked like a setting for an Arthurian legend, the shore nearly invisible. Zip felt invisible. He'd packed a cane pole, a couple brews
in a cooler of ice, and a cottage cheese container of night crawlers
he'd dug the night before. He was going bluegill fishing. Fresh
from the icy water of Lac Courte Oreilles they were delicious.
Even in the mist, he located his secret spot and quietly slid in the
cement anchor. But when he opened the container of night
crawlers, he found cottage cheese. If he went all the way back for
his bait, he'd lose the first light and the best fishing of the day.
Defeated, he raised anchor, and the boat drifted into acres of lily
pads, nosing sluggish bullfrogs into the water. Zip noticed tiny
green frogs camouflaged on the broad leaves, waiting for the sun
to warm them into life. He caught a few and put them in the ice
cooler. He'd seen bluegills come into mere inches of water along-
shore for frogs. Once they were paralyzed by cold, Zip had no
trouble baiting a frog on a hook one-handed. Returned to water,
the frog would revive. Zip swung his pole out, and his bobber
settled on the smoldering water. He watched for the dip of the
bobber, the signal to set the hook, while the mist thinned. Zip
was wondering where the bluegills were when the bobber vanished. He'd never seen one disappear underwater. Before he
could puzzle out what happened, the water churned and the pole
nearly jerked from his hand. The bamboo bent double, and he
locked it between his thighs and hung on. The fish leaped, and if
Zip hadn't known it was a muskie, he might have thought it was

an alligator. It wagged in midair and appeared to take the measure of Zip, then belly-flopped back into the lake and torpedoed beneath the boat. Zip braced, tried horsing it out, and the pole snapped, knocking him off balance onto his butt, crushing the Styrofoam cooler, but he still clung to the broken pole. The fish leaped again beside the boat, swashing in water. It seemed to levitate above Zip—he smelled its weediness—and when it splashed down, the broken pole tore from his hand and snagged on the gunwale. He lunged for it, almost capsizing the boat, then watched the stub of bamboo, tangled in line and bobber, shoot away as if caught in an undertow. It was too big a fish for a cane pole. Too big a fish for a one-armed man.

Zip drains the last of his Hamm's, sets the bottle on the bar, and stares at his left hand, the hand Joe Ditto wanted to shake. Blood pulses in his temples and a current of pain traces his right arm, and the thought occurs to Zip that if he ever has a heart attack, he'll sense it first in his phantom arm.

Whitey calls in the middle of a dream:

Little Julio is supposed to be in his room practicing, but he's playing his flute in the bedroom doorway. Julio's mother, Gloria Candido, is wearing a pink see-through nightie, and Joe can't believe she lets Little Julio see her like that because Little Julio is not *that* little and he's just caught Joe circumnavigating Gloria's nipples with his tongue and Little Julio wants some, too. "He's playing his nursing song," Gloria says. The flute amplifies the kid's breath until it's as piercing as an alarm. To shut him up, Joe gropes for the phone.

"Joe," Whitey says. "What's going on?"

Drugged on dream, Joe wakes to his racing heart. "What?" he says, even though he hates guys who say *what?* or *huh?* It's a response that reveals weakness.

"Whatayou mean what? What the fuck? You know *what*. What's with you?"

What day is this? Joe wants to ask, but he knows that's the wrong thing to say, so he says, "I had a weird night."

"Joe, are you fucken on drugs?"

"No," Joe says. He's coming out of his fog, and it occurs to him that Whitey can't possibly be calling about Gloria Candido. A confrontation on the phone is not how Whitey would handle something like that. Whitey wouldn't let on he knew.

"Well, what's the problem then?" Whitey demands.

It's Johnny Sovereign that Whitey is calling about, and as soon as Joe realizes that, his heart stops racing. "Ran into a minor complication. I went to see him yesterday and—"

"*Maronn'!*" Whitey yells. "Joe, we're on the fucking phone here. I don't care what the dipshit excuses are, just fucking get it done."

"Hey, Whitey, suck this," Joe says and puts the receiver to his crotch. "Who the fuck do you think you're yelling at, you vain old sack of shit with your wrinkled *minchia*? Your girlfriend's slutting around behind your back making a fucking *cornuto* of you. You don't like it I'll cut you, I'll bleed you like a stuck pig."

Joe says all that to the dial tone. Telling off the dial tone doesn't leave him feeling better, just the opposite, and he makes a rule on the spot: never again talk to dial tones after someone's hung up on you. It's like talking to mirrors. Mirrors have been making him nervous lately. There's a dress draped over his bedroom mirror, and Joe gets out of bed and looks through his apartment for the woman to go with it. That would be April. She's nowhere to be found, and for a moment Joe wonders if she's taken his clothes and left him her dress. But his clothes are piled on the chair beside the bed where he stripped them off— shoes, trousers with keys and wallet, sport coat with the .22

weighting one pocket. He's naked except for his mismatched socks. The stiletto is still sheathed in the black-and-pink argyle.

Yesterday was supposed to have been a cleanup day. His plan was to pitch the trash, drop his laundry at the Chink's, and then stop by Johnny Sovereign's house on Twenty-fifth Street. The plan depended on Sovereign not being home, so Joe called from a pay phone, and Sovereign's good-looking young wife answered and said Johnny would be back around four. Okay, things were falling into place. Joe would wait in the gangway behind Sovereign's house for him to come home, and suggest they go for a drink in order to discuss Johnny setting up gambling nights in the back rooms of some of the local taverns. Once Joe got Sovereign alone in the car, well, he'd improvise from there.

So around three in the afternoon, Joe parked beside the run-down one-car garage behind Sovereign's house. The busted garage door gaped open, and he saw that Sovereign's Pontiac Bonneville was gone. Bonnevilles with their 347-cubic-inch engines that could do zero to sixty in 8.1 seconds were the current bad-ass cars—in Little Village, they called them Panchos. Sovereign's splurging on that car was what made Whitey suspect he was skimming on the numbers. New wheels and already leaking oil, Joe thought, as he looked at the fresh spots on the warped, birdshit-crusted floorboards of the garage. If Sovereign wasn't careless and all for show, he'd have taken that Pancho to the Indian.

Johnny Sovereign's back fence was warped, too, and overgrown with morning glories. His wife must have planted them. She'd made an impression on Joe the one time he'd been inside their house. Johnny had invited him, and they'd gone the back way, the entrance Joe figures it was Johnny's habit to use. Johnny didn't bother to announce their arrival, and they caught his wife—Vi, that was her name—vacuuming in her slip. When she saw Joe standing there, a blush heated her bare shoulders before she ran into the bedroom. She was wearing a pale yellow slip. Joe had never seen a slip like that before. He would have liked to slide its thin straps down her skinny arms to see if her blush mottled her breasts the way some women flush when they come. Sovereign's Pontiac was yellow, too, but canary yellow, and Joe wondered if there was some connection between Vi's slip and the car.

He sat in the Bluebird and lit a cigarette, then unscrewed the top from a pinch bottle of scotch and washed down a couple of painkillers. Sparrows twittered on the wires and pigeons did owl imitations inside Sovereign's shitty garage. The alley was empty except for a humped, hooded figure of a woman slowly approaching in his rearview mirror—a bag lady in a black winter coat and babushka, stopping to inspect each garbage can. Except for the stink of trash, Joe didn't mind waiting. He needed time to think through his next moves. From where he'd parked, he could watch the gangway and intercept Sovereign before he entered the house. He'd ask Sovereign to have a drink, and Sovereign would want to know where. "Somewhere private," Joe would tell him. And then—wham—it came to Joe, as it always did, how he'd work it. He'd tell Sovereign, "Let's take *your* wheels. I want to ride in a new yellow Bonneville." He'd bring the bottle of scotch, a friendly touch, and suggest they kill it on the deserted side street where the dragsters raced, a place where Sovereign could show him what the Pancho could do. He couldn't think of a way to get the shotgun into Sovereign's car, so he'd have to forget about that. Joe was scolding himself for not thinking all this through earlier when a woman's voice startled him.

"Hi, Joe, got an extra smoke?"

"What are you doing here?" Joe asked.

"Trying to bum a Pall Mall off an old lover," April said. "You still smoke Pall Malls, don'tcha?"

Her hair was bleached corn-silk blond and she wore a dress the shade of morning glories. Joe wondered how she'd come down the alley without his seeing her. The scooped neckline exposed enough cleavage so that he could see a wing tip from the blue seagull tattooed on her left breast. She looked more beautiful than he'd remembered.

"I thought you went to Vegas," he said. "I heard you got married to some dealer at Caesar's." He didn't add that he'd also heard she'd OD'd.

"Married? *Me?*" She showed him her left hand: nails silvery pink, a cat's-eye on her index finger going from gray to green the way her eyes did. Joe leaned to kiss the pale band of flesh where a wedding ring would have been, but he paused when sunlight hit her hand in a way that made it momentarily appear freckled and old with dirty, broken nails. She lifted her hand the rest of the way and sighed when it met his lips.

"You used to do that thing with my hand that would drive me crazy," April said.

"Hey, we were kids," Joe said.

He worked back then for a towing service Whitey ran, and he'd met April when he went to tow her Chevy from a private lot off Rush Street. He'd traded not towing her car for a date. She was a senior at Our Lady of Lourdes High, still a virgin, and on their first date she informed him that she was sorry, but she didn't put out. That was the phrase she used. Joe had laughed and told her, "Sweetheart, it's not like I even asked you. And anyway, there's other things than *putting out*." "Such as?" April asked, and from that single question, Joe knew he had her. It was nothing about him in particular, she was just ready. "Imagine the knuckles on your fingers are knees and the knuckles on your hands are breasts," Joe had told her, extending her index and middle fingers into a V and outlining an imaginary torso with his finger. "Okay, I see. So?" she asked. "So this," he whispered and kissed the insides of her fingers, then licked their webbing. She watched him as if amused, then closed her eyes. Even after she was putting out three times a day, nothing got her more excited than when he kissed her hand. "Lover," she'd once told him, "that goes right to my pussy."

"Aren't you going to ask me if I'm still using?" April asked. "I'm clean. And I been thinking about you ever since I've been back in the neighborhood. I'm staying with my sister, Renee. Remember her? She had a crush on you, too. I dreamed last night I'd find you here, and when I woke I thought, Forget it, you can't trust dreams, but then I thought, What the hell, all that will happen is I'll feel foolish."

"You dreamed of meeting me *here*?"

"Amazing, huh? Like that commercial, you know? 'I dreamed I met my old boyfriend in an alley, wearing my Maidenform bra.' Nice ride," she said, gliding her fingertips along the Bluebird as if stroking a cat. She came around to the passenger side, climbed in, leaned back into the leather seat, and sighed. "Just you, me, and a thousand morning glories."

Joe flicked away his cigarette and kissed her.

"You taste like scotch," she said.

He reached for the pinch bottle and she took a sip and kissed him, letting the hot liquor trickle from her mouth into his.

"What are *you* doing here?" she asked.

"That information wasn't in your dream?"

"In my dream you were a lonely void waiting for your soul mate." April took another sip of scotch and swallowed it this time. "Maybe we should have a private homecoming party," she said.

He remembers driving with April down the alleys back to his place, stopping on the way at Bruno's for a fifth of Bacardi and a cold six-pack of tonic water, and later, covering his kitchen table with Reynolds Wrap and laying out lines of coke. He remembers the plink of blood on foil when her nose began to bleed, and April calling from the bathroom, "Joe, where's all the towels?"

"Forgot to pick them up at the Chink's."

"No towels, no sheets. Are you sure you live here? What's in the fridge? Anything at all? I dread to look."

They lay kissing on the bare mattress while darkness edged up his bedroom walls. How still the city sounded. Between shrieks of nighthawks, an accordion faintly wheezed from some open window. Joe's bedroom window was open, too, and the breeze that tingled the blinds seemed blued with the glow of the new arc lights the city had erected. Before the mirror, April, streaked by the same glow, undid her ponytail. Mimicked by a reflection deep in the dark glass, she slipped her dress over her head. No Maidenform bra, she was naked. He came up behind her and bit her shoulders. He could see what appeared to be disembodied blue hands—his hands—cupping her luminous breasts. Otherwise he was a shadow. His thumb traced the tiny seagull flying across her breast. In the mirror it looked graceless, like an insignia a gang punk might have India-inked on his forearm. Her reflection appeared suddenly to surge to the surface of the glass, and he saw that the mirror was blemished with hairline fractures superimposed on her face like wrinkles. She flipped the dress she was still holding over the mirror as if to snuff a chemical reaction. It snuffed the residual light, and in the darkness he could feel something flying wildly around the room, and they lost their balance, banged off a wall, and fell to the bed. She took his cock, fit it in, then brought her hand, smelling of herself, to his lips.

Joe remembers all that, but none of it—the booze, the coke, the Demerol, the waking up repeatedly in the dark already fucking—explains how it can be afternoon, or what her morning-glory dress is doing left behind. He yanks the dress off the mirror and is surprised to find a crack zigzagging down the center. Maybe it was the mirror they'd staggered into. He staggers into the kitchen and washes down a couple of painkillers with what's left in a bottle of flat tonic water, then palms Old Spice onto his face and under his arms, tugs on his clothes, and dials Sovereign's number. He knows it's not a good idea to be calling from his place, but that can't be helped. When Vi answers on the third ring, he asks, "Johnny there?"

"He'll be home around four," she says. "Can I tell him who's calling?"

Joe hangs up.

From the closet, he digs out a gym bag stuffed with dirty gym gear and canvas gloves for hitting the heavy bag. He lifts the mirror from the bedroom wall, bundles it up in the dress, totes it into the alley, and sets it beside the garbage cans, then throws the gym bag into the Bluebird. Joe drives down the alleys, formulating a plan for how to get the shotgun into Sovereign's car. Off Twenty-fifth, he scatters a cloud of pigeons and nearly sideswipes a blind old bag lady in a babushka and dark glasses who's feeding them. When he pulls up behind Sovereign's, Joe can smell the baking motor oil spotting the floorboards of the empty garage. Demerol tends to heighten his sense of smell. Wind rustling down the alley leaves an aftertaste of rotten food and the mildewed junk people throw away. He makes sure the alley is empty, then slips the sawed-off shotgun from under the seat and buries it in the gym bag, beneath his workout gear. The scotch bottle rests on top, and when he zips up the bag, the ghost of old gym sweat transforms into a familiar fragrance.

Marisol stands in the alley as if she's emerged from the morning glories. She has a white flower in her auburn hair. Her perfume obliterates the scent of pigeons, garbage, and motor oil he's come to associate with Johnny Sovereign. She's dressed in white cotton X-rayed by sunlight: a shirt opened a button beyond modest, tied in a knot above her exposed navel, and white toreador pants. The laces of the wedged shoes he used to call her goddess sandals snake around her ankles. Her oversize shades seem necessary to shield her from her own brightness.

"See you're still driving the B-bird," she says, sauntering to the car. "That's cute how you name your cars. Kind of boyish of you, Joe, though when you first told me your car had a name, know what? I thought, Oh no, don't let this be one of those pathetic wankers who names his penis, too. Hey, I like the color coordination with the sport coat. That splash pattern is perfect for eating spaghetti with tomato sauce. Recognize this shirt? It's yours. Want it back?"

She still speaks in the fake accent that when they first met had Joe believing she was from London. He's not sure he's ever heard her real voice, if she has one. He'd heard she broke her Audrey Hepburn neck in Europe when she blew off the back of some Romeo's BSA on the Autobahn. Who starts these rumors about dead babes? Maybe Sal told him; Sal's a know-it-all with a rep for spreading bullshit. Well, fucking *allora*, Sallie, if a very much alive Marisol, trailing perfume, doesn't get into the Bluebird, help herself to a smoke from the pack on the dash, and ask, "Know where a girl can get a drink around here?"

Joe unzips the gym bag, hands her the bottle of scotch, and she asks as if she already knows, "What else you got in that bag, Joe?"

"Whataya mean, what else? Gym stuff."

"Whew! Smells like your athletic supporter's got balls of *scomorza*," Marisol says. "But what do I know about the secret lives of jockstraps."

Joe looks at her and laughs. She always could break him up, and not many beautiful women dare to be clowns. Capri was funny like that, too, and no matter who he's with he misses her. Where's Capri now, with who, and are they laughing? Marisol laughs, then quenches her laughter with a belt of scotch and turns to be kissed, and Joe kisses her, expecting the fire of alcohol to flow from her mouth into his, but it's just her tongue sweeping his.

"What?" Marisol says.

"I thought you were going to share."

"Dahlink," she says in her Zsa Zsa accent, "you don't remember I'm a swallower?"

Joe remembers. Remembers a blow job doing eighty down the Outer Drive on the first night he met her at the Surf, a bar on Rush where she worked as a cocktail waitress; remembers the improv theater he'd go see her in at a crummy little beatnik space in Old Town where sometimes there were more people onstage than in the audience; just say something obscene about Ike or Nixon or McCarthy and you'd get a laugh—shit, he laughed, too. He remembers the weekend right after he got the Bluebird when they dropped its top and drove the dune highway along the coast of Indiana to Whitey's so-called chalet on the lake, water indigo to the horizon, and night lit by the foundries in Gary.

"So, luvvy, is here where we're spending our precious time?" Marisol asked, turning on the radio.

Joe shifted through the gears as if the alleys were the Indianapolis Speedway and pulled up to Bruno's. He left Marisol in his idling car, singing along with Madame Butterfly on the opera station, while he ran in for a fifth of Rémy, her drink of choice, then brought her back to his place.

"Where's all the sheets and towels?" she asked. "Joe, how the bloody hell can you live like this?"

"They're at the Chink's. I been meaning to get them, but I been busy."

"You better watch it before you turn into an eccentric old bachelor, luv. I think maybe you're missing a woman's touch."

That was all she had to say, *touch*, and they were on the bare mattress.

Her blouse, an old white shirt of his, came undone, and he

pressed his face to her breasts, anointed with layers of scent, lavender, jasmine, areolas daubed with oil of bergamot, nipples tipped with a tincture of roses. He recalled the single time she'd invited him to her place on Sedgwick and how, in her bedroom, a dressing table cluttered with vials and stoppered bottles smelled like a garden and looked like the laboratory of a witch. *Touch*, she said, and he straddled her rib cage, thrusting slicked with a bouquet of sweat, spit, and sperm between perfumed breasts she mounded together with her hands. *A woman's touch.*

When he woke with Marisol beside him it was night and his room musky with her body—low tide beneath the roses. An accordion was playing. It sounded close, as if someone in the alley below was squeezing out a tune from long ago. "Hear that?" he asked, not sure she was awake.

"They're loud enough to wake the dead," Marisol said. "When I was little I used to think they were bats and their squawks were the sonar they flew by."

"I didn't mean the nighthawks," Joe said. "Those new mercury vapor lights bring the bugs and the bugs bring the birds. Supposed to cut down muggings. Or at least line the pockets of a few contractors. I had to buy fucking venetian blinds to sleep."

"You need earplugs, too," Marisol said. She rose from the dark bed and crossed through the streaky bluish beams, then raised the blinds. The glare bestowed on her bare body the luster of a statue. "Liking the view in the vapor lights?" she asked. "Ever think of a window as an erogenous zone?"

"Always the exhibitionist," Joe said. "But why not? You're beautiful as a statue."

"Statues are by nature exhibitionists, even when they've lost their arms or boobs or penises. Where's your mirror? I want to watch statues doing it in mercury vapor."

"No mirror."

"You don't have a mirror? Don't tell me—it's at the Chink's."

"It's in the alley."

"That's a novel place to keep it. I may be an exhibitionist but I'm not going to screw in the alley."

"It's broken."

"Seven years' bad luck, Joe. Poor unlucky bloke doesn't get to watch the statues with their shameless minds."

"*Allora!*" Joe said. "It's not that broke."

He went down the back stairs into the alley. The mirror was still where he'd set it beside a trash can. April's morning-glory dress was gone; some size-six bag lady must have had a lucky day. The mirror no longer appeared to be cracked, as if it had healed itself. It reflected an arc light. Nighthawks screeched. No one was playing an accordion in the alley, not that Joe thought there would be, but he could still hear it, a song he'd heard as a child, something about blackbirds doing the tango that his grandpa played on Sundays when he'd accompany scratchy 78s on his red accordion. Joe listened, trying to identify the open window from which the song wafted. Every window was dark. The music was coming from *his* window. He saw the flare of a lighter, and a silhouette with its head at an awkward angle, gazing silently down at him.

Marisol was still at the window, smoking a reefer, her back to him, when he returned to the room. "You didn't get mugged. See, those new streetlights must be doing their job," she said.

He propped the mirror against the wall.

"I'll share," she said, and exhaled smoke into his mouth. He felt her breath smoldering along the corridors of his mind. She handed him the reefer, and the crackle of paper as he inhaled echoed off the ceiling. "That paper's soaked in hash oil," she said. The accordion pumped louder, as if it tangoed in the next room. Lyrics surfaced in his mind and dissolved back into melody. "*E nell'oscurita ognuno vuol godere* . . . in the darkness everyone wants pleasure." When he opened his eyes, he could see in the dark.

"*L'amor non sa tacere* . . . love can't keep silent . . ." She was in his arms, and he smoothed his hands over her shoulders, down her spine, over her hips, lingering on and parting the cheeks of her sculpted ass.

"Have any oil?" she whispered.

"What kind of oil?"

"Like you don't want me that way. Almond oil, baby oil, bath oil, Oil of Olay, Vaseline if that's all you got."

"Hoppe's Number Nine," he said.

"That's a new one on me."

He gestured with the reefer to the bottle in the ashtray next to the Old Spice on the bureau top. She picked it up and sniffed. By the lighter's flame, she read the label aloud: " 'Do not swallow. Solvent frees gun bores of corrosive primer fouling and residue. Preserves accuracy.' Jesus, Joe! Don't you have some good, old-fashioned olive oil? What-a kinda Day-Glo are you?"

"Maybe in the kitchen," Joe said.

Brandishing the lighter like a torch, she went to the kitchen. Joe waited on the bed, listening to the accordion playing with the mesmerizing intensity that marijuana imparts to music . . . "Love can't keep silent and this is its song . . . *la canzon di mille capinere* . . . the song of a thousand blackbirds . . ." when Marisol screamed. "God, what am I stepping in? What's leaking out of your fridge, Joe? You have a body in there?"

Wounded wing, how strange to fall from blue. Like a fish that suddenly forgets the way to swim. When men fly, they know, by instinct, they defy. But to a bird, as to a god, nothing's more natural than sky . . .

Needing somewhere to think about the words forming to a nonstop percussion in his mind, not to mention needing a cold brew, Teo gimps out of daylight into the Zip Inn. A slab of sunshine extends from the doorway. Beyond it, the dimness of the

narrow, shotgun barroom makes the flowing blue water of the illuminated Hamm's beer sign on the back wall look like a mirage.
The TV screen flickers with white static that reflects off the photos of the local softball teams that decorate the walls. Teo doesn't
remove his dark glasses. Zip, the folded right sleeve of his white
shirt fastened with a yellow clothespin, stands behind the bar before a bottle of whiskey and raises a shot glass.

"*Qué pasa, amigo!*" Zip says, a little loudly given there's just
the two of them.

"*Nada, hombre.*" Teo is surprised to see him drinking alone in
the afternoon, an occupational hazard of bartending to which
Zip has always seemed immune.

"Knee acting up? Have one with me," Zip says, filling a second shot glass.

"What's the occasion?" Teo hooks his cane on the lip of the
bar, carefully sets the bowling bag he's carrying onto a stool, and
eases onto the stool beside it.

"Today is Thursday," Zip says, "and if you ask me, and I know
nobody did, Thursday's a reason for celebrating."

"To Thursday," Teo says. "*Salud!*"

"*Na zdrowie,*" Zip answers. He draws a couple of beer chasers.

"Let me get the beers," Teo says, laying some bills on the bar.
Zip ignores his money. After a meditative swallow, Teo asks, "TV
broke?"

"No game today," Zip says. "Giants are in tomorrow. You
work Goldblatt's?"

"No, Leader Store," Teo says. He pushes a dollar at Zip. "At
least let me buy a bag of pretzels."

"I heard Leader's is going under. Any shoplifters even there to
pinch?" Zip asks, ringing up the pretzels.

"A kid in Pets trying to steal one of those hand-painted turtles.
A pink polka-dotted turtle."

"Give him the full nelson?" Zip asks.

"Only the half nelson. He was just a grade-schooler."

"I think the dress disguise actually reduces your effectiveness, my friend. I mean, if there was a problem in my tavern, you know, say, theoretically speaking, somebody pocketing eggs—"

"The eggs are free," Teo says.

"Then pretzels. Say I got a problem with some pretzel sneak-thief, so I hire you and you're sitting here, supposedly under-cover, in a polka-dot dress wearing a wig and dark glasses and a cane and maybe smoking a cigar. I mean, you wouldn't be fool-ing nobody. It might be a deterrent, but not a disguise. You might as well be sitting there in your secret wrestler's getup. Whatever the hell it is."

"Amigo, you really want to see the wrestler's outfit?"

"Why not?" Zip says. "Liven things up. This place could use a little muscle."

"You'd be disappointed. And, by the way, it was the turtle with the polka dots, not the dress."

Lately, Teo has been stopping at the Zip Inn on weekday af-ternoons when the bar is mostly empty. Zip seems to know when Teo is in a mood to sit scribbling or simply to sink into his own thoughts, and he leaves him alone then, but other times they swap stories. Zip has told Teo hilarious tales of the world-record muskies he's lost, and Teo, trying to make his story funny, too, told Zip how his knee was injured when he was thrown from the ring onto the pavement during an outdoor wrestling match.

"You mean like those masked wrestlers when they set up a ring on Nineteenth Street for *Cinco de Mayo*?" Zip had asked. "What are they called?"

"*Luchadores*," Teo told him.

"So, you're a . . . *luchador* . . . with a secret masked identity?" Zip had sounded genuinely curious.

"Not anymore," Teo had answered.

Now, from the bowling bag, Teo pulls the hem of the dress he dons occasionally as part of his store security job. It's the dress they gave him when he began working for Goldblatt's—blue paisley, not polka dots—and, contrary to Zip's wisecracks, Teo has caught so many shoplifters that he's begun moonlighting at Leader Store on his days off.

"Yeah, this one is more you," Zip says, fingering the fabric, then asks, "What the hell else you got in there?"

Teo lifts out the pigeon.

This morning, he tells Zip, on his way to work he found the pigeon, a blue checker cock—*columba affinis*—dragging its wounded wing down an alley, and took it with him to Leader's, where he kept it in an empty parrot cage in Pets and fed it water and the hemp seed he carries with him as a treat for his own birds. Teo thinks of it as the Spanish pigeon. He doesn't mention the message, in Spanish, that he found tied to its unbanded leg.

"So it ain't one of your birds?" Zip asks.

"No." Teo shakes his head. He's told Zip how he keeps a *palomar*, a pigeon loft, on the roof of the three-story building on Blue Island Avenue where he rents a room, but he hasn't told Zip about the messages arriving there. Teo hasn't told anyone but the sax player, and he's gone missing. Over the last month, Teo's pigeons have been coming home with scraps of paper fastened with red twine to their banded legs. The first message arrived on a misty day, attached to the leg of one of his bronzed archangels. It wasn't Teo who first noticed it but the sax player, Lefty Antic, who practiced his saxophone on the roof. Teo untied the message, and he and Lefty read the smeared ink: "Marlin."

"Mean anything to you?" Lefty Antic had asked.

"Just a big fish, man," Teo had told him.

"Maybe it's his name, Marlin the Pigeon," Lefty Antic said.

"No," Teo said. "They don't tell us their names."

The next morning, slipped under his door, Teo found two

hundred and fifty dollars in crisp bills rubber-banded in a folded page from a Sportsman's Park harness-racing form with "Merlin" circled in the fourth race and a note that read, "Thanks for the tip. Lefty."

Teo saved the winnings and the message in a White Owl cigar box. A few days later, out of a drizzle, a second, barely legible message arrived fastened to one of his racing homers. As far as Teo could tell, it read: "Tibet." He took the message and half his winnings and knocked on Lefty Antic's door. There was no answer, and Teo had turned to go when the door opened, emitting the smell of marijuana. The sax player looked hungover, unshaven, eyes bloodshot, and Teo was sorry he'd disturbed him, but Lefty Antic insisted he come in. Together they studied the harness races in the newspaper and found a seven-to-one shot named Tidbit in the fifth race. There was also a buggy driver, J. Tippets, racing in the third and eighth races. Lefty decided they'd better bet both the horse and the driver and went to book it with Johnny Sovereign.

That night Teo had a dream in which his cousin Alaina was riding him. She hadn't aged—the same bronze-skinned, virgin body he had spied on through the birdshit-splattered skylight on the roof in El Paso where his uncle, Jupo, kept a *palomar*. Uncle Jupo had taken him in when Teo was fourteen after his mother had run off with a cowboy. It became Teo's job to care for his uncle's pigeons. He was seventeen when Uncle Jupo caught him on the roof with his trousers open, spying on Alaina in her bath. His uncle knocked him down and smashed Teo's face into the pebbled roof as if trying to grind out his eyes, then sent him packing with eight dollars in his pocket. In the dream, Alaina still looked so young that Teo was ashamed to have dreamed it. The pain of her love bites woke him at dawn, and even after waking, his nipples ached from the fierce way her small teeth had pulled at his body, as if his flesh was taffy. Waiting under his door was an en-velope with eight hundred dollars and a note: "It was the driver. Thanks, Lefty."

The third message arrived in a rainstorm. "Lone Star." Teo woke Lefty Antic out of a drunken stupor. They pored over the harness races, but the only possibility was a driver named T. North whose first name, Lefty thought, was Tex, and whose last name suggested the North Star. Then they checked the thor-oughbreds at Arlington, and found a long shot named Bright Venus. "The Evening Star!" Lefty said, smiling. Track conditions would be sloppy, and Bright Venus was a mudder. Lefty had the shakes so bad he could barely get dressed, but, convinced it was the score they'd been building to, he went off to lay their bets with Sovereign. Teo bet a thousand to win.

That night he had a nightmare that he was in El Paso, where he'd begun his career as a *luchador*, wrestling on the Lucha Libre circuit at fiestas and rodeos. In the dream he was wrestling the fa-mous Ernesto "La Culebra" Aguirre, the Snake, named for the plumed serpent Quetzalcoatl, the Aztec god of human sacrifice. Lucha Libre wrestlers often took the names of superheroes and Aztec warriors, and Teo once really had wrestled the Snake, though not in El Paso. That match was in Amarillo, back in the days when Teo was making a name for himself as a masked *luchador* called the Hummingbird. He'd come upon his identity in an illustrated encyclopedia of the gods of Mexico. The Hum-mingbird was Huitzilopochtli, the Mayan sun god; the illustra-tion showed a hawklike warrior bird rising from a thorny maguey plant. According to the caption, the thorns symbolized the Hum-mingbird's beak, and after Spain destroyed the Mayan empire, the thorns of the Hummingbird became the crown Jesus wore. Huitzilopochtli's sacred colors were sun white and sky blue, so those were the colors of the costume—mask, tank top, and tights—that Teo wore. When Teo put on the mask, he'd feel transformed by a surge of energy and strength. As the Hummingbird, he defied the limitations of his body and performed feats that marveled the crowds. He flew from ropes, survived punishing falls, lifted potbellied fighters twice his size high off their feet and slammed them into submission. To keep his identity secret, he would put on his mask miles from the ring, and afterward he wore it home. The nights before bouts he took to sleeping in his mask.

It was at a carnival in El Paso that he saw Alaina again, standing ringside with a group of high school friends, mostly boys. It had been three years since his uncle had thrown him out without giving him a chance to say goodbye to her. The boys must have come to see the *rudo* billed as El Huracán—the Hurricane—but known to fans as El Flatoso—Windy—for his flatulence in the ring. El Flatoso, with his patented move of applying a head scissors, then gassing his opponent into unconsciousness, was beloved by high school boys and drunks. Teo had been prepared to be part of the farce of fighting him until he saw Alaina in the crowd. He could feel her secretly watching him through her half-lowered eyelashes with the same intensity that he knew she'd watched him when he'd spied on her through the skylight. Suddenly, the vulgar spectacle he was about to enact was intolerable. The match was supposed to last for half an hour, but when El Flatoso came clownishly propelling himself with farts across the ring, the Hummingbird whirled up and delivered a spinning kick that knocked the *rudo* senseless. He didn't further humiliate El Flatoso by stripping off his mask, and the boys at ringside cursed, demanding their money back, before dejectedly dragging Alaina off with them. But he saw her look back and wave, and he bowed to her. Later that night, there was a light rap on the door of the trailer that served as his dressing room. Alaina stood holding an open bottle of mescal. "Don't take it off," she whispered as he began to remove his mask. Though they'd yet to touch, she stood unbuttoning her blouse. "I don't believe this is happening," he said, and she answered, "Unbelievable things happen to people on the edge." She spoke like a woman, not a girl, and when she unhooked her bra, her breasts were a woman's, full, tipped with nipples the shade of roses going brown, not the buds of the girl he'd spied on. He knelt before her and kissed her dusty feet. She raised her skirt, and he buried his face in her woman smell. He wanted the mask off so he could smear his cheeks with her. "Leave it on," she commanded, "or I'll have to go." He rose, kissing up her body, until his lips suckled her breasts and their warm, sweet-sour sweat coated his tongue, and suddenly her sighs turned to a cry. "No, too sensitive," she whispered, pushing him gently away, then she opened his shirt and kissed him back hard, fiercely biting and sucking his nipples as if he were a woman. "My *guainambi*," she said, using the Indian word for hummingbird.

It was months before he saw her again, this time at a rodeo in Amarillo—a long way from El Paso—where he stood in the outdoor ring waiting for his bout with the Snake. The loose white shirt she wore didn't conceal her pregnancy, and for a moment he wondered if the child could be his, then realized she'd already been with child when she'd knocked on his trailer door. La Culebra, in his plumed sombrero, rainbow-sequined cape, and feathered boa, was the star of the Lucha Libre circuit, and it had been agreed that the Hummingbird was to go down to his first defeat in a close match that would leave his honor intact so that a rivalry could be built. But when Teo saw Alaina there at ringside, he couldn't accept defeat. He and the Snake slammed each other about the ring, grappling for the better part of an hour under a scorching sun with Teo refusing to be pinned, and finally in a clinch the Snake told him, "It's time, *pendejo*, stop fucking around," and locked him in his signature move, the boa constrictor. But the Hummingbird slipped it, and when the Snake slingshotted at him off the ropes, the Hummingbird spun up into a helicopter kick. The collision dropped them both on their backs in the center of the ring. "Cocksucker, this isn't El Flatoso you're fucking with," the Snake told him as he rose spitting blood. The legend surrounding La Culebra was that he'd once been a heavyweight boxer. He'd become a *luchador* only after he'd killed another boxer in the ring, and now, when he realized they weren't following the script, he began using his fists. The first punch broke Teo's nose, and blood discolored his white and blue mask, swelling like a blood blister beneath the fabric. The usual theatrics disappeared, and the match became a street fight that had the fans on their feet cheering, a battle that ended with the Snake flinging the Hummingbird out of the ring. The fall fractured Teo's kneecap, his head bounced off the pavement, and as he lay stunned, unable to move for dizziness and pain, the Snake leaped down onto his chest from the height of the ring, stomping the breath from his body, and tore off the bloodied mask of the Hummingbird as if skinning him, then spit in his flattened face. Teo, his face a mask of blood, looked up into the jeering crowd, but he never saw Alaina again.

In Teo's nightmare, the Snake humiliated him not only by tearing off his Hummingbird mask and exposing his identity to the crowd but by derisively shouting *"Las tetas!"* and tearing off Teo's tank top, exposing a woman's breasts weeping milky tears. At dawn, when Teo groaned out of his dream, with his stomped, body-slammed chest aching and his heart a throbbing bruise, there was no envelope of winnings waiting. That morning Teo knocked repeatedly on Lefty Antic's door without an answer. The thought occurred to him that the saxophone player had taken off with their money, not out of crookedness but on a drunken binge. It was only in the afternoon, when Teo bought a newspaper and checked the racing scores at Arlington, that he learned Bright Venus had finished dead last. He checked the harness results at Sportsman's, and there was a story about a buggy over-

turning in the third race and its driver, Toby North, being criti-
cally injured when a trotting horse crushed his chest.

It seemed as if a vicious practical joke had been played on
them all, but when the next message came, Teo knocked again
on Lefty Antic's door. He hadn't seen the saxophone player since
Lefty had staggered out to place their bets on Bright Venus.
There still was no answer, and Teo, filled with a terrible sense of
abandonment and foreboding, sure that Lefty Antic was dead inside, got the landlord to open the door, only to find the room
empty and orderly. Alone, feeling too apprehensive simply to ignore the message, Teo studied the racing pages looking for clues
as he'd seen Lefty Antic do. It seemed to him that the new rain-
smudged message, "delay plaza," referred to the mayor, Richard
Daley, and when he could find no connection whatsoever at any
of the race tracks, he took the El train downtown. There wasn't a
Daley Plaza in Chicago, but there was an open square near City
Hall, and Teo walked there, not sure what he was looking for, yet
hoping to recognize it when he saw it. But no sign presented itself, nothing was going on in the square but a rally for a young
senator from Massachusetts, an Irish Catholic like the mayor,
who was running for president in a country that Teo figured
would never elect a Catholic.

The messages have continued to arrive, and Teo continues to
save them, and the cigar box fills with scraps of paper his pigeons
have brought home from God knows where. Teo can't shake the
foreboding or the loneliness. His sleep is haunted by the recurrent
dream of a funeral that extends the length of a country of ruined
castles and burning ghettos. He's part of the procession following
the casket, ascending a pyramid, its steps dark and slippery with
the blood of what's gone before. He doesn't want to see what's
at the summit. Unable to return to sleep, sometimes he spreads
the messages on the table and tries to piece them together, to see
if the torn edges fit like the pieces of a jigsaw puzzle or if the

words can be arranged into a coherent sentence. He senses some story, some meaning, connecting them, but the words themselves baffle him: *knoll, motorcade, six seconds, bloodstone* . . .

And it's not dreams alone that disrupt his sleep. There's an increasing tenderness in his chest that waking doesn't dispel. In the darkness, his nipples ache as if they've been pinched with tongs; the palpitations of his heart resonate like spasms through soft tissue. His flesh feels foreign to his breastbone. He can feel his inflamed mounds of chest swelling beneath his undershirt, and he brushes his fingertips across his chest, afraid of what he'll find. He's put on weight, and his once sculpted chest has grown flabby, his weight lifter's pectorals drooping to fat. Come morning, he reassures himself that's all it is—fat, he's simply getting fat, and this strange pain will also pass. Better to ignore it. He avoids studying the bathroom mirror when he shaves.

Sometimes, after midnight, he thinks he hears Lefty Antic playing his saxophone softly on the roof, but it's only wind vibrating the rusted chimney hood, streaming clouds rasping against a rusty moon, the hoot of pigeons. He hasn't seen the sax player since they lost their stake on "Lone Star."

Teo has written his own notes—"Who are you? What do you want?"—and attached them to those pigeons of his who have brought the strange messages. Noah-like, he's sent them flying out over the wet rooftops to deliver his questions, but those pigeons haven't returned home, and it takes a lot to lose a homing pigeon. They fly in a dimension perilous with hawks and the ack-ack fire of boys armed with rocks, slingshots, and pellet guns. Fog and blizzards disorient them, storms blow them down, and yet instinct brings them home on a single wing, with flight feathers broken, missing a leg or the jewel of an eye.

Teo has decided that since his communiqués go unanswered and his birds don't return, he will refuse to accept further messages. All week he has kept his remaining pigeons cooped. And now this morning, attached to a strange pigeon, another message, the first in Spanish: *asesino.* "Murder" or "assassin," Teo doesn't know which.

He'd like to ease the loneliness, if not the foreboding, and tell Zip about the messages. But until this afternoon, when he found Zip drinking alone and obviously needing someone to talk to, Teo has been reluctant to talk about anything more personal than Zip's favorite subject: fishing. True, Zip was obviously curious about Teo's wrestling career, but it didn't seem right to tell the insignificant story of the Hummingbird to a man who is so careful never to speak of war wounds.

"This feels like we're in some kind of joke," Zip says, opening his palm and allowing the pigeon to step from Teo's hand to his.

"What do you mean?" Teo asks.

"You know," Zip says, "there's all these jokes that start: A man walks into a bar with a parrot, or a man walks into a bar with a dog, or a gorilla, or a cockroach. You know, all these guys walking into all these bars with every animal on the ark. So in this one, a man—no, a wrestler, a masked wrestler—walks into a bar with a pigeon."

"So, what's the punch line?" Teo asks.

"You're asking me?" Zip says. "It's *your* pigeon."

"No, not one of mine."

"Yeah, but you brought it in here."

"But the joke is your idea."

"Jesus, we got no punch line," Zip says. "You know what that means?"

"What?"

"We'll never get out of the joke."

Whitey calls.

Joe, lying on the bare mattress, naked but for mismatched

socks, doesn't answer. He knows it's Whitey on the phone. Joe
can almost smell his cigar.

What day is it? Must be Thursday, because yesterday was
Wednesday, a day's reprieve Johnny Sovereign never knew he
had. Joe can have the conversation with Whitey without bothering to lift the receiver.

—Joe, what the fuck's going on with you?
—Hey, Whitey, you ball-buster, *vaffancul*!

Are these ball-busting calls some kind of psychological warfare? Maybe Whitey knows about Gloria Candido, and the whole
thing with Johnny Sovereign is a setup. Maybe it's Whitey ar-
ranging for these women to distract Joe from doing his job, giving Whitey an excuse other than being a fucking *cornuto* to have
Joe clipped. Could Whitey be that smart, that devious? Maybe
Whitey has tipped off Sovereign to watch his back around Joe
and Sovereign is waiting for Joe to make his move. Or maybe
the women are good luck, guardian angels protecting him from
some scheme of Whitey's.

Joe quietly lifts the receiver from the cradle. He listens for
Whitey to begin blaring, *Yo, Joe, whatthefuck?* but whoever is on
the line is listening, too. Joe can hear the pursy breathing. It
could be Whitey's cigar-sucking, emphysemic huff. Joe slides the
stiletto from his right sock, holds it to the mouthpiece, thumbs
off the safety, touches the trigger button, and the blade hisses
open: *Ssswap!* Then he gently sets down the receiver.

Joe dresses quickly. The shirt he's been wearing since Tuesday
reeks, so he switches to the white shirt Marisol left behind even
though it smells of perfume. She's left a trail of rusty footprints
down the hall from the kitchen as if she stepped on broken glass,
and Joe splashes them with Rémy and mops them with the dirty
shirt he won't be wearing, then kills the bottle, washing down a

mix of painkillers. There's a soft wheeze from his closet, as if an accordion is shuddering in its sleep. When he dials Johnny Sovereign's number, Vi answers on the third ring.

"Johnny home?"

"He'll be back around six or so," Vi says. "Can I take a message?"

"So where is he?"

"Can I take your number and have him call you back?"

"Do you even know?"

"Know what?" Vi asks. "Who's calling?"

"An acquaintance."

"You called yesterday and the day before."

Joe hangs up.

The Bluebird is doing fifty down the cracked alleys, and when a bag lady steps from between two garbage cans, she has to drop her bag to get out of the way. Joe rolls over her shopping bag, bulging from a day's foraging, and in the rearview mirror sees her throwing hex signs in his wake. He pulls up behind Sovereign's, and there's that smell of trash, oil, and pigeons, compounded by a summer breeze. Joe can sense someone eyeing him from inside the empty garage, and he eases his right hand into the pocket of his sport coat and flicks the safety off the .22, uncomfortably aware of how useless the small-caliber pistol is at anything but point-blank range. A gray cat emerges from Sovereign's garage, carrying in its mouth a pigeon still waving a wing. The cat looks furtively at Joe, then slinks into the morning glories, and from the spot where the cat disappeared, Grace steps out. Morning glories are clipped to her tangled black curls. She's wearing a morning-glory-vine necklace, vine bracelets, and what looks like a bedraggled bridesmaid's gown, if bridesmaids wore black. Her bare feet are bloody, probably from walking on glass. "Long time, no see, Joey," she says. "I been with the Carmelites."

Joe recalls Sal asking if he was going to her closed-casket wake. "You had a thing with her, didn't you?" Sal had asked.

"No way!" Joe told him. "A little kissyface after a party once. I don't know why she made up all those stories."

"That whole Fandetti family is bonkers," Sal said.

Nelo, her father, a Sicilian from Taylor Street, operates an escort service, massage parlors, and a strip bar on South Wabash, but he brought his four daughters up in convent school. The official story was that Grace wasted away with leukemia, but rumor had it that it was a botched abortion. Now, Joe realizes old man Fandetti is even crazier than he thought, faking his daughter's death in order to avoid the humiliation of an illegitimate pregnancy. No surprise she's a nutcase. He wonders if they collected insurance on her while they were at it.

"If you stick your finger inside, you can feel the electric," Grace says and demonstrates by poking her finger into a flower. "That hum isn't bees. Electric's what gives them their blue. You should feel it. Come here and put your finger in."

"Where's your shoes, Grace?"

"Under the bed, so they think I'm still there."

"Still where? What are you doing here?"

"Come here, Joey, and put your finger in. You'll feel what the bee's born for. They're so drunk on flower juice!" She walks to the car and leans in through the window on the passenger side, and the straps of her black gown slip off her shoulders, and from its décolletage breasts dangle fuller than he remembers from that one night after a birthday party at Fabio's when he danced with her and they sneaked out to the parking lot and necked in his car. She'd looked pretty that night, made up like a doll, pearls in her hair, and wearing a silky dress with spaghetti straps. That was what she called them when he slipped them down and kissed her breasts. She wanted to go further, pleaded with him to take her virginity, but he didn't have a rubber and it wasn't worth messing with her connected old man.

"Know what was on the radio?"

"When?" Joe asks. He's aware that he's staring, but apparently still stoned on that hash oil, he can't take his eyes off her breasts. His reactions feel sluggish; he has to will them. He realizes he's been in a fog . . . he's not sure how long, but it's getting worse.

She opens the door and sinks into the leather seat and humming tunelessly flicks on the car radio. "I Only Have Eyes for You" is playing. "Our song, Joey!"

"Grace, we don't have a song."

"The night we became lovers."

"Why'd you tell people that?"

"You got me in trouble, Joey, and in the Carmelites I had to confess it to the bishop. We weren't supposed to talk, but he made me show and tell."

Joe flicks off the radio. It's like turning on the afternoon: birdsong, pigeons cooing, flies buzzing trash, the bass of bees from a thousand blue gramophones.

"All the sisters were jealous. They called me Walkie-Talkie behind my back. They thought I didn't understand the sacredness of silence, but that's not true. They think silence is golden, but real silence is terrifying. We're not made for it. I could tell you things, Joey, but they're secrets."

"Like what, Grace? Things somebody told you not to tell me?"

"Things God whispers to me. Joey, you smell like a girl."

"I think you can't tell 'cause you don't know. Tell me one secret God said just so I see if either of you knows anything."

"I know words to an accordion. If you turn on your radio you'll hear stars singing the song of a thousand crackles. I know about you and girls. I know what's in your gym bag."

"Yeah, what?"

"They're your way of being totally alone."

"What's in the gym bag, Grace?"

"I know you can't stop staring at my tits. I don't mind, you can see. Oh, God! Windshields glorify the sun! Feel."

"Not here, Grace."

"Okay, at your place."

"That's not a good idea," Joe says, but he can't stay here with her either, so he eases the car into gear and drives slowly up the alley. The top of her dress is down, and against his better judgment—almost against his will—he turns onto Twenty-fifth, crosses Rockwell, the boundary between two-flats and truck docks. He drives carefully, his eyes on a street potholed by semis, but aware of her beside him with her dirty feet bloody and her bare breasts in plain view. Rockwell is empty, not unusual for this time of day. They're approaching a railroad viaduct that floods during rainstorms. A block beyond the viaduct is Western Avenue, a busy street that in grade school he learned is the longest street in the world, just like the Amazon is the longest river, so they called it Amazon Avenue. Western won't be deserted, and across Western is the little Franciscan church of St. Michael's and the old Italian parish where he lives.

"I'm a Sister of Silence, so you need to be nice to me like I always was to you."

"I've always been nice to you, too, Grace."

"I could have had men hurt you, Joey, but I didn't."

They're halfway through the streaky tunnel of the railroad viaduct and he hits the brakes and juts his arm out to brace her from smacking the windshield. "I don't like when people threaten me, Grace. It really makes me crazy."

"Let's go to your place, Joey. Please drive. I hate when the trains go over. All those tons of steel on top of you, and the echoes don't stop in your head even after the train is gone."

"There's no train."

"It's coming. I can feel it in my heart. My heart is crying." She
squeezes a nipple and catches a milky tear on a fingertip and offers it to him, reaching up to brush it across his lips, but Joe turns
his face away. When he does, she slaps him. He catches her arm
before she can slap him again, and under the viaduct, minus the
glare of sun in his eyes, he sees her morning-glory-vine bracelets
are scars welted across her wrists. Whistle wailing, a freight hur-
tles over, vibrating the car. He releases her arm, and she clamps
her hands over her ears. Her bare feet stamp a tantrum of bloody
imprints on the floor mat.

"Get out!" Joe yells over the concussions of boxcars, and he
reaches across her body to open the door. She looks at him in
amazement, then mournfully steps out into the gutter, her breasts
still exposed. Without looking back, he guns into the daylight on
the other side, catches the green going yellow on Western, veers
into traffic, rattles across the bridge wheeled by pigeons that
spans the Sanitary Canal. He isn't going back to his place, he's
not heading to pick up his laundry, and until he finishes this job
he's not going to Fabio's or any of the hangouts where he might
run into Whitey. It's Thursday, and Joe's been seeing Gloria Candido on the sly on Thursdays, when Julio goes to his grandmother's after school, but Joe isn't going to Gloria's either. He's
in the flow of Amazon Avenue, popping painkillers, Grace's
handprint still hot on his face. He heads south to see what's at the
end of the longest street in the world. The radio is off as if he's
broken contact, and he'd drive all night if not for hallucinations
of headlights coming head-on. Finally he has to pull over and
close his eyes. When he wakes, not sure he was ever really asleep,
he's parked on a shoulder separated from a field by rusty barbed
wire netted in spider silk suspending pink droplets of sun. The
blank highway is webbed like that as far as he can see. He thinks,
I could just keep going, and at the next gas station, on an impulse, Joe decides he will keep going if she doesn't answer the

phone. But then he doesn't have enough change to make the call. "Make it collect, for Vi Sovereign," he tells the operator.

"Who should I say is calling?" the operator asks.

"Tell her a friend who's been calling, she'll know." And when the operator does, Vi accepts the call. "Where you calling from?" Vi asks. "I hear cars."

"A phone booth off Western Avenue. Johnny home?"

"You're calling early," she says. "He'll be home around noon or so for lunch."

"You don't know where he is or what he's doing? I can hear it in your voice. Did he even come home last night?"

"What do you keep calling for? If you're trying to tell me something about Johnny, just say it. You somebody's husband? What's your name?"

"Maybe we'll meet sometime. I'd pay you back for the phone call, but then you'd know it was me."

"I'll recognize your voice."

"Better you don't," Joe says, and hangs up.

Before noon, he pulls up behind Johnny Sovereign's. From the longest street in the world, he's back to idling in a block-length alley, and yet it's oddly peaceful there, private, a place that's come to feel familiar, and he's so tired and wired at the same time that he'd be content just to drowse awhile with the sun soothing his eyelids. He lights a smoke, chucks the crushed, empty pack out the window, checks the empty alley in the rearview mirror, and notices the handprint still visible on his face. He catches his own eyes glancing uncomfortably back, embarrassed by the intimacy of the moment, as if neither he nor his reflection wants anything to do with each other. He puts on a pair of sunglasses he keeps in the visor, and when he looks up through their green lenses, a tanned blonde with slender legs, in a halter top and short turquoise shorts, stands beside the morning glories. She's wearing sunglasses, too.

"Hi, Joe, they told me I'd find you here. I been waiting all morning, thinking how it would be when I saw you. I missed you so much, baby. I thought I could live without you, but I can't."

"Capri," he says.

She smiles at the sound of her name. "My guy, my baby."

"Oh fuck, fuck, not you, baby. I didn't care about the others, but not you, too." He hasn't realized until now that he's been waiting for this moment ever since, without warning, her letters had stopped, leaving a silence that has grown increasingly ominous. Her last letter ended: "Sometimes I read the weather in your city, so that I can imagine you waking up to it, living your life without me." After a month with no word, he'd asked Sal if he'd heard anything about her, but he hadn't. In all likelihood she'd met someone, and Joe thought he'd be making a fool of himself getting in touch. Even so, he tried calling, but her number was disconnected.

"I'm back, baby. Aren't you glad to see me?" She steps toward the car and removes her sunglasses. He can't meet her eyes any more than he can meet his own in the mirror. If he could speak, the words he'd say—"I'm crying in my heart"—wouldn't be his, and when she reaches her arms out, Joe slams the car into reverse, floors it, and halfway down the alley, skidding along garbage cans, hits a bag lady. He can hear her groan as the air goes out of her. He sees her sausage legs kicking spasmodically from where he's knocked her, pinned and thrashing between two garbage cans. Joe keeps going.

Nothing's more natural than sky.

From here railroad tracks look like stitching that binds the city together. If shadows can be trusted, the buildings are growing taller. From up here, gliding, it's clear there's a design: the gaps of streets and alleys are for the expansion of shadow the way lines in a sidewalk allow for the expansion of pavement in the heat.

With a message to carry, there isn't time to ride a thermal of blazing roses, to fade briefly from existence like a daylight moon. What vandal cracked its pane? The boy whose slingshot shoots cat's-eye marbles? The old man with a cane, who baits a tar roof with hard corn then waits with his pellet gun, camouflaged by a yellowed curtain of Bohemian lace?

Falcons that roost among gargoyles, feral cats, high-voltage wires, plate glass that mirrors sky—so many ways to fall from blue. When men fly they know by instinct they defy.

It's not angels the Angelus summons but iridescent mongrels with blue corkers in the history of their genes, and carriers, fantails, pouters, mondains—marbled, ring-necked, crested—tipplers, tumblers, rollers, homers homeless as prodigals, all circling counterclockwise around the tolling belfry of St. Pius as if flying against time. Home lost, but not the instinct to home. Message lost, but not the instinct to deliver.

From up here it's clear the saxophone emitting dusk on a rooftop doesn't know it plays in harmony with the violin breaking hearts on the platform of an El, or with the blind man's accordion on an empty corner, breaking no heart other than its own. Or with the chorus of a thousand blackbirds. Love can't keep silent, and this is its song.

"You need a fucken ark to get through that shit," Johnny Sovereign says.

The flooded side street is a dare: sewers plugged, hydrants uncapped, scrap wood wedged against each gushing hydrant mouth to fashion makeshift fountains.

"Think of it as a free car wash," Joe says.

"I don't see you driving your T-bird through."

"I might if it was whitewashed with baked pigeon shit. Go, man!"

They crank up the windows and Sovereign guns the engine and drops the canary yellow Pancho into first. By second gear, water sheets from the tires like transparent wings, then the blast of the first hydrant cascades over the windshield, and Sovereign, driving blind, flicks the wipers on and leans on the horn. By the end of the block they're both laughing.

"You can turn your wipers off now," Joe says. He can hear the tires leaving a trail of wet treads as they turn down Cermak. "Where you going, man?" Joe asks.

"Expressway," Sovereign says. "I thought you wanted to see what this muther can do opened up. You sure you don't want to drive?"

"I'm too wiped."

"You look wiped. Rough night?" Sovereign smirks. "Come on, you drive. A ride like this'll get the blood pumping."

"Yo, it ain't like I'm driving a fucken Rambler."

"No, no, your T-bird's cool, but this is a fucking bomb."

"I'll ride shotgun. But I want to see what it does from jump. I heard zero to sixty in eight-point-one. Go where the dragsters go."

"By three V's?"

"Yeah, three V's is good," Joe says. "Private. We can talk a little business there, too."

The 3 V's Birdseed Company, a five-story dark brick factory with grated windows, stands at the end of an otherwise deserted block. The east side of the street is a stretch of abandoned factories; the west side is rubble, mounds of bricks like collapsed pyramids where factories stood before they were condemned. Both sides of the street are lined with dumped cars too junky to be repoed or sold, some stripped, some burned. Summer nights kids drag race here.

"Park a sec. We'll oil up," Joe says. They've driven blocks, but he can still hear the wet treads of the tires as Sovereign pulls into a space among the junkers along the curb. Joe unzips the gym bag he's lugged with him into Sovereign's Bonneville and hoists out the scotch bottle. There's not more than a couple swallows left. "Haig pinch. Better than Chivas."

Sovereign takes a swig. "Chivas is smoother," he says. He offers Joe a Marlboro. Joe nips off the filter, Sovereign lights them up and flicks on the radio to the Cubs' station. "I just want to make sure it's Drabowsky pitching. I took bets."

"Who'd bet on the fucken Cubs?"

"Die-hard fans, some loser who woke up from a dream with a hunch, the DP's around here bet on Drabowsky. Who else but the Cubs would have a pitcher from Poland? Suckers always find a way to figure the odds are in their favor."

It's Moe Drabowsky against the Giants' Johnny Antonelli. Sovereign flashes an in-the-know smile, flicks the radio off, then takes a victorious belt of scotch and passes it to Joe. "Kill it," Joe says, and when Sovereign does, Joe lobs the empty pinch bottle out the window and it cracks on a sidewalk already glittering with shards of muscatel pints and shattered fifths of rotgut whiskey. Sun cascades over the yellow Bonneville. "Man, those mynahs scream," Sovereign says. "Sounds like goddamn Brookfield Zoo. Hear that one saying a name?"

In summer, the windows behind the grates on the fifth floor of 3 V's are open. The lower floors of the factory are offices and stockrooms. The top floor houses exotic birds—parakeets, Java birds, finches, canaries, mynahs. Sometimes there's an escape, and tropical birds, pecked by territorial sparrows, flit through the neighborhood trees while people chase beneath with fishing nets, hoping to snag a free canary.

"It's the sparrows," Joe says. "They come and torment the fancy-ass birds. *Cheep-cheep*, asshole, you're jackin off on the mirror in a fucken cage while I'm out here singing and flying around.' Drives the 3 V's birds crazy and they start screeching and plucking out their feathers. You ever felt that way?"

"What? In a cage?" Sovereign asks. "No fucken way, and I don't intend to. So, what's the deal?" He actually checks his jeweled Bulova as if suddenly realizing it's time in his big-shot day for him to stop gabbing about birds and get down to business. "Whitey say something about me getting a little more of the local action? Setting craps up on weekends?"

"Yeah, local action," Joe says. "That's what I want to talk to you about."

"I'm in," Johnny says. "I'm up for whatever moves you guys have in mind, Joe."

"There's just one minor problem to work out," Joe says. "Whitey thinks you're skimming."

"Huh?" Sovereign says.

"You heard me," Joe says. "Look, I know your mind is going from fucken zero to sixty, but the best thing is to forget trying to come up with bullshit no one's going to believe anyway and to work this situation out."

"Joe, what you talking about? I keep books. I always give an honest count. No way I would pull that."

"See, that's pussy-ass bullshit. A waste of our precious time. Whitey checked your books. He had Vince, the guy who set the numbers up in the first place, check them. They double-checked. You fucked up, Johnny, so don't bullshit me."

"I never took a nickel beyond my percentage. There gotta be a mistake."

"You saying you may have made a miscalculation? That your arithmetic is bad?"

"Not that I know of."

"Where'd you get the scratch for this car?"

"Hey, I'm doing all right. I mean, and I owe on it. The bank fucking owns it."

"More bullshit, you paid cash. Whitey checked. You been making book here, gambling it Uptown and losing, drinking hard, cheating on Vi . . ."

"Vi? What you talking about? She's got nothing to do with nothing."

"Why wouldn't you stay home with a primo lady like that? You're out of control, man. Your fucken Pancho's leaking oil. With your fear of cages, next you'll be talking to the wrong people. You're a punk-ass bullshitter and a bad risk."

"Joe, I swear to you—"

"You swear?"

"On my mother's grave. Swear it on my children."

"You cross your heart and hope to die, too?"

"Huh?"

"Like little kids say."

"I know how kids talk, Joe. I got a baby girl and a little boy, Johnny Junior."

"So, swear it like you mean it," Joe says, exhaling smoke and flicking his cigarette out the window. "I cross my heart . . ." Sovereign looks at Joe as if he can't be serious, and Joe stares him down.

"Cross my heart . . . ," Sovereign says.

"No, you got to actually cross your heart," Joe says, crossing his own heart, and when, to illustrate further, Joe reaches with his left hand to open Sovereign's sport coat, Sovereign flinches, then smiles, chagrined at being so jumpy. Instead of making a move to resist Joe touching him, Sovereign drags on his cigarette. "Nice pricey sport coat, nice monogrammed shirt," Joe says, holding Sovereign by the lapel. "Sure there's a heart in here to cross, Johnny?" Joe brings his right hand up to check for a heartbeat.

"Relax, I'm just fucking with you." Joe smiles, then touches the trigger on the stiletto he's palmed from his argyle sock, the blade darting out as he thrusts, slamming Sovereign back against the car door, the cigarette shooting from his mouth as he groans *uuuhhh*.

Sovereign's hands are pressed to where the blade is buried. He looks down at the bloodied pearl handle of the stiletto sticking from his chest, his eyes bulging, teeth gritted so that the muscles knot out from his jaw.

"Don't move, it's in clean," Joe says. "Just let it go."

"Oh, my God, oh, oh," Sovereign exhales, and an atomized spray of blood hangs in the sunlit air between them. The 3 V's birds raise a junglish chatter against the everyday chirp of sparrows. The hot car fills with Sovereign's gasping for breath and with the smell of garlic, of the mortadella sausage on the blade, and then an acrid smell, calling to Joe's mind a line of kindergartners. Sovereign has peed his pants. His right hand, smeared with the blood soaking through his monogrammed shirt, slips down his body, weakly feeling as if to brush away a burning cigarette. There's no cigarette, his cigarette has slipped between the seats. Joe guides Sovereign's hand back to his chest and Sovereign grits his teeth again and groans from the soul, then closes his eyes. Tears well out from under his red lashes. His skin has gone translucent white, making his liverish freckles stand out like beads of blood forced through his pores.

"Not Vi," Sovereign says. "Oh, please, not Vi. I got little kids." Blood gurgles in his throat, he tries to clear it and begins to choke and Joe clamps a handkerchief over his mouth and Sovereign keeps swallowing, breathing hard, but otherwise not struggling, as if the pain of the knife has pinned him to the door.

"I told you not to talk. Just let it go. I tried to do you a favor, man. Whitey wants you turned into hamburger. I let you off easy," Joe says, removing his bloodied handkerchief from Sovereign's mouth.

Sovereign is shaking his head no-no, trying to form words with his open mouth. A bubble of bloody spit breaks on his lips. All he can do is whisper. His body has slouched so that Joe looks into Sovereign's dilated nostrils, which are throwing cavernous shadows. Joe leans closer to hear what Sovereign's trying to say.

"Bullshit," Johnny Sovereign manages. The word sends up a hanging, reddish spray. "You just wanted to see if it worked."

"Fuck you," Joe says. "You got a reprieve you didn't even know you had. What did you do with the time?" But even as he says it, Joe realizes Sovereign is right. He wanted to see what the knife could do, and how stupid was that, because now he's stuck talking with a dying mook. He should have just put a couple into Sovereign's brain and walked the fuck away instead of getting cute, sitting here listening to birds chatter, beside a guy with his jaw grinding and red eyelashes pasted shut by the tears leaking down his cheeks as his life hemorrhages away, the muscle that once pumped five quarts a minute, a hundred thousand heart-beats a day—how many in a life?—no longer keeping time. Joe's not sure how long they've been here. He wants the knife back but worries that if he pulls it out Sovereign will start to thrash and yell, and the wound will gush. Sovereign makes a sound as if he's gargling, syrupy blood dribbles from the corner of his mouth as his head rolls to the side, and then he's quiet. Tears dry on his cheeks.

"Sovereign," Joe says. "Johnny? You still here?" Joe can hardly speak for the dryness of his own mouth. He's aware of how terribly thirsty he is, and of how suddenly alone. Heat rays in as if the windshield of the Pancho is God's magnifying glass. Now Joe can hear the name Sovereign was talking about—some 3 V's bird repeating *betty betty betty*. He can't sit any longer listening to the nonstop jabber of the last sounds Sovereign heard.

"Johnny."

Joe digs the shotgun out of the gym bag. His handkerchief is bloody so he uses his jockstrap to wipe down the sawed-off shotgun he'll leave behind, jammed in Sovereign's piss-soaked crotch. He tries to ease out the stiletto. Blood wells up without gushing. Joe tugs harder but can't dislodge the knife, maybe because his hands have started to shake. He's drenched with sweat, and takes his jacket off. How did his white shirt get spattered with blood? He removes his shirt. The lapels of his powder blue sport coat are speckled, too, but the splash pattern that's good for eating spaghetti makes it look as if the blood might be part of the coat. He wipes the car and knife handle down with the shirt. In the gym bag, there's a wrinkled gray tank top with the faded maroon lettering CHAMPS over an insignia of crossed boxing gloves. Joe pulls that on and slips his jacket over it, and then, for no reason, fits the jockstrap over Sovereign's face so that it looks as if he's wearing a mask or a blindfold. At the shotgun blast, flocks rise, detonated from the factory roofs, and Joe imagines how on the top floor of 3 V's the spooked birds batter their cages.

Friday afternoon, a red clothespin day at the Zip Inn. Ball game on the TV, Drabowsky against the Giants' Johnny Antonelli, top of the fifth and the Cubs down 2–0 on a Willie Mays homer. The jukebox, Zip apologizes, is on the fritz. No "Ebb Tide," no "Sing, Sing, Sing," no "Cucurrucucu Paloma."

Teo sits on a stool, balancing the quarters that he was going to feed to the jukebox on the wooden bar.

"One more, on the house," Zip says. His white shirt looks slept in, his bow tie askew, his furrowed face stubbled, eyes bloodshot. It's clear he's continued the pace from yesterday. Teo turns his shot glass upside down. Zip turns it back up. "To Friday," Zip says.

"We already drank to Friday." Teo turns his shot glass back down. "We drank to Friday yesterday, and to Saturday, Sunday, Monday, Tuesday, and Wednesday."

"We missed Thursday."

"Yesterday was Thursday, we started out drinking to Thursday."

"Yeah, but today's fucking special."

"Every day's special. Isn't that the point of drinking to them?" Teo asks.

"There is no point," Zip says. "That's the point."

Teo shrugs. "So why's today special? An anniversary?"

"*Special*'s the wrong word," Zip says. He looks as if the right word might be *doomed*.

Something is eating at Zip, but Teo doesn't know how to ask what. Yesterday, Teo stayed drinking with him until the after-work crowd started filtering in. By then, Teo was half-loaded. He put the wounded Spanish pigeon back in his bowling bag and went home, tended to the coop, then fell into bed and, for the first night in weeks, slept undisturbed by dreams. "Look, compadre, if there's something I can do . . ."

"Have a brew," Zip says. He sets a Hamm's before Teo, and a bag of pretzels, and rings up one of the quarters that Teo has balanced on the bar. "You bring your feathered friend with the bum wing?"

"No," Teo says, "but I got something you been asking about." From the bowling bag on the barstool beside him, Teo lifts out a blue head mask and sets it faceup, flat on the bar. The face has the design of a golden beak and iridescent white feathers that fan into flames around flame-shaped eyes. The luminous colors are veined with brownish bloodstains. "You wanted to see, so I brought it."

"Goddamn." Zip smiles, looking for a moment, like his old self. "This is what you wrestled in? Pretty wild. So, what was your ring name?"

"La Colibrí."

"Like the vegetable?"

"It's a kind of bird," Teo says.

"You got the rest of the outfit in there?"

Teo unfolds the matching blue tights, and Zip holds them up, smiling skeptically at Teo.

"They stretch," Teo says.

"Not that much they don't."

"Yeah, they do. I'm wearing the top. Same material." Teo unbuttons his checked short-sleeved shirt. Underneath, he's wearing an iridescent blue tank top. Its bulgy front is spotted with faded blood, like the canvas of a ring.

"I wish I could of seen you in the ring, amigo, must have been something." Zip picks up the mask. He looks as if he'd like to try it on if he had two hands to pull it over his head. "Can you actually see to fight out of this?"

"Sure," Teo says, "it's got holes for the eyes."

"Let's see." Zip hands the mask to Teo, and when Teo hesitates, Zip says, "Come on. What the hell?"

"What the hell," Teo agrees, and pulls it over his head. It's the first time in years that he's worn it, and he's amazed to feel a reminiscent surge of energy, but maybe that's merely the whiskey kicking in on an empty stomach.

"You are one fierce-looking warrior," Zip says. "You should come in here wearing the whole outfit, just amble in and sit down, open up your book, and if somebody asks, 'Who's that?' I'll tell them: 'Him? The new security. Guards the hard-boiled eggs—which are now a buck apiece in order to pay for security. Salt's still free.'"

On the TV, the Hamm's commercial, "From the land of sky blue waters," plays between innings.

"Can you drink beer through that?" Zip asks.

When Teo laughs, it's the mask itself that seems to be laughing, the mask that chugs down a bottle of Hamm's.

"Why's Goldblatt's got you disguised in a dress when they could have a goddamn superhero patrolling the aisles? You're wasting your talent. You could be a rent-a-wrestler, make up business cards. Headlocks for Hire, Half nelsons fifty percent off. I need an autographed picture for the wall. Hey, I could sponsor you, advertise on your jersey."

"Have a Nip at the Inn of Zip," Teo says.

"You're a poet!" Zip sets them up with two more cold ones and rings up another of the quarters Teo has balanced on the bar. "Can the Kohlrabi still kick ass?" Zip asks.

"Fight again?" Teo asks. Even wearing the blue tank top and the mask, even after the first good night's sleep in a long time, even with the sunlight streaming through the door and whiskey through his veins, on a Friday afternoon, and nowhere to be but here, drinking cold beer and joking with his new friend, Teo knows that's impossible.

"What if there was no choice?" Zip asks. "If it was him or you? Say you catch somebody stealing and he pulls a knife? Could you do whatever it took? Is it worth it? Purely theoretical, what if somebody hired you to watch their back in a situation like that?"

The undisguised undercurrent of desperation in these questions makes Teo recall the message from the Spanish pigeon: *"Asesino."* Murder. The slip of paper is still in Teo's pocket. There's an eerie feeling of premonition about it. He'd been thinking maybe of showing it to Zip to see what he made of it, but not now. "Purely theoretical, you keep protection back there?" Teo asks.

"Funny you should ask, I was just looking through my purely theoretical ordnance last night," Zip says. "Swiss Army knife,

USMC forty-five missing the clip. Ever seen one of these?" Zip reaches beneath the bar and sets a short, gleaming sword in front of Teo.

Teo runs his finger along the Oriental lettering engraved on the blade.

"Careful, it's razor sharp," Zip says. "Never found out what the letters mean, probably something about honor that gets young men killed. Guys said the Japs used to sharpen these with silk. I don't know if that's true, but all the dead Jap soldiers had silk flags their families gave them when they went to war. Made good souvenirs. GI's took everything you could imagine for souvenirs. Bloody flags, weapons, gold teeth, polished skulls until there was an order against those. Wonder what happened to all that shit? Probably stuffed away forgotten in boxes in basements and attics all over the country. Only thing I took was this. It's a samurai knife used for hari-kari. They'd sneak in at night and cut your throat, so we slept two in a foxhole, me and Domino Morales, one dozing, the other doing sentry. You'd close your eyes dead tired knowing your life depended on your buddy staying awake." Zip weighs the sword in his hand, then sets it back under the bar and lifts a length of sawed-off hickory bat handle that dangles by a rawhide loop from a hook beside the cash register. "This used to be enough," he says, "but the way things are these days you gotta get serious if you want to defend yourself. Whoa!" Zip exclaims, gesturing with the bat at the TV screen. "Banks got all of that one."

On the TV, Jack Brickhouse is into his home-run call: "Back she goes . . . way back . . . back! . . . back! Hey! Hey!"

"Hey! Hey!" Joe Ditto says. He stands in the emblazoned doorway in his sunglasses and factory steel-toes, his powder-blue sport coat looking lopsided and pouchy where the gun weighs down his right pocket. He's wearing the sport coat over a wrinkled gym top, and in his left hand he holds a gym bag. He's sweating as if he's just come from a workout. "Didn't mean to startle you, Mr. Zip. I thought you were going to brain your customer here. This masked marauder didn't pay his bar tab? You want I should speak to him?"

Zip hangs the bat back on its hook, and Joe sets the gym bag down and straddles a stool beside Teo. No introductions are made. On the right side of Joe's face, beneath a four-day growth of beard, there's a hot-looking handprint. "What's so interesting?" Joe asks, when he catches Zip staring. "You don't like the new look from the other side of Western?" He tucks in his Champs tank top as if it's his gym shirt–sport coat combination that Zip was staring at. "Fucken hot out there," Joe says. "I need a cold one. You need an air conditioner in here, Mr. Zip."

"They're too noisy," Zip says. "You can't hear the ball game."

"Hey, I'm not trying to sell you one," Joe says. He drains his beer in three gulps and slams down the bottle. Teo's remaining two quarters teeter onto their sides. "Hit me again, Mr. Zip. And a shot of whatever you're drinking. What's score?"

"Cubs down two to one. Banks just hit one."

"Drabowsky still pitching? You know where he's from?"

"Ozanna, Poland," Zip says like it's a stupid question. "He's throwing good."

"You bet on him?" Joe asks. When he raises the shot glass, his hand is so shaky that he has to bring his mouth to the glass.

"I don't bet on baseball," Zip says.

"Hit me again, Mr. Zip. And one for yourself." From a roll of bills, Joe peels a twenty onto the bar. "What are you drinking, Masked Marvel? Zip, give Zorro here a Hamm's-the-beer-refreshing."

Zip sets them up, and the three men sit in silence, looking from their drinks to the ball game as if waiting for some signal to down their whiskeys. Their dark reflections in the long mirror behind the bar wait, too. Teo glances at the mirror, where a man in a blue Hummingbird mask glances back. He knows the guy in the sunglasses beside him is mob, and can't help noticing that Zip has gone tensely quiet, unfriendlier than he's ever seen him. It makes him aware of how Zip set the samurai sword within reach, and of the message from the Spanish pigeon.

On the TV, Jack Brickhouse says, "Oh, brother, looks like a fan fell out of the bleachers," and his fellow sportscaster, Vince Lloyd, adds, "Or jumped down, Jack." Brickhouse, as if doing play-by-play, announces, "Now, folks, he's running around the outfield!" and Vince Lloyd adds, "Jack, I think he's trying to hand Willie Mays a beer!"

"That's Lefty!" Teo exclaims.

"Lefty? Lefty Antic?" Zip asks. "You sure?"

"The sax player. He's my neighbor."

"Here come the Andy Frain ushers out on the field," Brickhouse announces. "They'll get things back under control."

"Look at him run!" Teo says.

"Go, Lefty!" Zip yells. "He ain't going down easy."

Without warning, the TV blinks into a commercial: "From the land of sky blue waters . . ."

"Shit!" Joe says, "that was better than the fucking game. Guy had some moves."

"You know Lefty, the sax player?" Teo asks Zip.

"Hell, I got him on the wall," Zip says, and from among the photo gallery of softball teams with *ZipIn* lettered on their jerseys he lifts down a picture of a young boxer with eight-ounce gloves cocked. The boxer doesn't have a mustache, but it's easy to recognize the sax player. "He made it to the Golden Glove Nationals," Zip says. "Got robbed on a decision."

"That southpaw welterweight from Gonzo's Gym. I remember him from when I was growing up," Joe Ditto says. "Kid had fast hands." He raises his shot glass, and they all drink as if to something.

"Well, back to baseball, thank goodness," Jack Brickhouse says. "Vince, it's unfortunate, but a few bad apples just don't belong with the wonderful fans in the friendly confines of beautiful Wrigley field."

"Best fans in the game, Jack," Vince says.

"They didn't want to show him beating the piss out of the Andy Frains," Joe says.

"Lefty's good people. Hasn't put Korea behind him yet, that's all," Zip says.

Until yesterday, Teo couldn't gimp on his bum knee into the Zip Inn without wondering how Zip could put behind him the war that took his arm. Now he knows. Zip hasn't.

"Hit me again, Mr. Zip," Joe says. "A double. And get yourself and Masked Man, here." Joe turns Teo's shot glass up.

Teo turns it back down.

Joe turns it back up. "Hey, mystery challenger, we're having a toast." Joe props Lefty's photo up against a bottle of Hamm's. "To a man who knows how to really enjoy a Cubs game." This time, his hand steadier, Joe clinks each of their glasses.

"Gimme a pack of Pall Malls, Mr. Zip. So, what's with the mask?" Joe asks Teo. "Off to rob a savings and loan? A nylon's not good enough? Goddamn, you got the whole outfit here," he says, examining the tights that Teo hasn't stuffed back into his bowling bag. "You one of those street wrestlers on *Cinco de Mayo* or something?"

"Used to be," Teo says.

With his long-neck beer bottle, Joe parts Teo's open shirt to get a look at his tank top. "Who'd you fight as, the Blue Titman? Jesus, Mr. Zip, check the boobs out on this guy. That's some beery-looking bosom you're sporting, hombre. They squirt Hamm's? This might be the best tit in Little Village." Joe lights a smoke, offers one to Teo, who refuses. "Mr. Zip, hit me again, and Knockers here, too," Joe says. He's holding Teo's glass so that

Teo can't turn it over. Zip pours and Joe takes a sip of beer. Then his hand snakes along the bar and into Teo's bag of pretzels. Joe munches down a pretzel, and his hand snakes back for another, except this time it snakes inside Teo's shirt for a quick feel before Teo pulls away.

Zip appears to be busy rinsing out a glass.

"Ever go home after a hard day's wrestling and just spend a quiet evening getting some off yourself, or does there have to be a commitment first?" Joe asks. "I'm just fucking with you, friend. I used to love to watch wrestling when I was a kid. I didn't know it was a fake. You know, I didn't mind finding out Santa Claus was bullshit, but Gorgeous George and Zuma the Man from Mars—he wrestled in a mask, too—that hurt."

"It's not always fake," Teo says.

"What fucken planet are you from? How do you think Gorgeous George could have done against Marciano? Would you consider a little private contest that wasn't fixed?"

"I don't wrestle anymore," Teo says.

"See, but this may be my only chance to say I wrestled a pro. I'm just talking arm wrestling here," Joe says, and assumes the position, with his elbow on the bar. "We'll wrestle for a drink, or a twenty, or the world championship of the Zip Inn, whatever you want."

"I'm retired," Teo says.

"Come on," Joe says, "beside experience you got forty pounds on me. If your friend Lefty can jump out of the bleachers and take on the Andy Frain ushers, you and me can have a friendly little match. Mr. Zip has winner. Left-handed, of course. You can referee, Mr. Zip, and hey, that little matter of business for today, let's forget it. Another time, maybe. Who you betting on, or do you not bet on arm wrestling, either?"

"Twenty on El Kohlrabi," Zip says.

Teo looks at Zip, surprised.

"Purely theoretical," Zip, says, "but you can take him."

"Purely," Teo says, and smiles, then leans his arm on the bar and he and Joe Ditto clench hands.

"*Una momento,*" Joe says. He removes his sport coat and folds it over his gym bag, takes a puff of Pall Mall, then drops to the floor and does ten quick push-ups with a hand clap after each. "Needed to warm up."

Teo removes his shirt to free up his shoulder. Both men, now in tank tops, clench hands again. Joe is still wearing his sunglasses, and his half-smoked cigarette dangles from his lip. Zip counts one, two, wrestle! and they strain against each other, muscle and tendon surfacing along their forearms. Joe gives slightly, then struggles back to even, seems to gain leverage, and gradually forces Teo's arm downward.

The crowd at Wrigley is cheering, and Jack Brickhouse breaks into his home-run call: "Back she goes, back, back, way back . . ."

"Goddamn, come on, *luchador,*" Zip urges; his left hand slaps the bar with a force that sends the red clothespin flying off the sleeve folded over the stump of his right arm.

Gripping the edge of the bar with his left hand and grunting, Teo heaves his right arm up until it's back even, but his surge of momentum stalls. He and Joe Ditto lean into each other. They've both begun to sweat, their locked hands are turning white, arms straining, faces close together, separated by the smoke of Joe's dangling Pall Mall. "My friend," Joe says from the side of his mouth, "you smell like pigeons."

Out on the street, sirens wail as if every cop, ambulance, and fire truck in Little Village is rushing past. The lengthening ash of Joe's cigarette tumbles to the bar. Joe spits out the butt, and it rolls across the bar top onto the floor, where Zip grinds it out. Their arms have begun trembling in time to each other, but neither budges. Teo turns his face from Joe and finds himself looking into the mirror. A man in a blue mask looks back re-

proachfully; he won't allow another defeat. Teo closes his eyes
and concentrates on breathing, resolved to ignore the pain, to
welcome it, and to endure until Joe tires and he makes one last,
desperate move. Teo knows that final assault will be a sign of
weakness; if he can hold it off, he'll win.

"From the land of sky blue waters" tom-toms from the TV,
and Joe's left hand slowly snakes across the bar to Teo's tank top.
At its touch, Teo pushes back harder, but Joe won't give. His
right arm resists Teo's concentrated force while his left hand gently brushes, then fondles Teo's chest.

"Got you where I want you now," Joe says. "Cootchie-
cootchie-coo, motherfucker."

Our father figured that we'd want to see the sewer rat he'd cap-
tured, and he was right about that, so he waited to kill it until
Mick and I came home. It was a Saturday in summer, and I'd
taken Mick to the icy swimming pool at Harrison High. Our
hair, towels, and the wet swimsuits we wore beneath our jeans
still smelled of chlorine as we walked down the gangway into the
sunny backyard where Sir had an enormous rat imprisoned in a
glass canister. It had a wide-angled mouth and metal lid, the kind
of rounded jar that's often used for storing flour or sugar. The rat
filled it up and behind the thick convex glass appeared distorted
and even larger, with magnified beady eyes, buck teeth, handlike
rodent feet, and a scaly bald tail. I looked for rabies foam around
its whiskers. Sir had used the canister to store dago bombs. Every
few weeks, he'd lift the sewer cover over the pipe in the basement, light a dago bomb, and drop it down the sewer. The
echoey sewer amplified the explosion. Sir said the noise chased
off rats. The fireworks from the canister were gone; I'd been planning to pilfer a few for Fourth of July, but I never saw them
again. I don't know what Sir did with them, or how he managed

to catch the rat in the jar. I didn't ask at the time, maybe because we were too involved with preparations for its execution.

My father had me take the garden hose and fill the large galvanized metal washtub that he always referred to in Polish as the *balja*. We used the *balja* for mixing cement and, sometimes, for rinsing the mud out of crayfish we caught with string and chicken livers at the Douglas Park lagoon. When the *balja* was brim full, Sir brought over the rat-in-a-jar, as we'd begun to call it. I stood on one side of the tub and Mick on the other. Mick had stripped down to his bathing suit and cowboy boots as if he planned a dip in the *balja* himself. He'd put on his cowboy hat and was holding his favorite toy, a cork-shooting shotgun. Mick's toy box was an arsenal: matched six-shooters that shot caps, a Davy Crockett musket to go with a coonskin cap, squirt guns of various calibers, pirate swords and flintlock pistols, a Buck Rogers ray gun. They were mostly made of plastic, but not the shotgun. It had a blued metal barrel and a wooden stock, and broke at the center like a real shotgun. Breaking it was how one pumped it up enough to shoot the corks that came with it. If you jammed the muzzle into the dirt after a rain, it would shoot clots of mud. Holding the rat-in-a-jar with one hand on the bottom and the other on the lid, Sir lowered it into the *balja*. The rat looked worried. When the glass canister was entirely immersed, Sir slowly raised the metal lid so that water could seep in. Mick and I moved in closer on either side of him, trying to see. Sir lifted the lid a little more, and the rat shot straight up out of the tub and splashed back down into the water. Mick and I jumped back, but Sir grabbed the shotgun by the barrel out of Mick's hand, and as the wet rat scrambled over the side of the washtub, Sir knocked it back into the water. "Da-dammit!" Sir yelled. He was thwacking at the *balja*, sending up swooshes of water, and the rat squirted out between blows and ran for the homemade board fence separating our yard from the woodpiles and uncooped chickens in Kashka's yard next door.

We scrambled after it, and Sir managed to hack the rat one more time as it squeezed through the fence and crawled off into a woodpile.

We stood peering through the fence.

"Da-damn," Sir muttered.

"My gun!" Mick said. Sir handed it back to him. "You ruined my gun." A piece of the wooden stock had splintered off, and the connection between the barrel and stock was noticeably loose. One more good whack would have snapped it in two.

"Is that rat blood?" I said. There was a red, sticky smear along the side of the stock.

"I nailed it a couple good ones," Sir said.

Mick dropped the shotgun as if it might be carrying rabies and walked away, fighting back tears.

For a week or so the shotgun lay in the back yard where Mick dropped it, rusting in rain, bleaching in sun. Finally, Mick forgave our father enough to pick up the gun again. The bloodstain was now a permanent feature of the splintered stock, and though the gun was the worse for wear, it had acquired a mystique it hadn't had before its baptism in rat blood. It became Mick's favorite toy all over again, the weapon he'd always take with him when he went down the alley to play guns with his best friend, JJ—short for Johnny Junior.

Johnny Senior was Johnny Sovereign.

When Johnny Sovereign was found dead in his own car, with a jockstrap on his face and his balls blown off, it was big news in the neighborhood, but Mick knew nothing about the specifics. My parents and I never discussed the murder openly at home. Mick had simply been told that it wasn't a good time to go play at his friend JJ's house, that he should wait until JJ called him. But Mick got bored waiting, so after a few days he decided to sneak over to JJ's for a visit. He pulled on his cowboy boots, armed himself with the rat-blood shotgun, and snuck off down the alley. Alleys were secret thoroughfares for kids, and as long as Mick was sneaking away from our house, he decided he'd also sneak up on JJ. Surprise attack was one of their favorite games. He went past the garage where JJ's father parked the yellow car, but the garage was empty. As always, pigeons hooted from inside. At the Sovereigns' back fence, overgrown with morning glories and sizzling with bees, Mick paused, as he and JJ often did, to poke a finger inside a morning glory. He and JJ would pretend the flower was a socket, but unlike an electric socket, a morning glory was safe to stick your finger into. If you held it there long enough, you'd feel connected to the power coming through the tangled green wires of the vines.

Recharged with morning-glory power, Mick snuck past the back fence into the small patch of grassless back yard that led into a shadowy gangway. Instead of going to the back door, he sidled along the house, crouching under the back windows. He'd approached this way several times before to ambush JJ. He liked to catch JJ when he was least expecting it—still in his pajamas, eating Sugar Pops at the breakfast table.

The curtained kitchen window was partially opened, and Mick slowly rose and slid the barrel of the shotgun through the slit between the drawn curtains. He was into the make-believe of the game, and his heart pounded with a combination of tension and repressed laughter. When he heard the scream, he froze.

"Oh, God, no, please, please, I beg you," a woman's voice cried. "I don't know anything about what Johnny did. Please, I won't say anything. I have two little kids." It was JJ's mother, Vi, who'd always been nice to Mick. She was weeping hysterically, repeating, "Please, please, I wouldn't recognize your voice, you never called, I don't know who you are, it was all Johnny, for the love of Jesus, I'm begging you don't, please, I'm still young."

Mick will drop the shotgun and, crying hysterically himself, race through the alleys back home, but not before peering through a crack in the curtains and seeing JJ's mother on her knees on the kitchen linoleum, tears streaming down her face as she pleads for her life, unaware perhaps that the straps of her yellow slip have slid down her shoulders, spilling forth my brother's first glimpse of a woman's naked breasts.

Blue Boy

~~~~~~

Chester Poskozim's younger brother, Ralphie, was born a blue baby, and though not expected to survive Ralphie miraculously grew into a blue boy. The blue was plainly visible beneath his blue-green eyes, smudges darker than shadows, as if he'd been in a fistfight or gotten into his mother's mascara. Even in summer his lips looked cold. The first time I saw him, before I knew about his illness, I thought that he must have been sucking on a ballpoint pen. His fingers were smeared with the same blue ink.

On Sundays, the blueness seemed all the more prominent for the white shirt he wore to church. You could imagine that his body was covered with bruises, as if he was in far worse shape than Leon Szabo or Milton Pinero, whose drunken fathers regularly beat them. Unlike Szabo, who'd become vicious, a cat torturer, or Milton, who hung his head to avoid meeting your eyes and hardly ever spoke in order to hide his stammer, Ralphie seemed delighted to be alive. His smile, blue against his white teeth, made you grin back even if you hardly knew him and say, "Hey, how's it going?"

"Going good." Ralphie would nod, giving the thumbs-up.

When he made it to his eighth birthday, it was a big deal in our neighborhood, Little Village; it meant he'd get his wish, which was to make it to his First Holy Communion later that year, and whether Ralphie ever realized it or not, a lot of people celebrated with him. At corner taverns, like Juanita's and the Zip Inn, men still wearing their factory steel-toes hoisted boilermakers to the Blue Boy. At St. Roman Church, women said an extra rosary or lit a vigil candle and prayed in English or Polish or Spanish to St. Jude, Patron of Impossible Causes.

And why not hope for the miracle to continue? In a way, Ralphie was what our parish had instead of a plaster statue of the Madonna that wept real tears or a crucified Christ that dripped blood on Good Friday.

For Ralphie's birthday, I stopped by Pedro's, the little candy store where we gathered on our way home from school whenever any of us had any money, and spent my allowance on a Felix the Cat comic, which I recalled had been my favorite comic book when I was eight, and gave it to his brother, Chester, to pass along.

Chester and I were in the same grade at St. Roman. We'd never really hung out together, though. He was a quiet guy, dressed as if his mother still picked out his clothes. He didn't go in much for sports and wasn't a brain either, just an average student who behaved himself and got his schoolwork done. If it wasn't for his brother, the Blue Boy, no one would have paid Chester much attention, and probably I wouldn't be remembering him now.

Looking back, I think Chester not only understood but accepted that his normal life would always seem inconsequential beside his little brother's death sentence. He loved Ralphie and never tried to hide it. When Ralphie would have to enter the hospital, Chester would ask our class to pray for his brother, and we'd stop whatever we were doing to kneel beside our desks and pray with uncharacteristic earnestness. They were the same blood type, and sometimes Ralphie received Chester's blood. Chester would be absent on those mornings and return to school in the afternoon with a Band-Aid over a vein and a pint carton of orange juice, with permission to sip it at his desk.

Outside the classroom, the two of them were inseparable. I'd see them heading home from Sunday mass, talking as if sharing secrets, laughing at some private joke. Once, passing by their house on Twenty-second Place, a side street whose special drowsy light came from having more than its share of trees, I noticed them sitting together on the front steps: Ralphie, leaning against his brother's knees, his eyes closed, listening with what looked like rapture while Chester read aloud from a comic book. That was the reason I chose a comic as a gift instead of getting him something like bubble-gum baseball cards. His bruised, shivery-looking lips made me wonder if Ralphie was even allowed to chew gum.

The open affection between Chester and Ralphie wasn't typical of the rough-and-tumble relationships between brothers in the neighborhood. Not that guys didn't look out for their brothers, but there was often trouble between them, too. Across the street in the projects, Junior Gomez had put out the eye of his brother Nestor on Nestor's birthday, playing Gunfight at the O.K. Corral with Nestor's birthday present, a Daisy Red Ryder BB gun. In the apartment house just next door to ours, Terry Vandel's baby brother, JoJo, wrapped in a blanket, fell from the second-story window to the pavement. Terry was supposed to have been baby-sitting for JoJo while their mother was at work. Mrs. Hobel, walking below, looked up to see the falling child. For weeks afterward, while JoJo was in the hospital with a fractured skull, Mrs. Hobel would break into tears repeating to anyone who would listen, "I could have caught him but I thought the other boy was throwing down a sack of garbage."

As in the Bible, having a brother could be hazardous to your health.

For a while, the mention of twins or jealousy or even pizza would trigger a recounting of how, just across Western Avenue, in St. Michael's parish, the Folloni twins, Gino and Dino—identically handsome, people said, as matinee idols—dueled one afternoon over a girl. It was fungo bat against weed sickle, until Gino went down and never got up. Dino, his face permanently rearranged, was still in jail. Their father owned Stromboli's, a pizza parlor that was a mob hangout. Every time I'd ride my bike past the closed pizzeria on Oakley, and then past the sunken front yard where they'd fought, it would seem as if the street, the sidewalk, the light itself, had turned the maroon of an old bloodstain. I'd wonder how anyone knew for sure which twin had killed the other, if maybe it was really Dino who was dead and Gino doing time, ashamed to admit he was the one still alive. If they ever let him out, he'd go to visit his own grave to beg for forgiveness. Shadows the shade of mourning draped the brick buildings along that street, and finally I avoided riding there altogether.

Out on the streets, I kept an eye out for my brother, Mick, but at home our relationship was characterized by constant kidding and practical jokes that would sometimes escalate into fights. I was older and responsible for things getting out of control.

Once, on an impulse, while riding my bike with my brother perched dangerously on the handlebars the way friends rode—in fact, we called the handlebars the buddy seat—I hit the brakes without warning, launching Mick into midair. One second he was cruising and the next he was on the pavement. It would have been a comical bit of slapstick if he'd landed in whipped cream or even mud. I wasn't laughing. I was horrified when I saw the way he hit the concrete—an impact like that would have killed Ralphie. Mick got up, stunned, bloody, crying.

"Jeez, you okay?" I asked. "Sorry, it was an accident."

"You did that on purpose, you sonofabitch!" He was crying as much with outrage at how I'd betrayed the trust implicit in riding on the buddy seat as with pain.

I denied the accusation so strongly that I almost convinced myself what happened was an accident. But it was my fault, even though I hadn't meant to hurt him. I'd done it out of the same wildness that made for an alliance between us—a bond that turned life comic at the expense of anything gentle. An impulsiveness that permitted a stupid, callous curiosity, the same dangerous lack of sense that had made me ride one day down Luther, a sunless side street that ran only a block, and, peddling at full speed, attempt to jump off my J. C. Higgins bike and back on in a single bounce.

It was a daredevil stunt I'd seen in Westerns when, to avoid gunfire, the cowboy hero, at full gallop, grabs the saddle horn, swings from the stirrups, and in a fluid movement hits the ground boots first and immediately bounds back into the saddle. As soon as I touched one foot to the street, the spinning pedal slammed into the back of my leg and I tumbled and skidded for what seemed half a block while the bike turned cartwheels over my body. Skin burned off my knees and palms. I'd purposely picked a street that was deserted to practice on. But a lady who could barely speak English poked her head out of a third-floor window and yelled, "Kid, you ho-kay?" She'd just witnessed what must have looked like some maniac trying to kill himself. I waved to her, smiled, and forced myself up. Amazingly, nothing was broken, not even my teeth, although I had a knot on my jaw from where the handlebars had clipped me with an uppercut. I collected my twisted bike from where it had embedded itself under a parked car. Had it been a horse, as I'd been pretending, I'd have had to shoot it. If someone had done to me what I'd just done to myself, I would have got the bastard back one way or another. My brother let me off easy.

But years later, when he was living in New York, studying acting with Brando's famous teacher Lee Strasberg, Mick and I
spent an evening together, drinking and watching a video of
On the Waterfront. During the famous "I could have been a
contender" scene, when Brando complains about his "one-way
ticket to Palookaville" and tells his older brother, "Charley, it was
you. . . . You was my brother, Charley. You should have looked
out for me," Mick turned to me, nodded, and smiled knowingly.

Chester was anything but a tough, yet despite his quiet way,
you got the impression he'd lay his life on the line if anyone
messed with Ralphie. You could see it in how he'd step out into a
busy street, checking both directions for traffic before signaling
Ralphie to cross. Or how, whenever a gang of guys playing keep-
away with somebody's hat, or maybe having a rock fight, barreled
down the sidewalk, Chester would instinctively step between
them and Ralphie.

That willingness to take a blow was an accepted measure of
what the gang bangers called *amor*—a word usually accompanied
by a thump on the chest to signify the feeling of connection from
the heart—although in matters of *amor*, as in everything else, the
willingness to *give* a blow was preferred. There were guys in the
neighborhood who'd lay their lives on the line over an argument
about bumming a smoke, guys capable of killing someone over a
parking space or whose turn it was to buy the next round. There
was each gang's pursuit of Manifest Destiny: battles merciless and
mindless as trench warfare over a block of turf. There was the ca-
sual way that mob goons across Western Avenue maimed and
killed, a meanness both reflexive and studied—just so people
didn't forget that in capitalism on the street, brutality was still
the least common denominator.

Not that there weren't ample illustrations of that principle at the edge of the daily round of life where bag ladies combed alleys and the homeless, sleeping in junked cars, were found frozen to death in winter. Laid-off workmen became wife beaters in their newfound spare time; welfare mothers in the projects turned tricks to supplement the family budget; and it seemed that almost every day someone lost teeth at one or another of the corner bars.

The shout would go up—"Fight!"—and kids would flock in anticipation, especially if a couple of alkies were whaling at one another, because invariably loose change would fly from their pockets. The scramble for nickels and dimes would spawn secondary fights among us. And if we weren't quick enough, we'd be scattered by Sharky, a guy who'd lost his legs in Korea, or riding the rails to Alaska, or to sharks off Vera Cruz, depending on which of his stories you wanted to believe. He was a little nuts, and people wondered if he remembered anymore himself where exactly his legs had been misplaced.

Sharky mopped up late at Juanita's bar, but his main source of income was scavenging. He was also known as Gutterball for the way he'd rumble along alleys and curbs on a homemade contraption like a wide skateboard that he propelled with wooden blocks strapped over gloved hands, turning his hands into hooves. Late on summer nights, you could hear him clopping down the middle of deserted streets like a runaway stallion. Call him Gutterball to his face or get in his way, and he'd threaten to crack your kneecap with one of those wooden hooves.

It wasn't an idle threat, he'd been in several brawls. They usually started with a question: "What the fuck you looking at, ostrich-ass?"

Anyone with legs was an ostrich to Sharky.

"Huh?" came the usual response.

But Sharky wouldn't let it go at that. "Admit it, you rude motherfuck, you were staring at my bald spot, weren't you?"

Sharky did have a bald spot. He'd roll slowly toward the confused ostrich, who'd begin edging backward as Sharky's pace increased.

"You never seen a bald spot on wheels before? That it? I'm very fucken sensitive about my bald spot. Or is it something else about me that attracted your attention? Like, maybe, that I'm at a convenient height for giving head. You the kind of perv that wants a baldy bean doing wheelies while sucking your dick?"

By now, Sharky had gained momentum and was aimed for a collision if the ostrich didn't take off running, which he usually did, with Sharky galloping after him, raging, "Run, you perverted, chickenshit biped!"

Sharky obviously enjoyed these confrontations. What nobody suspected was that such spectacles were only a substitute for what he really craved: a parade.

There was no shortage of parades in Little Village. Most ethnic groups had one, and that must have figured in Sharky's thinking. St. Patrick's brought out the politicians, and St. Joseph's was also known locally as St. Polack Day since people wore red, the background color for the white eagle on the Polish flag. I never understood what was particularly Polish about St. Joseph, but I bought a pair of fluorescent red socks especially for the occasion.

The Mexicans had two big holidays. The first was El Grito, a carnival at the end of summer, when as part of the festivities a wrestling ring was erected in the middle of Nineteenth Street. There'd be pony rides, and Mick and I would try to time it so as to be in the saddle when the El roared overhead because the ponies would rear.

The Feast of Our Lady of Guadalupe, the patron saint of Mexico, was more solemn. Each December twelfth, no matter the weather, a procession wound through the streets led by a plaster likeness of the Virgin who'd appeared not to the Spanish conquerors but to a poor Indian, Juan Diego. She'd imprinted her mestiza image on his cloak—a miracle still there for all to see at the basilica in Mexico City. She'd told Juan Diego to gather flowers for her in a place where only cactus grew. When he did her bidding, he found a profusion of Castilian roses, and so all through Little Village people carried roses and sang hymns in Spanish to the Virgin whose delicate sandal had crushed the head of Quetzalcoatl, the snake god ravenous for human sacrifice. Even the alderman and precinct captains marched holding roses. And each year there was the fantastic rumor that the great Tito Guízar, the Mexican movie star of *Rancho Grande*—a singing cowboy like Roy Rogers—would arrive on a palomino to lead the procession through the barrio. His movies played at the Milo theater on Blue Island, where they showed films in Spanish. I'd study the posters I couldn't read and wonder if his rearing horse was a celebrity in Mexico, the way that Roy Rogers's horse, Trigger, was a star in America.

Then, one year, Tito Guízar actually showed. Down Washtenaw, heading for Twenty-second, he came riding right behind the Virgin, not on a palomino but on a prancing white horse whose mane blew in the feathery twirl of the early snowfall. The horse left pats of golden manure steaming in the street, while Tito Guízar, dressed in black leather chaps studded with silver, his guitar strapped across his back like a rifle, waved his sombrero, blessing the shivering crowd that lined the sidewalks to see him.

As the procession approached St. Roman Church, a motorcycle gunned to life, spooking the white horse, and while Tito Guízar whoaed at the reins, a Harley rumbled out of the alley beside the rectory. It was pulling Sharky, who was attached to the rear fender by a clothesline like a coachman commanding the reins of a carriage. The Harley was driven by Cyril Bombrowski, once known as Bombs. He'd been a motorcycle maniac until, doing seventy down an alley, he'd collided with a garbage truck. He had a metal plate in his head and didn't ride much anymore, as he was prone to seizures since the wipeout. Now people called him

Spaz, and when he rode down the street, it was a tradition that whoever saw him first would yell a Paul Revere–like warning: "Spaz Attack!"

No one yelled this time. Behind Spaz and Sharky, a procession of the disabled from the parish emerged from the alley. A couple of World War II vets, mainstays from the bar at the VFW Club, one with a prosthetic hook and the other with no discernible wound other than the alcoholic staggers; and Trib, the blind newspaper vendor; and a guy who delivered pulp circulars, known only as—what else?—the Gimp, pushing his wheelchair for support; and Howdy, who'd been named after Howdy Doody because his palsy caused him to move like a marionette with tangled strings.

It was a parade of at most a dozen, but it seemed larger— enough of a showing so that onlookers could imagine the battalions of wounded soldiers who weren't there, and the victims of accidents, industrial and otherwise, the survivors of polio and strokes, all the exiles who avoided the streets, who avoided the baptism of being street-named after their afflictions, recluses who kept their suffering behind doors, women like Maria Savoy, who'd been lighting a water heater when it exploded, or Agnes Lutensky, who remained cloistered years after her brother blew off half her face with a shotgun during an argument over a will.

With their canes, crutches, and the wheelchair, it looked more like a pilgrimage to Lourdes than a parade. They'd been assembled by Sharky and now marched, although that's hardly an accurate word for their gait, beneath the banner of a White Sox pennant clamped in a mop stick that the Gimp had mounted on his beat-up wheelchair. The Gimp never sat in his chair but rather used it like a cart, piling it with bags of deposit bottles and other commodities he collected while delivering the circulars no one read. Today, the chair was empty of junk.

Their flag bore no symbol of allegiance, no slogan of their

cause other than "Go Sox," but what must have fueled Sharky's outrage all along became suddenly obvious: they were at once the most visible and the most invisible of minorities. Instead of bit players out of the Gospels, fodder for miracles, the Halt and the Lame were in for the long haul, which required surviving day to day.

As they passed the church, Sharky raised a wooden hoof, not in blessing or salute—more as if scoring the winning goal—and on cue those parading behind him raised their fists. At that moment, Ralphie, wearing a cap and bundled in a checked scarf, stepped out of the crowd lining the curb, catching everyone by surprise, even Chester, who couldn't do anything more than exclaim, "Hey, where you going?"

By then Ralphie had put on a burst of speed—the first time I'd ever seen him run—and caught up to the Gimp, climbed up on the wheelchair, and raised his fist, too.

Ralphie died a few weeks later, on *Gwiazdka*. The word means "Little Star" in Polish, and it's what Christmas Eve was sometimes called in the parish. At midnight mass kids too young to be altar boys would file up the aisle to the manger carrying gold-painted stars on sticks. Had he been alive, Ralphie would have been among them. He was buried in the navy blue suit already purchased for the First Holy Communion he would have made that spring.

That was an observation made repeatedly at the wake, and afterward, at the Friday night bingo games in the church basement, and at bakeries and butcher shops and pizzerias and taquerias and beauty parlors and barbershops and corner bars: "Poor little guy didn't make it to his Holy Communion," someone would say.

And someone would likely answer, "They should of made an exception and let him make it early."

"Nah, he didn't want to be no exception. That's how he was. He wanted to make it with his class."

"Yeah, he was a tough little hombre, never wanted special treatment, never complained."

"You know it. Always thumbs-up with him."

"God should of let him make it."

"Hey! You start with that kind of talk and there's no stopping."

"Yeah, but just for this once, if I was God, that kid walks up there for his First Communion. Then, if it's his time, so be it."

"If you was God we'd all still be waiting for the Second Day of Creation while you slept off your hangover from the Big *Kaboom*. God knew he didn't want to be no exception. He made him that way."

"Yeah, he made him with blue fucking skin, too."

"Hey, maybe that was God's gift to us. Somebody too sweet for the long term in this world. Somebody to be an example—'A little child shall lead them,' like Father Fernando said at the service."

"Talk about hungover, that priest was still shitfaced. The night before he was pounding tequila at Juanita's till they eighty-sixed us out into the goddamn blizzard—snow piled so fucking deep we couldn't hardly get out the door. Me and Paulie have to help him back to the church, then Paulie falls in a snowbank, and while I'm digging Paulie out, Father Kumbaya decides to take a leak. I look up and there's our new padre waving his peter in the middle of Twenty-sixth."

"So, big deal, he's a human being. It was a beautiful service, he did a good job. I thought that older brother was a little weird, though, guarding the casket like a rottweiler. Somebody shoulda told him it was all right to cry. What's his name, anyway?"

"I don't remember."

"That little Ralphie was a saint. Don't be surprised if someday they don't canonize him."

"I think there's gotta be like miracles for that."

"Yo, that kid was a living miracle. Maybe that's it—why God put him here—what Little Village will be famous for: the Blue Boy! Mark my words, people will come from all over like they do to places in the Old Country . . . Our Lady of Fatima, the Little Infant of Prague. Know what I'm saying?"

"Yeah, somebody always figures out how to make a buck off it."

A year later there were yet to be miracles, at least none I'd heard about. But the Blue Boy wasn't forgotten. As we approached another Christmas vacation and the first anniversary of Ralphie's death, Sister Lucy, our eighth-grade teacher, assigned a composition on the meaning of Christmas, and dedicated it to Ralphie's memory. Chester was in our class, and at the mention of Ralphie, Sister Lucy smiled gently in his direction, but he just stared at his hands. He'd been a loner since his brother's death, and all but mute in school. We'd heard the rumor that Chester periodically showed up, only to be repeatedly turned away, at the blood bank on Kedzie where the alkies went to trade their blood for wine money.

"Do your best," Sister Lucy instructed our class. "This will be the last Christmas composition you will ever write."

The Christmas composition was an annual assignment at St. Roman, required from each class above third grade. The pieces judged best received prizes, and the top prize winner was read aloud at the Christmas pageant. Not that there really was any competition for top prize: it was reserved for Camille Estrada. She was the best writer in the school. Probably, before Camille, the concept of such a thing as a best writer didn't even exist at St. Roman. Camille was a prodigy. By fifth grade she'd already written several novels in her graceful A+ cursive and bound them in thread-stitched covers cut from the stays of laundered shirts. They were illustrated—she was a gifted artist as well. And they were filed, complete with checkout cards, in the shelves beside *Black Beauty*, *Call of the Wild*, and the other real books in the school library.

Camille's early works, mostly about animals, had titles like *The Squirrel of Douglas Park* and *The Stallion and the Butterfly*. I never actually checked them out, but I read them on the sly one week when I was exiled to the library for detention. Camille loved horses, and they often suffered terribly in her stories. They were the subjects of many of her illustrations: huge, muscular creatures with flared nostrils, often rearing, some winged, some unicorns.

By sixth grade she'd taught herself to type, and then the writing really poured from her. Camille became founder, publisher, editor, and chief reporter of our first school newspaper, *To Change the World*, as well as translator for an occasional Spanish edition. She represented St. Roman in the Archdiocese of Chicago Essay Contest, writing on why a Catholic code of censorship was needed for pop songs and movies like the Brigitte Bardot film *And God Created Woman*. It was a foreign film that would never have played in our neighborhood anyway. Still, although none of us had ever seen Bardot on screen, the B.B. of her initials—which also conveniently stood for Big Boobs—mysteriously appeared as a cheer scribbled on the school walls: *BB zizboombah!* When Camille's censorship essay won, she got a mention in the Metro section of the *Tribune*.

At the annual school talent show, where "Lady of Spain" pumped from accordions and virtuosos pounded "Heart and Soul" on the out-of-tune upright to the clatter of tap dancers,

Blue Boy 137

Camille would read an original poem written for the occasion. She wasn't a dramatic reader, but there was something inherently dramatic about her standing before the boomy mike, without a costume or an instrument to hide behind, her eyes glued to the page while she read in a quiet, clear voice.

I liked it when she read aloud because I could watch her without seeming to stare. I'd always been fascinated by the way her myopic eyes illuminated her thin face. Her long lashes drew attention like those on a doll. Beneath them, her liquid, dark eyes gazed out unblinking, serious, enormous. Her voice was colored with a slight Spanish accent. She spoke in a formal way that sounded as if she was cautiously considering each word in English, a language in which she was so fluent on the page. Her reserve made her seem older, though not physically older, like some of the boys who already had faint mustaches, guys like Brad Norky, who actually *was* older, having been held back. Once, at a talent show, I overheard two elderly women talking about the way Camille had read her poem about the ecstasy of St. Teresa.

"She has an old soul," one of the women observed, and the other said, "I know what you mean."

Even back then, in a way, I knew what she meant, too.

From seventh grade on Camille wore rouge that looked artificial against the caramel shade of her skin and made her appear feverish. She got glasses that year: ivory-sparkle cat frames that matched the barrettes clamping back the thick black hair she'd previously worn in braids. She was no longer quite flat-chested, though the rose-colored bra outlined beneath the white blouse of her school uniform hardly seemed necessary. She could have used braces.

In seventh grade, a gang of us proudly calling ourselves the Insane Fuckups would sneak off at lunch to our boys' club—the doorway of an abandoned dry cleaner's where we'd smoke Luckies, spit, and discuss things like the rumor that some of the girls were washing their school blouses over and over to make the fabric thin in order to show off their underclothes. I made the mistake of mentioning that even Camille Estrada's bra was showing, and, as if dumbfounded, Norky asked, "No shit? Estrada has titties! You think she might have a hairy pussy, too?" Then he burst into mocking laughter.

Even my best friend, Angel Falcone, couldn't resist breaking up. "Instead of BB's she's got bb's—bb*itas*," he said, making his voice tiny. "Hey, maybe she'll publish the news in her paper."

"Headline!" Norky shouted. "Stop the presses!" and with the chalk he carried to graffiti up our doorway, he printed in huge letters on the sidewalk: ESTRADA HAS bb's.

He chalked it on the graffitied tunnel wall of the viaduct on Rockwell, and along the bricks of the buildings we passed, and on the asphalt of the street where the little girls drew hopscotch courts alongside the school. It was one of those phrases that inexplicably catches on, and for the next couple of weeks it was everywhere—in the boys' bathroom, at the Washtenaw playground, on the concrete basketball court at the center of the projects: ESTRADA HAS bb's.

In class, when I'd sneak a glance at her, it seemed her rouged cheeks burned, but perhaps that was only a projection of my secret shame.

Near the end of seventh grade, my desk was moved out into the corridor, where I was banished after topping one hundred demerits in conduct. Then, our teacher that year, Sister Mary Donatille—the only nun who insisted we say the Mary in her name—introduced Partners in Christ. It was an experimental program, borrowing, perhaps, from AA, in that it teamed habitual bad boys with sponsors—good girls—so as to give the boys a taste of the rewards of behaving. I can't say what it was for the girls, torture probably; for the boys it was a subtle form of humiliation. Camille was assigned to be my Partner in Christ.

At St. Roman, two kinds of kids stayed after school, those in detention and the teachers' pets who were invited to help the nuns clean the classrooms. Detention time was spent copying chapters from the New Testament, but thanks to Sister Mary Donatille's experiment, instead of rewriting the Apocalypse, I got to clean the blackboard erasers with Camille. It was an honorary task: only pets were entrusted to take the erasers out behind the school and beat them clean against the wall. Although I'd been reassigned a seat beside Camille in class, we still hadn't spoken. We stood together, engulfed in chalk dust and an uncomfortable silence relieved only by the muffled thud of felt against brick. In blocky chalk impressions I pounded out *F-U-*

"I really like your vocabulary," Camille said.

"Real funny."

"No, I mean it," she said. "You have a neat imagination."

I looked at her, too puzzled to respond. I didn't know if she was putting me down or putting me on or applying some kind of condescending psychology, or if she was just spacey.

"That story you wrote for Christmas. About the ant. It was so cool. I wanted to publish it in the paper, but it was too long."

She was referring to "The Enormous Gift," which I'd written back in sixth grade for the Christmas competition. I frequently missed getting my homework in, but I'd found myself writing the story with an excited concentration I hadn't associated with schoolwork. The assignment that year had been to write a story about a gift brought to the baby Jesus in his stable at Bethlehem. In my story, the gift was a crumb of bread that weighed a thousand times more than my narrator, an ant, but he hoisted it nonetheless, and after narrow escapes involving spiders, sparrows, the hooves of oxen, and soles of sandals, he finally crept into the manger to offer his gift.

"After you read it I kept thinking about it and saw what you meant," Camille said. "How it was like a little miracle for the ant to bring the first bread to Jesus, who'd later make the big miracles of the loaves and fishes, and turn bread and wine into his body and blood."

I'd never thought about any of that. To me it was just the adventure of an ant.

"The Enormous Gift" had been chosen to be read aloud in class, but it didn't win the school competition. Camille won with "O Little Star of Centaurus," a story in which the Christmas star was revealed to be a spaceship in the shape of a winged horse. I couldn't help visualizing it as the fiery red Pegasus trademark for Mobil gasoline. It had traveled from the constellation Centaurus, where light-years ago Christ had appeared to redeem an advanced but brutal race of hooved aliens. The Centaurians, now converted to brotherhood and peace, had learned that Christ was traveling through the universe, redeeming world after world, and so in homage they followed him through time and space to witness each reappearance. The gleam of their ship was the star that guided the Wise Men, who in each new world came bringing gifts on each new night of Christ's infinitely repeated birth.

"Your story knocked my socks off," I said, not adding that, ever since I'd heard her read it, I'd wondered if the Christ on Centaurus had hooves like the other Centaurians. Her story didn't say, but it posed problems for his crucifixion.

"Thanks," she said, "but I thought yours should have won."

"No way. They should make yours into a movie. How'd you make that up?"

"How'd you think of the ant?"

"I don't know. I like to read about bugs and stuff," I said, not mentioning how during the summers I'd sneak off down the railroad tracks to the Sanitary Canal, where I hid a homemade net for collecting butterflies.

"I never purposely try to make things up," Camille said, sounding suddenly proper, the way she did when she spoke in class. "It just happens. It's not about made-up anyway, it's about feeling."

She looked at me for agreement, but the transformation in her voice put me on guard.

"It's about feeling, you know?" she repeated. "That's what's important," she insisted, as if I'd disagreed.

She went back to cleaning the erasers, clapping them together like cymbals, the poofs of chalky smoke surrounding her bronzed by the rays that shafted through the clouds massed over the convent. She stared at the two chalk-dust letters I'd pounded on the bricks, and back at me, then beat in a blocky *C*.

"Want to collaborate?" she asked.

I stood there, confused again, refusing to admit to myself that she intimidated me, but feeling hopelessly immature beside her all the same.

"So, come on," she said and beat out the slanted upper bar of the missing *K*.

I beat an impression of the straight staff. She added the lower slanted bar. Not much chalk remained on the erasers, and they left only the faded ghost of the word. I became conscious that my heart was beating.

She read our collaboration aloud as if it were composed of air flowing across her overbite, as if a whisper re-created its faintness on the bricks.

"Don't look so surprised. You don't know what I think," she said, then added, "I have stories I don't show anyone."

"Like what?"

"I don't think someone should be blamed for stories any more than they should have to confess their dreams. Boys don't have to confess their dreams. Do you?"

It was something I'd never thought about, and I wasn't sure what she was getting at. If she was referring to wet dreams, they were something I'd yet to experience. Later, in high school, I'd

think back to the two of us behind the school and realize that was
what she probably meant, but at the time all I did was shrug.

She hunched her skinny shoulders, mimicking me. "Maybe I'd
tell you if I thought you could keep a secret," she said.

"Sure I can," I told her.

"It would have to be a trade. First you have to tell me something you want me to keep secret."

"What if I don't have a secret?"

"Everybody has. But if you're an exception then make one
up."

I knew that collecting butterflies wasn't the kind of secret she
was after. Even at the time, it seemed strange to me that we'd
been in school together for years and hardly talked and now suddenly we were having a conversation of the kind I'd never had before with a girl or anyone, a conversation that, whether Camille
knew it or not, was already a secret I would keep. I laughed as a
way out of answering.

"What do you have to do penance for?" she asked.

"You mean the old five Our Fathers and five Hail Marys?" I
said. In my experience that was the penance no matter what you
confessed. I didn't know if it was the same for girls or not.

Camille looked at me unamused. "Have you ever written a
story that was a sin, one you had to do penance for?"

"Penance for a story?"

She gathered the erasers into an unbalanced stack and turned
to go inside, leaving me to pick up the erasers that dropped behind her. "You're a big help," she said sarcastically but added,
"Honest. I knew you weren't a loser."

That night, I went to sleep thinking about her—another secret—and looking forward to the following day, when we'd go
out together to beat the erasers. I didn't know what I'd tell her,
but I'd tell her something. But next morning, during the Pledge
of Allegiance, before class even began, Diane Kunzel, Norky's

Partner in Christ, let out a scream. Norky had Magic-Markered a smiley face on a white sausage-shaped balloon he'd worked through his open fly as if exposing himself. Sister Mary Donatille attacked him, slashing at his greasy d.a. haircut and stabbing at his balloon with the pointer she used during geography when she stood before the pull-down map that was green for Christian countries and pink for Communist ones. Partners in Christ came to a bitter end that morning.

"Don't cry, girls, these boys would try the patience of an angel," Sister Mary Donatille said.

Camille wasn't crying. She showed her teeth in a quick, re-gretful overbite smile and fluttered her fingers goodbye as I packed up. We boys were reassigned to seats at the perimeter of class, and for the remainder of seventh grade I never really spoke with Camille again.

But I still thought about her when in eighth grade we were asked to write our last Christmas composition and dedicate it to Ralphie. I wanted to write a story, not a composition, one that would be read aloud, so that Camille would hear it.

Unfortunately, I didn't have a story to write. I wanted a story that came out of nowhere, one I could get excited about the way I had when I'd written from the viewpoint of an ant, although writing about an ant seemed wimpy now. Sister Lucy had made it clear that dedicating our compositions to Ralphie didn't mean we were to write about him. Simply writing, as usual, about the true meaning of Christmas was all that was required. Yet, when I thought about Ralphie, already dead a year, tales about an ant or a red-nosed reindeer or a snowman come to life seemed the child-ish fantasies of a daydreamer, a term my father applied to me when he was feeling particularly contemptuous of my behavior.

"You better wake up and smell the coffee," he'd warn.

Getting desperate, I tried to write a story my father had told once about the first Christmas he'd spent as a child after his father had been sent to the state mental hospital, and how on a bitterly cold Christmas Eve he met a boy named Teddy Kanik, who became his best friend for life. It wasn't like any story my father had told me before. He told it after I'd accused him of being a Scrooge because of his cheapskate way of shopping for a Christmas tree. Before I could get to the story as my father told it to me, it seemed necessary to explain the annual ordeal that shopping with him for a Christmas tree had become. Each Christmas season, Mick and I would trudge after him from one tree lot to another in the cold. He was a comparison shopper. He insisted we drag along a sled for hauling back the tree, the way we had when we were little kids. Mick and I would argue over who got stuck pulling the old red Flexible Flyer, its rusted runners rattling over the partially shoveled sidewalks. It had become our family tradition—a terribly embarrassing one. My father loved to bargain, and everything, including the way he'd browse the rows of Christmas trees, shaking his head at their overpriced and undernourished condition, was part of a master strategy. His opening gambit on anything he bought, Christmas trees not excluded, was always the phrase "So how much you soak for it . . ."

That phrase was as far as I got in writing my father's story, because it occurred to me that if the story was read aloud in class, it would be as embarrassing as shopping for a tree with my father. Worse, each sentence I wrote about the shopping seemed to take me further away from the story as my father told it, and I knew why I was disgressing, treating it as a joke: his story about meeting Teddy Kanik one Christmas Eve so long ago depressed me. It seemed to have happened in a different world—the Chicago where my father had grown up as an immigrant, only blocks away but in an alternative universe, one forever sunk in a Great Depression. That wasn't a feeling I wanted to bring into a class where I had a reputation to uphold as a clown. I thought about

Camille confiding that she'd written stories she kept secret, and realized my father's story was better kept a secret, too.

By now it was late. I probably would have given up if all I'd wanted was to impress Camille, but writing a story was the only way I could imagine communicating with her. Despite what Sister Lucy had said about simply writing about the meaning of Christmas, I didn't seem able to concentrate on a story dedicated to Ralphie if he wasn't in it, so I tried writing about the funeral.

I hadn't ridden in the line of cars that left for the cemetery after Ralphie's requiem mass, but I'd stood on the church steps and watched the confusion of spinning tires and men in dark topcoats rocking a hearse piled with snow and flowers out of a rut along the curb. Then, the taillights of the cortege slowly disappeared down Washtenaw into a whiteout. I envisioned their headlights burrowing through the blizzard as they followed the hearse up Milwaukee Avenue, way out to the Northwest Side, where I imagined the snow was even deeper. I'd heard how, when they finally reached St. Adalbert Cemetery, they had trouble finding the grave site. In my story, the drifts were so deep that all but the crosses of the tallest monuments were buried. In that expanse of white, it was impossible to find Ralphie's plot, but as the procession of cars wound along a plowed road, they came to a place I described as "an oasis of green in a Sahara of snow." There, gaping from exposed grass, was a freshly dug grave. At my grandfather Mike's funeral I'd noticed a robin with a worm in its beak fly from his open grave, so in my story birds—robins, doves, seagulls—flew out of the hole as if a cage door had opened, and circled cawing overhead. When I reread that sentence, I scratched out "robins" and wrote in "blue jays." Only after the graveside service did snow drift over Ralphie's plot, which was marked—as I'd heard it actually was—with a simple gray stone that made no mention of his being a blue boy. But in my story, when the snow melted in spring, his gravestone had turned blue. I tried different shades: turquoise, cornflower, Prussian, all the blues in a giant 104 box of Crayolas. None seemed right.

It was long past my bedtime. Mick had gone to sleep in the room we shared, where I'd been writing cross-legged on my bed, so I'd relocated to the kitchen table. My father looked in on me before he turned in, obviously amazed to see me slaving over homework.

"Don't burn that midnight oil too late, sonnyboy," he cautioned.

Quiet in our flat was when the motor of the refrigerator grew audible. I could hear its hum, and the toilet trickling, the crinkle of cooling radiators and, from down the hall, a harmonica, maybe Shakey Horton or Junior Wells still faintly playing on the bedroom radio tuned to the black rhythm and blues station that Mick and I listened to on the sly before we went to sleep.

"I'm going down to the basement and put my blue light on," Sam Evans, the DJ, would announce at midnight.

What blue was that gravestone emerging from the dirty snow in spring? As blue as the blue light in Sam Evans's basement? The ghostly blue of Blue Island rising from the lake? Or the cold blue of the lake itself? Norky once described it as "turn-your-balls-blue" in an oral presentation. For a time after that we referred to Lake Michigan as Lake Blueballs.

It had actually offended Camille. "Sometimes people look but don't see what's beautiful all around us, like the lake," she wrote in *To Change the World*. "It's a melted glacier, an Ice Age turned to sweet water. I love its taste."

I slipped my jacket on and went out the back way and walked down the alley that led to an Ice Age so fierce the air felt crystallized, as if the snow tailing off the roofs might be flecks of frozen oxygen. It took a conscious effort to inhale its sharpness, yet instead of cursing the cold, I had a thought that maybe the purpose of winter was to make you realize with every breath that you were alive and wanted to stay that way. I thought about Ralphie and the other kids I knew who already were dead, some from accidents, some, like Peanuts Bizzaro, murdered. Peanuts had seemed indestructible. In winter, we'd all go to watch him fight at the steamy Boys' Club gym. He was a boxer who'd prided himself on not getting hit. He made boxing something daringly beautiful, like diving off a high board. One night I stood in an audience of guys outside the Cyclone fence surrounding the warehouse lot on Rockwell—a lot with floodlights mounted too high to bust with rocks—where Peanuts was dancing, jabbing, throwing combinations, and repeating, "I'm fast, I'm flashy," though under those lights and the bluish shadows they threw he appeared to move in slow motion as he methodically beat the piss out of a much beefier kid from the Ambros. The kid, called Dropout by the gang buddies cheering him on, had wanted to box at the Boys' Club, but he was obviously heavier than Peanuts's welterweight class, and when the boxing coach refused to let them put the gloves on, Peanuts offered to take it outside. Dropout wasn't even trying to box anymore. He was grabbing and kicking, and Peanuts was nicking him with his fists, calm and cool as a matador, asking, "Am I fast or what?" Then, from outside the fence, came a single pop that echoed off the stacks of oil drums. Guard still up, Peanuts went down to one knee. Dropout kicked him over, then scaled the fence and took off with his buddies.

Peanuts tried to climb the fence but slid back. Out of nowhere, his older brother, Tony, came running and nearly cleared the eight-foot fence in a jump. He wrapped his Levi's jacket around Peanuts, who was shivering, turning blue under the lighting, and repeating, "No fair, no fucken fair."

Ralphie never had a fighting chance. I thought of him, and of Peanuts, of Gino Folloni and the others all buried under earth frozen too hard to break with a spade. They couldn't feel the cold because they were the cold. Maybe they could hear the wind, but they couldn't see how even colder than earth the boulder of moon looked through the flocked branches of back yard trees. I stopped, made a snowball, hurled it, and the snow knocked from the tree maintained the shape of branches in midair for a moment before disintegrating. I wasn't wearing gloves, and my hands burned numb. Suddenly, I felt choked up, and I started to run as if I could outrun the feeling—which, in fact, was what I did, sprinting down three blocks of alleys without stopping to check the cross streets for traffic, but there weren't any cars and finally, when my nostrils and lungs felt at once frostbitten and on fire and I could no longer remember why I was running or if there even was a reason, I stopped and turned around, jogging home under streetlights that looked as if they, too, should have been exhaling steam.

The kitchen was filled with a dizzying warmth. It would have felt warm if the only sources of heat were the overhead light and the humming refrigerator motor. There, on the gray Formica table, lay my smeary blue ballpoint pen and three-holed loose-leaf papers, my story, and the scratch paper on which I'd listed various kinds of blue. I tried to reread my story and couldn't. The only thing left to make it feel right was to compress it in both hands like a snowball before throwing it into the trash bag under the sink.

Everyone handed in compositions but Chester and me. Sister Lucy didn't say anything to Chester, but she told me to sign my name on a blank sheet of paper, title it "Christmas Composition," and below that to write "Dedicated to Ralphie."

On the last day of class before Christmas vacation, when she returned the compositions, she handed the blank paper to me marked with a red *F*. Written in red ink was the comment "I see that your gift this Christmas was an ENORMOUS nothing."

After returning the papers, Sister Lucy placed a scratchy record of carols on the portable turntable, and while it played she announced what we all already knew, that Camille's essay would represent our class at the Christmas Pageant that year. As was customary, Sister Lucy asked Camille to read her story aloud for our class. Camille rose to read at her desk, but Sister motioned her to the front. Camille was to be our valedictorian, too, the first one ever at St. Roman, and Sister Lucy had begun coaching Camille on her oral delivery in preparation for her speech at graduation.

"A Christmas Carol for Ralphie: A True Story," Camille read, her quiet voice in competition with the "Ave Maria." She enunciated carefully, eyes glued to the page, rouge burning on her cheeks. She appeared to be overheating, and she partially unbuttoned the navy blue cardigan she'd taken to wearing over her school uniform.

"Try looking up at your audience from time to time," Sister Lucy suggested. "Eye contact, that's the secret."

Camille's composition opened with the sound of prancing hooves: not reindeer on a rooftop, she told us, but Tito Guízar on the white stallion following the Virgin down Washtenaw. Listening to her re-create the scene, I wondered if she'd been there. I didn't remember seeing her, but there had been a crowd of people on the sidewalk watching Tito Guízar. When she came to the part about Sharky leading his parade out of the alley, she looked up at us, her audience, and asked, "What if Charles Dickens, the author of *A Christmas Carol*—one of the greatest writers in the history of the world—was there in the crowd?"

She dropped her gaze back to her paper. "I think I saw him there that afternoon," she said, then deliberately making eye contact, asked, "If Dickens can transport us in time back to London, why can't we transport him to Chicago?"

Maybe eye contact *was* the secret, because it seemed as if she was asking me the question.

"You don't have to be transported to London on Christmas Eve a century ago to know that, as Dickens wrote, 'the business of Mankind is Man.' You don't have to be visited by the ghosts of Christmas Past, Present, and Future. But if you were, who would your ghost of Christmas Past be?" she asked. "Each of you has one. What would your spirit of Christmas Present look like?"

She paused as if waiting for an answer, and though I now realized her technique was to make eye contact whenever she asked a question, the question nonetheless seemed directed at me, as if there were a secret connection between us.

Before I could think who my ghost might be, Norky turned in his seat a row over and whispered, "Brigitte Bardot," then shook his fist as if jerking off and made a demented face, which confirmed the ill effects of masturbation. Otherwise, the class was quiet, everyone intent but Chester, who'd buried his head in his arms as if asleep at his desk.

"Maybe the ghost might be disguised as a blind man who sells newspapers or, instead of dragging chains, comes rattling on a little cart with hooves strapped to his hands," Camille suggested.

However different our ghosts might be, she said, she guessed that everyone in our class had the same Tiny Tim—Ralphie—and that we needed to be inspired by his example to change the world. To change the world, we first had to change ourselves. We had to make Christmas in our hearts and love one another.

Norky turned, caught my attention, and raised a sheet of paper on which in big letters he'd scrawled: "Estrada has BB's."

I hated to admit he was right—maybe it was an optical illusion, but whenever Camille paused for breath, her white blouse beneath her blue sweater seemed to strain against the swell of her breasts as if she were developing before our eyes.

She took a deep, breast-heaving breath and said that a blue boy was not so different from Tiny Tim with his crutch. And that Tiny Tim with his crutch was not so different from Jesus with a cross.

She said that on that day last December when he ran to join the band of disabled marchers, Ralphie "mounted the wheelchair like a prince assuming his throne." She said he raised his blue fist not in triumph or, as some claimed after he died, to wave goodbye, but as if to cheer as Tiny Tim would, "God bless us every one!"

"That's not what happened," Chester said quietly.

He lifted his head from his arms and, without asking permission, half rose at his front-row desk.

"Chester, do you want to add something?" Sister Lucy asked, giving him the floor, though it wasn't necessary, because Camille had immediately stopped reading and now stood as if trapped before the class, more uneasy than I'd ever seen her.

Chester sat back down. "Lots of little kids chase parades," he said. His voice trembled. "How come for once in his life Ralphie couldn't just do what other kids do without somebody making it a big deal?"

"Of course he could," Sister Lucy said. "What Camille meant was—"

"She shouldn't make stuff up about him," Chester interrupted, rising to his feet with a force that jarred his desk and sent the needle on Sister's portable player skipping across vinyl. "He wasn't joining anything!" he shouted at Camille. "He wasn't like them. His fist wasn't blue. That's bullshit. What do you know?" he demanded. "You don't know shit! And he hated being called Blue Boy. That wasn't his goddamn name. He wasn't some fucking freak. He wasn't some crip in a story. He didn't want your fucking feeling sorry for him. We don't need it. What do you know? You don't know fucking dogshit! Go fuck your four-eyed self!" he yelled after her as Camille ran from the room.

"How much you soak for it?" my father asked, studying the tree with a characteristic combination of suspicion and contempt.

His appraisal was accurate, it wasn't much of a tree. The lots were already picked over. Each year we'd shop later in December in order to get a better deal. I'd begun to suspect that, if he could, he would buy a tree on sale after Christmas the way he bought Christmas cards.

"You don't unload these trees soon and you'll be stuck with them. You won't be able to give them away." As usual, he marshaled his arguments before getting down to talking turkey, applying what he called "psychology," even though the kid he was bargaining with didn't own the lot. He was a sullen-looking teenager in a hood who kept his eyes on his own stamping feet. The unclasped buckles of his galoshes jangled; I could smell the resin on his oversize canvas mittens. While we'd wandered through what was left of the tiny pine forest, he hadn't bothered to leave the flickering, illusory warmth of the garbage can where he stood smoking a cigarette and burning boughs.

During summer, lots like this were eyesores, clotted with trash, ragweed thrusting from bricks and broken bottles. But each December they were transformed—strung with colored bulbs and plastic pennants like used car lots. A horn speaker, blaring maniacally as any from an ice-cream truck in July, crackled "Here Comes Santa Claus."

"*Maybe* I'd go a fin on this one," my father grudgingly offered.

"I don't make the prices, mo', " the kid told him.

"Well, just between us, what do *you* think it's really worth?" my father asked. "If you were shopping for it."

"Whatever the tag says, mo'. "

That second *mo'* caught my attention. The first time, I'd thought maybe he'd mumbled "man," but it was *mo'* as in *mo-fo* as in *motherfucker*. I wondered if he was high. My father seemed not to have noticed. His general obliviousness to gang etiquette in the neighborhood had always alarmed me.

"Suppose the tag fell off," my father prodded. "Trees don't grow in nature with price tags, you know."

The kid shrugged as if it wasn't worth talking about. "Look, mo', you buy it or you don't."

"I offered a fin . . . with an extra six bits in it for you if you saw the stump," my father said, conspiratorially.

"Why you come here and insult me for, mo'?"

"What? You want I go see what the competition has to offer? Maybe you haven't noticed, but they got a very nice selection of trees down the block, and another down the block from that," my father said, not letting on that we'd already cased every lot in an eight-block radius before he decided this lot had the cheapest trees—no doubt because they were the scruffiest. "There's more trees out there than customers," my father informed him, amused by the irrefutable laws of capitalism now working to his advantage.

"So go fucken waste their time."

Mick and I looked at each other and back at the guy.

"What you looking at? How you like I shove that sled up your ass, kid?" he asked me.

We walked off, me dragging the sled.

"I didn't like his attitude," my father said.

I didn't say anything. I was furious. All the other times my father had embarrassed me returned in a rush: the way he'd stop his beater in traffic to pick a piece of scrap he thought might be worth something off the street; how I'd unpack my lunch in school to find he'd made me what my friends called "a puke on white"—last night's chop suey on now dissolved slices of Wonder bread; how at Maxwell Street, or Jewtown, as it was called with typical Chicago ethnic sensitivity, at the outdoor market my father haunted where endless haggling was the rule, while I tried on trousers behind the makeshift dressing room of a windblown sheet, he'd yell, "Do they fit in the crotch?" I was banging the sled over curbs as if yanking the leash on a dog I was trying to kill.

"Pa-rum-pa-pum-pum," Mick hummed to himself as he had the entire time we'd been out. "Me and my drum."

"Hey, take it easy on that sled," my father said. "If you can't make something, don't break it."

I gave the sled a jerk that slammed it along a building so its metal runners sparked off the bricks, and my father stopped, challenging me to try it again. "Someone having a problem here?"

"You are really a Scrooge, mo', " I told him, and braced for an attack that, this time, didn't come.

Later that night, while Mick helped Moms bake gingerbread, my father and I strung the Bubble Lites on a Scotch pine to a burble of carols courtesy of the Lawrence Welk orchestra. It was the first long-needled pine we'd ever had, and it seemed exotic— a pedigreed Persian cat of a tree. It still had pinecones on it. The bushy needles made stringing the lights trickier, my father observed, then we continued working in silence.

"Be a good night for some homemade eggnog," he offered. "The real thing made the old-fashioned way." He prided himself on his eggnog; it was the best I've ever had. He began talking about his father—my grandfather—whom he never mentioned and whom I'd never really met. I thought of him as my father's father rather than as my grandfather. My father remembered how at Christmastime his father would send him to a barrelhouse—a tavern where beer barrels served as a bar—with a pail to bring back a special holiday brew. Everybody at the tavern knew his father. There were local prize fights back then, one tavern's champ against another's, and his father, whose name was Michael, fought every Friday night. He fought as the Wild *Goral*, which sounded like an abbreviation for "gorilla," but meant the wild man from the Tatra mountains—although, my father added cryptically, Mike might have been half Jewish and no hillbilly at all. He told me how once his father came home late with his front teeth broken and how he sat groaning, slugging from a fifth of whiskey and spitting blood into the beer pail as he worked at his teeth with a pair of pliers, trying to pull the stubs out of his bloody gums so he wouldn't have to pay a dentist. Finally, he tried to get my father to yank out what was left of his teeth, and when my father wouldn't, Mike got furious and chased him, trying to brain him with the whiskey bottle until he escaped by running out of the house.

Long past midnight on one of those Friday nights, drunken men brought the Goral home, half-conscious, blood running from his nose, mouth, and ears, his paycheck gone. He lay moaning in bed for a day, then slept for two more, and when he regained consciousness he was dazed, speechless, nearly helpless, and finally, after weeks that way he was taken to Dunning, the state mental hospital, a Palookaville from which he never returned.

My grandmother Victoria barely spoke English. She worked at home as a seamstress during the day. After they took Mike away, she got a second job at night scrubbing floors in a downtown office building. My father was eleven at the time, the oldest of the six kids, so as the man in the family, he had to work several jobs. He rose at five a.m. to deliver milk, then delivered newspapers, then attended grade school, and immediately after school he headed for the flower shop on Coulter Street, where he worked until suppertime. The shop was closing late on the Christmas Eve of the first year of Mike's incarceration when the florist told my father there was a rush order on a wreath—not a Christmas wreath but a funeral wreath. They made it from pine boughs anyway, stuffed with wet sphagnum moss and tied with a black ribbon; my father helped work on it and the florist sent him to deliver it. The address was in a neighborhood my father wasn't familiar with. He went through the city in the dark, half lost on the snow-drifted streets, holding the wreath out before him. He didn't have gloves, and when he finally found the address, on a street that has since been erased by an expressway, he couldn't knock because his hands were frozen to the wreath. He had to kick at the door.

A boy his own age answered, the son of the man who had died. The family couldn't afford a funeral home so the body, dressed in a Sunday suit, was laid out in a small living room, or parlor, as my father called it—he always referred to living rooms as parlors. When the kid who answered the door saw that my father couldn't let go of the wreath, he invited him in and sat him down beside the oil stove. There was a pan of water on top of the stove, and the kid, Teddy Kanik, brought a washcloth and towel and bathed my father's hands until they thawed. He made him a cup of tea. They were best friends from that day on.

It's a story I heard my father tell twice: once that evening as we strung the Bubble Lites on the Scotch pine, and then again, thirty years later, after he'd retired from his job at the foundry. He'd retired in Memphis, Tennessee, where he'd been transferred when the Harvester plant closed in Chicago. I was visiting after he'd had a stay in the hospital for the kidney ailment that would ultimately take his life. We were telling stories, laughing about all the crazy people from the old neighborhood, and I tried to get him to tell what he remembered about Poland. He was very young when, to use his phrase, "they came over on the boat." Instead, he told the story about his father again, and when he reached the part about kicking at Teddy Kanik's door, hands frozen to the funeral wreath, unable to knock, he broke into tears, something I'd never seen him do, excused himself, and rushed from the room.

At my father's funeral, when there might have been an opportunity to pay a few words of respect, that story set in the dead of winter returned to my mind. It was summer in Memphis—"a scorcher," my father would have called it—and his story seemed even more foreign there. Not the actual feeling itself, but the recollection of an old feeling from childhood, one for which I still don't have a name, returned: an inexpressible protectiveness toward my father, a concern that, despite his faith in hard work and practicality, he'd never wholly appraised the reality of the country we lived in. We shared a home, we shared a life, but there was a dimension separating us. He inhabited another America, a distant place like Dickens's London or Gogol's Moscow. He feared that we, his sons, would go wanting, and that fear had set him at odds with us. I thought of telling his Teddy Kanik story at the wake but wasn't sure what the point might be; the story wasn't a way he'd want to be remembered in public, or a way of saying goodbye. And yet the story itself diminished anything else I could think of to say, and so, to my shame, I left my father unprotected and sat silently and listened to the priest mouth the usual clichés.

Mick had flown in from New York for the funeral toting a huge, bulging soft-sided plaid suitcase. Before his flight, he'd rushed to the Lower East Side to buy containers of pierogi and borscht, jars of herring, garlic dills, horseradish, kraut, links of fresh and smoked kielbasa—sausages my father loved and wasn't able to eat in his last years because of his restricted diet. Mick knew that after the funeral a meal would be required. He stuffed in a bottle of *wisniowka*—a cherry brandy—and a bottle of 150 proof Demerara rum, then, at LaGuardia, checked the suitcase through to Memphis. Everything but the *wisniowka* and rum arrived broken and run together.

The rum was for Mick's private tribute. He'd worked as a bouncer at a strip club on Forty-second Street and lived with one of the dancers, a striking Puerto Rican woman who'd introduced Mick to Santeria. He'd become an initiate and wanted to become a santero. He wore his *caracoles*—a shell necklace no one was allowed to touch—and brought a thick black candle inscribed with esoteric symbols that he erected before our father's tomato patch as if we had buried him in the back yard. It was an offering made to Oya, patron of whirlwinds and cemeteries, to ease the entrance to the world of the dead. Oya's syncretic form, he explained, to ease our mother's misgivings, was Our Lady of Montserrat. Beside the candle, he set a shot of rum; Oya, fiercest of the female orishas, liked her drink strong. In the humid, bug-roaring darkness of Memphis, the orange candle flame flickered eerily off the tomato netting until Moms went out and drenched it with a blast from the garden hose.

The rum that Oya didn't require Mick and I killed driving around at night between barbecue places and country bars in my father's gold Chrysler. We ended up in a pool hall. My father had been a skilled pool player. Neither Mick nor I had inherited the gene. Maybe it was the similarity of our inept play, but people kept asking if we were twins. No, we told them, just brothers.

After the funeral we served a meal of Memphis barbecue and Lower East Side Polish sausage to my father's surviving brother and three of his sisters, who'd all traveled from Chicago. We said a brief prayer and downed a *wisniowka* in a silent toast to my father's memory.

I sat beside my aunt Olga, my father's youngest sister.

"When we were kids, your father kept us all going," she told me. "One year, when we barely had enough to eat, he somehow managed to show up with a tree on Christmas Eve, because, he said, our family shouldn't be without one. He was a good brother. He was a good guy."

"He never told me about that," I said.

She dabbed her eyes. "There's a lot he didn't talk about."

That was the first of times to come when missing my father took the shape of being startled that he was no longer there to answer a question regarding a past I knew so little about, to which he'd been my only link. I wished, with an intensity that ambushed me, that I could have asked him for the details on how he'd come up with the tree. It sounded like another story that might have made Charles Dickens proud.

When, in her composition, Camille Estrada told how she'd seen Charles Dickens standing on Washtenaw, I too saw him, a familiar face among the crowd watching Tito Guízar ride by. Camille might have argued that if Tito Guízar could actually appear parading through Little Village behind the miraculous Virgin, then why not Charles Dickens? The appearance of the Mexican cowboy star, complete with stallion, sombrero, a guitar strapped across his back, was barely less remarkable than that of an old British writer would have been. Dickens was the man in a starched collar with a blue cravat that matched his worn, serious eyes; his auburn hair was thinning, his flowing beard was the kind one saw on hoboes who lived by the railroad tracks. That was how Dickens was pictured on the card in Authors, a game our family played. Dickens shared the deck with Shakespeare, Sir Walter Scott, James Fenimore Cooper, Washington Irving, Longfellow, Tennyson, Louisa May Alcott, Twain, Poe, Hawthorne. At bedtime, our mother would read from those authors to Mick and me.

"No wild stuff," she'd caution, "this is reading time."

It was the closest thing Mick and I had to sacred time.

On the Dickens card, beneath his likeness, four books were listed: *Pickwick Papers, David Copperfield, Oliver Twist, A Christmas Carol*. Of those, Moms read *Oliver Twist*. We owned a set of 78 rpm records of a dramatized reading of *A Christmas Carol* starring Basil Rathbone, who was also Sherlock Holmes. My father had gotten a good deal on it at Maxwell Street.

Camille had tried to summon up the authority of Dickens's fiction to justify the true story of Ralphie she wanted to tell, a story destined to end with the hopelessly pathetic fact of a boy dying on Christmas Eve. On some level she must have asked herself, who would read *A Christmas Carol* a second time if Tiny Tim died at the end? She needed a rebirth, a resurrection. A year had passed without a single miracle. Although parishioners had prayed *for* the Blue Boy so long that it had become a habit, they were bound to give up praying *to* him. It would occur to them, as it had to me the one shameful time I prayed to Ralphie and asked him to help me make the basketball team, that if Ralphie's wish to make his First Holy Communion hadn't been granted, why would he have the clout to intercede for anyone else? Gradually, but sooner than had ever seemed possible, he would be forgotten.

Camille needed to summon the timeless power of Dickens's story in order to superimpose what remained of Ralphie's spirit on the streets of Little Village. Her borrowing of images from Dickens wasn't so different from the local spray-can artists who painted murals on the crumbling walls, as if Diego Rivera–like visions might shore up what urban renewal had not. There was a permanence to Dickens's story that Camille aspired to. And in that, her tribute was not unlike the tributes of the gang bangers who sometimes tattooed an indelible blue tear at the outside corner of one eye in memory of a wasted homey. That was what Tony Bizzaro did after his brother, Peanuts, died.

It's about feeling, Camille had told me that one afternoon when we were Partners in Christ.

She refused to settle for a tribute that took the shape of silence. She failed for want of accuracy, but not of feeling. Not for want of *amor*.

I don't know what became of Camille Estrada. After Christmas break that year in eighth grade, a rumor spread that beneath the blue cardigan buttoned to the top no matter what the weather, Camille was wearing falsies. Sister Lucy didn't inquire about the matter directly. Instead, she asked Camille not to wear the sweater during class, it wasn't part of the school uniform. Camille correctly observed that by eighth grade the uniform code wasn't strictly enforced, and besides, she was cold. So Sister Lucy offered to move her to a desk beside the radiators. Camille thanked her politely and said that wouldn't be necessary, in the future she would leave her sweater at home.

But the following day, Camille still wore the blue sweater. After morning prayer, Sister Lucy reminded Camille that she'd promised to leave her sweater at home and asked her to hang it in the wardrobe—immediately. Camille remained seated, composed, silent, defiant. Sister Lucy observed that such behavior was hardly what she expected from the class valedictorian. The class went quiet. There'd never been a hint of confrontation between Camille and any of the nuns before.

"I want you to remove your sweater now," Sister said, taking a step down the aisle toward Camille.

Camille replied softly in Spanish.

"What did you just say?" Sister Lucy demanded. The previously inconceivable possibility that Camille might have just cursed her stopped her in her tracks.

I, too, wondered if Camille had cursed. But later, Angel told me what she'd said was a proverb he'd heard his *abuela* use: *"El hábito no hace al monje."* The habit doesn't make the monk.

Camille didn't repeat the words. Almost wearily, she began unbuttoning her sweater, but Sister Lucy stopped her.

"Camille, I want to speak with you in private. Please go to the principal's office and wait there for me."

This time, Camille complied immediately. As she rose and left class without another word, the half-unbuttoned sweater gave us a flash of a bosom worthy of Marilyn Monroe. It didn't look nat-

ural on her, but I remember thinking, What if those aren't falsies
Camille was concealing?

"BB zizboombah!" Norky saluted, and Camille's lips retracted
in what may have passed for a smile.

Afterward, we learned that, instead of the principal's office,
Camille had gone to our small school library, where a senile nun
named Sister Angelica presided over the books. Camille didn't
demand her old illustrated novels back. She checked them out on
library cards and left, never to return. That was the last time I saw
her, but hardly the last time I thought about her.

By junior year in high school, my earlier fascination with stories from Greek mythology evolved into an addiction to science
fiction. I'd read on the bus to and from school, and sometimes
late into the night, and each Saturday I'd stop for a new fix of
sci-fi at the Gad's Hill Library, which had also been my father's
neighborhood library. Sometimes, I'd imagine him going there
when he was my age. He'd told me that as a kid he'd read every
Hardy Boys mystery on the shelves but that, after reading a biog-
raphy of Andrew Carnegie, he realized reading novels was im-
practical, a way for daydreamers to waste time. I decided to read
every book in the science fiction section.

One sleeting, gray afternoon, sitting at a window table in
Gad's Hill, reading Ray Bradbury's *Illustrated Man*, I came upon
a story called "The Man," about earth voyagers to a distant planet
who just miss Christ's appearance there. The captain vows to
keep questing after the Man until he finds him. "I'll go on to another world," he says. "And another and another. I'll miss him by
half a day on the next planet, maybe, and a quarter of a day on
the third planet, and two hours on the next, and an hour on the
next, and a minute on the next. But after that, one day I'll catch
up with him!"

There were no hooved Centaurians, but the idea of following
Christ from world to world was so reminiscent of Camille's story

that I couldn't help wondering if she'd stolen it. Or if, by seventh grade, her imagination was already the equal of Bradbury's. I recalled the afternoon when the two of us stood beating erasers, and Camille confided that she'd done penance for stories—stories that I'll never know if she wrote or only imagined writing. She'd wanted me to tell her a secret from my dreams, a secret from dreams I hadn't had as yet, and so I didn't quite understand what she was after.

"It's about feeling," Camille had insisted.

I didn't understand then that she was talking about risk.

There's a recurrent dream that visits me less and less frequently. I first had it after my father took ill. In the dream, I'm pulling the red sled, but not loaded with a Christmas tree. What I'm hauling is an automobile battery, just as we actually did once in winter when my father's Plymouth died at the factory lot. Rather than spend money to have a wrecker come out and jump it, he unbolted the Atlas battery and caught a ride home with a fellow employee. He left the battery at a gas station to be recharged, and after supper we walked to the gas station with the sled. The grease monkey—as my father called mechanics—said he couldn't guarantee the battery would hold a charge, and in this subzero weather the safest thing was to buy a new one. My father didn't even bother to ask what he soaked for it.

The old sled creaked when my father set the battery on it. He cautioned that we had to be very careful not to tip out the battery acid and told me to center the battery on the sled. I couldn't even budge it.

"You practice lifting that, sonnyboy, and you'll become Charles Atlas." He laughed. "Nobody will kick sand in your face." Then he repositioned it and we began the long trek back to the factory lot.

A curfew of cold had emptied the streets. It was probably approaching my bedtime—unusual for my father to have kept me out late, but that was how it happened, as if something important was going on. We crossed Rockwell, a border between blocks of apartment buildings and blocks of factories. Past Rockwell, the total absence of trees gave the industrial-strength streetlights a bluish glare that made the temperature seem to drop another few degrees. Even in summer the cracked, fissured sidewalks could be treacherous, as if a localized quake had occurred along these miles of truck docks, warehouses, and abandoned factories. Snow piled up unshoveled all winter. We took turns tugging the sled through the drifts and over mounds of dirty ice, one of us pulling, the other steadying the battery. I secretly wouldn't have minded the sled tipping, as it repeatedly threatened to, because I wanted to see the reaction between battery acid and snow. Wind bored to marrow, and my feet in rubber galoshes and fingers in rabbit-fur-lined gloves went achingly numb. My face felt raw and chapped from the woolen scarf I'd raised like a mask, and I began worrying that the battery would be dead when we got to the car, that the engine wouldn't turn over, and that we'd have to lug the battery all the way back to the gas station. I don't remember a word of what we said as we walked, if we said anything at all, and yet there wasn't a time when I felt closer to my father.

In the dream, I'm tugging the sled alone, and, without my father along, the effort seems increasingly senseless. Knee-deep in drifts, navigating mounded ice, I glance back to make sure the load hasn't tipped, and in the squint of streetlights realize that it's my father, blue with cold and reduced to an ancient child the compressed weight of a battery, which I'm pulling.

Who knows why certain humble objects—a bike, a sweater, a sled—are salvaged by memory or dream to become emblems of childhood? Childhood, an alternative universe expanding into forgetfulness, where memory rather than matter is the stuff of creation.

At the end of each day at St. Roman, classes would be released in order of seniority, so Chester would have to wait for Ralphie's class to let out. He'd wait for Ralphie on the corner by the church. If it was raining, he'd have an umbrella already opened. Chester was the only boy at school with something as sissyish as an umbrella. At least it was a black umbrella. Then, he and his brother, Ralphie, walked home down Washtenaw together, engaged in their secret conversations.

Once, the spring after Ralphie died, I was released early from detention because the April afternoon was darkened by the total eclipse of a thunderstorm. The corridors were empty, all the classes had already fled home. Outside, I noticed from a half block away that Chester stood on the corner waiting with an open umbrella. He must have stayed to watch the younger kids file out. And he was still there waiting after they'd gone. Although I saw Chester in school every day, I really hadn't talked to him since Ralphie died. We'd paid our condolences as a class, but I'd been feeling vaguely guilty around Chester for not having said something on my own, though of course there seemed nothing to say. It was raining hard enough that when I held my history book over my head I could feel as well as hear the drumming rain. I didn't realize until I walked past him that Chester was crying. Maybe he thought no one would notice in the rain. Or maybe he didn't realize it himself, as he made no attempt to conceal his tears.

"You're getting soaked," he said and gave the umbrella a little lift meaning that he'd share it.

"I'm okay," I said. "I got my book, but thanks."

"All right," he said and gave me the thumbs-up sign that probably he'd taught to Ralphie.

I gave it back. And for no good reason, as I walked away, I felt forgiven for having prayed that one time to Ralphie as if death had turned him into something other than himself.

How many others back then pretended to pray when what they were doing was crying in secret—in secret even from themselves? Or praying as an alternative to futile tears? Or perhaps, praying because they thought they should have cried or should continue to cry for what they'd forgotten or would forget. Praying because one grief connects with another, and feeling insists upon being expressed, even if only in secret as prayer. A prayer for the brother of whom one might have been a better keeper; a prayer for the father one might have loved more gently; a prayer prayed the way children do, as if making a wish, as if hot tears are streaking a wild, cold heart; a prayer for all of God's blue boys.

Orchids

All that road rolling and all those people dreaming in the immensity of it.
—Jack Kerouac, on *The Steve Allen Show*, 1961

I could begin with sitting at the kitchen table on the way to Mexico, speeding on uppers, and typing to the sound of Stosh's Merc circling the block. But it seems only right to start with the dawn. So I'm going back a year earlier, to Stosh and me fasting from sleep at the counter of the Economy restaurant on the first night that Stosh smuggled Dexadrine out of the Rexall where he worked after school. It's two a.m. and everything looks brilliant. The scuffed Formica sparkles with blue-green iridescence, the buzzing neon of ECONOMY in the window radiates a halo I've never noticed before and reflects like flame across the nickel-plated coffee urns. We're dipping fries in salsa and drinking from bottomless cups of coffee, not that we need the caffeine. My heart is pounding as if I've run a 440.

"Call this salsa? It ain't hot," Stosh complains, then blasts his fries with lethal green splats of El Yucateco. "Ah!"—he exhales—"that cleans out the sinuses. Now I'm ready."

"For what?" I ask.

"To party like this till dawn."

"You ever actually seen the dawn?"

"Now that you mention it, no," Stosh admits.

"Ever notice how everyone's always writing songs and poems about the Dawn—capital *D*—like it's this big magic moment, but I just realized I never seen it either."

"So, let's go find it," Stosh says.

We drive to an alley behind a high-rise that overlooks the lake, and pound on the metal doors until Stosh's uncle Hunky lets us in. He's the night watchman, and Stosh occasionally does him a favor and pulls his Merc up to the same back entrance so Uncle Hunky can fill the trunk with stolen goods.

We ride the freight elevator to the roof. Neither of us knows what time dawn is supposed to arrive, but we figure we'll wait it out, although the wind, unimpeded twenty-five stories up, cuts into our enthusiasm. Backs against a chimney, collars raised, hands jammed in our pockets, we take turns peering out to see if anything is happening yet to the east over the black expanse of water.

To the west, the city sprawls sketched in light. I sort out the expressways, and try to trace the unlit gap of the Sanitary Canal back to where I guess our neighborhood lies, twenty blocks to the southwest. I want to know what it looks like from the Gold Coast.

"Katman, check this out," Stosh calls. He's gone over to the edge of the roof in order to piss on the world below.

Far out over the dark lake, where the horizon might be, there's a reddish aura as if an enormous coal we still can't see is glowing.

We stand watching, waiting for the coal to peep over the rim of black water and crack into crimson and gold. But dawn seems stuck, glimmering just out of sight beyond the curve of the planet, whose rotation we can feel in the numbing wind that buffets the chain-link fence bordering the roof. The speed in our systems makes us shiver faster. We're staring out, not so much shivering as vibrating like the fence, when Uncle Hunky joins us, and we point out the glow.

"Dawn? Dawn ain't for at least two hours. You're looking at the furnaces across the lake in Gary," he starts to explain, then pauses, snorting laughter. "You two *dupas* thought Gary, Indiana, was the dawn!"

We were going to Mexico.

Every day brought the border a little closer. We were getting ready to cross: practicing our Spanish by reading aloud the signs over the bodegas, cantinas, and taquerias as we cruised along Twenty-sixth Street in Stosh's Merc with the Brave Bulls blaring on the tape deck.

Hot afternoons, we'd sit before the window fan in Stosh's upstairs room listening to flamenco guitar, Miles wailing on "Sketches of Spain," or Jack Kerouac reading to the tinkle of blues piano on the Heathkit stereo that Stosh had built in electronics class, and drinking Tecate with lime—ReaLime, actually, squeezed out of the plastic green fruit his mother kept in the fridge. A Tupperware lime, Stosh called it, as in, "Toss that Tupperware lime over here, amigo."

Stosh spent his evenings behind the counter at the Rexall where he'd worked part-time since junior year. He'd already won the scholarship offered to employees, and he'd been accepted into the prepharmacology program at the University of Illinois for the fall. When he wasn't working, he was scavenging for parts and tinkering with the 383 Chrysler engine he'd dropped into his Merc. It was the car we were depending on to take us to Mexico.

There was no point looking for a full-time job until I got my diploma, so I was "landscaping," which meant that each morning I'd wait on the corner across from the projects on Twenty-sixth for the day labor truck from Manpower that drove through the

neighborhood rounding up an assortment of illegal aliens, laid-
off guys, borderline winos, and teenagers. The truck, if and when
it showed, never came to more than a rolling stop, and I'd swing
aboard the lowered tailgate and find a place among the guys
smoking and sipping carryout coffees, using the mower engines
as seats. Trailing the scent of yesterday's cut grass, we'd rattle
down the Eisenhower out to the western burbs—Oak Park, Elm-
wood, River Forest—where the truck would drop us off armed
with mowers, weed whackers, and hedge trimmers, then pick us
up again in the late afternoon. All it paid was minimum wage,
but at least it kept my father off my back. I'd even started a travel
fund, not that I'd saved much, but I'd heard things were cheap in
Mexico.

Evenings, I'd head over to the cinder field under the lights at
Harrison Park looking for a pickup softball game. It felt like my
last summer for playing ball. I'd get back home after everyone
was in bed, and then it would be time to set up my Smith-
Corona at the kitchen table and get to work on the semester's
worth of term papers I had to finish before St. Augustine High
would grant the diploma they'd withheld and set me free.

It felt vaguely disorienting to be sitting at the Smith-Corona
that was supposed to have been my graduation present, typing,
to the accompanying clack of summer insects, papers that had
been due months earlier when I was still in high school.

I couldn't recall those months back in winter without envi-
sioning them as a private world opaque with frost and breath-
steamed windows in which I wandered lost in dreams of Laurel
Elaina Levanto. The temptation was to daydream about her now,
except that the last time I'd seen her had been so humiliating it
was painful to think about her. I'd awakened abruptly from my
dream state just in time to tally up the damages: in the few
months since I'd met Laurel, I'd managed to fail most of my sub-

jects, mess up my college entrance tests, and lose whatever slim chance I had for a track scholarship. Fortunately, she had no idea.

She didn't know that instead of memorizing Spanish verbs or writing a civics paper I had stayed up late at night working on songs about her that I never managed to finish, ballads I sounded out on the sax I'd inherited from my uncle Lefty and wrote down on music paper note by painstakingly tooted note. She didn't know I lost races I should have won, coming slow motion out of the starting blocks, floating over the high hurdles in a self-induced fog, while the coach raced after me along the inside oval of the track yelling, "Get your head into it, Katzek!" Nor did she know how I'd wait in the cold just to board the Archer Avenue bus she rode to her dance lessons. If she wasn't on the first bus, I'd get off at the next corner and wait for the next one. Sometimes, I'd have to board three or four of them before I timed it right. I must have had a reason, but looking back I no longer knew why I'd thought that meeting her had to continually seem like a coincidence, or fate.

It was on the Archer Avenue bus that I first saw her. She was wearing leg warmers and pinning up her hair, lifting the dark, silky weight of it in both hands in a way that exposed her neck and made me feel I'd seen something I shouldn't have. Later, she'd tell me that Miss Lilli, her dance teacher, required her students to wear their hair up. I worked for weeks on a song called "Bus Girl," and one of the few things I still felt thankful for was that I'd never mailed it to her, as I almost had any number of times.

> The way your arms raise over your head
> kinda knocks me out
> kinda knocks me dead

>   And when you sweep your hair up
>   offa your neck
>   my heart starts pounding, hey, what the heck . . .

I tested the lyrics out in the Economy one night on Stosh and Angel—fortunately, I wrote them on a napkin rather than singing them aloud. My friends exploded into laughter, anyway.

"Try it this way," Angel said, scribbling on a napkin.

>   When you sweep your hair up
>   offa the floor
>   it-a always makes-a me pound offa more.

"No," Stosh said. "Better like this." He grabbed my napkin and scratched out my lines so that the verse read:

>   When you sweep your hair up
>   my pecker thinks, Hey, aw, shucks!
>   How about it if we fucks?

I crushed the napkin, which made them laugh all the harder.

"I'm worried about you," Angel said. "You're getting carried away."

"Yeah, wake up, Katman, before you're in over your head," Stosh said. "I mean, *what the heck*, I don't know if you're ready for an older woman."

They were kidding, but it was true. I was seventeen, younger than they, and Laurel had graduated from high school the year before and was enrolled part-time at Loop Junior College. She worked as an organist at weddings and funerals. I couldn't deny it: my still being in high school *did* have something to do with the way I was acting around her, which is probably why I sud-

denly told Stosh, "Fuck you," and fired the balled-up napkin in
his face, then stood up. We'd been sparring partners when we
were both freshman lightweights on the boxing team, but I'd
dropped boxing for track, and Stosh had gone on to win the
CYO middleweight championship. He had a fierce temper that
he'd learned to harness and could probably have mopped up the
Economy with me, but he remained seated in the booth, holding
his bowed head in disappointment.

Now, sitting before the typewriter in the middle of the night,
my jaws grinding on Dexadrine, I listened to the 383 engine
backfiring at stop signs as Stosh circled the neighborhood.
Maybe he was high on some potion he'd concocted in the pharmacy, and probably he was grooving to Beethoven—he'd gone
from Ray Charles and the blues to Beethoven with nothing in between. Then his tires would squeal and I'd hear him revving
through what seemed like an infinite number of gears, playing
the Merc like a virtuoso as he faded off into one of his exploratory drives toward the blast furnaces of South Chicago or
north along the dark curve of the lake to the place we called
Baha'i.

I was down to my last paper, a report on a book I'd chosen
about a Frenchman named Marcel Libert, who, while still a college student, had trekked alone down the coast of Quintana Roo,
discovering what he called "the lost world of the Mayas." Marcel
hiked along blazing beaches and hacked through jungle, coming
upon overgrown ruins of temples and hidden villages with names
that sounded like the cries of tropical birds: Xcalet, Yalcu, Xcalak.

I wanted a cry like that for a postmark on the letter I'd write
to Laurel when I made it to Mexico.

Usually Stosh would stop by late to see how the typing was
going. Ever since the beginning of summer, he'd been on a sleep
fast. It was his contention that sleep was something They—with a

capital *T*—had conditioned you to do ever since kindergarten
nap time in order to keep you quiet. He claimed it could be cut
back like any bad habit.

"It's holy to fast from food, so why not sleep?" he argued.
"Think about it, man, it's a plot against us. For all practical purposes sleep is a rehearsal for being dead."

"Sleep is the opiate of the people," I agreed.

Stosh estimated that with the two of us conditioned to stay
awake and driving nonstop we could make the border in three
days.

"One drives while the other sacks out," he figured.

"Save on motel bills," I said.

"*Motel* bills! Are you kidding, hombre? Spend money on mo-
tels when we can sleep in the car if we have to? What kind of
bourgeois, gringo idea is that?"

"Maybe Angel will come, then there'd be another driver."

"Yeah, don't count on it. Angel's doing the van Gogh," Stosh
said, making a sound like a tubercular old man hacking up a gob
of phlegm, which was how we uttered van Gogh's name after Angel corrected our pronunciation.

Angel Falcone, Stosh, and I had hung around together
through high school, but Angel had been expelled in the middle
of senior year, and we hadn't seen much of him ever since he
started taking classes at the Art Institute.

Stosh didn't need to go to Mexico to sleep in his car. He'd
been getting into fights with his father for the last year, and
sometimes rather than go home he'd park the Merc behind a factory and sleep in the backseat. Some mornings, when I'd wake up
to catch the Manpower truck, I'd find Stosh sacked out on the
sagging musty couch on our back porch. I'd make us a couple of
instant coffees to start the day.

That's where I found him one morning, stretched out, wearing his Ray Charles shades, a single purple flower resting on the middle of his chest.

"What's with the corsage?" I asked.

"I walked into the jungle, Willy, when I was seventeen, and when I walked out I was twenty-one and, by God, I was rich!" Stosh said, quoting the line we both loved from *Death of a Salesman*, which we'd read in senior English class. He raised his sunglasses, and I noticed a welt under one eye as if he'd stepped into a left hook.

"What happened to you?" I asked.

"Orchids"—he smiled—"I found fucking wild orchids."

There wasn't time for instant coffee.

"Screw the landscaping," Stosh said. "Come on, *ese*, we may never have to work again."

"What are you on anyway?"

"Hey, how much did you waste on that orchid for your ill-fated prom night? Eighteen bucks a pop! Every spring my uncle Hunky goes to the cemetery and picks morel mushrooms off the graves. A pound of them dried goes for twenty bucks, so what do you think a pound of orchids goes for? Fuck pills and pot; we'll be orchid dealers."

We jumped into the Merc and riding on fumes sped six blocks and swerved into the Marvel gas station on Western.

"I thought orchids only grew in the tropics," I said.

"Obviously not," Stosh said, spitting out the orchid that he held between his teeth. "Here, don't let Bigbo get a whiff of this or he'll get carried away." He handed me the orchid, and I inhaled expecting perfume, but its scent was too faint to compete with the smell of gas. I fit it in with the pink dice dangling from the rearview mirror.

Bigbo was standing by the gas pumps, blowing his nose into a paper towel that looked as if he'd just used it to wipe a dipstick. With his free hand he felt for his balls, lost in the folds of his greasy coveralls. No matter what else he was doing, the Bo always kept one hand checking his balls. His shaggy head barged into the window before Stosh came to a stop.

"How she runnin, man?" Bigbo wanted to know.

He'd helped Stosh cram the 383 into the old Merc body and was in love with the idea of something that looked like a primered junker being able to fly.

"Needs a fuel pump," Stosh said.

"I'll see what I can do," Bigbo told him. No one mentioned it, but we all knew the Bo was connected with the Perido brothers, who ran a chop shop in a deserted lumberyard off Ashland Avenue. Gordo, Stosh's motorpsycho younger brother, had been getting involved with the Peridos, too.

The engine was too big for the hood to close completely, and Bigbo unwired the hood while Stosh pumped the gas.

"Look at this fucken bomb," Bigbo crooned, massaging his balls. "Rev the muther, Kat," he said to me.

I toed the pedal, and the Merc began to percolate.

"More!" Bigbo hollered over the thunder, pulling on his crotch as if headed for an orgasm.

I pressed the pedal halfway, and it felt as if the Merc would shake apart if it couldn't squeal off. Stosh vanished in the blue cloud of exhaust smoke. I could hear him yelling, but not what.

"Lemme," Bigbo demanded, tugging himself balls first into the driver's seat and stomping the accelerator. "Had to cut through the fire wall to cram in this monster, pushed back the trannie, drilled through the floor for the Hurst, braced the front end, installed a Bendix, quads, headers . . ."

Mouth against my ear, which was the only way he could make himself heard over the engine, he recited the inventory of parts as if chanting a litany. I didn't know if it was the engine roar flushing them, but I could see a cloud of blackbirds rising from the viaduct where the strip of wilderness that bordered train tracks passed unnoticed through the neighborhood. There was a marsh hidden back there alive with turtles, frogs, dragonflies, where once we'd seen a blue heron lifting off; a pterodactyl couldn't have filled us with more wonder. Stosh, Angel, and I discovered it back in grade school when we hung out on the tracks, hitching rides, clinging to the ladders on the sides of boxcars rocking through the neighborhoods and prairies behind factories, destination unknown.

"Bo, you fucken demento!" Stosh yelled, reaching in to switch off the ignition. Even the semis barreling toward the expressway and the freight train that had rousted the blackbirds and now racketed over the viaduct sounded peaceful by comparison.

"You need some weight to hold the ass end down, babe," Bigbo said.

"I need a goddamn fuel pump," Stosh said, shaking his head dismally. "Keeps dying on me. Not to mention that everything I eat lately tastes like gas from sucking on the fuel pump to get it running again."

"As long as it's just fuel pumps you're sucking," the Bo said, winking at Stosh and rapping his shoulder.

"I was making out the other night and the girl kept complaining my breath smelled like Texaco," Stosh complained.

Bigbo rolled out of the Merc chuckling, holding himself as if he'd been kicked in the groin. "She even knew the flavor, huh?"

"No, it was Marvel. Sometimes she can be so wrong."

"Chicks! Too fucken much! Here, man," he said, digging deep in his coveralls and extracting a thin, grease-imprinted twist of paper that he slipped into Stosh's shirt pocket. "A little taste for later . . . dynamite shit, babe. Don't say I never gave you nothin."

"Hey, I'm afraid to light matches around my mouth, but

thanks anyway," Stosh said, ducking under a Bigbo embracio—so Bigbo gave his ass a pat instead.

Stosh slid into the car, handed the gas money out the window, adjusting his shades.

"Hey, man," the Bo asked, catching a glimpse of Stosh's bruised eye. "Who coldcocked you?"

Stosh merely shrugged.

"So where you guys off to this early? Scare up some puzzy?" He pronounced it "puzzy," the way some guys in the neighborhood called sewers "zewers."

"Picking orchids . . . here, don't say I never gave you nothin," Stosh said, tossing him our orchid, then popping the Merc into first so we shimmied off on a streak of rubber.

We were in third doing fifty through the pinging dust along the curb, passing semis on the right.

"Does need some weight in the ass end," Stosh said.

I slid a few bucks across the dash.

"What's this?" he asked, dumbfounded.

"For gas." Since Stosh had the wheels, Angel and I kicked in for gas whenever we went riding.

"Has it come to this?" Stosh asked, pushing the money back with distaste as if he was through honoring a tradition that was beneath us. Ever since getting out of high school he'd been in some higher gear: Beethoven, the sleep fast, Mexico, now no gas money was all part of it. "The bullshit is over," he'd said into the microphone when they'd handed him his diploma, then added ominously, "You must change your life." He'd read that somewhere. Stosh had been reading a lot. The backseat of the Merc was a clutter of paperbacks.

We fishtailed left on Thirty-first, gunning past the Hospital for Contagious Diseases.

"I always hold my breath when I go by so I don't inhale the plague or something," Stosh said.

By the next block we'd slowed to a crawl, hugging the curb as we passed the city auto pound. Stosh checked the pound regularly for parts we'd strip at night.

"I'd rather luck into a pump here than get one from the Bo," he said.

"He'd like to give you a pump all right." I leered with a Bigbo-like wink and tugged at my crotch.

"Just as long as it's your own balls you're grabbing, babe."

Halfway down the three-block span of wrecks we spotted a black Chrysler, or what was left of one. Scorched, front end mangled, it appeared to have collided head on with a train.

"No fuel pump there . . . ," I started to say, when a greasy Doberman that looked as if it might have been feeding on the corpses lunged out snarling through the busted windshield. We'd never seen a watchdog at the auto pound before. "Goddamn!" I said, my eyes fused to the dog's, which were hot with fury. "I wouldn't want to be surprised at night by that."

"Don't look! Don't say anything," Stosh cautioned. "If the gods don't think we've seen it, then it can't be used against us as a fucking omen."

He stomped the gas, and we bounced over the rail tracks at Twenty-sixth just as the gates were dinging down. We followed the curving grade of the tracks along a deserted cobblestone street, then pulled into a concrete tunnel that ran under the railroad embankment. I jumped out and lifted a padlocked metal gate off its rusted hinges, and Stosh drove through the tunnel and onto an oiled cinder road that wound among mountains of scrap metal, coal, rock salt, sand, gravel. He stopped beside a cliff of bricks and broken concrete hauled from demolition sites all over the city and dumped here on the shore of what we referred to as the Insanitary Canal or, more simply, Shit Creek.

We hefted hunks of cinder block into the open trunk to balance the back end against the weight of the engine. No matter how we rearranged the blocks, it seemed to me the car was listing, but I didn't mention it. Stosh took setbacks with the Merc too hard.

He was rocking the car, woefully shaking his head. "What it really needs now is goddamn heavy-duty shocks," he said.

"As long as we're here, we might as well check out the cop cycles," I suggested, hoping it didn't sound like a vote of no confidence in the Merc.

Stosh's brother, Gordo, had told us that beyond the Fire Truck Graveyard there was another junkyard, the Cop Cycle Burial Ground, where old police three-wheelers went to die. According to Gordo, the three-wheelers were taken off the streets after a certain number of miles and not all of them were burned out. They had big Harley engines, and Gordo figured it might be possible to fire them up and drive off with a couple.

I didn't bother pointing out that tooling around on a stolen three-wheeler with the Chicago Police Department seal on it might be a little conspicuous. But later the idea occurred to me that we could spray-paint them black, drive back streets out of the city in the dead of night, and by dawn have made our getaway to Mexico.

The Fire Truck Graveyard was deserted as always. We'd discovered it back in grade school when we'd pedal our bikes to explore along Shit Creek. The faded red enamel of the rusting trucks looked polished in the baking sun. At their sides, weathered wooden ladders still hung at the ready along with frayed, cracked hoses. A few trucks had big chrome bells waiting to clang. There were fire trucks so old you could see the hitches that had attached them to galloping teams of horses. It was a place where the tangible presence of history inspired a kind of reverence—not a feeling frequently encountered in Chicago—like an outdoor museum but better, because we could clamber around, crank the old hand pumps and winches, sit in the perch on the hook and ladder where the tillerman steered, and no one would bother us.

I could smell the familiar scent of milkweed laced with the creosote reek of the canal, but instead of the usual elation, I was feeling uneasy. The last time I'd been here had been with Laurel, and now it felt as if I'd ruined the place for myself.

I had wanted to sing her song, "Bus Girl," to her while clanging a fire bell. Just thinking about it made me cringe inside.

I'd shredded the sheet music, not that it erased the scene from my mind. The only thing about the song I'd managed to forget was the original melody, which I'd dreamed one night back in winter. In my dream, she was dancing along the aisle of an empty bus with frosted windows that I was blindly driving, and when I woke I could still remember how lovely the song she was dancing to had been, but the melody itself was vanishing like one of those subatomic particles that decay as soon as they're created.

Maybe everything with Laurel should have remained a dream. Trying to make it real had ruined it. Maybe my instincts had been right: if we'd just kept meeting as if by accident I'd never have had to wake from that private world of frosted windows. Maybe we could have sustained the intimacy of that corner booth, beside a window blurry with steam and rain, at the neighborhood Chinese restaurant where we took to meeting after her dance class. We'd sit sipping little cups of tea and talking. I loved listening to her, watching the expressions flash across her elfin eyes while she talked. I wasn't aware I was staring until she observed, "You know, we've both got green eyes, except yours are a green brown and mine green blue."

It was in the Chinese restaurant, sharing the garlic shrimp, that I told her how much I detested high school, especially after they'd expelled my buddy Angel, and that I was boycotting the prom, and Laurel kiddingly said, "Are you sure it's not because you don't have a date?"

Kind of kidding back, I said, "Well, now that you mention it, want to go?"

"Okay," she said, which shocked me, "as long as we don't end up in the same places everybody else does. I've done the prom bit already."

"I know this jazz club, the Blue Note."

"Sounds neat. You've been there?"

"Sure," I said, though actually I'd only heard about it from my uncle Lefty, who'd once seen Miles Davis there.

Thinking about her now, I wished that, rather than traipsing down an aisle of obsolete fire trucks beside the Insanitary Canal, I was hacking through jungle, exploring an unmapped river while monkeys yammered and macaws screamed.

Stosh and I crossed an unfenced field where other city vehicles—ambulances, squad cars, paddy wagons—sat junked in the weeds. Beyond them, lined up in a row that bordered the canal, were the three-wheelers.

"Now I understand why cops have to have such fat asses," Stosh said.

The saddles were huge. We climbed onto a couple and sat working the gears, wringing the accelerators, and squeezing the hand brakes as if racing neck and neck. In the hot sun, with insects and birds twittering from the brush, and the fecal brown canal drifting by in glittering slow motion, more like lava than water, it felt as if we were already somewhere else. I could picture Stosh, Angel, and me, three abreast, tooling down an empty, blazing highway.

"These would be perfect, man," I said. "They even have trunks. We could keep all our travel shit back there."

"What travel shit?"

"Blankets, pots and pans, extra clothes . . ."

"Pots and pans!" Stosh said. "You don't even have a pot to pee in."

"That's exactly what my old man tells me."

"He's right. Why the fuck would we bring pots and pans? You know how to cook?"

"I can heat up chili."

Mexico had been my idea, and every so often, especially when the Merc was causing problems, Stosh could get a little negative. He'd lose sight of it: the three of us on our cop cycles, gunning off the highway onto a dirt road past the glowing Texaco pumps of a small gas station somewhere in Oklahoma maybe, pitching camp beside a river, cooking supper over an open fire, knowing the next day we'd make the border.

"You know how to make Mexican chili?" Stosh inquired.

"Dare I ask?"

"Stick an ice cube up his keister."

"I don't get it—too subtle."

"My old man, the world's greatest bohunk wit, shared that with me when I told him we were going to Mexico. He suggested we could save ourselves some serious time and money by just walking along Twenty-sixth Street and watching the beaners paint their houses orange and purple."

"What's he got against a little local color?"

"I was up in my room playing that Sabicas album and he comes in and tells me he's sick of hearing *flamingo* guitar."

"There it is: the man hates bright colors."

Stosh shook his head pessimistically. "These beat-out cop sickles wouldn't make it to Indiana, *ese*," he said. "Let's go north to freedom. Get some orchids."

We took Cermak to the Outer Drive, heading north to freedom along the lake. We hadn't spent much time on the North Side un-

til last fall, when, aimlessly cruising, we'd come upon the fili-
greed, illuminated dome of the Baha'i Temple rising, like a vision
from *The Arabian Nights*, incongruously over the dark, suburban
trees of Wilmette.

We were equally amazed by its incongruity and the fact that
we'd never heard of the temple. It was as if, like everyone in
Chicago, we knew about Sox Park, Wrigley Field, and the stock-
yards, but had failed to take notice of the Taj Mahal. Our amazement still hadn't worn off, so Baha'i became a destination,
enough of a reason in itself for us to jump in the car and head
north.

"I think I've become a Baha'i," I'd announced one night when
Stosh, Angel, and I circled through the terraced gardens surrounding the temple. "Maybe I've always been one and didn't
know it."

"How come, if they're so interested in universal brotherhood,
they didn't build the temple on the South Side, where there's a
little more ethnic diversity, not to mention good old-fashioned
all-American race wars?" Angel asked. "It would look great
sprayed with gang graffiti, rising out of the projects on Twenty-
sixth."

Later, he painted a picture of the temple's simple interior:
spiritual light streaming onto a basketball court where a couple
guys in gang colors were shooting baskets at a hoop attached to a
cross while a freight train disappeared Magritte-like into a portal.
The painting, along with the nightscapes which made the mills in
South Chicago look like travel posters for the Inferno, became
part of the portfolio that won Angel a scholarship to the Art
Institute.

The North Side felt almost like another city, one zoned with
residential streets in mind, rather than factories and truck docks.
It wasn't fragmented by demolished blocks of urban renewal and

stitched together by railroad tracks. Glassy high-rises, courtyard apartment buildings, and elegant hotels overlooked the parks, beaches, and indigo lake.

Off Bryn Mawr we always watched for one hotel in particular, with coral roof tiles and matching windowsills. We didn't know its name, but it looked like something from some more glamorous past, the twenties, maybe.

"A perfect place for an affair between a mysterious, beautiful, very rich older woman of exquisite taste and a young, gifted artist," Angel had observed.

"A young artist with a nose like a hose covered in zits and a beard that looks like he's Krazy-Glued hair from his rectum onto his chin?" Stosh inquired.

"An artist who in a fit of jealous madness cuts off a piece of his hose-nose and then paints a portrait of himself with a huge bandage on what's left of his prehensile beezer?" I added.

"I should have known better than to bring up something romantic in the company of those warped by Catholic education," Angel said.

This time, as we passed the coral hotel, Stosh looked at me and started laughing.

"That's where you should of taken Bus Girl after the prom," he said, "instead of taking her—" He tried repeatedly to finish his sentence but couldn't without breaking up. "Instead of taking her to fucking Shit Creek," he finally managed to spit out. "Whatever possessed you to take her down to Shit Creek on prom night? You are the last of the great romantics!" He was beating the steering wheel, driving in a way that made it feel as if the car was propelled by his laughter.

I gazed out the window and watched the harbors and beaches whiz by. Sailboats staked out the horizon. A skywriter doodled across blue sky. We were on the inner lane doing sixty, and I leaned out squinting against the cool rush of wind. I could smell the lake and the suntan lotion from thousands of opened tubes and, within the boom of traffic, could hear what sounded like snatches of the same Top Forty song blaring from a blur of radios. For a fleeting moment it sounded like the lost, elusive dream melody of Laurel's song, and I wondered what it would be like to be standing at a coral-silled window stories up gazing down on the patchwork of beach blankets and press of bare bodies. A woman would be standing beside me, her hair up, but it wasn't Laurel Levanto. It wasn't anyone I knew yet. Out of nowhere the thought occurred to me that the person I was at this moment in the speeding Merc wasn't ready for that hotel room either.

"Teeming with peons out there today," Stosh was saying. He swerved into the next lane, the cab behind honking. The lane we'd been in was stalled behind a rusted station wagon full of kids, smoke spewing from its open hood. Their father, a black guy who'd taken off his shirt and wrapped it around his hand, seemed to be doing a sort of dance, hopping toward the radiator cap, giving it a twist, hopping away.

"Poor joker," I commented.

"Oh, no! Did you have to admit to noticing that? Did we stop to help our fellow man? No. Now you've done it, *cabrón*."

"What?"

"Attracted the attention of the Immortals. 'As flies to wanton boys are we to the gods, / They kill us for their sport.' " That was another of Stosh's favorite lines. He'd memorized it from *King Lear*, the other play we'd had to read in senior year.

"The car's running fine."

"Holy shit! He didn't mean it," Stosh screamed at the heavens. "He knows not what he speaks. Give us a break just this once. All we want to do is pick a few measly fucken orchids."

"You're sure these orchids are even there?" I asked. "I hope this isn't going to be another wild-goose chase like seeking the dawn."

"The dawn! You're going to bring that up? Orchids, I tell you. After shelling out fifteen bucks for my promster corsage, I know orchids when I see them—they're a kind of obscene orchid color, like they're exposing their privates. Don't you start molesting them either. You look like an orchid fucker to me, hummingbird dick."

"I hate it when you call me that."

"Hummingbird penis! Hummingbird penis!"

"That's better. I just don't want to be involved in another fiasco like the boat ride."

"First the dawn and now you have to bring up the boat ride. Pretty low. I thought we'd agreed never to speak of it. *You* were the rectum who wanted to go on the boat ride as I remember. *I* was hesitating."

"He who hesitates is lost."

"Very profound."

I could tell from the way Stosh's ears flushed that even kidding about the boat ride still bothered him. He'd learned to control his quick temper, but the blood still rushed up his neck whenever he felt his dignity threatened. After he won the CYO championship, his dignity, at least at St. Augustine High, didn't get threatened too often. People felt that, even if he wanted to, it was nearly impossible for Stosh to back down.

He looked like a boxer. Partly it was the way he carried himself. I could easily outrun him, but he was lighter on his feet, better balanced. Where his nose had been broken, a slight ridge remained, which gave him a profile off a Roman coin. His usual shadow of stubble highlighted a thin scar along his jawline from a fight on a CTA bus in freshman year when, wearing the colors of the Ambros, a gang he'd belonged to for a while, he'd been slashed. His forearms, one of them still tattooed with the pachuco cross from his brief gang membership, were scarred from fending off the knife in the same fight. He'd carried a switchblade ever since.

In senior year, after Angel was expelled, Stosh and I pretty much dropped out—though, unlike me, Stosh managed to graduate. He would have lost his Rexall scholarship if he hadn't. The last months of school we'd show up in the mornings, then cut classes after lunch and joyride. That's what we were doing on a springlike day in April when we drove to Lincoln Park and hung around watching people get their yachts back into the water. All we knew about boats was that having one was the ultimate dream.

We were walking away from the boat slips when a guy called, "Say, lads, if you have some time I could use help with a boat."

His white hair was visible beneath a blue captain's cap. He wore white canvas shoes, a blue blazer, and yellow ascot. Stosh and I glanced at each other. He didn't seem to fit any of our immediately recognizable categories of weirdo.

"Come on, it's a perfect day for a boat ride," he said and set off briskly.

We shrugged and followed.

He led us through the park, keeping a purposeful, nautical pace as he circumvented rain puddles on the winding walkways, explaining to us over his shoulder the differences between ketches and yawls. It was a walk leading away from the harbor, and just about the time we got suspicious enough to stop, he paused. We stood outside a fence surrounding the manmade lagoon that bordered Lincoln Park Zoo. On the other side was a rental stand for bright yellow, molded plastic pedal boats.

"I'm a little short today, fellows," the captain said, "but if you could pick up the rental, I'd be happy to pedal."

We crossed Howard Street into Evanston, a border marked only by the last liquor store on the Chicago side, and followed Sheridan Road as it swerved beneath an archway of shady trees, past mansions, and the campus of Northwestern, which stretched for blocks along the lake. The thwack of tennis balls echoed from courts, and the school with its trimmed lawns and ivy walls had a country-club look. Students in polo shirts and Bermuda shorts wandered the grounds; summer classes must have been in session. When we stopped at a light before one of the frat houses that lined the street, a red Porsche convertible with three guys wedged in pulled out of a driveway into the lane beside us. They were grinning; the driver gunned the engine like they wanted to drag.

"What Greek youth gang do you lads belong to?" Stosh inquired.

They shouted something that sounded more like "greaser" than Greek initials, impossible to make out because Stosh had tromped the gas and the Merc stood vibrating like an airliner about to sprint down the runway. A cloud of blue smoke engulfed the intersection. The guys in the Porsche clutched their throats and pretended to retch over the side of the car. The light flashed green, and while Stosh was still thundering at a standstill, they raised a whiskey bottle in salute and shot away.

Stosh popped it into first, and the Merc lurched forward, coughing and choking as it crawled across the intersection, then backfired into second, caught, and pinned us back in our seats. By third we were coming up on them fast with no traffic between us. Two of them whirled around to look back at us and the driver goosed it, but the Merc kept gaining. I glanced at the speedome-

ter and cheap tach bandaged to the dash, but they were jiggling
too much to read; then the four-barrel kicked in, and the Merc
bolted forward as if it had discovered an extra gear. Stosh down-
shifted, whining into a curve, and on the next straightaway,
rather than passing them, hung on their rear bumper as if to say,
"Can you snap it up?" I could see their shoulders hunched, waiting for a blow. The white dome of Baha'i suddenly rose up over
the trees, and we braked into a tire-peeling left onto a cobblestone side street, and rolled to a stop along the curb. When Stosh
cut the engine, there was an immediate twitter of birdsong
and the sense of peace that the temple imposed on the space
around it.

"At least the ass end didn't skate all over the street," Stosh said
as we slammed out of the car doors.

It was the middle of the week and no one was around, no
guards—we'd never seen a guard there. Flights of gulls and pigeons circled the polished dome. Even the pigeons looked exotic.

Everything about Baha'i seemed to circle: the stairs rising past
terraced gardens, each garden planted with different flowers to
symbolize the beauty of unity in diversity. That all was explained
in a brochure I'd picked up during one of our first visits. We'd expected the brochure would be yet another attempt to collect
money while saving our souls, but mainly it detailed the design
of the temple. The dome rose from a circular-looking nine-sided
base—nine because that number symbolizes comprehensiveness,
oneness, and unity. The nine doorways were framed by pylons
engraved with mystical symbols: the hooked Zoroastrian cross—
which we were afraid was a swastika until we read the brochure—
the Star of David, the Christian cross, the star and crescent of
Islam, and the nine-petaled rosette of the Baha'is. At Baha'i, every
detail was symbolic.

But it wasn't the gardens or the temple itself we'd come to
visit. Instead, we jogged back across Sheridan and, ignoring the

locked gate and rusted No Trespassing sign, flipped the fence and followed a path that led past a maintenance building polished the same satiny white as the temple. Behind it, a stand of willows concealed a grassy dune sloping to the lake.

The beach was hidden, screened by willows. We'd never noticed any evidence that anyone besides the sandpipers used it. The powdery sand was dazzling white. Our theory was that the sand was quartz, one of the materials that gave the temple its luster, and that the construction crew had dumped what had been left over on the beach. It was gradually washing away, leaving the coarser, natural sand behind. From the shore, the temple dome ascended above the willows as if Wilmette didn't exist. For us, the beach was the locus of the place we called Baha'i.

We piled our clothes on the sand and weighed them down with our shoes. The mouse below Stosh's eye looked purple when he set down his shades. We waded out along a sandbar, the shallow water lukewarm with sunlight. When it sloped off we dove under, swam out, then, treading water, turned to face the beach, where we could see the dome over the dune and keep an eye on our clothes.

"Ah! This is the life," Stosh said. "No jammed parking lots, no lifeguards trying to save you, no *peons* peeing in the water."

"Speak for yourself."

He gave me a look of horror and began splashing wildly. "Is not even Baha'i sacred?"

"I'm experiencing unity and oneness."

I swam out farther, each stroke another stroke away from the muggy nights of typing overdue papers, the mornings of waiting for the Manpower truck to show, the question of what to do now that high school was over. Out where it was deep, I kicked down through progressive levels of cold that took my breath away, then shot up cleansed, bobbing on the surface of what felt like the eternal present: gently rocking water nearly indistinguishable

from the sparkle of sunlight and reflection of cloudless blue sky.
Gulls wheeled, yipping, and I yipped back silently. Stosh swam
over, and we floated on our backs.

"I finally brought Dahl out here last night," he said. "Ever since
fucked-up prom night she's been saying, 'Take me to Baha'i.' " He
caught Dahl's Lithuanian accent without seeming to mimic her.

"So, how'd she like it?"

"We got into a fight. I think we broke up."

"Yet again?"

"Yet again," Stosh said. "It was an evening doomed from the
start. She waited until my trousers were down to tell me she's
pissed about my going to Mexico. Then she adds she's heard
maybe I'm already in Mexico—namely one Nita Rosario."

"Uh-oh. What did you tell her?"

"The old standby: Huh? 'You heard me,' she says. 'Did you
bring her here to fuck, too? I know when you're with other girls.
I can smell them on you. It changes my period. I see what you do
in my dreams.' Does that sound a little spooky?" Stosh asked.

"Perfectly normal," I said, not adding that any number of
things about Dahl seemed spooky. She'd once threatened to light
herself on fire if they broke up.

"So, trying to salvage Baha'i, I say, 'Look, let's just inhabit the
present, drink some vino.' And she says, 'Yeah, inhabit the present,' and when I pass her the vino she takes a long swig, then spits
it in my face and clocks me with the bottle. Dahl's a violent
person."

"Couldn't convert her to the peaceful Baha'i way: a little unity
in oneness and diversity, eh?"

"Not when she's trying to brain me with a bottle, screaming,
'I'm not some little twat born yesterday.' "

"You know, that's got a certain ring to it. Could be a hit."

"*Little Twat Born Yesterday?*"

"No, *Unity in Oneness and Diversity*."

Sudden swells, perhaps from some enormous freighter that had passed long before and too far out for us to see, were slowly washing us back toward shore. Stosh, floating on his back, was singing in a falsetto voice meant to imitate black girl singers. Gulls yipped. I added a bass line.

> Unity and oneness in diversity
> dum dum dum dum . . .
> A little twat born yesterday . . .

I checked the beach for our piled clothes. They were covered by sandpipers.

Baha'i was our final destination on prom night. Laurel and I were supposed to have met up there with Dahl and Stosh after the Blue Note. Stosh and I had loaded towels, blankets, and three bottles of Lancers into the trunk of the Merc. The wine would chill in the lake while we gathered driftwood for a fire on the beach. In the darkness, the illuminated dome would rise over the dune as if the temple housed a moon.

"We can swim, drink wine, dance by the fire," Stosh said, "stay up all night . . ."

"Until Gary, Indiana, rises in the east," I told him.

It sounded perfect, especially since Laurel had said she wouldn't go to the same old places crowded with promsters. She said the only thing she liked about proms—or funerals or weddings, for that matter—was the flowers. I couldn't tell if she meant that literally, but I ordered a corsage just in case.

I didn't mention the beach. I wanted to surprise her the way I'd been surprised with the sight of the glowing temple. If we went for a night swim, I hoped she wouldn't mind not having a swimsuit.

I spent the entire day of the prom working on my father's Rambler. First, I removed the customized carriers he'd attached to the roof. He used them to haul scrap from demolition sites to our backyard for possible use later in repairs on the six-flat he owned. It was a standard set of carriers from Sears that he'd strengthened with two-by-fours and secured to the roof with a complex system of duct tape, coat hangers, and ropes that ran up from the bumpers. Removing the carriers exposed a roof covered in black suction marks that were baked into the slime-green paint as if the Rambler had done battle with a giant squid, an impression reinforced by the smell of smoked fish exhaled by the trunk. My father delivered smoked chubs and kielbasa on weekends for my uncle Vincent's meat market, and I couldn't eradicate the smell despite applications of undiluted Pine-Sol.

I gave up on the roof and trunk and slid under the car to wire a second coat hanger behind the one my father had already used to secure the dragging muffler. Next, I tried to turn off the heater—my father believed that riding with the heater blasting even in summer saved wear on the engine—but it was stuck. I vacuumed the seats, Windexed, mopped, hosed, and applied numerous coats of Turtle Wax. The cleaner the Rambler got, the worse it looked for trying.

By now I was sweating, not with exertion, but in desperation. I'd lost sight of the image of the beach at Baha'i, and cursed myself for getting into this. I'd never intended to go to the prom. I'd come to hate high school in general and St. Augustine's in particular, especially after they'd expelled Angel. Instead of spiffing up the Rambler, I should have been spray-painting SAINT A'S SUCKS across the hood. It was only because Laurel had surprised us both by agreeing to be my date that I was going through this agony.

It would have been easier if, instead of meeting later with Stosh and Dahl, we were all going together in the Merc, but I knew that wasn't an option. There was a powerful aloofness

about Dahl. She was tall and athletic looking—lean, not wil-
lowy—and the way her long hair fell across her face, as if she was
peeking past a blond curtain, gave Dahl the look of one of those
Swedish actresses who utter, "I vant to be alone."

Stosh and Dahl were too unpredictable together. They could
be private, almost secretive, her finger hooked through a belt
loop of his jeans, their faces close together, partly hidden in her
hair, speaking in whispers. Or they could fall silent, pointedly ignoring each other before erupting in an argument. Even when
they were getting along, they brought out a craziness in each
other; there was a continual sense of dare between them. They'd
been arguing, breaking up, and getting back together since freshman year, when Dahl had sent Stosh a letter on a sheet of three-
ring loose-leaf paper she'd decorated along the margins with
drawings of vines and flowers.

> Oh last night when you held me in your arms your kisses
> took my soul away and I knew I would love you forever. I
> want you to hold me like that again, to kiss me, to fuck
> me.
>
> xxx, Dahlia

Stosh had shown me the letter in the locker room after a boxing practice that had left me with a bloody nose. "What are you
going to do?" I asked, astonished.

"Double Trojans and a tube of rubber cement," he said.

The last time they'd broken up was in winter, on a night, driving around with Angel in the backseat, when Dahl went nuts
about being outvoted on the choice of radio stations, smashed
her boot heel into the radio, then tried to brand Stosh with the
car lighter.

She'd called Stosh out of the blue a couple weeks before the
prom, and as always they started up again. Dahl warned him that

she wouldn't be wearing anything under her prom dress, and that after the dance she wanted him, wearing his tuxedo, to screw her on the edge of the roof of St. Augustine High.

"As long as my tux comes with a safety belt," Stosh told her.

"No safety belt and no net," she'd answered.

Even at my lowest point with the Rambler, I knew that doubling with Stosh would have been a bad idea.

Instead of renting formal wear, I wore a tux that, along with my tenor saxophone, I'd inherited from Uncle Lefty. He'd once played for weddings in a combo called the Gents. I hadn't realized until I unfolded it that it wasn't a tux: It had tails. I tried pinning them up and I tried tucking them into the trousers, but neither worked. By then I was running late. I stopped by the florist and picked up the orchid corsage I'd ordered, then, flooring it, drove, as much like a speed demon as was possible in the Rambler, to Laurel's neighborhood.

She lived out toward Midway Airport, and I promptly got lost in a maze of side streets. When I finally pulled up beside the bungalow with her address, Laurel, shouting something over her shoulder, slammed out of her front door before I could get out of the car. She looked flushed, and I had the feeling she'd just been arguing. True to her word, she wasn't wearing a typical prom gown. Her dress was silky black with thin shoulder straps, and it clung to her slim body. She wore a single strand of pearls, and pearls were threaded through her hair, which was up in the way that had thrown me into a trance on the Archer bus before I ever knew her name.

"You look great," I said, handing her the corsage.

"Thanks. I got tired of prom gowns that made me feel like a bridesmaid," she said. "You're looking pretty dapper yourself— perfect for being fashionably late. I mean, you don't see many guys these days sporting the Fred Astaire look. You must be a really good dancer, huh?" She was undoing the corsage from its backing of ferns. She tilted the rearview mirror so she could watch as she pinned the flower in her hair.

"What do you think?" she asked. "Kind of a jazz singer look. I'm ready for the Blue Note." She gave me a peck thanks on the lips that turned into a kiss, and suddenly, spontaneously, we were making out. I could feel her tongue tracing a cursive like the curlicue letters on chocolates, and the vibration of airliners coming in low for landings, and I thought my prom night would be memorable after all.

"Oh, God," she sighed, pulling away finally, "not in front of my house."

We made it about a half block from Laurel's before the engine ground into a sound like corn popping and smoke huffed out from under the hood.

High heels and all, Laurel insisted on helping me push the Rambler to the curb. I raised the hood and stared into the smoke and spattering oil as if I might have some idea as to how to fix things. Either my maniacal driving had been too much for the Rambler or the carriers had been more integral than I thought.

"Usually, you're supposed to have car trouble at the *end* of the evening," Laurel said.

"Really sorry," I apologized. "There's a pay phone by the Dairy Queen. I'll call us a cab."

"Then how will we cruise around later? I thought you had this big surprise planned, that we were going to stay out till dawn—capital *D*."

Laurel insisted we borrow her mother's Olds. She also insisted that I wait outside with the Rambler. "You don't want to meet my mother in that tux just now," she explained, "and she doesn't want to meet you."

The prom was where it was always held, at the South Shore Country Club, which was nowhere near the shore, and by the time we found it in the dark the dance was in full swing, which

meant that hardly anyone was left on the dance floor. The real
party was going on in the parking lot. Guys had positioned their
cars to form an arena lit by an inner ring of headlights. Car radios, all tuned to the same station, blared, and drunken promsters gyrated, eyes closed against the blaze of high beams, while
along the perimeter, groups stood smoking and passing bottles.

Stosh and Dahl were already gone. Apparently, we'd missed
the high point of the evening: Stosh's first fistfight since freshman
year. He'd gotten into it with a guy named Lusk, a wiseass on the
basketball team who mostly rode the bench. The story I heard
that night was that Stosh and Dahl, who looked like a model in
her filmy low-cut gown, had showed up already high. Stosh had
been threatening to mix up some special pre-prom cocktail at the
Rexall. Dahl had stripped off her high heels and, clapping them
overhead like castanets, danced barefoot in the parking lot. With
the headlights blazing through her dress, it was clear that she
wasn't wearing underclothes. The other dancers opened a space
for her. She was dancing alone for Stosh when Lusk drunkenly
cut in and tried copping a look up her dress by doing the limbo
between her legs. Dahl nailed him with one of her spiky heels.
Lusk scrambled to his feet, said something to Stosh about con-
trolling his crazy bitch, and Stosh hit him with a combination
that knocked him down. Like most of the daily fistfights at St.
A's, that was the end of it. Or should have been, except that Lusk
came back with his buddies, snuck up on the Merc, where Dahl
was giving Stosh a blow job, and started rocking the car. Stosh
put it in reverse, drove over their feet, and just kept going. Later,
I found out from Stosh that he'd broken his hand on Lusk's jaw
and finished prom night in the emergency room while Dahl slept
passed out in the Merc.

It was one of those nights: puke spattered on rented patent-
leather shoes, guys who were buddies one second duking it out
the next.

"You know what's gross?" somebody's date commented. "A nosebleed on a cream-colored tux."

"That about sums it up," Laurel said.

Before the cops came, Ken Guletta, the class valedictorian, climbed up on the hood of a car to give a speech about how our class was disgracing the tradition of St. Augustine.

"This is the only senior prom we're ever going to have," he shouted. "Is this how you want to leave high school? Is this how you want to remember it?"

The question hung in a momentary lapse of any sound other than the bass throb of car radios. Then the cry went up, "Pants him!" They were on Guletta before he could escape inside, dragging him twisting and pleading into the arena of headlights and tearing off his trousers.

"I can see why this place has the reputation of the Beast School," Laurel said. A tendril of her hair had come undone. Ever since she'd seen my tails she'd wanted to dance, and we'd been swaying against each other in our own little space between cars, sipping from the steady round of bottles being passed, and from the silver flask that I'd found empty in the jacket of Uncle Lefty's suit and filled with Bacardi. Laurel was a little drunk, calling me Freddy, and I was calling her Gin.

"Take me to the Blue Note, Freddy," she said, and handed me the keys to her mother's Olds.

I had a fake New York driver's license I hoped would get me in. But I never got to test it out. It hadn't occurred to me that seating was by reservation only. "Come back for the late show at one a.m.," the doorman told us.

"I'm sorry," I said to Laurel. I could see she was disappointed. "Want to get something to eat?"

"I'm too tipsy. Just drive us somewhere neat. Where's this Baha'i I keep hearing about? It sounds like an island in the Pacific."

Baha'i was too far if we were going to try the Blue Note later, but there must have been dozens of places I could have taken her, and yet, with an entire city to choose from, I suddenly couldn't think of anywhere to go. I found myself driving through Little Village. I'd meant only to turn off briefly and cruise by with a beautiful, slightly drunk girl beside me. But once back on those streets I had the impulse to show her the river, where the factories billowed veils of smoke across floodlights as if they were manufacturing fog. I wanted her to see the reflections that the furnaces scorched across oily water, the fireworks of acetylene blue splashing into red-hot sparks behind smudged foundry windows, all the incredible places where Angel and I had walked at night. In a way that I couldn't explain to her, or to myself for that matter, it was preparation for Baha'i.

We ended up at the Fire Truck Graveyard, the car parked so that its front bumper almost touched the Cyclone fence, its headlights spraying across the battered shapes of old fire trucks. I stepped out and shook the flask. It felt as if only a couple swigs were left. Laurel's eyes looked enormous, as if they'd grown in order to see in the dark.

"We could finish it on the seat of the hook and ladder," I suggested.

"Are you serious? Perry, where are we?"

"I bet you never saw anything like this before."

"I have to admit it's a first. Is that smell the Sanitary Canal?"

"You honestly don't think it's kind of cool?"

"Maybe if we were here for a drug deal or to dump a body, sure. Oh my God! Is that a rat? I think I saw a rat. I'm terrified of rats."

"C'mon," I said, although now I was feeling jumpy, "no rats. I've never seen a rat. There's probably fire engines here your parents chased as kids."

"My parents grew up in New Jersey." She'd slid over to the

open door on the driver's side and sat facing out with her legs crossed. They seemed to glow with the light of the polished temple. I could see she was thinking it over. "How do you propose to get over the fence? There's barbed wire on top."

"No problem." I demonstrated, giving myself a boost off the bumper and flipping the fence. It was a maneuver I'd had down since I was a kid, but this time the tails on my tux caught on the barbs, yanking me back in midair, and, jacket shredding as I crashed, slammed me to the ground.

"Oh my God! Are you all right?" Laurel cried.

I stood up, brushed the cinders out of my palms, checked my skinned knee through the tear in the trousers, picked up the flask that had clattered off, and raised it in a toast. "Just kidding around. I got a little carried away," I assured her. "There's actually a gate you can squeeze through."

"No," Laurel said. "No there isn't. There's no gate. There's no Blue Note, no Baha'i, and if Baha'i is like this I don't want to be there." She swung her legs back into the car, slammed the door, and leaned out the window.

"I don't want you to take this the wrong way, Perry, and think it means I don't like you, or that I never want to see you again, because I really do like you, and I know I could get to like you a lot more, and I do want you to call me someday as soon as you get some professional help." Then, she put the Olds into reverse, swung a U, and I watched the red taillights disappear.

Stosh and I toweled off with our T-shirts, dressed, and headed up the beach toward the break in the trees where a dry streambed led to the North Branch of the Chicago River. We crashed out of bramble and followed the river, ducking under an old concrete bridge. I'd never been farther upstream than that.

"Are you sure you can find your way back to these orchids?"

"I went into the jungle, Willy, and, by God, came out rich. Rich, I tell you, rich!"

Beyond the bridge the banks got steep. We rolled up our jeans and waded in over the tops of our gym shoes, keeping to the muddy ledge before the water dropped off. Cottonwoods angled out, and we picked our way over fallen trunks. Mosquitoes buzzed from marshy patches of shade.

At a bend, the river divided around flat, bleached slabs of limestone. We hauled ourselves up on a rock close to the bank. Stosh arranged a pack of matches, a crushed pack of Kools, his knife, and the twisted greasy reefer between us.

"Do you realize that this joint was made with one hundred percent pure Bigbo spit?" Stosh asked. "Not a pretty idea." The secluded river seemed far away from Bigbo and the rumble of Western Avenue. Stosh held up his hands as if he'd just scrubbed for brain surgery, then delicately massaged a Kool over the water, letting the threads of tobacco float off until he was left with a hollow tube of cigarette paper.

"You know what's spooky," Stosh said, "is that every time Dahl and I break up, I know that should be it, but I don't feel free. It's like the breaking up is a stronger part of us being together than the actual being together . . ." He gave up as if it was beyond explaining and continued carefully untwisting the joint, concentrating on his task, not looking up. I'd never heard him talk about Dahl that way before and suddenly realized that things with her were bothering him more than he'd let on, and that of the two of us it was Stosh who was in over his head. He slit the joint with his knife and funneled the weed into the tube of cigarette paper, twisted the end, and handed it to me.

"The Bo always has dynamite weed, but personally, I'd rather not smoke Bigbo spit," Stosh said.

The match flared and the tip of the reefer crackled as I inhaled. I held in the smoke the way I held my breath swimming under water.

"Did you ever think," I asked, exhaling, "that it might be Bigbo spit that's the active ingredient?"

We passed the joint, surrounded by a stillness in which the birds chirped louder and more musically and the reflections of trees shimmered like a green glaze on the olive river. Sunlight sparkled off floating motes of scum and the drizzle of invisible insects. When we waded off the rock into the reflections of the trees along the bank, it felt as if we were moving like mimes. I could see the wakes of the water spiders we disturbed fanning away from us. I was thirsty. My mouth felt too dry to talk. It seemed we'd been slogging a long time.

"We're lost, aren't we?" I finally asked. "We'll never find these orchids."

"Two braves from the Fugowi tribe go hunting," Stosh said. "They go for miles, many moons, deep into the forest until they realize they're lost. 'Hey, not to worry,' one of them says and climbs to the top of a towering tree, scans the landscape, and yells, 'Where the Fugowi?' "

"Your father tell you that one, too?"

"As a matter of fact it's a pharmacy joke."

"You'll probably have a seminar in those when you get to pharmacy school."

Stosh sadly hung his head. Although he'd won the Rexall scholarship, he didn't want to study pharmacy, but it was that or having to work his way through college.

We both flinched at the shadow of a vampire bat that became a tiger swallowtail gliding over our heads as if leading us upriver before disappearing into a haze of light. It was hard to tell how long we'd actually been slogging. I remembered other times stoned when it seemed to take all night just to walk up a familiar alley.

"Hey, Katman," Stosh asked as if we'd been having a conversation, "so what are you going to do?"

"I'm going to Mexico."

"Right. But what if we don't get it together, or even if we do, when we get back wearing our huaraches, then what?"

"I have my prospects," I said, "a position in the ice-cream sector."

"You mean like pedaling an ice-cream cart?"

"And then there's cans. America will always need more cans." I'd worked on the production line at the American Can Company briefly the summer before. The one thing it taught me was that I didn't want to spend my life as my father had, on a production line.

The bank turned increasingly swampy. Cattails and reeds sprouted waist high. We balanced along partially submerged logs and hopped from rock to rock, sending frogs and turtles plopping in. Stosh suddenly sank in ooze up to his thighs. I leapt to the steep bank, grabbed his flailing arm, hoisted hard, and the mud made a smooching sound as he floundered free. His jeans were entirely slimed in mud.

"Sonofabitch," he said. "I lost a fucking shoe."

"I went into the jungle, Willy, and, by God, I came out without my shoe," I managed to choke out before doubling over.

"Oh no, not a fucking laughing fit! You goddamn dope addicts have no compassion," Stosh said, breaking up, too. We collapsed side by side in the weeds on the bank under the sun, howling while the birds in the trees chittered back.

"Shhh," Stosh said. "I hear celestial music."

"You're hallucinating on Bigbo spit."

"No, listen."

We clawed up the steep bank toward the sound and peered through a screen of brush. An expanse of perfect lawn, bounded by sculpted hedges that would have employed a truckload of

Manpower workers to maintain, stretched to a turreted mansion that made the great houses lining the streets of Evanston look like so many bungalows. In a formal garden, a string quartet played beside a fountain. White-gloved butlers in livery that resembled my Gents evening suit transported flashing trays of cocktails to the guests stroking croquet balls. A woman with a sleek, muscled Doberman was strolling across the lawn. The dog broke from its leash, loped in circles, then froze and, from the distance, locked on to my eyes. For the second time that day I felt the fury in a stare.

"They're setting the dogs on us," I whispered.

We scrambled back down the hill as if we were guilty of trespassing and hurried upriver.

"You realize who they were?" Stosh asked, limping along on his single shoe.

"The Fugowi?"

"The Ruling Class. At play in their back yard. You ever seen anybody that stinking rich? They're usually too wily to let you see what real money is."

"Yeah, but money can't buy happiness. That look like happiness to you?"

"Very profound. One thing they don't know is that while they're having their lawns trimmed and petunias fertilized there's fucking orchids sprouting wild under their stuck-up snouts."

We had entered an atmosphere of gnats. Clouds of them reshaped themselves to fit the outlines of our bodies. They stuck to sweat. I was afraid if I inhaled I'd feel them buzzing in my lungs.

"Where the Fugowi?" I bellowed. It echoed off the river.

"Cool it," Stosh cautioned. "If the Rich find out we're here for orchids they'll pass an ordinance that says they own them."

"Speaking of orchids, where the fuck are they?" I demanded.

Stosh stopped. The plague of gnats evaporated. We stood knee-deep in ferns at a bend where the river pooled.

"They're here, muchacho." He gestured. "Everywhere."

For a moment I thought he was putting me on, then among the reeds along the bank I saw them, vivid slashed violet banners, their funnels striped orange and yellow, tiger-furred bees zooming about them.

We had our knives out, cutting bouquets. We took off our shirts and piled the orchids onto them, then insulated them in ferns. Cradling our shirts, we sloshed back along the bank.

The car was sweltering. I was afraid the orchids would wilt. They filled the backseat, where we carefully piled them. Radio blaring the Latin station, we raced to the next stoplight on Sheridan, where the engine died. Stosh tried cranking it, then sat bashing his forehead against the steering wheel.

"*Chinga, chinga, esta caro chingau.*" He groaned. "And you, Señor Simpático, had to say something about that poor joker broken down on the Drive. You couldn't just ignore him like everyone else. I told you the gods wouldn't let us get away with that. You know what we are to them? Gnats!"

"Look at it this way, better it happened now than later, in the Yucatán."

"Ah! the every-cloud-has-a-silver-lining theory beloved by nuns. Very profound!"

Traffic jammed the lane behind us while we unwired the hood. Stosh leaned into the huge, hot engine with a wrench, unbolting the fuel pump.

"Move the heap," a guy in a Beamer hollered as he swung around us.

I flipped him the finger.

"You want a fucken orchid up your rectum?" Stosh raged after him. He disconnected one end of the plastic hose from the fuel

pump, sniffed for gas, and made a face as if ready to barf. "I can't
go on."

"Hurry up before the orchids wilt," I told him.

He glanced balefully at me, then sucked on the hose and spit
out a mouthful of gas. He was still spitting out the taste when the
Porsche with the frat guys swung even and braked for a moment,
all three of them grinning. "Wanna drag?" the driver taunted and
spun rubber. Stosh waved at their rear fender with the wrench.
There was a crunching sound from the taillight. "Oops!" Stosh
said. The Porsche kept going.

I rewired the hood while Stosh slid behind the wheel, and the
engine turned over with an explosive backfire.

"Tijuana or bust." Stosh grinned as I jumped in.

"All that road rollin," I said, "and all those people dreaming in
the immensity of it."

Two lights down, an Evanston cop pulled us over.

He was an older guy with a gray crew cut. His partner sat in
the squad car listening to calls.

"I'm sure you both know the drill. Let's see some ID. Better
yet, get out of the car and assume the position," the cop said.

We stood with our legs spread and hands leaning on the hot
car while he studied Stosh's license without bothering to frisk us
down. Maybe Stosh's jeans looked too filthy. "Take those sunglasses off, so I can determine if this is you, Palacz."

Stosh propped them up on his forehead.

"You been fighting, Palacz?" the cop asked, looking at Stosh's
black eye. "You been rolling around in the mud like a pig?"

Stosh said nothing.

"What's with the one shoe?"

"There a local ordinance against one shoe?" Stosh asked.

"You know how many laws this vehicle is probably breaking?
What are you troublemakers doing up here, anyway?"

"Worshiping," I said. "We're Baha'is."

"You smarting off with me, Katzek?" he asked, reading the name off my license. He looked in the car. "What the hell's in the backseat?"

"Nothing," Stosh said at the same time I said, "Orchids." Stosh gave me a disgusted look as if I was a snitch.

"Norm, come look at this," the cop hollered to his partner, but Norm waved him off. Norm looked impatient to get moving.

"Where'd two characters like you get a carload of orchids?"

I looked at Stosh, and he raised his eyebrows in the crazed Groucho way he had each time he'd repeated "I went into the jungle, Willy," but he said nothing.

The cop was jotting in a notebook. "Names and license numbers," he said. "We'll know where to come looking."

By the time we hit the neighborhood, the shadows of doorways had edged down the front stairs and out along the sidewalks. After the blue lake and green-reflecting river and the gardens of Baha'i and shady lawns of Evanston, the streets looked narrow and shabby. Even the golden wash of late afternoon couldn't transmute the colors of concrete and faded housepaint. I wondered how it would look when we got back from Mexico.

The scratches along my arms from the thorny underbrush we'd slogged through welted up and burned.

"You know what poison ivy looks like by any chance?" I asked.

"Stop whining, we're rich," Stosh said. "Figure, if we sell these to flower shops at say six bucks a pop, how many of them are back there? At least fifty. How many pesos is that? Plus we can always go back for more."

"You're serious?"

"Why not? We could probably sell these at the Fulton Market, where the fruit peddlers go to buy."

We wheeled down Washtenaw, yelling, "Orchids, hey! Orchids!" as if hawking tomatoes or watermelons.

"Pull over," I said, and Stosh swung to the curb where an old *babka* dressed in black and wearing a babushka despite the heat was sweeping the sidewalk before a two-flat.

"*Jak sie masz, Pani,*" I greeted her. "Would you like an orchid?"

She stopped sweeping and regarded us suspiciously.

"Maybe she thinks you're running the old orchid scam," Stosh said. "Tell her no strings attached."

"That was the extent of my Polish," I told him. I handed an orchid out the window and, when she refused to take it, dropped it where she'd swept. As we drove away, I turned to see her pick it up and smile, revealing a mouth of missing teeth.

"There was someone who needed an orchid, all right," Stosh said. "Just because we're entrepreneurs doesn't mean we need to be greedheads. Let's give a few away."

We cruised the bars along Washtenaw, past Harrison High and its cinder ball field, past the motorcycle shop on the corner of Marshall Boulevard where Stosh's brother, Gordo, hung out. Nobody was around. It was that lull in afternoon for which there's no name, when the streets seem composed of shadow and the drawn shades of golden foil, an hour only weekdays have, just before the near riot of traffic when, freed from toil, people rush back to their lives. The Merc, rumbling low and liquid in second gear as if Stosh was trying to drive quietly, rolled into a space across the street from a frame house sided in imitation brick where Dahl lived with her mother. The blinds in the windows of their flat were drawn.

"Probably not home yet," Stosh said. "She got a job working at a bakery."

He sorted through the flowers on the backseat until he found the one he wanted, then crossed the street, climbed the stairs, and fit an orchid into the handle of the storm door.

"No note?"

"She'll know who," he said and took off as if we were making a getaway. "Hey, we're on a roll. How about an orchid run to Bus Girl's?"

I looked at our mud-caked jeans, at Stosh's missing shoe; despite the elation we were riding, it sounded impossible.

"Nah, I'm dying of thirst," I said, which was true.

"So let's go celebrate. I got a couple *cervezas* tucked in the fridge."

The sudden idea of seeing Laurel again after thinking about her continually since prom night made me feel as if I'd just taken a hit of speed. In my daydreams, I planned on calling her when I got back from Mexico with something pretty I'd bought for her—I didn't know exactly what—something you could only get in Mexico. We splished down Twenty-fourth Place, our windows open to the spray as the Merc windshield-wipered through the car wash of an erupting hydrant. I tossed an orchid to a little girl wading in the flooded gutter. We turned onto Rockwell, cruising along the truck docks and factories, and as we passed the block length of Spiegel's warehouse I noticed a shift of women filing out of work.

"Hold up," I yelled, and Stosh braked and double-parked before the employee entrance. I scooped up an armful of flowers and squeezed between the parked cars into the group of women.

"Who's that wild-looking bouquet for, honey?" a poker-faced redhead with a hillbilly accent asked.

"Ladies, good afternoon!" I announced. "The Management of Spiegel's has declared this Women Workers' Day and asked me to distribute these tokens of appreciation. This is for *you*," I said, presenting the redhead an orchid.

"Why thanks, sugar," she said, cracking a smile, then gave me a peck on the cheek.

"And this is for you and you and one for you," I repeated, handing out flowers. They mobbed around me, laughing and kidding and popping gum. Another group of women filed out the door and came over to see what was going on.

"What you giving away, boy? Ooooh, cool!" one of them exclaimed.

"Plenty more where these came from, ladies," I said, handing over the last of my flowers.

A driver in a semi stuck behind the Merc was leaning on the horn. I could see Stosh gesturing to me.

"Sorry, gotta run," I said.

"Bye-bye!" The ladies waved. "Thank you, thank you!"

I climbed in, and we shot away as if propelled by the horn blasts of the enraged trucker.

"You're giving away all the profits, man!" Stosh laughed.

I looked in back. The pile had been diminished. "There's still plenty, and we can go back and get more."

"I guess a little free advertising never hurt. You probably could have sold them. See what I mean? There was mass orchid madness, an orchid feeding frenzy. I thought they were going to gang-rape you."

"Hey! I think I might have found my calling: the Orchid Man!"

"All right, Orca Man, let's go get a brew."

"Yeah, and we better get the rest of these in water." I could almost feel their thirst. I could visualize them in a vase of cool water—a tall, clear vase on a bureau beside the bed in Laurel's room. Sunlight filtered through her sheer curtains and the glass of the vase. She'd wake and the flowers would be the first thing she saw. I didn't know how I'd sneak them in there, but she'd rise wondering who left the flowers and go to the mailbox and it would be full of orchids, too. There'd be orchids fit into the knocker of her door, stuffed in keyholes, scattered over her front steps, clipped like parking tickets under the windshield wipers of her mother's Olds. And if I didn't have enough flowers for all that there were more along the river, growing out of the ooze, surrounded by the drone of insects and songs of birds, still undisturbed, secret.

We were riding down Twenty-sixth, and what was left of the day had come alive. Shoppers whirled from the revolving doors of department stores; mariachi music blared out of bars; at stands under awnings outside groceries, women were breaking bunches of plantains from green stalks; on the corner of Spaulding, a vendor scooped black seeds from freshly sliced papayas. There was the fragrance of tacos and *cabrito* smoldering on spits. The street names were in English, but the rest of Twenty-sixth read like a Spanish lesson: *Frutería, Lavadero, Se Habla Español*. I repeated the signs to myself, practicing, and when I noticed the Mayan features of an old woman whom Stosh had stopped to allow to cross the street, it suddenly was clear, in a way it had never been before, that whether I got there or not, Mexico had already come to me.

We parked on Stosh's street in the rubble lot beside his two-flat.

"Tecate!" he said, to the refrain of "Tequila." He carefully gathered up the remaining orchids from the backseat.

"They keep them in a cooler at the florist," I said. "You think we should put them in the fridge?"

"I don't know. My old man might think they're a salad and eat them."

I picked up a couple he'd dropped and did an Orchid Man dance with them down the gangway to the rear of the house.

"Oh no, the fucken Orkin Man is getting carried away again," Stosh said.

Even before we climbed the back stairs to the kitchen, I could smell the coffee wafting through the screen door and hear the women's voices.

The kitchen was full of women dressed as though it was Sunday. They were sitting around the kitchen table, sipping coffee and nibbling the remains of the devil's food cake that Stosh's mother served on the afternoons when she hosted Tupperware parties. This party looked nearly over: ashtrays piled with lip-sticked butts, countertops lined with half-empty Tupperware bowls of dip and chips. All shapes and sizes of Tupperware were displayed on card tables in the dining room, where the formal presentation had been. I recognized a few of the women from the parish: Mrs. Lalecki, whose son, Larry, had dropped out of grade school when Stosh and I went there; Mrs. Sosa, who led the choir at St. Roman and whose son, Hector, had been paralyzed by a bullet in a gang shooting; Mrs. Corea, who got up once during a sermon and denounced the priests as Svengalis after her beautiful daughter, Lima, insisted on joining the Carmelites; Mrs. Martoni, who once, wearing only a slip, was locked out of the house in the dead of winter by her drunken husband. Along with the other women, they'd spent the afternoon at the Tupperware party, and we'd barged in on their confidential conversation.

"Excuse us," Stosh said, giving me a Groucho look that I knew meant the beer is trapped. He stood there sweaty, shirtless, covered in dried mud, holding the flowers as if delivering a bouquet.

"You boys want some cake?" Stosh's mother asked. "Stanley, where's your shoe?"

"We could use a Tupperware vase for these," Stosh said.

"What you have there?" one of the ladies asked.

"Orchids," Stosh said.

"Orchids don't grow around here," Mrs. Lalecki said authoritatively.

"Yeah, that's what they all say," Stosh told her, nodding a look at me and shaking his head condescendingly. "So, what do you call these?"

"Irises," Mrs. Corea said.

"What do you mean irises?" Stosh said, flushing suddenly the way I'd seen him do in fights. "They're orchids."

"Stanley, sweetie, they're irises," his mother said. "I got them growing in the back yard."

"I like the carnations better for the house," Mrs. Corea said. "The irises are pretty, but they don't last."

"Irises," Stosh repeated, looking at me, then glancing away.

I shrugged, drained for a moment of everything but thirst.

"Let's split," he said and slammed out of the screen door.

"So long," I said to his mother and the ladies.

"Stanley!" his mother exclaimed, looking past me out the door. "Oh, honey, don't!"

I heard the hiss against the screen and turned to see the violet blur of his arm sweep down and smash the bouquet off the banister, violet petals exploding, and almost in the same motion their headless green stems scattering out over the yard. In the dazzling afternoon light it seemed as if the arc of an orchid aura hovered around Stosh before I realized the flowers had left a streak when he'd whipped them across the rusted screen of the back door.

Lunch at the Loyola Arms

By winter I had acquired a table and chair, but that late September I liked the place as bare as I'd found it, and was content to spread my lunch on the white kitchen windowsill and eat while staring out at the street below.

The street was bounded by the El tracks and a neighborhood cathedral, the name of which I didn't know. It was a shadowy street with the amplified quiet of a dead end, except for the occasional clatter of the El and, at noon, the uniformed kids from the Catholic grade school playing during lunchtime recess in the cul-de-sac. The cross-tipped shadow of the steeple creeping along the pavement seemed to add an eerie dimension of echo, which made the lighthearted banter of their voices sound all the more riotous.

The window I sat propped in had been painted open. White paint slapped over cobwebs still foamed in the corners of the sash. Tiny white worms of paint uncoiled from the hinges of the kitchen cabinets. I'd snapped a butter knife prying at the painted drawers, trying to stash the silverware I'd borrowed, along with a pair of salt and pepper shakers, from a cafeteria.

The entire apartment wore this fresh coat of white, through which the inscriptions that generations of former tenants had left behind—bottle rings, phone numbers, initials carved into the woodwork—slowly reemerged. I wondered who my predecessors were, tried to imagine all that might have happened here, but there were no ghosts, no history other than what was waiting to happen, merely two unfurnished rooms, empty except for my saxophone case and portable typewriter, and the suitcase, heavy with too many books, that I'd dumped in the center of the floor.

I was living in exile from Little Village, in a place called the Loyola Arms Hotel, although it obviously hadn't operated as a hotel for years. The rusted, burned-out neon sign in front had never been removed. It was my first apartment. The rent was cheap but still beyond my means after my friend Stosh, who was a Trotskyite that year and was to have been my roommate, moved into a place across town, closer to the University of Chicago, at the invitation of a Thai girl he'd been seeing. I didn't blame him.

Had we split the rent as planned, I could have made it to next spring—at least by my most optimistic calculations—stretching out the money I'd managed to save while living with my parents. They'd been uprooted from Chicago, transferred to Memphis, when the plant where my father had worked for thirty years shut down and moved south. My father had managed to get me a job for the summer in the foundry with his company in Memphis—a situation I was desperate to escape.

So I left and came back to Chicago, ostensibly to return to school, and moved in anyway, imagining that I could live off the city like some form of urban wildlife—alley cat, rat, sparrow. I thought I could slip between the seams like the homeless foreigners who'd roamed through the South Side neighborhood where I'd been raised. I'd grown up studying them: tramps, bag ladies, panhandlers scavenging the alleys in summer like beachcombers; old black hobos fishing along the Sanitary Canal; urban hermits like the bearded mute known only as the DP, who lived in a cave hollowed out under a sidewalk on Twenty-first and Washtenaw, or the Mexican known as the Pigeon Man, who lived with the pigeons in a nest of cardboard cartons that he'd wedged among the girders of the Western Avenue bridge.

My plan was to live on Cheerios and baked potatoes. How much money did one really need, after all? Supermarkets offered free samples and bruised fruit. There were books and records in libraries, paper and pens in banks, toilet paper and paper towels in public rest rooms, soap and socks left in Laundromats. There was Army Surplus and Goodwill. It was September in America, days hazed in gold, streets lined with the largesse of produce stands and flower stalls; the city, to quote Stosh, loaded with bargains at the world's expense. "In this country," he said, "what amounts to merely surviving off the crumbs would be a life of privilege most anywhere else on earth."

But my lunches were becoming extravagant. Picnics on a windowsill: braunschweiger, Jewish rye, mayonnaise, raw onion, potato salad blushing with paprika, a cold beer, an enormous garlicky sea green pickle tonged just minutes before at the corner deli by a young woman with high cheekbones and a Slavic accent, her golden hair stranding from turquoise combs that could hardly contain the weight of curls, ample breasts so loose they had to be bare in the sleeveless blue sundress she wore, and the blond hair growing profusely under her arms flashing as she dipped into a huge glass crock where a school of kosher pickles darted away and tried to hide amidst the dillweed, roiled seeds, and wheeling peppercorns.

Did she realize, looking at me when she seized a pickle and, raising it victoriously, smiled, that there are times in a life when a flash of the natural, humble hair beneath a woman's arms can seem like a forbidden glimpse, a promise, of further mystery?

I'd walk back to the hotel, my lunch tightly wrapped in white butcher paper sealed with the strip of brown tape she'd licked. It was windy that fall, and the neighborhood smelled of whitecaps off the lake. The echo of noon bells from the church-locked street swirled in the vortex of doorways and mingled with the rasp of leaves and dust; pigeons and sheets of newspaper kited over the wooden platform of the Loyola station. The blind accordion player in an abandoned newsstand caught my arm as I passed, saying he smelled garlic.

"Take me to the turnstiles," he said. "It's so windy I can't hear where I'm going." And when I left him at the entrance to the El, he started pumping notes just as the northbound train slammed overhead like a part of the song catching up.

Late at night, through the painted-open window, I could hear the El train, stations away, rocking over the hollow viaducts of the North Side—Argyle, Thorndale, Granville, stops with names like English butlers—as I lay on the twangy, flop-out Murphy bed that a girlfriend once referred to as "the debilitated bicep of the Loyola Arms."

Well, not a girlfriend exactly. She was the same girl who told me that she'd faithfully kept a diary from the time she was a child but that now she wrote down nothing, because recording things as they happen—exactly as they are—means that one is merely a journalist, and she was living her life like a novel.

"The Great American Novel?" I asked, but before she could answer I guessed that no, it was probably a Russian novel—pages of drifting snow, suffering, endless vodka-addled philosophical arguments, and at the end an appendix with a family tree that was necessary in order to follow the generations of characters with their unpronounceable names, names that required you to move your lips while reading.

She said she didn't know what kind of novel it was, because she—then she changed that to *we*—were only on Chapter One.

She said that without the least bit of irony, and though that frightened me a little, I liked her all the more for it.

"You may have noticed we have different thought processes," she said.

"How so?"

"I love the connections, the overview of novels. And you . . .

you think that life is a Great Moments collection. Look at all these undernourished-looking books of poetry," she said, gesturing to where my typewriter sat on the platform I'd erected on the worn carpet from a stack of library books. "How can you type sitting on the floor, anyway?"

"I'm living my life like a haiku," I said. "Syllable by syllable."

"The best teacher I ever had in high school once wrote on one of my papers 'Sarcasm is the final defense of the weak.' And this saxophone—do you ever play it or is it just for decor?"

"I'm practicing to be a musician of silence," I told her, quoting a line I'd read just the night before in a book of translations of Mallarmé.

She merely gave me one of those looks that says if there's one thing more tedious than being a bore it's being a pretentious asshole.

I knew she was impressed.

We'd met in the New World, a socialist bookstore that had just moved up to Rogers Park after a mail bomb had blown out the windows in its former downtown location. Stosh, who frequented the place, had told me that the owner, Lew Merskin, had fought in the Spanish Civil War. I'd wandered in on the evening of the first day I'd moved back to the city, and meeting her there seemed like a good omen.

Her name was Melody—but after our discussion about life as a Russian novel, I began calling her Natasha, a name she seemed fond of. She had the soulful eyes to carry it off, though that quality might have been enhanced by her violet eye shadow. Her face was framed by dark hair, wisps of which she constantly brushed away from her eyes and away from our mouths when we kissed.

I didn't have a phone and would never know when she was coming over, or if she was coming at all. The day we'd met I'd told her where I was living, never expecting her to drop by, especially when she didn't even offer her phone number. All she'd told me was that she lived in Evanston.

Later, she mentioned that she was attending Northwestern, which I'd assumed, somehow, but I never found out where she was living, whether alone or with a boyfriend, in a dorm, or at a sorority house she was embarrassed about. Or was she slumming and didn't want her friends to know? Once, when I asked her how I could get in touch, she said, "Let's just leave it this way for a while—both free, okay?"

"Fine by me," I said.

The lobby buzzer didn't work. I lived on the top floor, down a dingy corridor dark with burned-out overhead bulbs. There'd be a knock at my door—I never quite learned to recognize her knock—and a chemical change too immediate to control would surge through me. If it turned out to be merely one of my friends, Stosh or Doolin, I'd feel foolish standing there at the door with a pounding heart. But sometimes, usually in midafternoon when she'd cut class and take the train from Evanston, it would be Melody, looking Natasha-like in the black raincoat she wore whether it was raining or not. Jeans or a denim skirt, blouse opened at the throat, and underneath a colored bra—violet, ivory, mint, smoke, rose, Capri. A bra from what she referred to as her Italian underwear hobby, which she blamed on the corrupting childhood experience of collecting wardrobes for her Barbie. Whatever the color of the day, she took to dangling her bras from my saxophone as if it was a coatrack, not a horn.

When the flop-out bed would begin twanging melodiously beneath us, the old woman in the apartment below would beat the ceiling with what I guessed was the handle of a broom.

"I wonder what chapter she's on?" I said.

"That's sad, not funny," Natasha said.

"At least my typing late at night never seems to bother her."

"And what is it that you're typing so late?"

"Maybe *my* diary."

"Oh really, and do you write about us? About this? How do you describe it?"

"Well, I usually start out, 'Dear Diary . . . ' "

"I wouldn't know what words to use," she said. "Certainly not the clinical ones, but not the dirty ones either. And certainly not the bodice rippers. *Throb* or *tumescent*—God, that's truly disgusting."

"I thought diaries were supposed to be private, like confession."

"No fair. I share my stories with you."

It was true, she'd tell me stories—strange, amazing stories like the one about her first real sexual experience, when she was a freshman in high school, in a suburb outside Cleveland. It happened with a young man named Armando, who was painting the condo where she lived with her family. Not that she and Armando actually did anything much but talk, she explained, but the things they talked about were a sin. Simply talking with Armando was more intensely erotic than what she called mashing, which came later with high school boys. He was the first man who made her realize that men could be beautiful, and once she saw that, Armando was all she could think about.

He'd tease her, refer to her as Lolita or Ms. Jailbait, and then his voice would drop and he'd begin a litany of what he'd like to do if she were legal. Once, when he was painting the inside hallway, she brought him an ice-cold Coke and he climbed down from his ladder—the way she described it made it sound like Michelangelo descending from the ceiling of the Sistine Chapel—and took a long swig, then kissed her with his ice-cold lips. It was the first kiss for which she opened her mouth. Lips still cool, he kissed her throat and down her body. It was summer, she was dressed in a halter top and shorts.

"If you were a woman, this is how I'd kiss your breasts," Armando said, kissing gently through her clothes. "And this is how I'd kiss you here," he said, sliding to his knees.

"Jeez, what a pervert," I said.

There was more. She woke the last morning the painters were there to find that Armando had lowered the scaffold outside to the level of her bedroom window. He perched there, five stories up, looking in. "I was watching you sleep," he said. She remembered that she was wearing shorty pajamas of a nearly transparent cotton.

"What would you do now if I wasn't here?" he asked.

She stood before the window, yawned, stretched, and then unbuttoned her pajama top.

"I am a woman," she told him.

"Thank you," Armando whispered. "I'll always remember you in the morning light." Then, he reached in past her curtains with his paintbrush and very lightly drew a streak of white paint down her chest.

She stood for what seemed an hour under the shower letting the water slowly wear the paint from her skin.

All through her next year in high school, she told me, she'd unexpectedly feel that streak of paint, and feel the almost irrepressible urge to open her blouse and see if it had reappeared—an urge so strong that if she was in class she'd slip her fingers between the buttons, touch her skin, and check her fingertips for paint. And if she was at home, she'd stand before the mirror and unbutton her blouse, pretending that Armando was at the window, watching her.

Sometimes, looking into the mirror, she told me, she'd be startled to notice that tears were running down her face.

"Why were you crying?" I asked.

"Because I'd heard that while painting another building Armando fell to his death."

Probably peeping at someone, paintbrush in one hand and dick in the other, he lost his balance, I wanted to say.

And I might have, had I already heard her other stories.

They were all about firsts: that first *real* sexual experience, with Armando; the first time naked with a boy in a hotel room (that was at the state forensic finals in Dayton, and the boy, a forensic powerhouse known and feared as Motormouth, turned out to be more awkward and shy than she was); first time with a woman—Maria, a defector from Hungary, who was hired as the gymnastics coach at the all-girl Catholic high school during Melody's junior year there, which, in a weird way, led to her first time with a divorced man—the Laingian psychotherapist to whom she was sent during the scandal about the gymnastics coach, which had ensued after Melody's mother read the diary in which Melody recorded the entire lesbian encounter with Maria from the date of their first seemingly innocent back rubs.

After that, Melody stopped keeping a diary.

There was a price to pay in all her stories. The therapist, she said, simply went missing one day—later they learned he'd disappeared into a religious cult—and the overmatched naked boy in the hotel room won state and went on to nationals, only to crack during the finals and attempt suicide.

"What about that teacher who wrote about sarcasm on your paper?"

"What about him?"

"Did he die, too?"

"What's that supposed to mean?"

"Accidents, death, deportation, disappearances, madness, suicide, and all that before Chapter One. Some prologue. It doesn't bode well for me."

"I wouldn't worry," she said. "You're obviously a survivor."

"I'm just glad it's a novel and not a diary we're talking about."

"I guess I shouldn't have told you."

"Hey, I never said I didn't like listening to your stories."

"I'm sure. What's to like anyway?"

"I like the line from your high school teacher. I like the one about how, after the first time a girlfriend described oral sex to you, you had a dream about it so intense you woke and, gymnast that you were, tried having auto-oral sex."

"I told you *that*?"

"Remember? That afternoon I had the jug of Paisano courtesy of my friend Doolin?"

"Damn that Doolin and his Paisano! Sicilian LSD. God! Why do I tell you such things?"

"To drive me crazy?"

There'd been a knock one night, too late to be Melody. A little late even for Stosh.

When I opened the door, Doolin, returned from Europe, stood there holding two enormous jugs of Paisano the way a traveler stands balanced between suitcases.

"I heard you were back," he said, stepping in, looking around appraisingly. "Very minimal, very understated."

"I'll give you the grand tour: and this is the kitchen."

"A little breezy, no? But I love the way that tree branch is growing in through the window. Good place to hang your hat."

Which, in Doolin's case, was a beret. His worn gray corduroys were now supported by a pair of green suspenders. He'd only just returned to Chicago himself, he said. Europe had wiped him out financially, and for the time being he was living at his mother's.

"Man, you should of come," he said. "You'd have loved it. Winding cobbled streets out of a Pisarro painting. You got any glasses around here?"

"They're on back order."

We sat, backs to the wall beside the window, passing the gallon jug of thick, dark Paisano. With each swig, wine dribbled down Doolin's red beard and beaded off the chin hairs onto the frayed collar of his shirt. He was telling me about Paris, about visiting Debussy's house off the Avenue du Bois de Boulogne, as I'd asked him to; and he'd gone to Debussy's grave as well, at the cemetery at Passy, and left a flower for me. Then, after Paris, it was on to Rome, riding the train that runs along the coast past Nice, and Bordighera—names of fantasy places picked up from the paintings we'd stood before at the Art Institute, breathing as if we could inhale their atmosphere.

"I got off at Rapallo because Pound went crazy there."

Outside, an El streamed by, a strip of blue-lit film.

It was on the train through Italy, Doolin said, after the stop at Rapallo, that the flash of a single word came to him like a revelation and he realized it was the name of a literary magazine that he had to start: *Obscurity*.

"Hmmmmm," I said, but not enthusiastically enough.

"You don't think *Obscurity* says it all?" Doolin asked. "What's missing? That certain *je ne sais quoi*?"

I shrugged. We'd been drinking excitedly, too fast, but still weren't halfway through the first jug, though it had grown easier to heft. "What are you working on?" I asked, changing the subject.

"Mayakovsky," Doolin said, "*A Cloud in Trousers*. A new translation for our generation."

Back braced against the wall, he slid up to a standing position to recite, the slightest hint of a Russian accent edging into his voice:

> The world breaks into a cold sweat
> when I roll out of bed and bellow,
> I'm twenty-two.
> Get off the street, motherfuckers.

"That's Mayakovsky?"

"Is now." He unzipped his fly and took a leak out the window. "Very convenient setup you have here, Perry," he said and began pacing.

When I stood, the Paisano hit me, and I could see why Doolin was pacing. It kept him from staggering. He paced to the typewriter on the living room floor, ripped out the sheet I'd been typing when he knocked, and read aloud in the booming Welsh-inflected tones of a Dylan Thomas record:

Chapter 1: You, me, a secret concealed like a baloney-and-cheese sandwich smuggled in a secretary's purse as she rides the express to work, something she wants to devour now, that makes waiting for lunch impossible— I'm famished like that, or as you say ravished, when you mean ravenous, and lunch turns out to be a kiss that leaves a speck of mustard on your lips . . .

"Perfect for *Obscurity*," Doolin said. "I'll be your first publisher. You'll be in good company with Mayakovsky."

We slammed out of my door and with what was left in the first jug of Paisano sloshing between us staggered down the back stairs and out the alley entrance. The pavement seemed unsteady, pitted like the face of the moon; the alley, a narrow Parisian back street—the rue de Lune. A glint beneath a streetlight caught my eye.

"A good-luck penny!" I said, stooping for it. "One cent closer to making the rent." A Rasputin-looking Lincoln stared up from my palm.

"Let's make a wish," Doolin said and grabbed, knocking the coin from my hand. We watched it roll along the gutter and down a sewer.

On Columbia Beach, whitecaps blew in, atomized spindrift

misted like drizzle above the breakwater. We passed the Paisano, having to yell over the racket of waves. Wine and words both tasted of grit. "Who's the woman in Chapter One?" Doolin shouted.

"A gymnast named Natasha. She defected . . . from Ohio."

"I got it!" Doolin cried.

"Got what?"

"*Obscurity and a Penny.*"

"You said," she wrote to me one day, "that you won't feel you really live here until you get a letter. Will a story about a journey to which a woman has become somewhat addicted do? I could draw a map with the stops at the stations along her way: Howard, Jarvis, Morse—good English butler names—but a map wouldn't tell how far she really travels, or how it feels to wait at the edge of sunlight on a wooden platform in the company of pigeons to board the train.

"Hello again, she tells the pigeons. Hello again, she tells herself.

"Picture the shades along the route in the apartment buildings that face the tracks, all drawn, golden in the sun, no other window standing open like yours. It's two in the afternoon and the city feels almost deserted, everyone at work or school, and here she is alone on an Indian summer day, coat off, a lilac bra visible through her white blouse, which is reflecting light like a golden shade. Usually you raise it slowly, but sometimes let it fly from your hand.

"She never goes the back-alley way, even though she believed it when you told her that it's a Paris street by night. She's loyal to the way she came the first time, when she felt a little lost. Can you imagine what she felt—the crazy chance she was taking?

"Do you believe she actually came—walked past the phantom

doorman, past the desk clerk, who, if there was one, would be dressed in black like the desk clerk in 'Heartbreak Hotel'—you know, the one who's 'been so long on lonely street' he'll never come back. And the bellboy in his little suit would be a wizened old man by now.

"The dusty lobby doesn't need phantoms, it has gutted mailboxes instead. You complain that you never get any mail. Could it be that's because you haven't bothered to tape your name to one of those mailboxes still scrawled with the names and numbers of people who lived here years ago? If you had a mailbox, you'd find this there, rather than slipped under your door.

"She climbs the stairs with their carpeting worn from countless footsteps, some of them hers from earlier visits, and makes her way down a corridor that's dark even in midday. Do you believe *this* story—you who were so worried to find yourself in Chapter One, as though beginnings aren't always the best part?

"Consider this a letter, although it's turning into a flashback. Doesn't every novel need one? Do you have them after she's gone? What words do you use to describe the two of them when you think of times together like that afternoon it stormed?

"This flashback is like a déjà vu I have each time I climb the stairs again: an image of that woman, standing as she did the first time, wondering whether to knock, listening at your door. On the other side she can hear wind, an El train going by, chiming bells, an interval of silence played by a saxophone at rest."

The afternoon it stormed, it seemed as if we were able to make the rain go faster. Her moans like a countdown; her lilac-painted fingernails pinching her pink nipples. Had she painted them to match her bra?

There seemed always something new to invent between us;

even after she'd gone there was always one more thing I wanted to tell her.

I wanted to tell her what I'd heard on the night it turned cold—the kind of crisp, breath-steaming cold that I'd sometimes tried to imagine during days back at the foundry in Memphis. In summer, the workday there would begin at five in the morning, an attempt to deal with the heat; by nine we'd be popping salt tablets.

Shivering on the flop-out bed, wound in the bedspread, I was trying to read to the sound of Mr. Davi, the Albanian janitor, who labored to get the heat going. I pictured him in the furnace room whacking with a crowbar, as if he could beat the stubborn old furnace into action. On one occasion when I'd been doing my laundry in the basement, Davi showed me his collection of the flotsam he'd skimmed from the garbage he hauled—skin magazines, compromising photographs, torn panty hose. Having shared this confidence, he wanted to know about college girls.

"I should have gone to college and become a doctor or an engineer, but I came to America instead and now look," he said with the corrosive bitterness of a man employed below his station.

Davi and his family lived in the basement apartment, behind what sounded like a half dozen locks, as if they were expecting the KGB. At least it felt that way the one time I'd knocked on his door to ask if he could come up and help me get the window unstuck. It was Melody's theory that Davi pounded the pipes to convince the tenants the cold radiators were on—"the psychosomatic heat of the Loyola Arms" she called it. She called him "Salvador Davi, the surrealist janitor" after he'd opened the door on us one afternoon.

I wasn't even aware it had happened until, later, Melody said, "You're a cool customer."

"What do you mean?" I asked. Cool was hardly the way I felt toward her.

"The janitor comes in and you don't miss a beat."

"Mr. Davi?"

"Who else? A paunchy guy with a mustache, standing there with a crowbar. I waited for you to say something. He just stood with his mouth open watching us mating, and finally gave this apologetic little bow and turned and went quietly out the door. You didn't notice?"

"You think I would have simply continued?"

"See, I misread you. You are a romantic after all."

Wrapped in a bedspread, listening to the psychosomatic heat that first night in fall, when the wind off the lake smelled of its glacial past, I recalled a grade school day in Indian summer. I was returning to school from lunch, taking a meandering roundabout way and trying to work up the nerve to cut that afternoon and hang out on the railroad tracks with Angel and Stosh, when I saw the alkies were back. They'd been away. Trucks from Manpower would come to the neighborhood every fall and take them off to Michigan to pick apples. Now they were back with bags of apples and money for booze, gathered around a hydrant that trickled along the side street of broken glass where old cars were dumped. Some of them lived there during the summer, sleeping in junked cars the way campers might use a tent. The street dead-ended in the 3 V's Birdseed Factory, and from the factory's screened windows came the exotic cries and chatter of parakeets, canaries, mynahs, and Java birds singing out, perhaps in response to the excited twittering of sparrows who were bathing in the sky-reflecting pond that spread from the hydrant. Some of the alkies were bathing, too, mopping water-soaked kerchiefs over their heads. I watched them awhile, then headed for the railroad tracks.

I wanted to tell her how, when the radiators stopped their metallic knocking, I'd heard another dull pounding—one I hadn't heard for over a week—and I'd begun to wonder if I'd ever see

Melody again. It was the old woman in the flat below, banging with her broom handle the way she did those afternoons when Melody would come over and we'd end up in bed. This time, alone, I sat perfectly still upon the bed. Thump, thump, thump, it continued, as if the woman downstairs was trying to communicate through some code. I decided that if she was healthy enough to stand on a chair and pound the ceiling with a broom, then it wasn't an SOS. Maybe she was simply a little cracked, like whoever had that voice I could hear traveling up the pipes in my bathroom late at night keening the same nearly unintelligible phrase—"Don't you wanna, don't you wanna"—although it could just as well have been someone calling a name—Donna—over and over.

Night brought out moans like that in the old hotel, sounds I hadn't noticed at first, growls of insatiable hunger from the guts of the place. Maybe they were ghosts; maybe they were flashbacks left behind. If so, I had my own to contribute: the way Natasha looked that afternoon when we heard the windblown slant of rain beating glass panes and pattering the linoleum in the kitchen. "As if the floor was tile," she said later. Racing against my ear, her breath became part of the hiss of rain, her hands rose to her breasts, pinching her nipples, making herself cry out again and again. True or not, I wanted to tell her that I knew why the old lady pounded the ceiling. Because she was lonely, and what we'd assumed were raps of disapprobation had actually been applause.

I would spread the white butcher paper out on the windowsill and pop open a long-neck beer.

On the street below, a schoolgirl in a white patrol belt stood on the curb at the border of shadow, ringing a bell while games disintegrated around her. Lunch hour was ending.

Children, herded by billowing nuns, jostled into lines.

The pigeon-launching church bells tolled one o'clock, if a single ring can be considered a toll. Its reverberation filled my apartment.

That was lunch at the Loyola Arms Hotel—on one or another of those days when nothing happened really but lunch—and yet I don't remember ever feeling more free, or more alone, than when I'd watch the children marching into school, surrendering the street back to the pigeons and shadow until it was empty and quiet again, and I sat propped in the window, draining the foam, with the length of an entire afternoon still before me.

We Didn't

~~~~~~

We did it in front of the mirror
And in the light. We did it in darkness,
In water, and in the high grass.
                    —Yehuda Amichai, "We Did It"

We didn't in the light; we didn't in darkness. We didn't in the
fresh-cut summer grass or in the mounds of autumn leaves or on
the snow where moonlight threw down our shadows. We didn't
in your room on the canopy bed you slept in, the bed you'd slept
in as a child, or in the backseat of my father's rusted Rambler,
which smelled of the smoked chubs and kielbasa he delivered on
weekends from my uncle Vincent's meat market. We didn't in
your mother's Buick Eight, where a rosary twined the rearview
mirror like a beaded, black snake with silver, cruciform fangs.

At the dead end of our lovers' lane—a side street of abandoned factories—where I perfected the pinch that springs open a
bra; behind the lilac bushes in Marquette Park, where you first
touched me through my jeans and your nipples, swollen against
transparent cotton, seemed the shade of lilacs; in the balcony of
the now defunct Clark Theater, where I wiped popcorn salt from
my palms and slid them up your thighs and you whispered, "I
feel like Doris Day is watching us," we didn't.

How adept we were at fumbling, how perfectly mistimed our timing, how utterly we confused energy with ecstasy.

Remember that night becalmed by heat, and the two of us, fused by sweat, trembling as if a wind from outer space that only we could feel was gusting across Oak Street Beach? Entwined in your faded Navajo blanket, we lay soul-kissing until you wept with wanting.

We'd been kissing all day—all summer—kisses tasting of different shades of lip gloss and too many Cokes. The lake had turned hot pink, rose rapture, pearl amethyst with dusk, then washed in night black with a ruff of silver foam. Beyond a momentary horizon, silent bolts of heat lightning throbbed, perhaps setting barns on fire somewhere in Indiana. The beach that had been so crowded was deserted as if there was a curfew. Only the bodies of lovers remained, visible in lightning flashes, scattered like the fallen on a battlefield, a few of them moaning, waiting for the gulls to pick them clean.

On my fingers your slick scent mixed with the coconut musk of the suntan lotion we'd repeatedly smeared over each other's bodies. When your bikini top fell away, my hands caught your breasts, memorizing their delicate weight, my palms cupped as if bringing water to parched lips.

Along the Gold Coast, high-rises began to glow, window added to window, against the dark. In every lighted bedroom, couples home from work were stripping off their business suits, falling to the bed, and doing it. They did it before mirrors and pressed against the glass in streaming shower stalls; they did it against walls and on the furniture in ways that required previously unimagined gymnastics, which they invented on the spot. They did it in honor of man and woman, in honor of beast, in honor of God. They did it because they'd been released, because they were home free, alive, and private, because they couldn't wait any longer, couldn't wait for the appointed hour, for the right time or temperature, couldn't wait for the future, for Messiahs, for peace on earth and justice for all. They did it because of the Bomb, because of pollution, because of the Four Horsemen of the Apocalypse, because extinction might be just a blink away. They did it because it was Friday night. It was Friday night and somewhere delirious music was playing—flutter-tongued flutes, muted trumpets meowing like cats in heat, feverish plucking and twanging, tom-toms, congas, and gongs all pounding the same pulsebeat.

I stripped your bikini bottom down the skinny rails of your legs, and you tugged my swimsuit past my tan. Swimsuits at our ankles, we kicked like swimmers to free our legs, almost expecting a tide to wash over us the way the tide rushes in on Burt Lancaster and Deborah Kerr in *From Here to Eternity*—a love scene so famous that although neither of us had seen the movie, our bodies assumed the exact position of movie stars on the sand and you whispered to me softly, "I'm afraid of getting pregnant," and I whispered back, "Don't worry, I have protection," then, still kissing you, felt for my discarded cutoffs and the wallet in which for the last several months I had carried a Trojan as if it was a talisman. Still kissing, I tore its flattened, dried-out wrapper, and it sprang through my fingers like a spring from a clock and dropped to the sand between our legs. My hands were shaking. In a panic, I groped for it, found it, tried to dust it off, tried as Burt Lancaster never had to, to slip it on without breaking the mood, felt the grains of sand inside it, a throb of lightning, and the Great Lake behind us became, for all practical purposes, the Pacific, and your skin tasted of salt and to the insistent question that my hips were asking your body answered yes, your thighs opened like wings from my waist as we surfaced panting from a kiss that left you pleading *Oh, Christ yes*, a *yes* gasped sharply as a cry of pain so that for a moment I thought that we *were* already doing it and that somehow I had missed the instant when I entered you, entered you in the bloodless way in which a young man discards his own virginity, entered you as if passing through a gateway into the rest of my life, into a life as I wanted it to be lived *yes* but Oh then I realized that we were still floundering unconnected in the slick between us and there was sand in the Trojan as we slammed together still feeling for that perfect fit, still in the *Here* groping for an *Eternity* that was only a fine adjustment away, just a millimeter to the left or a fraction of an inch farther south though with all the adjusting the sandy Trojan was slipping off and then it was gone but *yes* you kept repeating although your head was shaking *no-not-quite-almost* and our hearts were going like mad and you said, *Yes. Yes wait . . . Stop!*

"What?" I asked, still futilely thrusting as if I hadn't quite heard you.

"Oh. God!" You gasped, pushing yourself up. "What's coming?"

"Gin, what's the matter?" I asked, confused, and then the beam of a spotlight swept over us and I glanced into its blinding eye.

All around us lights were coming, speeding across the sand. Blinking blindness away, I rolled from your body to my knees, feeling utterly defenseless in the way that only nakedness can leave one feeling. Headlights bounded toward us, spotlights crisscrossing, blue dome lights revolving as squad cars converged. I could see other lovers, caught in the beams, fleeing bare-assed through the litter of garbage that daytime hordes had left behind and that night had deceptively concealed. You were crying, clutching the Navajo blanket to your breasts with one hand and clawing for your bikini with the other, and I was trying to calm your terror with reassuring phrases such as "Holy shit! I don't fucking believe this!"

Swerving and fishtailing in the sand, police calls pouring from their radios, the squad cars were on us, and then they were by us while we struggled to pull on our clothes.

They braked at the water's edge, and cops slammed out, brandishing huge flashlights, their beams deflecting over the dark water. Beyond the darting of those beams, the far-off throbs of lightning seemed faint by comparison.

"Over there, goddamn it!" one of them hollered, and two cops sloshed out into the shallow water without even pausing to kick off their shoes, huffing aloud for breath, their leather cartridge belts creaking against their bellies.

"Grab the sonofabitch! It ain't gonna bite!" one of them yelled, then they came sloshing back to shore with a body slung between them.

It was a woman—young, naked, her body limp and bluish beneath the play of flashlight beams. They set her on the sand just past the ring of drying, washed-up alewives. Her face was almost totally concealed by her hair. Her hair was brown and tangled in a way that even wind or sleep can't tangle hair, tangled as if it had absorbed the ripples of water—thick strands, slimy looking like dead seaweed.

"She's been in there awhile, that's for sure," a cop with a beer belly said to a younger, crew-cut cop, who had knelt beside the body and removed his hat as if he might be considering the kiss of life.

The crew-cut officer brushed the hair away from her face, and the flashlight beams settled there. Her eyes were closed. A bruise or a birthmark stained the side of one eye. Her features appeared swollen, her lower lip protruding as if she was pouting.

An ambulance siren echoed across the sand, its revolving red light rapidly approaching.

"Might as well take their sweet-ass time," the beer-bellied cop said.

We had joined the circle of police surrounding the drowned woman almost without realizing that we had. You were back in your bikini, robed in the Navajo blanket, and I had slipped on my cutoffs, my underwear dangling out of a back pocket.

Their flashlight beams explored her body, causing its whiteness to gleam. Her breasts were floppy; her nipples looked shriveled. Her belly appeared inflated by gallons of water. For a moment, a beam focused on her mound of pubic hair, which was overlapped by the swell of her belly, and then moved almost shyly away down her legs, and the cops all glanced at us—at you, especially—above their lights, and you hugged your blanket closer as if they might confiscate it as evidence or to use as a shroud.

When the ambulance pulled up, one of the black attendants immediately put a stethoscope to the drowned woman's swollen belly and announced, "Drowned the baby, too."

Without saying anything, we turned from the group, as unconsciously as we'd joined them, and walked off across the sand, stopping only long enough at the spot where we had lain together like lovers, in order to stuff the rest of our gear into a beach bag, to gather our shoes, and for me to find my wallet and kick sand over the forlorn, deflated Trojan that you pretended not to notice. I was grateful for that.

Behind us, the police were snapping photos, flashbulbs throbbing like lightning flashes, and the lightning itself, still distant but moving in closer, rumbling audibly now, driving a lake wind before it so that gusts of sand tingled against the metal sides of the ambulance.

Squinting, we walked toward the lighted windows of the Gold Coast, while the shadows of gapers attracted by the whirling emergency lights hurried past us toward the shore.

"What happened? What's going on?" they asked without

waiting for an answer, and we didn't offer one, just continued walking silently in the dark.

It was only later that we talked about it, and once we began talking about the drowned woman it seemed we couldn't stop.

"She was pregnant," you said. "I mean, I don't want to sound morbid, but I can't help thinking how the whole time we were, we almost—you know—there was this poor, dead woman and her unborn child washing in and out behind us."

"It's not like we could have done anything for her even if we had known she was there."

"But what if we *had* found her? What if after we had—you know," you said, your eyes glancing away from mine and your voice tailing into a whisper, "what if after we did it, we went for a night swim and found her in the water?"

"But, Gin, we didn't," I tried to reason, though it was no more a matter of reason than anything else between us had ever been.

It began to seem as if each time we went somewhere to make out—on the back porch of your half-deaf, whiskery Italian grandmother, who sat in the front of the apartment cackling at *I Love Lucy* reruns; or in your girlfriend Tina's basement rec room when her parents were away on bowling league nights and Tina was upstairs with her current crush, Brad; or way off in the burbs, at the Giant Twin Drive-In during the weekend they called Elvis Fest—the drowned woman was with us.

We would kiss, your mouth would open, and when your tongue flicked repeatedly after mine, I would unbutton the first button of your blouse, revealing the beauty spot at the base of your throat, which matched a smaller spot I loved above a corner of your lips, and then the second button, which opened on a del-

icate gold cross—which I had always tried to regard as merely a
fashion statement—dangling above the cleft of your breasts. The
third button exposed the lacy swell of your bra, and I would slide
my hand over the patterned mesh, feeling for the firmness of
your nipple rising to my fingertip, but you would pull slightly
away, and behind your rapid breath your kiss would grow distant, and I would kiss harder, trying to lure you back from wherever you had gone, and finally, holding you as if only consoling
a friend, I'd ask, "What are you thinking?" although of course
I knew.

"I don't want to think about her but I can't help it. I mean, it
seems like some kind of weird omen or something, you know?"

"No, I don't know," I said. "It was just a coincidence."

"Maybe if she'd been farther away down the beach, but she
was so close to us. A good wave could have washed her up right
beside us."

"Great, then we could have had a ménage à trois."

"Gross! I don't believe you just said that! Just because you
said it in French doesn't make it less disgusting."

"You're driving me to it. Come on, Gin, I'm sorry," I said. "I
was just making a dumb joke to get a little different perspective
on things."

"What's so goddamn funny about a woman who drowned
herself and her baby?"

"We don't even know for sure she did."

"Yeah, right, it was just an accident. Like she just happened to
be going for a walk pregnant and naked, and she fell in."

"She could have been on a sailboat or something. Accidents
happen; so do murders."

"Oh, like murder makes it less horrible? Don't think that
hasn't occurred to me. Maybe the bastard who knocked her up
killed her, huh?"

"How should I know? You're the one who says you don't want to talk about it and then gets obsessed with all kinds of theories and scenarios. Why are we arguing about a woman we don't even know, who doesn't have the slightest thing to do with us?"

"I *do* know about her," you said. "I dream about her."

"You dream about her?" I repeated, surprised. "Dreams you remember?"

"Sometimes they wake me up. In one I'm at my *nonna*'s cottage in Michigan, swimming for a raft that keeps drifting farther away, until I'm too tired to turn back. Then I notice there's a naked person sunning on the raft and start yelling, 'Help!' and she looks up and offers me a hand, but I'm too afraid to take it even though I'm drowning because it's her."

"God! Gin, that's creepy."

"I dreamed you and I are at the beach and you bring us a couple hot dogs but forget the mustard, so you have to go all the way back to the stand for it."

"Hot dogs, no mustard—a little too Freudian, isn't it?"

"Honest to God, I dreamed it. You go back for mustard and I'm wondering why you're gone so long, then a woman screams that a kid has drowned and everyone stampedes for the water. I'm swept in by the mob and forced under, and I think, This is it, I'm going to drown, but I'm able to hold my breath longer than could ever be possible. It feels like a flying dream—flying under water—and then I see this baby down there flying, too, and realize it's the kid everyone thinks has drowned, but he's no more drowned than I am. He looks like Cupid or one of those baby angels that cluster around the face of God."

"Pretty weird. What do you think all the symbols mean?—hot dogs, water, drowning . . ."

"It means the baby who drowned inside her that night was a

love child—a boy—and his soul was released there to wander through the water."

"You don't really believe that?"

We argued about the interpretation of dreams, about whether dreams are symbolic or psychic, prophetic or just plain nonsense, until you said, "Look, Dr. Freud, you can believe what you want about your dreams, but keep your nose out of mine, okay?"

We argued about the drowned woman, about whether her death was a suicide or a murder, about whether her appearance that night was an omen or a coincidence which, you argued, is what an omen is anyway: a coincidence that means something. By the end of summer, even if we were no longer arguing about the woman, we had acquired the habit of arguing about everything else. What was better: dogs or cats, rock or jazz, Cubs or Sox, tacos or egg rolls, right or left, night or day?—we could argue about anything.

It no longer required arguing or necking to summon the drowned woman; everywhere we went she surfaced by her own volition: at Rocky's Italian Beef, at Lindo Mexico, at the House of Dong, our favorite Chinese restaurant, a place we still frequented because when we'd first started seeing each other they had let us sit and talk until late over tiny cups of jasmine tea and broken fortune cookies. We would always kid about going there. "Are you in the mood for Dong tonight?" I'd whisper conspiratorially. It was a dopey joke, meant for you to roll your eyes at its repeated dopiness. Back then, in winter, if one of us ordered the garlic shrimp we would both be sure to eat them so that later our mouths tasted the same when we kissed.

Even when she wasn't mentioned, she was there with her drowned body—so dumpy next to yours—and her sad breasts, with their wrinkled nipples and sour milk—so saggy beside yours, which were still budding—with her swollen belly and her pubic bush colorless in the glare of electric light, with her tangled, slimy hair and her pouting, placid face—so lifeless beside yours—and her skin a pallid white, lightning-flash white, flash-bulb white, a whiteness that couldn't be duplicated in daylight—how I'd come to hate that pallor, so cold beside the flush of your skin.

There wasn't a particular night when we finally broke up, just as there wasn't a particular night when we began going together, but it was a night in fall when I guessed that it was over. We were parked in the Rambler at the dead end of the street of factories that had been our lovers' lane, listening to a drizzle of rain and dry leaves sprinkle the hood. As always, rain revitalized the smells of smoked fish and kielbasa in the upholstery. The radio was on too low to hear, the windshield wipers swished at intervals as if we were driving, and the windows were steamed as if we'd been making out. But we'd been arguing, as usual, this time about a woman poet who had committed suicide, whose work you were reading. We were sitting, no longer talking or touching, and I remember thinking that I didn't want to argue with you anymore. I didn't want to sit like this in hurt silence; I wanted to talk excitedly all night as we once had. I wanted to find some way that wasn't corny sounding to tell you how much fun I'd had in your company, how much knowing you had meant to me, and how I had suddenly realized that I'd been so intent on becoming lovers that I'd overlooked how close we'd been as friends. I wanted you to know that. I wanted you to like me again.

"It's sad," I started to say, meaning that I was sorry we had reached the point of silence, but before I could continue you challenged the statement.

"What makes you so sure it's sad?"

"What do you mean, what makes me so sure?" I asked, confused by your question.

You looked at me as if what was sad was that I would never

understand. "For all either one of us knows," you said, "death could have been her triumph!"

Maybe when it really ended was the night I felt we had just reached the beginning, that one time on the beach in the summer when our bodies rammed so desperately together that for a moment I thought we did it, and maybe in our hearts we did, although for me, then, doing it in one's heart didn't quite count. If it did, I supposed we'd all be Casanovas.

We rode home together on the El train that night, and I felt sick and defeated in a way I was embarrassed to mention. Our mute reflections emerged like negative exposures on the dark, greasy window of the train. Lightning branched over the city, and when the train entered the subway tunnel, the lights inside flickered as if the power was disrupted, though the train continued rocketing beneath the Loop.

When the train emerged again we were on the South Side of the city and it was pouring, a deluge as if the sky had opened to drown the innocent and guilty alike. We hurried from the El station to your house, holding the Navajo blanket over our heads until, soaked, it collapsed. In the dripping doorway of your apartment building, we said good night. You were shivering. Your bikini top showed through the thin blouse plastered to your skin. I swept the wet hair away from your face and kissed you lightly on the lips, then you turned and went inside. I stepped into the rain, and you came back out, calling after me.

"What?" I asked, feeling a surge of gladness to be summoned back into the doorway with you.

"Want an umbrella?"

I didn't. The downpour was letting up. It felt better to walk back to the station feeling the rain rinse the sand out of my hair, off my legs, until the only places where I could still feel its grit were in the crotch of my cutoffs and each squish of my shoes. A block down the street, I passed a pair of jockey shorts lying in a puddle and realized they were mine, dropped from my back pocket as we ran to your house. I left them behind, wondering if you'd see them and recognize them the next day.

By the time I had climbed the stairs back to the El platform, the rain had stopped. Your scent still hadn't washed from my fingers. The station—the entire city it seemed—dripped and steamed. The summer sound of crickets and nighthawks echoed from the drenched neighborhood. Alone, I could admit how sick I felt. For you, it was a night that would haunt your dreams. For me, it was another night when I waited, swollen and aching, for what I had secretly nicknamed the Blue Ball Express.

Literally lovesick, groaning inwardly with each lurch of the train and worried that I was damaged for good, I peered out at the passing yellow-lit stations, where lonely men stood posted before giant advertisements, pictures of glamorous models defaced by graffiti—the same old scrawled insults and pleas: FUCK YOU, EAT ME. At this late hour the world seemed given over to men without women, men waiting in abject patience for something indeterminate, the way I waited for our next times. I avoided their eyes so that they wouldn't see the pity in mine, pity for them because I'd just been with you, your scent was still on my hands, and there seemed to be so much future ahead.

For me it was another night like that, and by the time I reached my stop I knew I would be feeling better, recovered enough to walk the dark street home making up poems of longing that I never wrote down. I was the D. H. Lawrence of not doing it, the voice of all the would-be lovers who ached and squirmed. From our contortions in doorways, on stairwells, and in the bucket seats of cars we could have composed a Kama Sutra of interrupted bliss. It must have been that night when I recalled all the other times of walking home after seeing you, so that it seemed as if I was falling into step behind a parade of my former selves—myself walking home on the night we first kissed, myself on the night when I unbuttoned your blouse and kissed your breasts, myself on the night when I lifted your skirt above your thighs and dropped to my knees—each succeeding self another step closer to that irrevocable moment for which our lives seemed poised.

But we didn't, not in the moonlight, or by the phosphorescent lanterns of lightning bugs in your back yard, not beneath the constellations we couldn't see, let alone decipher, or in the dark glow that replaced the real darkness of night, a darkness already stolen from us, not with the skyline rising behind us while a city gradually decayed, not in the heat of summer while a Cold War raged, despite the freedom of youth and the license of first love— because of fate, karma, luck, what does it matter?—we made not doing it a wonder, and yet we didn't, we didn't, we never did.

Qué Quieres

~~~~~~

My brother, Mick, crossing the country on a Greyhound Ameri-pass, has stopped in Chicago and stands before the old apartment building on Washtenaw where we grew up. Out in front, loung-ing on the cracked, concrete steps as we used to, five *chicos*—teenagers wearing gang colors—stare in his direction. Maybe they're Satan Disciples, maybe Two-Twos, maybe La Raza; the gangs in this neighborhood come and go, leaving the RIP of graffiti behind.

"*Qué tú quieres?*"—What do *you* want?—one of the Disciples asks him.

Mick is on his roundabout way to Memphis, where our father, who has never missed a day of work to illness, is scheduled to have exploratory surgery. That's what they're calling it, but the doctor took me aside to say, "Be prepared, because, frankly, we're not sure what we're going to find when we open him up."

Mick says he wants to be there when Sir wakes from the anes-thetic, to be by his side in case the doctor's diagnosis sounds more like a sentence.

But Mick also wants to take advantage of the Ameripass that he purchased with what should have been the rent money for his bath-down-the-hall flop in a rooming house for men only. It's across from a block of porno places in Hell's Kitchen, and it's where he's been living since a fire totaled his apartment on De-lancey Street.

"Who needs a fucking rip-off dump? I can live on buses," he told me.

Mick has decided that as long as he is, so to speak, traveling back in time to visit our father, he might as well "visit other shrines of memory"—his phrase, irony intended.

On this trip, he's already stopped in D.C., where he once camped in a tent city of civil-rights activists and was twice arrested protesting the war in Vietnam. From D.C. he rode to Pittsburgh, where he was hoping to find Joy, a Cambodian woman to whom he was married for a month—in fact, she's still legally his wife; they never bothered with a divorce. That was years ago, in New Orleans, when, as a favor to a friend, Mick married Joy to get her past Immigration. Mick was living with another woman at the time and, after a month, Joy moved on as planned to stay with relatives in Houston. After she'd gone, Mick realized that she haunted him, that though he'd never touched her, he'd fallen in love with her. He's been looking for Joy off and on ever since, and whenever he does, I know something isn't right in his life. Over the years he'd heard that she was in San Diego, in Portland, in Denver, but this time he had an address for her on Kish Way in Pittsburgh. He couldn't make out any of the names scribbled under the mailboxes when he found the apartment building, but the hallways smelled like Asia. He began knocking at doors. Behind some of them, people shouted back, but the doors didn't open; other doors remained silent. Finally, he jotted a note saying he loved her on the back of one of the Chinese take-out menus piled in a corner, and slipped it beneath a silent door, the one that a flash of intuition told him was hers, then got back on the Greyhound.

Mick's plan is to visit our father in Memphis, then to continue on to New Orleans, a city where he lived for seven years before moving to New York—years of working on the barges that travel the Gulf Coast, of tending bar, waiting tables, becoming an actor. New Orleans is another place where he's seen the inside of a prison.

But now Mick is back in Chicago, the city where he was born. He left it when he was fourteen, at the end of his freshman year in high school, when our father got transferred to Memphis. For me that had been an opportunity to move out and stay behind on my own; Mick had no choice but to transfer to Memphis, too. In Memphis, they lived in a ranch house, not an apartment building, and Mick slept alone in a bedroom furnished with our set of twin beds from the flat on Washtenaw. He piled the bed that had been mine with the books in which he'd lose himself—Dostoyevsky, Proust, Kafka, Jung. At school, he was getting into fights and failing most of his classes. I remember Moms, whom we'd rechristened Mammy after the move south, telling me how sometimes she'd check on Mick at night and find him poring over a Chicago street map spread open on his desk.

He's bought our father a present, a souvenir of Chicago—a kielbasa. That was the first thing Mick did after finding his way from the Greyhound station back to our old neighborhood: buy two long links of smoked Polish sausage from Slotkowski's, which, Mick unerringly recalls, was our father's favorite butcher shop. Mick prides himself on having a photographic memory. He claims he can remember actually being born. Mick has become a devotee of Santeria, and his santero in the Bronx has encouraged him to recall his childhood through dreams. Each night Mick sets a half-full water glass beside his bed—it's a charm that promotes significant dreams. He is seeking a moment in childhood that will explain the shape his life has taken. He dreams of our old cold-

water flat on Eighteenth Street, where his crib stood in the dining room; he remembers me staring in at him through the
wooden bars, whispering, "Shut up, crybaby"; he remembers our
father lifting him from the crib, rocking Mick in his arms over to
the open fourth-story window, and holding him out beyond the
ledge, still rocking him, perhaps considering whether to throw
him out or maybe just soothing his diaper rash in the night
breeze. There's something about our father Mick is trying to
summon up. Maybe it resides in the recurring dream in which Sir
stands above the crib at midnight when the household is asleep,
striking sulfurous blue-tipped stick matches and holding the
flame close to Mick's face, while Mick, awake in the dark, stares
up in silence. In the dream, he knows he must remain silent. His
life depends on it.

"That never happened, Dad wouldn't stand there wasting
matches," I said when Mick implied that at some point Sir
wanted to kill him.

"How would you know?"

"Hey, he's only my father, too."

"Yeah, and don't you think it's a little weird that you, the first-
born, get Anglicized to Perry like you're some fucking admiral,
and I get named after our crazy DP grandfather who they left to
rot in the state madhouse."

Even before his conversion to Santeria, Mick and I often disagreed about which of us more accurately recalled the past. He'd
tell me about Sir dangling him in outer space above Eighteenth
Street, and I'd remember the fire escape under the window. I'd
recall a family vacation at Eagle Lake, a weedy little Michigan lake
with a mud beach and leeches in the reeds—bloodsuckers, we
called them. We called Mick the Lifeguard of Eagle Lake for the
way he'd windmill his arms as he bounded through chest-deep
water, convinced he was swimming. But what Mick remembers is

Sir burning leeches off our bodies with a cigarette, a scene that I think we actually both saw in a movie about explorers in the jungles of Borneo.

"That never happened," I'd insist. "You always make it out more dramatic than it was."

Mick would look at me, shake his head condescendingly, and give me the Sir salute, a dismissive wave of the hand our father used whenever he felt someone was trying to gyp him. "By any chance you familiar with the term 'repressed memory'?" Mick would ask.

"You're not talking about memory. You're talking about half-empty water glasses and dreams."

"You don't think dreaming is a kind of remembering? And if it is, then why wouldn't memory be a kind of dream?"

Where we've never disagreed is over our memories of food. We can recite every detail of meals we shared growing up, like those meatless Friday dinners: fried frog legs Sir brought home from the fish house beside the Sanitary Canal—we joked that the frogs came out of the canal—or potato pancakes with applesauce; or one of Sir's favorite dishes, potatoes mashed with browned onion and served steaming in a bowl of cold buttermilk. We both remember our father cooking his special Sunday breakfast, slices of smoked kielbasa scrambled with eggs, peppers, potatoes. Mick would pile a huge portion between slices of toasted rye slathered with catsup, a creation known as the Stuff-a-Mouth Delight. The Polish sausage that Mick carries now is wrapped in brown butcher paper. From where they're sitting, the gang bangers probably can't smell the strong aroma of garlic or see how fat has seeped through the natural casing and left glistening spots on the butcher paper. For all they know, Mick might have a weapon wrapped in brown paper, a jumbo lead-cored sap.

"*Qué tú quieres*," the kid asks my brother again, then lights a

cigarette with a lighter snapped open like a switchblade, and
blows the smoke in Mick's direction.

Mick shrugs: How to explain to guys who've probably never
been out of the hood why someone would come back for a look?
They're all lighting up and Mick wouldn't mind a smoke. In fact,
he's dying for one, but something tells him now is not the time to
ask. He's given up smoking since he burned down the apartment
in New York he'd shared with Mirza.

The fire happened only a few weeks after she'd packed a suitcase of her stuff and moved to her mother's in Astoria. He still
thought then that she might be coming back. True, she'd taken
their borzoi, Diablo, but undergarments that retained her scent
of gardenias were left in the laundry bag, her leather winter coat
still hung in the closet above rows of high heels, and the tapes of
music to which she practiced dance routines were stacked beside
a boom box. She wouldn't leave for good without taking her music or her shoes. Mick was counting on that. Those abandoned,
beautiful shoes for which she'd shopped compulsively became his
altar of hope.

Mick had worked a double at the mob-owned clam bar in
midtown where he waited tables and had come home drunk to
his fifth-floor walk-up on Delancey. Head pillowed by the shirt
and trousers he'd removed, he lay on the bare kitchen table, the
table they'd swept clean and then made love on the night before
she left. He hadn't known that she was fucking him goodbye. He
covered his face with a slip she'd left behind and inhaled the oils
of her skin. The pearly fabric brought back winter nights when
her bare skin made him feel feverish—they'd cling so tightly together that he couldn't tell which one of them was trembling—
and he remembered how the room would fill with the scent of
gardenias the way it's said the attar of flowers precedes stigmata.

With an ashtray balanced on his stomach, and the slip veiling his eyes against the streetlight, Mick drowsed off to the reverberation of the boom box dialed to the Latin station: Tito Puente. He woke choking, blinded by smoke, rolled off the table and crawled along the floor between boxes of their belongings that were shooting up flames. His pillars of books were burning, and it seemed as if the ideas he'd lived by were burning, too. The scent of gardenias from the laundry was burning, not simply her underclothes but the fragrance itself fuming into toxic smoke. He could hear their possessions popping in the fire and thought of her shoes shriveling into ash as he felt along the wall for the door—the metal doorknob hot to the touch—and staggered out onto the stairwell in his underwear. His lungs felt scorched. He knelt, his eyes tearing as he gagged on his own sooty breath. Between spasms of dry heaves, he heard sirens and screams and suddenly realized the screaming was Leon, his cat, holed up somewhere in the apartment. He tried to go back in after the cat, but the smoke was too thick, the heat intense. "Leon! Leon!" he shouted to guide his cat through the smoke, then remembered the cat was deaf. From inside the apartment he could hear the radio still blaring, and even recognized the song "Hojas Blancas," a song Mirza loved. She had the tape by El Gran Combo, a tape that was melting into lethal fumes of acetate. He could hear the jazzy, lilting chorus. "*Están cayendo hojas blancas en mi cabello*": white leaves are falling on my hair. He heard Leon and shouted back, but only the Spanish lyrics answered— maybe he only imagined them mixed with the furious crackle of fire:

> *There arrives a moment in which I feel very happy*
> *for the good I have done in my life,*
> *and then there comes a moment of grand repentance*
> *for all the errors I have committed.*

"You know that expression, tearing your hair out?" Mick asked when he told me the story. "Well, it ain't just an expression. I didn't know that was what I was doing till a fireman pulled me away and told me to take it easy."

I'd met Leon, a blue-eyed, white male Persian, when I visited Mick for a weekend after he moved to New York to study acting. I rode a train from Chicago, got in on Friday night, and Mick, who'd taken the weekend off from work, was waiting at Penn Station. We walked down Broadway, him toting my backpack and telling me how he'd found Leon at three a.m. on the tracks in a downtown subway station. Mick loved cats; we both did, as did our father. Sir never let us have a dog, but we'd had cats.

"Cats, swimming, getting a bargain, and food—the man loves to chow down," Mick said, totaling up Sir's favorite things. "I think that about covers it."

"He loves to sing."

"Oh yeah, there's that."

We simultaneously launched into a chorus of "Memphis, Memphis, Memphis," a song Sir composed when Harvester, where he'd worked most of his life, closed its Chicago plant. He was fifty at the time, and moving to Tennessee must have seemed like salvation next to the alternative of being out on the street— the fate of most of his co-workers. Sir sang the song adding a blat of Al Jolson to his baritone voice, his idea of a Southern accent. The lyrics went "Oh, Memphis, Memphis, Memphis, Tennessee . . .," repeated ad infinitum.

We were on a fifth chorus when Mick cautioned, "Not so loud or someone will hear what a catchy tune it is and rip it off and then we'll be in a real mess." It was a concern of our father's that someone might steal his song and get rich.

We began to graze our way through the Lower East Side—a Caribbean place for conch fritters, a restaurant in Chinatown whose display window featured a swampy aquarium filled with croaking frogs, baby eels in olive oil at a tapas bar, giant clam in a basement sushi place, borscht at the Ukrainian National Home, Sicilian cheese cake at Venieros, palacsinta at the Veselka Coffee Shop . . .

Grazing through an evening was a private ritual carried over from the times I'd visited Mick in New Orleans, when we'd hike the city from restaurant to restaurant or drive into the Spanish moss–festooned countryside, to all-night truck stops serving Cajun food and zydeco joints in Delacroix on the bayou, where the oysters were fresh off the boat.

We were alternating rum and espresso on Mick's yin-yang theory that an equilibrium could be achieved between alcohol and caffeine. By two a.m. we were speeding drunk. We hid our money in our shoes and, still schlepping my backpack, headed down Ninth, a street along which drugs bloomed like night flowers in the spring air. A shadowy gauntlet of dealers murmured, "Smack it up man, smack it up, dust dust, got what you need, got what you want, rambo, coke, sunshine . . ."

We bought a dime bag from a black kid singsonging "sens, sens, sensamilla," and walked to a fenced park off Avenue A where a basketball game—as much a symptom of spring as lilacs—was going on by streetlight. In the shadows, three drummers beat congas and chanted.

"Does this weed smell like oregano to you? I hope we didn't get rooked," I said, employing one of Sir's signature words for being taken.

"Hear that?" Mick asked, passing me the reefer he'd expertly rolled. "They're chanting the name of Obatala, the supreme divinity on the terrestrial plane."

"The terrestrial plane! No shit?"

"His day of the week is Sunday, his color the purest white. Sacrifice to Obatala requires a white female goat or a white canary."

"And I always thought canaries were by definition yellow." I took a drag and held in the smoke. It wasn't oregano.

"His favorite fruit is *guanábana*, and unlike Chango, whose offering is always rum, Obatala hates alcohol. His water comes from rain." There was no stopping Mick now. He could go on reciting the secret attributes of the gods for hours, just as he could recite recipes, historical facts, conspiracy theories, jokes, verbs in a half dozen languages . . .

Maybe it was the sens, but, after a few hits, my brother's litany began to seem interconnected in a web of chant with the *congaceros* at its center. Car horns and sirens and shouts in the dark were part of it, too, threads of an invisible network of sound discernible in the way that the miles of spider silk connecting every weed and wildflower in a field become momentarily visible on dewy mornings at a certain angle of dawn. The rumble of traffic, the scuffle of gym shoes, the ball reverbing across asphalt, gonging off the metal backboard, and slithering through the chimes of the chain-link net, were a counterpoint to the drum-beat. It struck me then that such connections were the way Mick had come to perceive the world. He believed reality was coded and that there were wise men who could read its mysterious sub-text, wizards who could discern the eternal designs beneath the daily chaos, shamans, all the grander for their humble surround-ings, whose arcane knowledge could influence fate.

"This city is so fucking strange," Mick was saying. "Look up and there's all these lights and even though we're at the edge of a dark ocean, not a single star. Empty skyscrapers squandering elec-tricity just so everyone knows that in the undeclared capital of the modern world there's power to burn, and here, just blocks away in the middle of junkie heaven and hell, they're calling on the an-cient Yoruba deities. It seems all the wilder and more primitive for the incongruity."

There wasn't much night left by the time we finally got to

Mick's flat on Delancey. Mick had told me about Leon, his deaf albino tom, but overlooked mentioning Mirza, so I wasn't prepared for the sight of a woman asleep. The place seemed furnished in anarchy. A boom box resonated Latin music. Partially unpacked boxes spilled their contents, pillars of books piled against walls threatened to topple and bring the walls down with them. The only seats were at a kitchen table cluttered with empty bottles, plates that served as ashtrays, and dirty pots from some exotic feast Mick had cooked up, perhaps days ago. Beneath the table the eyes of Diablo the borzoi glared out like a wolf's from its lair. But, unlike all of Mick's previous disordered places, this flat smelled faintly floral. A bare mattress, crammed into what probably was meant to be a pantry, extended out beyond the doorway. A woman was asleep on the mattress, although given the surrounding mess, the blaring radio, the flickering fluorescent kitchen fixture, it seemed more likely that she was passed out. All I could see of her were long legs in black net stockings and red high heels—one red shoe, to be exact, the other presumably kicked off. The immobile perfection of those tawny legs sticking from the doorway made it appear wholly possible that my brother was bedding down with the bottom half of a mannequin. Mick didn't seem to notice anything out of the ordinary.

"You didn't mention a roommate. You sure it's all right for me to crash here?"

"No problem. My girlfriend, *mi amiguita*, Mirza," he said by way of introduction. "Mirza, meet *mi 'mano*, Perry."

The legs didn't stir.

"See," he said. "She's totally cool with it." Then he dropped his voice. "If she asks how old I am don't tell her."

"Why not? Why would she ask me?"

"She's very curious about my family. Don't tell her anything. She'll misinterpret it. We're having our little squabbles lately."

For what was left of the night, I slept in my clothes on a

musty pile of drapes wedged between boxes on the bare floor, with Leon curled purring on my chest and Diablo snarling, his fangs bared at my throat each time I shifted, futilely searching for a comfortable position.

When I woke to Saturday, light was defogging the grated, unwashed windows. Leon sat perched on the refrigerator observing Mirza, who, dressed in a tank top and jogging sweats, stood at the stove with her back to me, whisking canned milk and cinnamon into a pot of coffee. From the pantry doorway, Mick's bare, hairy legs stuck out over the mattress as Mirza's had the night before. The radio played Bach, and the borzoi gnawed at something under the table.

"*Buenos días,*" Mirza said, glancing over her shoulder. I was struck by how broad her shoulders were. She had the build and muscle tone of a gymnast. Her kinky hair was cropped short, dyed bronze, a shade that matched her skin. She wasn't pretty so much as beautiful in a handsome way.

"Good morning," I said.

She handed me a steaming mug. "I can see the family resemblance. Especially in the cheekbones. You are Yimmy's brother."

"Whose brother?" I asked.

"Yimmy."

I was groggy and wondered if Yimmy was some Caribbean term of endearment. "You mean Mick?"

"Mick? No, Yimmy. Yimmy Delacroix."

"Yeah, *mi hermano,*" I said.

Not only had Mick neglected to tell me about Mirza but he'd forgotten to mention that in New York he was no longer Mick Katzek. Later, he'd clue me in that he'd changed his identity and assumed a stage name for his acting career. The name had belonged to an old Cajun he'd worked with on the boats out of New Orleans, a man without any family of his own who befriended Mick, taught him how to make gumbo on a galley stove, to tie nautical knots, to cable barges together without losing his fingers, and to play bourre, a mean card game with dramatically rising stakes. Bourre was played each payday on the docks, and Mick also learned the phrase—*Je bourried la vie foutu*—and the attitude that went with it: I bourried my fucking life. Delacroix's heart gave out suddenly on one of their trips down the Gulf Coast, and he was buried in the Seaside Cemetery in Corpus Christi, in a pauper's grave beneath a marker on which the date of neither his birth nor death appeared. It simply read: JAMES DELACROIX OF LOUISIANA.

His name was the last thing he taught Mick.

"*Di qué tú quieres?*" the gang banger asks again.

That the question is oddly formal and more insistent—"Say what you want"—is not lost on my brother. German and Spanish were his double major before he dropped out of Memphis State. Years ago he lived briefly in Mexico, just before the FBI caught up with him in New Orleans for draft evasion. Mick has an ear for languages. He doesn't dream in Spanish but does lapse into it when he gets drunk. One of Mick's many theories is that the fastest way to learn a language is to live with a woman who speaks it. "Of course," he concedes, "your vocabulary will be a little skewed."

Besides Spanish he speaks a bit of German, Cambodian, Italian, French, Portuguese, Haitian Creole, Polish, Chinese. Not that he's learned all those from women—our father spoke Polish, and in the restaurants where Mick has been employed for most of his working life English is often a second language.

He got involved with theater by following a woman. She was strikingly beautiful, Mick said, her hair glowed with a sheen he'd seen before only on race horses. He saw her on a street in New Orleans and the song "Tennessee Stud," with its chorus "The Tennessee stud was long and lean, The color of the sun and his eyes

were green" popped into his mind. Humming the song, he followed her for blocks into the Garden District, to a bar where actors had gathered for an audition in the back room. When Mick
followed her in, they thought he'd come to try out for *The Glass
Menagerie*. Playing along, he read for the part of the narrator,
Tom Wingfield, from the play's opening speech: "Yes I have tricks
in my pocket, I have things up my sleeve. But I am the opposite
of a stage magician. He gives you illusion that has the appearance
of truth. I give you the truth in the pleasant guise of illusion . . ."

Mick had read only to the line "In memory everything seems
to happen to music" when the director gave him the lead.

"What about the Tennessee mare you followed?" I asked.

"She was a beauty, but I'm afraid she couldn't say 'Pass the
bread,' " Mick said. "Got sent home in tears without a part."

Over the next four years Mick played leading roles at most of
the theaters in New Orleans, until he felt there were no chal-
lenges left there. Local theater didn't pay the bills, and Mick, who
was waiting tables, had never saved a cent, but he managed to put
away enough for a one-way bus ticket to New York, and to stake
himself for the month he figured it would take to get resettled.

It was winter when he left for New York; he'd forgotten what
real winter was like. He was crashing in the one-room flat of an
old activist friend on Mott Street and running out of money fast.
One night, half frozen as he aimlessly explored the city, he wandered into the Kit Kat, a strip bar off Forty-second Street, and
saw Mirza dancing topless before a blue foil curtain on a lilac-
lit stage. She was dusted in glitter, and the lighting seemed
appliquéd to her muscular body. Instead of disco, she was
dancing—writhing—to Coltrane's *A Love Supreme*. If she'd been
stripping to the "Ave Maria" it wouldn't have seemed more sacri-
legious to Mick. He watched spellbound, the sinuous supplica-
tion of Coltrane's tenor sax aching along the byways of Mick's
body, and suddenly he understood that, in this glitzy low-life bar,

her dance was daring to preach something beautiful and so, inescapably, something spiritual as well. Before the night was over, Mick, claiming he was a prize fighter, had talked himself into a job as a bouncer at the Kit Kat Lounge.

My brother is a middleweight, not the typical bouncer build, but he'd actually had a few semipro fights in New Orleans and been coached by Willie Pastrano, the onetime light heavyweight champ. In a way, it was Pastrano who was responsible for Mick's moving to New York. Theater types had repeatedly told Mick that New York was where he needed to go if he wanted a real acting career, and that his vague physical resemblance to James Dean was something he could cash in on. But he didn't buy it until Willie Pastrano said, "Mick, I can't keep training you unless you make the decision to turn pro. Think it over, because people will pay to see a white kid who looks like that dead fuckup actor James Whatshisface." That was the permission—the omen—to start anew as Jimmy Delacroix, to move to New York in the dead of winter and enroll in the Actors Studio, where Brando, Montgomery Clift, and James Dean had studied with Lee Strasberg.

"*Qué quieres?*"

The Disciple removes his sunglasses as if for emphasis, then rises to his feet like someone tired of sitting, in need of a stretch. He's a handsome kid with a shadow of mustache, and now that he's removed his sunglasses, Mick notices that what he took to be a mole on the kid's cheekbone at the corner of one eye is a tattooed blue tear. The tear, Mick knows, is a tribute to a gang buddy who was killed. Every kid in this gang-graffitied neighborhood could probably be crying the same blue tear.

"*Qué quieres, hombre?*" Whataya want, man? the kid asks for what must be the fifth or sixth time. Now that he's on his feet, it's clear he has no intention of sitting back down.

"I grew up here, too. I thought I'd come back to see if the old place was still standing," Mick answers in Spanish, and smiles. In New York, the surprise of a blond-haired, blue-eyed guy speaking rapid-fire street Spanish usually eases the reflexive hostility. In the Bronx neighborhood of his santero, Mick is known as the *jíbaro rubio*, the blond hillbilly. But here, no one smiles back. Before Mick can continue explaining, the kid repeats the question.

"Qué quieres?"

We were at the Village Vanguard on Saturday, the second night of my visit to New York, when Mick told me the story of how he'd moved from New Orleans. We'd gone to hear Gato Barbieri, an Argentinean sax player with a tone like the screak of some great tropical bird. On the Vanguard's stage, a stage that seemed too cramped for the club's legendary stature, Barbieri soared in ecstatic flurries above a joyful racket of drumskins, maracas, and a berimbau. Between sets, Mick chain-smoked and chain-talked. He kept offering me cigarettes, and I kept telling him I'd quit. Finally, he observed that quitting must have agreed with me as I was looking fit, then insisted we arm-wrestle for drinks even though he could wrestle only with his weaker left arm. His right elbow was still healing from a break that had required surgery. Since I'm left-handed, it wasn't a fair match.

"How'd you ever get them to hire your Yimmy Delabaloney ass as a bouncer?" I kidded, after pinning him a few times.

"I simply told them the truth, that the job of bouncer demands psychology, not brute strength. Being a bouncer is about acting."

It was another of Mick's ever-fomenting theories that life was essentially about playing roles. It seemed a dangerous idea to put to the test if the role was that of bouncer on Forty-second Street.

His elbow was injured outside the Kit Kat when he was stomped in a brawl he didn't see coming with a party of crazed UFO conventioneers—some dressed like Star Trek characters. "Wouldn't think Trekkies could be such mean fucks," Mick said. "Whatever happened to 'Live long and prosper'?"

After the cops broke up the fight, Mick went back into the Kit Kat and began pounding shots of Barbancourt rum. A Haitian friend had once told him there was a saying in Haiti that "Barbancourt can cure even peg leg." Mick couldn't bend his right arm, and the bad timing of the injury was ominous: his first real audition since arriving in New York was scheduled for the next morning. He was to read for a role in Tennessee Williams's *Summer and Smoke*, a play he had done in New Orleans. He'd long regarded Williams as his lucky playwright, and luck was something Mick increasingly courted. He'd become superstitious since moving to New York, addicted to lotto—a game he'd previously condemned for bilking the poor. You couldn't pursue a career in acting, he now argued, without accepting that your life would be governed by chance.

The Kit Kat closed at three a.m., and by then Mick's elbow was so swollen that he couldn't roll down the sleeve of his bloodstained white shirt. Drunk, out of subway tokens, Mick hurdled the toll bar at the Times Square station. The exertion made the blood throb in his right arm as if the elbow joint might explode. He was dizzy, nauseous with pain, and figured he'd better get himself to an emergency room. The subway platform was empty except for a homeless guy asleep on one of the benches and an elderly Asian man doing tai chi. When the man saw Mick cradling his arm and woozily staggering, he paused in his exercises to ask what was wrong.

"I think it's broken," Mick said.

The old man gently traced his fingertips over Mick's elbow; he studied Mick's face as if examining his eyes.

"Will be all right," the man concluded. "You need *yunnan baiyao.*"

"What?" Mick asked.

"*Yunnan baiyao,*" the old man said and had Mick repeat it. "It's what the Viet Cong used on their wounds when they fought America."

"Where can I find *yunnan baiyao?*" Mick asked.

As if sharing a secret, the old man told him an address in Chinatown.

Instead of going to the emergency room, Mick rode the train to Chinatown and wandered the shuttered streets. At six a.m., he stopped for tea in an all-night Shanghai place and, deciding soup might be medicinal, ordered a ginkgo-nut congee, and when he noticed on the menu something translated as "embroidered fish balls," he ordered that, too, out of sheer curiosity. At eight a.m., he was waiting in the doorway when the Chinese herbalist came to open his pharmacy. Mick stepped into the shop's alien atmosphere of dried herbs and powdered animals and inhaled a smell that seemed in itself curative.

Perhaps things would have gone differently if Mirza, who'd been taking classes at NYU, hadn't been away at a weeklong dance seminar at SUNY, Purchase. She'd left a note dusted with glitter and embossed with a lilac impression of her lips, wishing Jimmy luck on his audition. Alone, Mick took the first dose of *yunnan baiyao* and washed it down with rum; then he settled onto the mattress in the pantry and fell into a fitful sleep with Leon purring against his wounded arm. It was as if the cat understood he was injured and would help heal him. For the next two days Mick lay tended by Leon, religiously taking the *yunnan baiyao* and rum, but otherwise fasting. By the third evening, when he dragged himself to work at the Kit Kat, his right elbow was the size of a melon and turning shades like rotting fruit. Vince, the bartender, took one look and hailed a cab to rush Mick to the ER at Lenox Hill. There, they had to put him under and rebreak the elbow in order to pin it together. Mick said he never fathomed the word *pain* until he woke from the anesthetic.

The injury ended his career as a bouncer. When he got out of the hospital and recovered enough to return to work, Mick found a job at a midtown clam bar. He was back to waiting tables, a role he'd already played for too many years in New Orleans. Mirza was through with the Kit Kat as well. She'd been accepted as an understudy in the Alvin Ailey company, and was devoting herself full-time to her dream of becoming a serious dancer.

"I know that dream stuff sounds like corny Hollywood shit, but I don't know what else to call it," she'd told Mick on the very first night they'd met at the strip club. And Mick said, "No, not corny, *dream* is a beautiful word—*sueño, träumen, marzenie*—a word we'd die without. You can't let cheeseballs fuck it up for you." It had taken only a few weeks from that freezing night when Mick first saw Mirza dancing to Coltrane for them to move in together.

When Mick told me that they'd been "having their little squabbles lately," I guessed that probably meant they'd been at each other's throats. They didn't argue during my visit, but they couldn't conceal the tension. In contrast to Mick's manic humor, Mirza brooded. Yet it was obvious she was still nuts about him. I could hear it in the teasing way she called him Yimmy as we roused Mick that Saturday morning from the mattress in their pantry bedroom. The way she called his name made him sound like a different guy than the kid I'd grown up with.

We roused Mick up, and the three of us, with the borzoi in tow, hailed a cab on Delancey and rode all the way uptown so Diablo could romp in Central Park, and from there we walked to a *mercado* on the West Side where Mirza bought the ingredients for *pastellas*. We spent the rest of Saturday afternoon rolling *pastellas*, which reminded Mick and me of the *gowumpki* Moms used to make, except that instead of a cabbage leaf, the filling was wrapped in a banana leaf. The *pastellas* were for a baptism party the next day in Astoria. The baby's mother was Mirza's younger sister, Chiqui. Mick was to be *padrino*. As his brother, I was welcomed, too.

Mirza's family lived on welfare and couldn't afford both a church service and a party after, so the priest performed the ceremony at the kitchen sink. He baptized the infant Milton Jimmy Marrero—Jimmy after his *padrino*, Jimmy Delacroix. That Sunday, on the Marreros' little concrete patio decorated with balloons, beneath the canopy of low-flying jets from LaGuardia, it looked like my brother had found himself a new life complete with adopted family.

Mirza hadn't asked me his age or anything about him, but at the christening party, on that last day of my visit, while Mick salsaed with her wide-hipped *tías*, two at a time to the tape of El Gran Combo, Mirza told me as if confiding, "When he's not acting crazy, your brother is so sweet and has such a big heart. So generous! Chiqui loves him. He got her a job in the restaurant where he works and helped her sign up for night school." Then she asked, "Perry, does your father like to drink?"

"He's not much of a drinker," I told her, and left it at that rather than explain that our father was the child of a brawling drunk who'd died in the state mental hospital, a father he never talked about.

"I guess I don't even know if that's good or bad news so far as Jimmy. I don't know what he's looking for or running from."

From what Mick had told me the night before at the Village Vanguard to the yawp of Gato Barbieri's sax, the problems with Mirza began after he broke his elbow. Mick implied that his inability to get roles was corroding their relationship. After too many drinks he'd referred to himself as "just another fly on the wall of the New York theater scene" and ranted about actors be-

ing treated like "the niggers of the art world," phrases of a kind
I'd never heard from him before. But Mirza told me that what
worried her was that Jimmy wasn't doing the things necessary to
help himself, the way she was in pursuing her dream of dancing.
He still hadn't arranged to have a set of publicity pictures made,
or typed a résumé, or contacted an agent, and he refused to audition for what he called shitwork—which included anything other
than serious drama.

"You're his older brother, maybe you can tell him he needs to
be more practical," she said.

"I'm afraid that's exactly the lecture our father constantly gave
us," I said, laughing.

She seemed to recoil, and I was sorry I'd laughed, as I could
see she was by nature proud and private and wouldn't be having
this talk if it wasn't terribly serious to her.

"Did Jimmy tell you how he got involved in Santeria?"

"No."

It hadn't occurred to me that anything in particular was necessary to get Mick interested in Santeria. He'd always felt most alive
when crossing borders, most at ease in the foreign outposts of
America. Our father was an immigrant, but Mick was the one
who seemed to feel foreign—foreign in the church and Catholic
schools we went to as children; foreign in Memphis, Tennessee;
foreign in the face of My-Country-Right-or-Wrong and the gov-
ernment that jailed him for refusing to fight a war he believed
was a crime against humanity.

"Once, after a terrible argument with Jimmy," Mirza said, "I
felt so bad I went to see the santero. It was something I hadn't
done since high school. It's supposed to be private, like confession, but when I came home Jimmy wouldn't leave me alone until I told him what the santero said. So, finally, I broke down and
told him: 'You are living with a man cursed by his father.' That's
what the santero told me. And when I told Jimmy that, it was

like I'd stabbed him in the gut, and then he began to laugh that crazy laugh and he became like happy, and he said, 'Now I understand.' "

"Qué quieres?" the Disciple demands. Though he's taken only a few drags, he drops his lit cigarette and grinds it beneath his high-topped basketball shoes.

"Just wanted to walk around the old hood," Mick tells him in Spanish, "check out our old building, take a look at the back yard where we used to play. You know that oil shed back there? My old man built it out of scrap wood we stole after urban renewal bulldozed a square block on Cermak and Western. I saw there's a big Jewel on that corner now. Me and my bro used to sneak out after supper and smoke behind that oil shed. It was our secret place. But it really pissed us off when our father first built it because that little back yard had been our baseball field, you know, when we were small and couldn't hit a ball farther than we could spit. It seemed as big as Sox Park to me then. A home run was over Kashka's fence. You guys probably never heard of Kashka. See that parking lot next door? It used to be a falling-down old house surrounded by a wooden fence where this crazy, fat woman named Kashka Marishka lived. She kept chickens even though it was illegal. Her fucken rooster would wake us up every morning—"

It's too long a story to tell them now, even for my brother, who can talk nonstop all night, but he's remembering Kashka's old house, and how the cops had to come the day it was scheduled to be wrecked in order to tear Kashka away from its warped rooms. Her enormous body bulged through rips in the slip she was wearing. She was cursing in English and Polish, weeping and screaming and fighting the cops, while a bulldozer mowed down her crooked home-run fence, and her chickens flapped a getaway down the alley with the cops in pursuit. Mick remembers watching the spectacle with the rest of the neighborhood, and feeling sorry and ashamed, knowing it was Sir who'd finally bribed the alderman to get Kashka's house condemned.

"*Qué quieres?*"

It was Sir who bribed the cops to keep an arrest off Mick's record after Mick was clubbed and detained when an antiwar rally he'd helped organize in his freshman year at Memphis State turned into a riot. Our father drove a bloodied Mick from the police station to a deserted industrial lot that overlooked the Mississippi. There, he told Mick that all his life he'd lived with the dread that "the family curse," the madness responsible for his own father's incarceration in a state mental hospital, would be inherited by his sons. Then, our father apologized to Mick for passing it on to him.

It was Sir who gave Mick's address on St. Philip Street in New Orleans to the FBI.

Two feds in suits and ties showed up at the house in Memphis looking for Mick. He'd dropped out of Memphis State, lost his student deferment, and was evading the draft. Not just evading the draft but sending his draft board a steady stream of antiwar literature—posters of Che Guevera, the poems of Ho Chi Minh, all of which were by law required to be kept in his file. One of the agents said to Sir that it must be sad to no longer hear from his runaway son, and Sir replied that sure he heard from Mick, he'd received a letter just the other day. The agents told him they'd have to confiscate the letter, and he handed it over. On the envelope was Mick's address in New Orleans.

As letters go, it wasn't particularly incriminating:

Dear Folks, Don't worry that you haven't heard from me.
I was in Mexico. Now I'm back here, doing okay. Got a
job cleaning ships. The food in this town is sure good.

                                                    Peace, Mick

Mick was in bed with a nun when the FBI broke down his
door, which was unlocked, and stormed in with guns drawn.
They made Mick and the nun lie facedown and naked on the
floor while they cuffed Mick. The nun—her name was Sister
Claudia—was in the process of leaving her order. Mick had met
her at a protest rally. U.S. marshals took Mick to the New Orleans Parish Prison, where he was thrown in with the general
population. He was twenty-one, blond, and really did bear a resemblance to the dead actor James Whatshisface.

I didn't know what had happened until several days later,
when I got a message to call a Sister Claudia, whom I'd never
heard of. I was teaching at a junior high in the Caribbean; I'd
finally made it from Blue Island Avenue to a real blue island.
She'd had a hard time tracking me down.

"You have to get him out," Sister Claudia pleaded on the
phone. "His cell mate, who's in for murder, is a psychopathic
weight lifter covered in Klan tattoos. Mick's fighting for his life
every night in there. They broke his nose, they knocked out one
of his front teeth." She began to cry.

I telephoned our father immediately.

"A little time in there might straighten him out," he said.

"Are you nuts? Do you know what goes on in prison? They'll
gang-rape him."

"What the hell are you talking about?" he said.

"Don't you know what happens in prison to young guys,
Dad?"

Then I realized he didn't know, or didn't want to. I pictured
him after dinner sitting before the TV, Mammy darning socks

while he pondered his monthly issue of *Forbes*, calculating market forces for investments he never made. And then, although the events weren't connected, I recalled how, long ago, when he was told by the nuns that, given his IQ scores, Mick should be sent to a special school, our father became alarmed. He thought they were talking about reform school.

"It's true what I'm telling you," I said. "Look, I can't do anything from here, but I'll fly in and get him a lawyer."

"What's wrong with you guys?" he asked. "I don't understand my own sons. If it ain't one mess, it's another."

One mess or another—an expression we'd been raised with, not that it applied strictly to Mick and me. When our father was hospitalized, bleeding internally and awaiting exploratory surgery, I called from the airport, on my way to Memphis, and asked, "How you doing, Dad?" and he answered, "I'm in kind of a mess here, sonnyboy."

I didn't have to return to the States to try to get Mick out of prison. After talking to me, Sir packed a suitcase, got in his gold Chrysler, and drove in the middle of the night to New Orleans. He hired a lawyer and had Mick out two days later, then took Mick to the dentist and got him a new front tooth.

"*Qué quieres?*" the Disciple demands.

The kid hasn't indicated that he's understood one word Mick has said in Spanish, but now he makes a gracious gesture toward the gangway, inviting Mick to step into it and visit the back yard he's been describing. Mick glances toward the gangway—a narrow, shadowy corridor between apartment buildings. At the end, bounded on three sides by the brick walls of apartment buildings, a square of trampled mud is crosshatched by shadows of clothesline and power wires. It's the patch of earth Mick has come here to stand on again. He can still predict the angles of ricochets off the brick wall of the building next door, whose mortar was knocked loose years ago by the countless hours of pounding he gave it with a rubber ball. And down the crumbling, cobwebbed basement steps that smell of leached lime, he knows by heart the recesses where spiders, rats, and alley cats harbor their wildness in the musty darkness. Behind the oil shed Sir built, under the rafters, are caches where we hid cigarettes and lighters, pints of muscatel the winos bought for us, dirty playing cards, illegal fireworks, a Wham-O slingshot and a bag of ball bearings with an affinity for factory windows, a throwing knife we'd practiced with on Kashka's fence. He wonders whether any of our treasures are still hidden there. What might he remember standing in the back yard? He can visualize how the shadows of clothesline and hanging laundry are swallowed as the deeper shadows of the brick walls extend across the yard. It's a place composed more of shadow than of earth. Shadows familiar enough to be recognized by their smell, the smell of a past that sometimes seems more real than the present, a childhood in which degrees of reality were never a consideration, when reality and the sense of identity that went with it were taken for granted. That unquestioned conviction as to who they are is the advantage the Disciples on the front steps have over him.

Their eyes follow his, looking into the gangway. Perhaps something back there has meaning for them, too. Surely one of them must have descended the back stairs some winter night, maybe lugging a sack of garbage out to the alley, and stopped to stand looking up into the random patterns of snow, letting the flakes melt against his face. *Están cayendo hojas blancas* . . . white leaves are falling . . . Perhaps he imagined them as cold flecks of soot that had floated through infinite space from burned-out stars, or imagined how, above the cloudy snow, the gorgeous, terrifying blizzard of the cosmos wheeled over the back yard. Mick remembers such nights, when he gazed up aware that he was just another speck adrift in stardust on the absolute zero breath of God, and yet that lonely awareness made him feel more intensely alive and, in a strange way, free—a freedom by which he's determined to live his life. But when he looks from the gangway to the gang staring at him, Mick loses any desire to step off the street into its shadow.

"*Qué quieres?*" the Disciple demands.

"*Qué trais, pendejo?*" a heavyset guy, the oldest-looking of the group, with a rat-tail braid of the kind favored by featherweight boxers, adds in an exaggerated drawl of Mexican Spanish: What do you bring, asshole?

"A dildo *para te metas, pinche puto,*" a kid with a scholarly, Indian face mutters. He's the only one besides my brother wearing glasses. His comment draws snickers.

Mick catches that they're joking about how he might abuse himself with the kielbasa and tries joking back. "*Es mi amigo,*" he tells them, brandishing the kielbasa. He's begun slowly backing away, talking as he does: "*Mi amigo* and I go everywhere together and now it's time for us to catch a bus to Memphis, Tennessee. *Hasta la vista.*"

"*Está hablando español boricua chingau. Aquí es un barrio Mexicano,*" the heavyset guy says: You talk like a fucking PR. He stands and flicks the lit butt of his cigarette at Mick, and the other guys on the stairs spark theirs at him, too.

And only now does my brother realize what he should have picked up on immediately—his accent is Puerto Rican, not the best impression to make on Mexican guys wary of rival Puerto Rican gangs. He can't explain his theory that the way to learn a language is to fall in love with a woman who speaks it. He can't tell them how the language becomes indistinguishable from her, internalized, permanent as any gang tattoo, that even when she's gone for good she's there in the feel of the words in his mouth. He knows what they'd say to that or anything else he might tell them.

"Qué quieres?" the Disciple asks, and takes a step toward Mick.

They're all standing now, representing as if practicing some spastic tai chi, throwing gang hand signs as if hexing Mick or warding off evil, speaking as if one in a mute language whose lexicon, if their facial expressions are any indication, consists entirely of obscenities.

"You know what I conveniently forgot?" my brother asks in English, moving off faster, still walking backward so as not to turn his back, "I forgot how sometimes I fucking hated it here."

"Qué quieres?" the kid barks, following after Mick, with his homies behind him.

"Nada," my brother answers.

As soon as he rounds the corner, he begins to run down Twenty-fifth Street, through a boozy blast of *conjuntos nortentos* from an open bar that used to be Metric's—in memory everything seems to happen to music—past JJ's and the driveway where, in summer, Señor Hot Tamale, the name painted in flames on his little white cart, sold incendiary tamales. He kept an iguana on a leash, and his beautiful wild daughter, known on the street as Tamalita, could be momentarily glimpsed clinging to the backs of motorcycles that Mick, eight years old and madly in love with her, would chase for blocks.

Qué quieres?

I want to be wringing the throttle, winding through gears, saddled to the chromed sky-rocket of a Triumph 650.

He turns down Rockwell, past the defunct 3 V's Birdseed Factory, whose windows once broadcast the cries of caged exotic birds. Its walls are spray-painted in the style of Siqueiros. The peeling murals make the factory appear to be disintegrating along with its superimposed bandoliered angels and peons who ride rearing Quetzalcoatls auraed in fire, its mariachi whose guitars gush at their center holes into rivers of blood and orchids, and its olive-skinned Virgin of Guadalupe. Mick's reflection flees across her enormous, mournful eyes.

Qué quieres?

I want to hide among the martyrs and heroes; I wish this factory, bankrupt of birds, was a cathedral that offered sanctuary.

Down the flooded side street where Johnny Sovereign had his balls blown off, a street that might have issued from the mural, Mick splashes upstream through the current of an open fire hydrant, scattering gulls lured from garbage dumps by the water. The street is deserted but for a young girl in a wet dress who utters aloud the name of God as a loco blond man races past with a drooping, wind-resisting Polish sausage.

Run, Jimmy Delacroix, breath ragged, a stitch in your side. Don't look back to see what's gaining. Run until the city beneath your feet becomes a blur, run propelled by fear, familiar fear—the fear by which you know you're home. Don't stop for traffic, stop signs, red lights, don't stop for shrines or to kneel beside the pauper's gravestone where your name's inscribed in the Seaside Cemetery, a graveyard where the sprinklers throw salt spray and the markers are seabirds that fly away at night.

Qué quieres?

I want winged shoes, my old PF Flyers, I want to be wearing the invisible clothes of wind, to be trailing a comet tail of songs: *"A love supreme, a love supreme . . . Those redskin boys couldn't get my blood cause I was a-ridin' on a Tennessee Stud . . ."*

Qué quieres?

I want to change smoke into a perfume of gardenias.

A Minor Mood

~~~~~~

The concertina sleeping beside Lefty has started to wheeze. It's the middle of the night, even the streetlights have their misty blinders on, and the concertina can't seem to catch her breath. In the dark Lefty listens to her ragged sighs. He can't sleep to the concertina's labored breathing. He's worried. He can't help thinking about what happened with the glockenspiel, how he would wake to find her place beside him on the bed empty, and then, from the other side of the locked bathroom door, he'd hear her heart hammering arrhythmically and flat, a dissonant rise and fall of scales. Once it began, it went on like that night after night. The neighbors complained; finally, he lost his lease. And one day at dusk, he found himself standing on a street of pawnshops and tattoo parlors, with nowhere to go and only a pawn ticket to show for what had been his life. He'd wandered out with a tattoo—not a rose or an anchor or a snake or a heart, but a single note of indelible blue, a nameless note without a staff, only an eighth note, really—stung onto his shoulder.

Afterward, he spent a long and, in retrospect, mournful time alone before becoming entangled with the tuba. He met her at a tuba fest, and for a while it seemed as if they were destined for each other, until the dreams started. Disturbing dreams in which he ran lost and breathless through twisting corridors, dreams he'd wake from in the dark to a borborygmus of gurgled moans, blats, grunts, drones, which seemed drawn out longer each night, like the vowels of whales—melancholy whales. At first, he tried to tell himself that it was only gas. But the signs and symptoms were undeniably clear, and this time he didn't wait for landlords or court orders to tell him it was over. He'd already been evicted from sleep. One afternoon, while the tuba was away for a valve job, Lefty, groggy with insomnia, packed what he could fit into a suitcase that once cushioned a saxophone and left the rest behind.

In the years that followed, home was wherever he set that suitcase down—a sad succession of flophouses and transient hotels, dumps that seemed tenanted by fugitives from the collective unconscious: Depression Deco lobbies; ill-lit corridors lined with doors emitting smells like whispers and whispers like smells; restless, rheumatic rooms that creaked and groaned under their own dingy weight, rooms that came furnished with desperation, and wallpapered with worn, fitful dreams. He carried a sax case but was past his time for saxophones and their slinky, sultry, seductive ways; their nocturnal predilections and swanky pretensions were for breaking the hearts of younger men. On his deathbed, his father had gestured him closer and before dying whispered in his ear, "The wallflowers, son, go for the wallflowers. They'll appreciate it." But his father was wrong about that as he was about everything else. The wallflowers were a vain, angry, neurotic, and anything but appreciative lot. Sometimes, in a fog, down by the docks, he'd hear sounds echoing the warning that lights could not convey—buoys dinging their bells, the moody moans of foghorns—and he'd think about the glockenspiel, recalling the sensitive touch of her mallets, and the patterns her glittering vertebrae left along his skin. He'd feel the blue tattoo ache like a bruise from bite marks on his shoulder. He'd think about the tuba until he could feel again a ghostly impression of her hard, cool mouthpiece and taste the brass against his lips (a taste not unlike that of his own blood after a fistfight), and then he'd recall the way his breath flowed into her, as if there was no filling her up, as if she was sucking it from the deepest pocket of his body, leaving him hollow. He had carried that hollowness within him for years; he didn't want to feel hollow any longer. Whatever came after the tuba would have to arrive on a breath of its own.

Now, he listens to the concertina wheeze, and perhaps to find a little respite from his worries, Lefty remembers nights as a child when his lungs sounded like wind blowing past a tattered shade, and his bronchial tubes gave recitals of the croup. While his father was God knows where, and his mother was at work, his grand-mother would come to nurse him. It was a large family on his fa-ther's side, and his grandmother managed to love them all and yet showed such special affection toward Lefty—maybe because his father was always God knows where—that everyone called her Lefty's Gran, even if she was their grandmother, too.

Lefty's Gran would show up whenever he was sick, carrying her green mesh shopping bag. She always carried that bag in case she suddenly had to do some shopping, or on the chance she stumbled upon something valuable lying in the street. Even if it served no other purpose, it was good for carrying her purse in. When she came to see Lefty, the shopping bag would also con-tain the chartreuse protrusions of a half dozen lemons and the blue-green bulge of an economy-size jar of Vicks VapoRub, against which other, lesser bottles clinked.

The sight of her would set Lefty coughing.

"So, Louis," his gran would say—oddly Lefty's Gran refused to call her grandson Lefty—"So, Louis, I hear you got the Krupa again."

The lemons and Vicks were part of her cure for the Krupa. But before unloading the shopping bag, before doing anything else, Lefty's Gran would fill the apartment with steam. She'd go from room to room, balancing pie pans and cookie trays on the tops of radiators, and as she set them up they'd bang like cymbals punctuating her stream of muttering: "Kid's got the Krupa (*Bang!*) the Gene (*Bam!*) the drummer man (*Boom!*) Krupa (*Crash!*).

"Hey, Louis (*Wham!*), whatayou got?"

"The Gene Krupa."

"You can say that again (*Blam!*)."

"The Gene Krupa."

"Ha!" Lefty's Gran would expel a laugh resounding like a cymbal clap, as if he'd just said something surprisingly hilarious even though she had taught him the you-can-say-that-again routine. "You can bet your *dupa* (*Bing!*) you got the Krupa (*Bong!*)."

She'd fill the pie pans and cookie trays to the brim with water; she'd set kettles and pots on every burner of the stove and let them boil; she'd turn the shower on hot in the bathroom and let it pour down clouds of steam; she'd hook the vaporizer up beside Lefty's bed, fuel it with a glob of Vicks, and aim its snorky exhalations in his direction. The entire flat began to heave with breath.

While the steam rose like genies rushing out of bottles, Lefty's Gran would rub camphor oil on his chest and on his neck, where his glands were swollen; she'd dab a streak of Vicks along his upper lip as if she was drawing a mustache. Then, she'd undo the babushka that she wore whether she was outside or in. She'd whisk it off with the flourish of a magician doing a trick, and years would disappear. When he saw her blurred in steam, minus her babushka, Lefty could imagine his grandmother as a girl. He wondered if she kept her head covered because her hair looked younger than she did. It was a lustrous ash blond, so springy with curls that it looked fake, as if she might be wearing a wig. This girlishness that she kept hidden was like a secret between them.

She'd twine her satiny babushka around his throat, and over the babushka she would wrap a rough woolen scarf that was reserved for these occasions and known as the croup scarf. The scarf, a clashing maroon-and-pea-green plaid anchored at one end by a big safety pin, retained past smells of camphor and Vicks. Its scratchy wool chapped his chin where his skin wasn't protected by the babushka.

By then, the flat was expanding with steam. Mirrors disappeared in the mist they reflected. Through the mist, the wallpaper, a pattern of vines and flowers, opened into three dimensions and came alive like flora in a rain forest. The background noise of outside traffic transformed into screeches of monkeys and tropical birds. Steam smoldered along the insides of windows and made them sweat; it condensed on the ceiling into beads that hung like rain above Lefty's bed. He was sweating, too, sweating out the fever; germs were fleeing his body through the portholes of his pores.

In the kitchen, lost in steam, Lefty's Gran was squeezing lemons. He could hear the vigorous, musical rattle of her spoon as she stirred honey and a splash of boiling water into syrup, then added lemon juice, and last, but not least, a dash of whiskey—Jim Beam—which was the brand of choice for all his relatives, by tradition referred to simply as Beam. *Beam* as in a ray of light.

Even stuffed up, Lefty could smell its fiery perfume.

The apartment was filling with aromas: pie tins and cookie trays baking on top of merrily knocking radiators; menthol, eucalyptus, camphor, lemon; and through the steam, like a searchlight glancing through fog: Beam. Lefty's Gran stirred the lemon and honey concoction together in a coffee mug but served it in jigger-size portions, although they referred to a jigger as a shot glass— another family tradition. It seemed an apt name, as far as Lefty was concerned, for a glass that had the shape, density, and sometimes the wallop of a slug.

He'd sip his medicinal drink until it was cool enough, then belt it down as if drinking a toast: *Na zdrowie,* germs, take this!

When the shot glass was empty, his gran would bring a refill on the theory that he needed fluids. She'd have a couple belts herself on the theory that she needed fluids, too.

"*Na zdrowie,*" she'd say—bottoms up!

"*Na zdrowie,*" he'd answer—down the hatch!

On such white winter mornings—white steam on one side of the pane, white snow on the other—propped on a throne of pillows with the babushka like a raja's turban wound around his swollen glands; with menthol, eucalyptus, camphor, lemon, and through the steam, his gran materializing with a mug in one hand and a bottle of Beam in the other—on white mornings like that, how could a boy not conclude that being sick might almost be worth the joy of getting well? Those were mornings to be tucked away at the heart of life, so that later, whenever one needed to draw upon a recollection of joy in order to get through troubled times, it would be there, an assurance that once one was happy and one could be happy again.

Sometimes, on those mornings, Lefty would wonder how his room, its window clouded as if the atmosphere of Venus was pressed against the pane, must have looked from the street. He wondered how it sounded to strangers passing by. Could they hear the vaporizer hissing like a reed instrument missing a reed? Could they hear his gran, who was now sipping Beam straight from the bottle, singing "You Are My Sunshine" in her Polish patois? She loved that song. "Not to be morbid," she'd say, "but sing 'Sunshine' at my funeral."

Not to be morbid, but when that time came, Lefty played it on the sax, his breath Beamy, played it to heaven, his back braced against the steeple of St. Pius.

She taught Lefty to play the measuring spoons like castanets in accompaniment to her gypsylike singing. She was playing the radiators with a ladle as if they were marimbas. Lefty was up, out of bed, flushed, but feeling great, and in steam that was fading to wisps, he was dancing with his gran. Her girlish curls tossed as around and around the room they whirled, both of them singing, and one or the other dizzily breaking off the dance in order to beat or plunk or blow some instrument they'd just invented: Lefty strumming the egg slicer; Lefty's Gran oompahing an empty half gallon of Dad's old-fashioned root beer; Lefty bugling "Sunshine" through the cardboard clarion at the center of a toilet-paper roll; Lefty's Gran chiming a closet of empty coat hangers; Lefty shake-rattle-and-rolling the silverware drawer; Lefty's Gran Spike Jonesing the vacuum cleaner; Lefty, surrounded by pots and lids, drum-soloing with wooden spoons; while Lefty's Gran, conducting with a potato masher, yelled, "Go, Krupa, go!"

How would it look to some stranger who had crept to the window and seen a boy and his gran carrying on as if they'd *both* been miraculously cured of the croup, doing the hokeypokey face-to-face with the babushka between their teeth?

It would have looked the way it appears to him now, peering in at the memory, like a stranger through a blurred window, straining to hear the beat of pots and the faint, off-key rendition of a vaguely familiar song.

And how would it look to the boy and his gran if they were peering in on him now, watching at the window while an unshaven stranger with a blue note on his shoulder worriedly paces in his dirty underwear, in the dead of night, to the sickly wheeze of a concertina? For a moment, Lefty almost expects to see their faces at the window, though the window is four stories up. He almost feels more like the boy staring in than the unshaven man who is pacing the floor. The boy and his gran seem more real to him than his room in the present. Suddenly, it's clear to him that memory is the channel by which the past conducts its powerful energy; it's how the past continues to love.

He moves directly to the suitcase buried in the back of the

closet and rummages through it until he finds a scarf. It's not the old scarf of maroon-and-pea-green plaid anchored with a safety pin; this scarf is navy blue. Nor is it redolent of camphor and Vicks; this scarf smells of mothballs. But it's woolly and warm and will have to do. He gently wraps the scarf about the concertina, and immediately her labored wheezing softens and is muffled.

He doesn't own enough pots to constitute a drum set, or to occupy all four burners, but he fills the single pot he has and, with the fanfare of a cymbal crash, he sets it to boil.

He doesn't know about the concertina, but as the water rumbles into steam, *he's* feeling a little better already—less anxious. He's been worried about the concertina, and his worries have made him feel helpless. He should at least have recognized that something was wrong before it came to this. The concertina has been in a minor mood lately, one that Lefty's found contagious— wistful, pensive, melancholy, heartsick by turns—a mood that, for lack of perfect pitch, words can't exactly convey. Even music can only approximate—a G minor from a Chopin nocturne, per- haps; or the D minor of a Schubert quartet, the one called "Death and the Maiden"; or, at times, an airy, disorganized noodling in no discernible key at all, like an orchestra tuning up; or a squeal like a bagpipe with a stomachache; or a drone as if the concertina were dreaming in a scale that only a sitar would find familiar. She's been in a minor mood that turns a polka into the blues, a jig into a dirge, a tarantella into a requiem. And a tango—how long has it been since he's heard her slink into the stylized passion of a tango?

Polka, jig, tarantella, tango . . . wistful, pensive, melancholy, heartsick . . . *menthol, eucalyptus, camphor, lemon.* He's found a mantra on which to meditate, a talismanic spell to chant.

He rifles through the cupboard, but he's out of honey. Not out, exactly; the fact is that he's never owned a jar of honey in his life. He opens the arctically austere cell of his refrigerator: a bottle of catsup, a jar of pickles, a couple containers of Chinese takeout that need to be pitched, but no lemon, not even a plastic citrus fruit ripening in there.

Fortunately, he does possess a shot glass and a bottle of whiskey—not Beam—but memory is, at best, approximate, and he bets Old Guckenheimer will do the trick. In honor and imitation of his gran, he belts down a couple quick doses to test its efficacy, and a couple more for the sake of fluids.

There's that fiery perfume!

Now it's the concertina's turn. Even distressed, the concertina looks lovely in the navy blue scarf. It heightens her complexion of mother-of-pearl. Oh, he thinks, little beauty, sweet companion, the one I didn't realize I was searching for, who almost came to me too late; little squeeze box who taught my fingers to sing, who taught me how to close my eyes and let the music flow.

He loves her pliant fit between his palms, and the way her body stretches as she yawns rhapsodically. He loves to feel the pumping of her breath. It's like a summer breeze warmed by the bellows of her heart—although *bellows* has never seemed to him a word suited to her. There's nothing bellowy about her, no puffed-up sentiments, no martial clamor that might accompany the lock-step or goose step of a march, no anthems for football halftimes, or for saluting flags while windbags swell with their own rhetoric; and though, a few times in her company, he's heard angelic whispers—an echo of some great medieval organ—no hymns. Hers has always been a song of earth, of olive trees, vineyards, blossoming orchards melodic with bees.

Na zdrowie, little squeeze box.

He watches as, delicately, she inhales the fumes of whiskey—tiny sips starting at *do* and slowly ascending through *re, mi, fa, sol,* to a tremulous *la-ti*. And after the shot glass has been drained repeatedly, he lifts her gently from the bed and they begin to dance to a tune they play together, a tune whose seesaw rhythm is like the panting of lovers. Not a polka, jig, tarantella, or even a tango. They dance to a dance they've just invented, an ancient dance they've just recalled.

If there are strangers on the street at this late hour, they've stopped to listen as if, like dogs, they can cock their ears. They listen, inhaling the cool air, with their heads thrown back against the night. Their breaths plume; their eyes are locked on the faint wisps of dissolving constellations. And though it's a dark, American city street on which they've stopped, they know there isn't the need to feel afraid because, instead of danger, tonight the air carries music.

Na zdrowie, strangers.

Na zdrowie, music.

Then, in the long diminuendo of a sigh, the concertina folds up quietly, peacefully, exhaling a sweet, whiskey breath, and Lefty lies down on the pillow beside her, covers them both with a bedspread, and closes his eyes.

Sleep, like a barcarole, carries him away.

~~~~~~

The woman had stopped to browse at the perfume counter. It was Christmas season, Marshall Field's was mobbed with shoppers, and the counter was a clutter of opened samples—exquisite bottles of myriad shapes and colors. She sorted through them without stopping for so much as a sniff until she found what she was looking for and, raising an atomizer, sprayed a poof into her brunette hair. Then she glanced around to see if anyone was watching, and I pretended to be studying the display of pearl earrings at the jewelry counter so that she wouldn't catch me staring. Not that if she caught me she would have noticed. Even dressed as I was, in a suit and tie under the old tweed topcoat imported from England that had belonged to my uncle Lefty, I still would have looked like a kid to someone like her.

When I looked up again, she was unbuttoning her coat. She was dressed like a clarinet, reedy thin in a black dress with silver buttons, a silver belt, and a matching necklace. She sprayed one wrist, inhaled the fragrance, then glanced around again, almost furtively, and the thought suddenly occurred to me that this elegantly beautiful woman was about to shoplift a bottle of perfume. Witnessing her theft would make me an accomplice, a partner in crime she didn't know she had. I found the thought exciting. The two saleswomen in the perfume section were on the opposite side of the counter, busy with customers. It was the perfect moment for the woman to slip the bottle under her coat. Instead, she opened two buttons on her dress, exposing a flash of cleavage and black lace, and quickly sprayed a puff over her breasts. Then, just as quickly, she buttoned up and turned away from the counter into the flow of shoppers.

As soon as she left, I stepped to the spot where she'd been standing. The atmosphere around the perfume counter was heady and thick, all the competing scents merging into a single fragrance that permeated the store. One could smell it immediately upon coming in from the cold through the revolving door. It was like an antidote to the clouds of incense in the church that I'd fled earlier in the day, when the smell of the requiem mass for my uncle Lefty grew suddenly nauseating. I'd left the church in the middle of the service, on the verge of a gagging fit that made my eyes tear. I'd been sitting by myself toward the rear of the church, so neither my mother nor any of the other relatives saw me leave, and if they had they would probably have figured that I needed to get back to my high school classes. The only person who noticed was a middle-aged black woman standing in the vestibule, looking in on the service. She was wearing sunglasses and a filmy black scarf over what may have been a wig. If it was her hair, then she'd dyed it a metallic color that brought out the bronze of her skin. Her fur coat, the kind my mother called Persian lamb, nearly matched the shade of her hair. I'd never seen her before, but as I went past she removed her sunglasses to catch my eye. Her eyes were green, not brown, and she smiled as if she knew me.

"That sharp topcoat don't quite fit you in the shoulders yet," she said in a husky voice.

"I guess" was all I could stammer.

"You take care now, Perry," she said, calling me by name.

Then I was out the huge, ornate door into the blast of frigid downtown air, feeling the exhilaration of an escapee, but at the same time feeling as if I was running out on Uncle Lefty, leaving him to the stink of incense and the insipid organ music he would have despised, and to the sentimental tributes he would have ridiculed. When the head of the local VFW, decked out in his ribbons and medals, and repeatedly referring to Lefty as Louis—a name Lefty hated—called him a war hero and a belated casualty of Korea, Lefty would have countered with his standard line that he was just a guy unlucky enough to get sunk in crap up to his neck and lucky enough not to drown.

I picked up the atomizer the woman had been holding. It was cobalt blue, and I could only imagine the color of the liquid inside. I pumped a blast into my cupped palm, inhaled, and the profusion of fragrances hovering over the perfume counter retreated. Its scent was powdery, not heavy, but deep as the fragrance of vanilla is deep, and it had a quality that couldn't be described simply in terms of smell, something that evoked the mysterious manner of the woman I'd just seen. I glanced around as the woman had in order to see if anyone was watching, and then, as she had not, I slipped a turquoise-and-gold box of Je Reviens—surprisingly expensive, though not much larger than a cigarette pack—from the display behind the cobalt atomizer into my topcoat and hurried off to follow the woman through the crowd.

Perhaps from the moment I went into Marshall Field's I was looking for something to steal. Not that it was a conscious intention. I hadn't even planned to end up in the store. I'd merely intended to walk around the block to clear the incense and testimonials out of my head. Laddy Bruscziec, the Bruiser as people called him, who was the drummer in the Polka Gents, a band in which Lefty made his comeback, was giving a eulogy when I left. Instead of talking about Lefty in a way that made him not quite recognizable, as a corpse in a casket is not quite recognizable, the Bruiser told a little story about a phrase that Lefty had a habit of using: "I'll never forget you for that." It was something I heard Lefty say plenty of times myself. Lefty might be in a greasy spoon, flirting with a waitress as usual, and when she'd bring him a refill for his coffee, he'd look up at her with his hooded eyes somewhere between dreamy and sad, and he'd point at her and say, "Thanks, I'll never forget you for that." It was a wisecrack, but Lefty could make it sound like he meant it.

After telling his Lefty story, the Bruiser stood at the pulpit for what seemed a long time, silently gazing down at the casket draped with the American flag. The family had got a good deal on a used metal casket, my aunt Zena had proudly confided to me at the wake. It was dented, she said, but with the flag over it, nobody would see. I thought of asking her if *used* meant that they'd dug it up and in the process maybe dinged it with the shovel, but I didn't. The casket rested in the center aisle of the church. Tall candles stood at attention on both its sides; at its foot, an altar boy waved a censer, and the church filled with the smoke of incense as if someone had uncorked the breath of the Dark Ages.

"Lefty, old bud," the Bruiser finally said, jabbing a finger toward the casket, "I'll never forget you for that."

His voice broke, and I was up and out of my pew, feeling sick, my eyes burning.

If the funeral mass had been held where it should have been, at St. Procopius on the South Side, where Lefty had grown up, I'm sure that after a walk around the block I would have gone back to the church. But the old neighborhood was getting rougher. The stained-glass windows were pocked with bullet holes, gang graffiti were spray-painted along the church walls, and besides, most of the family had moved out to the burbs, so the requiem mass was held at St. Peter's, the fancy downtown church. Once I was out the door that opened onto Madison, locked in step with the bustle of Christmas shoppers along streets lined with holiday lights and giant candy canes and Santas ringing bells, I just kept walking.

I walked thinking about Uncle Lefty, my godfather. When I was little and he was just back from the POW camp in Korea, he used to take me along on his rounds of the neighborhood taverns. I was considered good therapy for him back then. Later, after he started playing in public again, I'd sometimes go to hear the Gents play wedding receptions held in the back halls of corner taverns. I'd wait for that moment when Lefty switched from his cheap metal clarinet to the tarnished tenor sax that had spent the evening on the bandstand, armed with a number $4\frac{1}{2}$ Rico reed and draped with a white towel Lefty called his spit rag. Swaying drunkenly at the edge of the bandstand, Lefty would launch into a solo with the Bruiser behind him slamming the foot pedal of the bass drum as if flooring the gas and driving his red sparkle Ludwig kit over the edge of the stage, taking the rest of the Gents with him. The dancers whooped and whirled and stomped, but finally were defeated by the tempo and stood on the dance floor gaping and panting while the bridesmaids stumbled dizzily in their disheveled taffeta like deposed prom queens. Lefty blew, possessed and oblivious to the rising imprecations of the wedding guests, who stood on their folding chairs shouting for dance music. Even the pleas of his fellow Gents, all of whom with the exception of the Bruiser had stopped playing, couldn't silence him, leaving them no recourse but to drag Lefty, still wailing on his horn, off the stage.

In his sober interludes back then, Lefty tried, mostly unsuccessfully, to teach me to play the saxophone. After he died, besides his English topcoat, I inherited his tarnished Martin tenor sax. He'd owned an alto, too, but they couldn't find it or the metal clarinet, and figured he must have pawned them, though the pawn tickets never surfaced amid his mess of papers.

He was the only guy I knew who patronized pawnshops. A few times he took me pawnshopping with him. Once he bought a pair of teardrop-shaped green and violet earrings.

"Who are they for?" I asked.

"For good dreams," Uncle Lefty said. "Touch them to your eyelids before you go to sleep and no nightmares."

"Are those emeralds?" I wanted to know.

"Peridots from Africa and amethysts from the Amazon," the pawnbroker answered. He had unfolded a black velvet cloth on the counter, arranged the earrings on it, and was squinting at them through a jeweler's loupe.

"If you look up my butt with that maybe you'll discover the Hope diamond, too," Lefty told him.

The pawnbroker didn't seem offended, and I listened as they dickered back and forth until Lefty got him down to the price he wanted.

"I'm letting you steal from the mouths of my children," the pawnbroker complained.

"Yeah, thanks," Lefty said. "I'll never forget you for that."

As long as Lefty was dealing, I tried to talk him into buying something for me: a switchblade with a bone handle from a menacing display of knives and bayonets. Instead, he bought me a harmonica—a mouth harp, he called it.

"Perry, you take care of this," Lefty told me, "and it will be a better friend to you than a goddamn blade."

After I rinsed it out under the hot-water faucet about a hundred times in order to kill the germs of whatever degenerate had pawned it, I found that I actually had a knack for playing it that I lacked for a real horn.

Sometimes we went to Sportsman's Park, as we had when I was little. Lefty would stake me so that I could bet on the sulkies. Stuffed in the inside pocket of his English topcoat, I found a roll of seventy-two dollars, mostly in the crisp two-dollar bills bearing Jefferson's picture that I saw only at the track. I hadn't mentioned finding the roll to anyone. Besides the money there were stubs of old racing tickets on which Lefty had tried to hit trifectas, the kind of bet he'd always taught me was for suckers.

As his drinking got heavier, I saw less of him. He was in and out of VA hospitals, though for what specific ailment no one seemed to know. He went out to California and returned sporting an eighth note tattooed in blue on his shoulder and a Vandyke beard that gave him a beatnik look.

The first time he was committed was after he fell out of the bleachers at Wrigley Field while trying to welcome Willie Mays to Chicago by handing down a Hamm's beer. He'd galloped like a broken-field runner across the outfield grass, fighting off the ushers and cops who'd rushed to cart him out of the ballpark, and was sent to a psychiatric hospital on the far Northwest Side.

Each time he was committed my mother and I took a two-hour ride by El and bus and visited him. The hospital, which Lefty insisted we refer to as the Booby Hatch, was surrounded by a high, spiked iron fence painted a fir-tree green as if it were a natural feature of the wide expanse of lawn. Lefty referred to himself as a POD, Prisoner of Doctors, and I remember thinking that he'd been a POW in Korea, dreaming of escape and all the things he would do if he ever made it back to the States, little things like going to a ball game or buying himself a warm winter coat, and now he was home and imprisoned again.

The first few times he escaped, the hospital called my mother and we waited thinking that Lefty might show up at our house, but he never did. He'd disappear for weeks at a time and refuse to say where he'd been. My mother had a theory that Lefty had a girlfriend somewhere in the city, but the few times she hinted around to Lefty about it he just gazed silently at her with those hooded eyes.

His last escape was during a mild spell when December felt deceptively like April, misty and wet. They found his body on the morning after the night that it turned bitter cold again. Wearing the light sport coat that he'd escaped in, Lefty had tried to climb back into the Booby Hatch during the night over the locked front gates, and, blind drunk, had apparently fallen from the top of the gate and landed facedown in a puddle. The autopsy determined he'd drowned in three inches of muddy water. By morning the puddle had frozen around him, and they had to chip his body free from the ice. If he had to die in such a way, I wished that at least he had been climbing out instead of back inside.

I thought of the woman in the bronze wig, standing at the back of the church. Perhaps she had been Lefty's secret girlfriend, maybe a woman he had met at the track or at some bar where he'd gone to listen to music, or a waitress on whom Lefty had used his I'll-never-forget-you-for-that line. But the woman, wearing her sunglasses as if they were a sign of mourning, had looked too regal for a waitress. There was a fiery blush of rouge warpainted along the bronze of her high cheekbones. I tried to recall if she was wearing earrings, tried to imagine how those earrings that Lefty had bought might look on her. They'd have matched her oval eyes. Maybe it was her place where Lefty hid out during his escapes; maybe she was what kept him escaping. It hadn't occurred to me before that Lefty needed something to escape *to* as well as *from*, and when I realized that, I wanted to see her again, to see her from Lefty's point of view. I wanted to know what happened, why he hadn't stayed with her that night when it turned cold, what drove him back to the Booby Hatch, though even in my fantasy of tracking her down, I knew we'd never have that conversation.

The cold had cleared my head. I wasn't feeling sick any longer. In fact, I was starving. I almost turned back; then, walking down Adams, I passed Berghoff's, a restaurant with an annexed stand-up bar that Lefty used to talk about. It was one of his favorite hangouts for celebrating when he hit it big at the track, a state of affluence he called "being in the peanuts and caramel." Standing at the polished oak bar, he'd eat cold hard-boiled eggs, and Thuringer sandwiches on rye spread with brown mustard and horseradish, and wash them down with steins of Berghoff's private-label dark beer. Probably he'd stood at the bar wearing the very topcoat that I was wearing now. Instead of heading back to St. Peter's, I stepped into Berghoff's.

Three bartenders were working the long bar, where business-men, some still in their topcoats and scarves, stood packed together eating sandwiches and plates of hash and quaffing foamy steins. A line of men, shaking off the cold, waited for sandwiches from a server dressed in chef's white, who expertly wielded a carving knife against the grain of mountainous roasts.

I noticed a *Tribune* left behind at one of the high, wooden tables along the wall where men stood as an alternative to crowding at the bar. I picked up the newspaper, which was folded to the market report, and wished I was smoking a cigar. No, I thought, that would be overdoing it. Instead, I snuck the butt of a half-smoked filter cigarette from an ashtray and struck a light from a handy Berghoff matchbook. I raised my topcoat collar up around my face, wedged in at the bar, and assumed the nonchalant pose of a man on a late lunch immersed in the financial section. My heart had begun to race. I was counting on the suit and Lefty's topcoat to help me pass for legal drinking age; after all, there was no telling how many drinks that topcoat had been served in here.

"What'll it be?" a gray-haired bartender with moles on his face and a German accent asked me, scooping up the tip from the man beside me who'd just left.

I inhaled as if considering, blew a cloud of smoke, and very deliberately stubbed out my cigarette in the ashtray on the bar.

"I'll take one of those eggs," I said, and went back to studying the market report.

He brought the egg, a plate for shells, a napkin, and salt and pepper shakers.

"Anything to drink?" he asked.

"Just a stein," I said, without looking up from the paper.

I could feel him staring at me, not just with his eyes but with his moles as well, but he didn't ask for my ID.

I peeled the egg, my hands steady, though I was sweating under the weight of the topcoat. I felt as if Uncle Lefty was at my shoulder like a guardian angel, as if instead of my abandoning him, his spirit had followed me out of the church and was here at the bar rather than transported off in a hearse running red lights, towing a line of funeral cars in a last ride down Milwaukee Avenue, way out to the Northwest Side, past the forest preserves, to the family plot in St. Adalbert Cemetery, a place that Lefty called the Old Polack Burial Ground. There would be a brief service at the graveside, that all-too-fertile-looking black rectangle gaping from a snow-clotted lawn. Then the living would retire to the White Eagle Restaurant, conveniently located across from the cemetery, for a huge spread of chicken, roast beef, kielbasa, kraut, pierogi, mashed potatoes, cucumbers in sour cream, and for dessert, platters of kolacky.

I salted and peppered my egg, applied a dab of horseradish from one of the bowls along the bar, and glanced up at my reflection in the gleaming mirror that ran the length of the bar. I watched myself loosen my tie. Already a plan was hatching: I'd finish the egg and order another, and with it another stein, then stand in line for a Thuringer sandwich on rye with a dill pickle. And for dessert, a boilermaker featuring a shot of Berghoff's aged bourbon from one of the bottles reflected along the base of the mirror—a private toast to Uncle Lefty.

The bartender hammered a stein down before me, mopped the foam with his white apron, and I peeled off a couple crisp two-dollar bills and slapped them on the bar. He picked them up without batting an eye at the unusual bills and walked over to the register.

I raised the egg I'd dressed in pepper and horseradish to my mouth. It tasted better than anything I'd ever bit into before. Then I lifted the heavy stein, with its dark brew and beige head of foam, and took a swallow.

It was root beer.

"Everything okay?" the bartender asked when he returned with my change.

"Fine," I said.

I finished the egg in another bite but left the root beer. When I was little and Uncle Lefty took me with him to neighborhood bars, root beer was what he'd always buy me.

"Excuse me," I said to the bartender.

"Yah?" he asked as if we were speaking German.

"Do you have something to write with?"

He handed me the pencil from behind his ear.

"Thanks," I said.

I slid the cardboard coaster emblazoned with the red Berghoff emblem out from under the stein of root beer, flipped it over, and on its blank side carved GO FUCK YOURSELF, and left it for a tip.

Outside, it had begun to snow, ticking grains that turned the afternoon as gray as a rainstorm would have. An icy wind off the lake funneled down Adams. I could hear the flags on the corner of State whipping the way my topcoat whipped around my knees. Instead of sticking, the snow blew off like grit, though behind display windows along State Street, sequined flakes suspended by threads gathered in cotton drifts around elves and reindeer.

On the other side of the expressway, downtown turned into blocks of pawnshops and strip bars displaying pictures of women in G-strings and pasties who were presumably disrobing inside. In the spirit of the season, some of the women were pictured wearing Santa hats. When Uncle Lefty took me pawnshopping with him, he'd blinder my eyes with his hands when we passed the strip bars, saying, "You're too young yet." Now, I was simply too cold. The streets that had seemed forbidden and exciting looked sleazy and dismal. I turned around and walked north back into downtown.

If not for the cold I could have kept walking. I wasn't wearing a hat, and my ears burned numb. My hands felt raw from taking turns holding the topcoat closed at the throat, where it was missing a button. When I passed Marshall Field's, I went in to get out of the cold.

The revolving door spun into a rush of steam heat and perfume, and I was drawn into a current of shoppers that led inevitably to the great Christmas tree at the center of a rotunda domed with Tiffany glass. To view the tree properly, you rode up the escalator, gaping over the edge to take in the lavish decorations—a dizzying sensation I recalled from childhood. A trip to Field's, as my mother familiarly referred to the store, was a pilgrimage we made each holiday season. Instinctively, I followed the old route my mother and I would take to the toy department on the fifth floor. I wanted to see if the knights were still there. Until about sixth grade I'd obsessively collected them. They were miniatures made of metal, not plastic, imported from Europe and found only at Field's. Their armor gleamed like newly minted nickel, their helmets had working visors that opened to reveal individual faces enameled with the intense expressions of combat. They swung broadswords, maces, battle-axes; some were jousters on armored steeds. I dreamed of amassing an army, but they were too expensive for me to acquire more than one or two each Christmas. At that rate, childhood would be over before I could marshal my forces. I wondered if I'd ever thought back then about stealing one. Probably not with my mother waiting patiently while I agonized over my choices. I wanted them all.

It was too late to buy them, even though I had Uncle Lefty's wad of money. I wondered if there was anything in Field's I wanted as much now. I began to browse, looking not for something to steal, exactly, but for something that I wanted enough to steal for. I rode the escalator as high as it went and worked my way down, drifting through aisles of furniture, crystal, china, clothing. I was back on the main floor, checking out jewelry, when I saw the woman at the perfume counter.

It was an impulse to take it. I had it in hand before I'd dared myself to do so; a flush of alarm at what I was doing shot through my body like an amphetamine. Beneath my topcoat the box of perfume felt pasted by sweat to where I'd pinned it between my arm and ribs. I backed away from the counter convinced that people were staring accusingly, yet it wasn't getting caught that I was most worried about. In the instant during which I'd snatched the perfume, I'd lost sight of the woman in the crowd.

Jostling past shoppers laden with packages, I hurried along the aisle to catch up to her, trying not to look like a thief fleeing the scene of the crime. She had vanished. I stopped and surveyed the store, but picking her out of the milling crowd was impossible. Perhaps she was already riding the escalator up to women's apparel. It seemed better to take a wild chance on finding her there than to stand paralyzed with a box of perfume under my coat. I turned for the escalator, and suddenly saw her straightening up from a drink at the water fountain.

After the panic of losing sight of her, simply to be following her through the store felt like incredible luck. She headed directly for the Washington Street exit, and I thought I could almost follow her by the scent of her perfume, although probably what I was smelling was the perfume that I'd blasted on my palm.

Even back out in the cold I caught her scent through the diesel fumes of buses and wafts of caramel corn and roasted nuts, as if I'd been blessed with a dog's power of smell. The wind had let up, and the floating snow collecting on the windshields of cars parked illegally along the curb now resembled the snow behind display windows—hanging flakes that sparkled in the lights.

She turned south on Wabash and waited for the signal to cross the street. I caught her profile bathed in the green of the traffic light. Her breath steamed. She wore the same intensely private expression that I'd noticed as she stood before the perfume counter. Not a dreamy look—the opposite, really, though I couldn't have described it at the time: the look of someone so alerted to her inner life as to be detached from the world around her. She wasn't part of the bustling crowds, she wasn't shopping, she wasn't stopping to browse.

The light changed, we crossed the street. An El racketed overhead, balanced precariously at the edge of the tracks, scraping blue sparks from the third rail. My mind raced with plans for what to do next. I thought of simply running up behind her and, as I went by, wishing her Merry Christmas and handing her the box, then rushing off. Or perhaps it would be better to say, "Excuse me, miss, you dropped this," and before she could recover from her surprise enough to say anything or try to hand it back, I would be racing off as if I was late for an important engagement, glancing over my shoulder and waving at her as she stood there puzzled but smiling while the rush-hour crowd parted around her.

Whatever my strategy, she'd be surprised, but then I considered that it might not necessarily be a pleasant surprise to have some guy in a topcoat that was too big for him, and wearing a Robert Hall suit purchased for the Sophomore Hop and already outgrown, running up out of nowhere and handing her a perfume she'd just surreptitiously sprayed along her breasts.

It would be better if, in passing on the street or stopped at a traffic light, we were jostled together in the crowd, and in that instant I slipped the perfume into the pocket of her black coat. She was walking bareheaded with her coat unbuttoned, one hand thrust in a pocket, and the hem flaring open with each stride. Slipping the perfume into her coat was a plan that would work only if I was a pickpocket, as deft as one of those kids under the tutelage of Fagin in *Oliver Twist*. Whatever I settled on had to be unobtrusive, and, as I hadn't arrived at a workable scheme, I merely followed her down Wabash.

We caught the light on Madison and crossed. In the middle of the block, a Salvation Army band played "O Come, All Ye Faithful" to the accompaniment of blaring traffic. The closer we got the more off-key the band sounded. The trumpet player, a gangly kid in wire-rim glasses, was the worst offender. His acne scars were violet in the cold, and his tone broke repeatedly like an adolescent's voice. I would have sympathized with him if each time he flubbed a note he hadn't blown louder. Beside him a tuba player oompahed a bass line that would have made him a natural in the Polka Gents. There was an old guy wearing woolly white earmuffs, thumping a bass drum with a matching woolly mallet, and a fellow with a beard off a Smith Brothers cough drop box playing an ice-cold-looking glockenspiel. They all looked cold, and remarkably they all looked as if they were smiling, even the two brass players.

The woman's gait slowed as she approached them. She glanced at her watch, then joined the small group of people who stood listening to the carol. The band roused to a crescendo on "sing choirs of angels, sing in exultation," and the trumpet player hit a flat note that had passersby shaking their heads, but he simply raised the bell of his horn higher into the falling snow and continued to play. Behind his thick glasses, his eyes were squeezed closed, and I noticed that the woman, too, had raised her face to the snow and closed her eyes so that the snowflakes crumbled on her lashes.

Amidst the small gathering, I had edged just beside her, closer than I'd dared before, close enough to catch the scent again. Inside my coat pocket I clutched the box of perfume, still waiting for the right moment. The carol hung suspended on the last refrain, drawing out the notes before raggedly collapsing to a conclusion. There was a smattering of glove-muffled applause and the tink of donations. She dug into her coat pockets as if searching for a coin, but came up with only a rumpled Kleenex. I took the opportunity to step forward, peel a bill from Uncle Lefty's wad, and drop it into the collection pot, and she turned, gazed directly at me, and smiled. Then, glancing at her watch again, she continued down Wabash, and the moment dissolved like the scent of her perfume as I watched her walking away.

I should have stopped right there and watched her disappear into the crowd, content with the acknowledgment of her smile, but the musicians launched into "The First Noel," and suddenly it felt so lonely there listening to them by myself that I started after her again.

She was already across Monroe, and I had to cross against the

light and dodge through traffic. She stopped at the Wabash entrance
to the Palmer House hotel, and a bellman with a luggage cart
pushed by, momentarily shielding her from view. I sped up so as not
to lose sight of her as I had in Field's, but she remained standing before the entrance, watching an airline bus with dark windows load
up passengers while guests returning from shopping sprees bustled
around her. A doorman in green livery, with a whistle piercing
enough to carry over the roar of the El, hailed a Checker cab,
opened the passenger door, and gestured toward her. For a second I
thought she was going to get into the cab, and I had an impulse to
rush up and toss the perfume in after her, though what I did was
stand there frozen. Then another woman and a man, both dressed
for the theater and laughing uproariously over some private joke,
dashed past her and grabbed the cab instead. It swerved off into
the snow, taking their merriment with it, and she turned as if a decision had been made for her, and walked through the entrance.

I trailed behind her past an arcade of shops, then up a broad
flight of marble stairs to the vaulted lobby on the second floor,
with its coral-and-green expanse of carpet. Mirrors and marble
reflected the electric candlelight of the brass sconces. A Christmas
tree, not the equal of Field's but magnificent all the same, rose up
to a mezzanine. At a grand piano, a pianist rippled Christmas
tunes as if they were Chopin. Gone was the bustle at the outside
entrance, the lobby seemed serene. I was no longer one of a
crowd on a snowy street. Since she'd smiled at me outside, I'd
lost the camouflage of anonymity integral to my impossible
schemes.

She went straight to the front desk and spoke with the clerk,
then crossed the lobby to the elevators. For a moment outside the
hotel she'd looked nervous, indecisive, a little lost. Now, she had
that air again of someone absorbed in her own private world.

She stood alone at the bank of elevators, smoothing back her
hair, then pressed the button and the doors opened. Had there

been a crowd waiting I might have squeezed in with them, but not with just the two of us. I didn't want her to look at me as if I was some weirdo. She looked out at me without the slightest hint of recognition. She was freshening her lipstick. I could imagine the elevator filling with her perfume. The doors slid closed. I'd been acting weird, but I knew what was really crazy was my feeling that I missed her.

I watched the ascent on the panel of lighted numbers. When the elevator stopped on the nineteenth floor and began to descend, I walked to the front desk. In the time it had taken the elevator to rise I had formulated my best plan yet, not just some fantasy but one I knew would work.

I waited while the desk clerk whom the woman had just spoken with gave an elderly guest a room key, then stepped to the desk.

"Can I help you?" the clerk asked, somewhat curtly, I thought. He had a way of enunciating that fit with the intimidating lobby.

"I want to leave something for one of your guests," I said, suddenly conscious of my own enunciation.

"And that would be for whom?" he inquired, cocking an eyebrow.

He was dressed in a gray suit, his striped tie cinched so tightly against his white button-down collar that it made his face look flushed, as if he was slowly strangling. And then I recognized that particular flush, the capillaries purple and broken beneath the rawness of a close shave. I'd seen it often enough from childhood when I'd gone to the taverns with Uncle Lefty. It was the complexion of a drinker, and that boosted my confidence.

"It's for the woman you were just speaking with. The woman on nineteen. Could you just put this in her box?" I took the turquoise-and-gold box out of my pocket and placed it between us on the counter.

"And you are Mr. ——?" he inquired.

"Mr. Perry. But it isn't necessary to include a name," I hastened to add when he started writing it down. "She'll know who it's from. She's expecting it."

"That's Perry with a *y* or an *i*?"

"An *i*, but no note needed, thanks. Just please place it in her box."

He eyed the perfume suspiciously, as if I might be smuggling in a bomb. He still hadn't touched it.

"I'm afraid that's not possible, Mr. Perri," he said, accenting the last syllable of my name as if it was the city in France.

"Why not?"

"I'm sorry to say, Mr. Perri, that hotel policy prohibits anything that might intrude on the privacy of our guests."

"You don't take messages?"

"I'd be happy to take a message, Mr. Perri. Who is it for?"

"I explained that," I pleaded, but I could see that pleading with this guy was the wrong tactic. "Look," I said more confidentially, in a way I thought Uncle Lefty might handle the situation, "it's a surprise gift." I thumbed what felt like five of the bills from the wad in my pocket and slid them, folded under my hand, across the counter.

"I thought she was expecting it," the desk clerk said, but his voice was lowered and he took the bills.

"It's one of those surprises that you don't know you've been expecting until you get," I explained, pushing the perfume toward him the way I'd slid the money.

The money disappeared as if by sleight of hand into his trouser pocket.

"I'm sorry to say, Mr. Perri, that as much as I would like to accommodate you, I still can't deliver your . . . gift."

"But you took the money," I whispered.

"Mr. Perri, for your kindness I *am* going to share privileged information. I cannot deliver this," he said, his manicured fingertips nudging the perfume back to me across the counter, "because the lady in question is not a guest at this hotel."

"Bullshit! I saw her going up to her room," I said louder than I meant to.

"It wasn't *her* room that she went up to. Now please, Mr. Perri, don't require me to call security. Put this expensive little box that you got from God knows where back into your pocket and leave."

"I see. Thanks," I said, stuffing the perfume back into my coat pocket. I felt ridiculously obtuse.

"If you'll excuse me then," the desk clerk said and turned to answer a buzzing phone.

I headed directly for the exit. I wanted to get back to the anonymity of the downtown streets.

"Mr. Perri!" the clerk called urgently behind me as if one of us had forgotten something.

I turned without stopping, walking backward.

"Happy holidays, Mr. Perri!"

I hurried down the marble stairway, through the arcade of shops that were shuttering their windows, and past the doorman warming himself inside the door and gazing out on the snowy street, where the traffic had thinned. Snow was accumulating on sidewalks and streets now that rush hour was over. It muffled the lights and the church bells chiming a carol. Perhaps the woman was looking out over the misted lights, watching it snow from the nineteenth floor and hearing the bells. They were probably the bells from St. Peter's. Far across the city, the snow by now would have drifted over the empty lawns of St. Adalbert, erasing a new grave. Grates were drawn over display windows, shop lights blinked out. Down the block, the Salvation Army musicians had disbanded. Almsgiving, like shopping, was over for another day. I walked to Field's, but the revolving doors were already locked. Only a single door remained opened, where a guard was ushering stragglers out of the darkened lobby, and I kept walking, unable to return the gift in my topcoat pocket, unable to give it away.